SPIRIT

An Andrea Kelley Mystery
The Archivist Book 2

ELLE ANDREWS PATT

Blue Beech Press
Knoxville, Tennessee USA

Cover design by Alexandre Rito

ISBN (PB AZN): 978-1-7347544-4-5

ISBN (PB D2D): 978-1-960974-98-3

ISBN (EBK): 978-1-7347544-3-8

ISBN (HB): 978-1-7347544-7-6

Published by BLUE BEECH PRESS

5923 Kingston Pike #161

Knoxville, TN 37919

Spirit/An Andrea Kelley Mystery/The Archivist Book 2 -- 1st ed. Nov 2021

ALSO BY ELLE ANDREWS PATT:

NOVELS

GHOST: An Andrea Kelley Mystery

(The Archivist Book 1)

WRAITH: An Andrea Kelley Mystery

(The Archivist Book 3)

BLIND MICE BITE: A Matt Loose Mystery

SHORT FICTION

MISSING: PRELUDE TO A MURDER CONVICTION

The Prometheus Saga: MANTEO

The Prometheus Saga 2: REMUDA

Return To Earth: SOMEDAY LOYAL

The Masters Reimagined:

REGARDING MR. BULKINGTON

The Masters Reimagined 2:

AMONG THE BLUE HORSES

ACKNOWLEDGMENTS

Thank you to all of you who have been kind and constructive as you've helped this series into existence, that includes all of you, the readers, who have left honest reviews online, commented on posts, or written me emails to share your enjoyment of The Archivist Book 1, Ghost.

On Spirit, extra thanks to First Reader and Editor, Kelley Walters, Editor Dustin Bilyk, Copy Editor Patricia Lee, and astute readers, Lindsey Patt, Bria Burton, and Ken Pelham. The book would not be half as good without you. And thank you, writers of the #5amWritersClub for the support and camaraderie, especially super cheerleader and volunteer organizer Ralph Walker. Thank you, Keith Short, for the night we got the EVP.

As in Book 1 of this series, thank you to the people of Charleston, West Virginia. I have taken fictional liberties and created dramatic circumstances but have strived to show how much my characters love their town. To all the historians and authors who have shared their knowledge of American slavery in all its forms, the Civil War, and law enforcement, thank you. To all of those past and present who have shared first person accounts of the same, I commend you for making your stories public so that others will know your truths.

As always, thank you to my husband and family for giving me the space, time, and patience that allows me to write. Thanks for forgiving the squeaky floorboards when I make coffee at five am!

—EAP

SPIRIT

1

The woman, bundled in a wet and filthy blanket, a dark blue hoodie pulled over her loose black hair, lay crumpled in a heap against the alley wall. An unnatural paleness gave the brown skin of her bare feet and legs, bloody hands, and exposed lower face a grey cast. Dark patches and streaks of blood covered the front of the hoodie, crusted the sleeves.

Stomach turning over on itself, Andrea slid her fingers under one of the gaping bloody cuffs of the hoodie to feel the woman's wrist anyway. Her skin was cold, her flesh stiff, the blood dry.

Still.

Andrea ducked down to see the woman's face. Just in case. Dark eyes, half-open and glazed over. Her mascara had run, and eye liner smudged her temples. Dark berry-stained, bee-stung lips, the lower one torn. Bruising across one high cheekbone. In her twenties, maybe. Latina, maybe. And dead.

As she let go, Andrea's fingers grazed a rough section of skin. She pushed the hoodie's cuff up an inch to see the uneven scars that encircled the dead woman's wrist. Something silver lay on the pavement below her forearm. Andrea lifted the hoodie's oversized sleeve with the back of her hand. A silver metal lighter. Folded cash in a money clip embossed with a marijuana leaf. A fifty on top. She let the woman's sleeve fall back over them and stood up, aware of Jesus, Louie's kitchen manager, at her back. "She's dead."

Her breath rose. Not the same, at all, as the lingering white mist that had twisted itself from the deeper shadows against the alley wall and rose into the cold air earlier. That hadn't been the woman's breath.

"She's dead," Karie echoed into her phone, her voice small. She was a paranormal investigator at Waltham-Young Community Library, where Andrea also worked as an archivist.

Aaron, the ghost haunting Louie's Gastropub, the current bane of Andrea's existence, and the one who'd led them to the dead woman, was gone to wherever ghosts go when they aren't around.

They retreated to Louie's kitchen door as a group. Jesus ducked inside. There were only two other employees in the kitchen this early in the morning. Karie shivered beside her. Andrea should go back in for her coat.

When Jimmy stepped out into the alley from the kitchen door a few minutes later, an unexpected frisson of relief loosened Andrea's clenched muscles. "Hey," he said.

"How'd you know?" Karie asked.

A state cop with the Bureau of Criminal Investigations, Jimmy wasn't exactly Andrea's boyfriend, but they'd spent a lot of time together since they met a few weeks ago. And Jimmy knew about Aaron and Andrea's ability to see him, for all the good that did. She'd not been able to help Aaron at all so far.

"Taka heard dispatch send units and called me. I was already in the garage, coming to see you." Jimmy rubbed his hands up and down the upper part of Andrea's crossed arms. "Louie's manager said she's out here?"

"Between the bins," Andrea said.

Karie added, "She was hidden by those pallets."

The pallets lay out in the alley now, a scrap of dark blue cloth flapping from a splintered board. Jesus had dragged and dropped them after Andrea shoved each one at him to get to the girl. And that's what she was, really, at twenty-something. A girl. Would anyone miss her at Christmas? Did she get Thanksgiving with family last week?

Jimmy gave the pallets a wide berth and crossed the alley to look but didn't go between the bins. He stood right where Aaron had.

Since that first, glorious contact, Aaron had been tongue-tied, unable to hear what Andrea asked him, and only partially visible at best. None of Karie's paranormal tools had helped so far, although his presence and ability to manipulate them proved that ghosts could indeed set them off. Karie, ever the scientist, had been elated, but explained just because ghosts *could* use them didn't prove ghosts *were* using them in other settings.

They had the advantage of Andrea watching Aaron set them off. But they didn't help Aaron hear her or her hear him except in one-word static bursts across the radio frequencies on the spirit box. "Wrong" and "Georgia" and "Alley" weren't helpful.

And neither was Detective William Taka, her best and oldest friend. Based on Andrea's first paranormal experience with little ghost Billie Mae, and how Aaron had spoken so easily in his first interaction with her, Karie's working theory was that Andrea needed Taka present to boost Aaron's ability to communicate with her.

She'd asked for his help, twice, but he refused to be drafted into any more interactions with ghosts. He hadn't been to Louie's since Aaron appeared. After the trauma life after death had already caused him, Andrea hadn't pushed him again.

"What were y'all doing out here?" Jimmy asked, coming back to them.

"Aaron."

"Ah. You need a better reason than a ghost and fast."

Andrea blanked, but Karie said, "We're documenting Louie's for Waltham-Young."

"Even the alley?"

"Yes," Andrea said. "His disposal practices, including recycling and composting. Plus the other businesses surrounding him and the appearance of the historic buildings on either side of the alley."

Jimmy nodded. "Good."

Emergency lights flashed at the mouth of the alley. Finally. Andrea might be able to roll the lingo of her job off her tongue, but... "How do I explain you?"

One side of his mouth lifted in that crooked smile that made her heart hit a double beat every single time. "Concerned boyfriend?"

"You or Taka?" Karie quipped, the snark ruined a bit by the chatter of her teeth.

Jimmy looked to the heavens and sighed, but Andrea squashed an errant laugh into a sharp escape of breath and quick smile. Jimmy shook his head at her. She loved that about him, that he reacted with affection rather than anger when it came to her and Taka and their inseparable friendship that, until October, equated to a platonic marriage.

A Charleston Police Department patrol officer came out the back door, followed by Jesus and the sous chef. Andrea and Karie took their jackets from Jesus with thanks as the officer said, "Where's the body?"

So harsh.

Jimmy glanced at Andrea. It'd be better coming from her, that look said. She took the lead, taking the officer over to where Jimmy had just been, so he could see the woman. A second patrol officer walked through the alley to join them. Andrea was glad to recognize Eric, a uniform she knew from department functions. She made introductions and explained their involvement. She knew she'd have to repeat it ad nauseam.

A woman in jeans and an apron opened the back door of the bakery next door, a huge garbage bag at her feet. Her eyes went wide at the sight of them. "I'm going to have to ask you to stay inside, ma'am," Eric said. "I'll come explain everything in a few minutes."

She nodded and shut the door.

As more officers showed up, they were taken inside Louie's and separated to give their individual statements. Jimmy gave her a nod and mouthed "call me" when he left a half-hour in. Louie came in, his whole being somber. Karie left a few minutes later. Under the watchful eye of the uniform at the front door, Andrea moved from a table in the gastropub's great room to the Christmas-lights-draped bar. Maybe Aaron would show, though it hardly mattered at this point unless he'd seen something related to the woman's death and could communicate it.

She studied the ring on her right middle finger, the intertwining curves of the several horseshoe nails twisted together. It was Louie's, passed down from his great-grandfather. Only days after Billie Mae crossed over in October, Aaron had stolen the ring from where Louie kept it and dropped it burning hot onto the old wooden bar in front of her.

She looked up, at the spot it had fallen from, but there was still nothing to see.

She'd been with Jimmy and Taka, Louie standing behind the bar, all of them confused. And then she'd noticed Aaron standing near the beer taps. In his mid-twenties, wearing a blue chambray button-down shirt, white waist apron, and dark blue trousers, he resembled Louie with his square jaw, piercing dark eyes, and expressive face. She'd assumed that maybe he was one of Louie's many nephews. They often passed through, acting as barback or waitstaff for the night.

But when she'd drawn Louie's attention to him, no one else could see him. And then he said, "Tell him Aaron needs to clear a few things up."

And winked out.

Louie's family history held that a father had forged four rings, one for each son. The design itself signaled the enduring nature of that relationship. The one she wore had been handed down through the sons of Louie's line. Louie didn't know who Aaron was by name or where he fit on the family tree, if he was family at all. Andrea had narrowed the prospects over the last few weeks, but Aaron was still basically lost in time.

Pete Tamarin, the CPD detective assigned to the case, pushed through the kitchen's swinging half-doors. "Andrea," he said by way of greeting. He set his open tablet on the bar and sat down beside her, his belly brushing the bar. "Hey, tough morning."

She nodded.

"Taka said to call him when you're done. It's a damn shame. That family's old money. They could tie him up a couple of years if mediation fails."

After a grand jury declined to indict him for the shooting death of a murder suspect at the start of the painful mess that was October, Taka was hoping to be reinstated to regular duty by the new year. But three days ago, a civil lawsuit filed by the suspect's family took the wind out of his sails and meant he'd remain on desk duty indefinitely.

"The suspect did kill someone," she reminded him.

"But under the circumstances . . ." Pete shook his head.

There was no sense in talking to Pete about any of it. "Did she have ID on her?"

"No."

"Did Louie know her?"

"No, says he never saw her before," Pete said, scrolling through his tablet. "Help says the same. Have you? Maybe on the street? In the parking garage after hours?"

"You think she's homeless?"

"I'm not thinking nothing. I'm asking. That's what I get paid to do."

"No. I'd think I'd remember that hair. And those cheekbones."

He finally looked up at her. "You'd think, but probably not. Women can look real different with a different do and some makeup."

That sounded like experience speaking.

"And dead," he added. "They can look real different dead."

"If you're trying to shock me," Andrea said, "it's too late. I'm already in shock."

"Geezus," Pete said, face softening into concern. "I'm sorry. I just— that was inappropriate. I forgot you aren't just Andrea today. Are you okay?" He stood halfway up, looking around for Andrea didn't know what. "You need a drink?"

"No, I'd just really like to get to work."

Tapping on the tablet with a beat-up stylus, he ran her through the morning's timeline, checking her answers against his notes—and everybody else's answers, she presumed—and asking her to tell him why they were in the alley and how she happened to notice the body.

Just as they were wrapping up, Detective Raymon Fields came in from the back.

"You know Fields?" Pete asked.

She nodded. Taka had introduced them once. Fields was CPD's only Black detective and the most recent transfer into the Criminal Investigations unit. He and Taka, of mixed race, including Black, were among the very few people of color on the force, which made them highly recognizable. "Your first murder?"

"My first death investigation," Fields corrected her. "As a primary investigator."

"You're in experienced hands under Pete." Pete and Tracy Manners were the alternating leads on death investigations. Taka would have been the natural successor to Tracy Manners, his most frequent partner, but not now, placing Pete under a lot of pressure until another detective with Tracy's level of investigative knowledge could be hired.

The uniform let her out, locking the door again behind her. A few people were loitering out in front of Louie's, talking in low voices about the cop cars and the ambulance, its doors wide open and waiting to receive the woman.

Andrea hitched her small leather backpack over one shoulder and walked around the corner to the Huntington Square garage and her FX. After climbing inside and locking the door, she sat in the silence with her eyes closed, seeing the wispy rise of, what? A spirit? Aaron's lowered head, his praying hands, the pallets falling away from the woman. The ashy pallor of her face.

Music rose from her phone, Train's "Hey, Soul Sister" refrain. She really needed to change Taka's ringtone in fairness to Jimmy, though Jimmy had only laughed when he'd heard it and said, "Y'all really are soul sisters with your sleepovers and meal planning."

They were still feeling each other out, both wary with their glued-together hearts. Hers because of Chuck's death shortly after their engagement and him because his girlfriend of three years demanded he choose between her or his job. On their first real date, just them over steaks at Bricks & Barrels, Andrea had enlightened him about her job as an archivist at Waltham-Young and the satisfaction that filled her when ferreting out and compiling details to form whole historical records that let anyone with an interest immerse themselves in the past. Jimmy shared his drive to solve even the smallest of criminal puzzles and the overwhelming sense of justice done he felt when closing a case.

And over a shared Chocolate Brick for dessert, Andrea had spelled out the facts of her complicated friendship with Taka and that she'd never give him up just to keep a man in her life.

Jimmy had leaned forward, spoon frozen above the half-demolished block of chocolate-encased ice cream. "What about for the love of that man. Or your love for him?"

She'd read the sincerity of the question in his eyes, his openness. He wasn't being aggressive or trying to shut them down before they'd ever really started. He was curious. He was being a cop, his interest in human nature on full display.

"I don't know." And she'd not even known what words she'd say until she was hearing them. "Not for him. Definitely. But for me? Maybe for my love of him? If it was better for us all? Maybe that makes me a narcissist."

"No," he said, spell broken. He scooped up a bite of ice cream. "That makes you disgustingly mentally healthy. You do you for you. I'll do me for me. And where we overlap, we'll find our common ground and go from there." He popped the ice cream in his mouth. Savored it. "If you'll keep seeing me, that is, because damn if I don't want to keep seeing you."

He said all the right things. He was patient and accepting. He was undeniably her type. She couldn't stop thinking about his lips. So why did she still feel anxious every time she thought of them together?

The phone fell silent. Whoops.

But Taka just rang it back again.

She thumbed it open. "Hey."

"Hey. Pete said he let you go. You okay?"

"Yeah."

"Jimmy said Aaron took you to her."

He'd already spoken to Jimmy? "You've been busy."

"Not really, that's why I have time to text around the block to find out what's going on."

"I think I saw her."

"You mean, like ghost her? Or the woman herself, before she died?"

"Ghost her, only not. I saw—her spirit?" And even as she questioned, she saw again the rising spirit, Aaron's praying hands. "I saw her spirit rise from the alley."

"Well maybe she won't come knocking on your door then."

"I need you to help me with Aaron, Taka. Just come stand beside me. Please."

The silence between them sat heavy in her throat, on her heart.

"I know Karie has that idea I'm a 'conduit' for you, but why me? Can't we look for someone else? Maybe a medium or somebody like that?"

"Why are you so scared, Taka?"

"Why *aren't* you scared, Ands?"

2

Taka thought she wasn't going to answer him. He'd known her since middle school, and nothing scared her. She might have a few anxious moments that drove her to up her monthly savings a few extra dollars or buy some extra canned food before winter got cranking, but true irrational fear, no.

She took her own spiders out.

And made bacon for ghosts.

And killed a man to protect him, William Taka, a guy who still had to shove down his dread just to take a shower.

A snapping startled him.

Not knowing he'd closed them, Taka opened his eyes.

Karl's hand in front of his face, fingers poised to snap again.

Taka batted his hand away.

"I gotta go, Andrea," he said into the silence.

"I don't know, Taka." The words tumbled out in a rush, like she was afraid he'd hang up on her. And okay, maybe that was something they were both afraid of, their friendship being irrevocably broken because he couldn't freaking deal.

Karl continued to stand in front of him.

He hadn't been there when she fell and tweaked her brain, so how he became her damn conduit for channeling ghosts, he had no idea. "I've really got to go. I'll call you later."

After she made him promise, she let him go.

Karl thrust the files in his hand at him. "Horton's wanting you to review these, make up a priority action report."

Aside from a short be-on-your-best-behavior briefing before his official return, Detective Chief Ronnie Horton had had nothing to say to Taka so far. "What are they?"

"I don't know, man," Karl said over his shoulder, headed for the bullpen door. "I'm on my way to a witness interview. Horton caught me on the stairs."

The top file tab read "Admin Inventory." Taka's phone rang. Jimmy. "I just talked to her. She okay?"

"Yeah," Jimmy said, his voice muffled. "What've they got you doing?"

"Reviewing video."

A dull thud. "Better than checking patrol cars in and out."

"True." He'd been back a total of four days on light duty per his therapist, spending eight hours a day on surveillance tapes. Two hours dawdling through the assignment and then an hour fast-forwarding on the traffic cams for his own secret project. "What's up?"

"Did she tell you she found the body?" His words burst on Taka's eardrum, suddenly crisp. "Karie was there, but Andrea found it. Said Aaron took her straight to it. She needs Aaron gone, Taka, and she needs you to do that."

"I've heard."

"Louie needs a better security setup. You know he doesn't have a camera on the alley?"

Louie didn't have a camera anywhere. His only security was his grandfather's hunting whip hanging in the bar and nine-one-one. "Why are you telling me?"

"Louie doesn't know me, not really. You know him, you know the business. You could moonlight. Tell him how useful video would've been to run down whoever killed that woman."

"And then I'd just happen to be there to help Andrea with Aaron."

"My thought exactly. Without having to, I don't know, reverse your stance."

"Why does everyone think she needs my help?"

"Dude. I was there."

"So maybe you can be her fucking conduit."

"I tried."

Well, shit.

"And Karie's tried, too. You know what we saw before you picked up Billie Mae? Before we all saw Bruten standing there plain as day?"

Taka didn't trust himself to speak. Two ghosts, as real as anyone. Bruten Wilder had been his training officer at the Academy. Jimmy's, too. With Billie Mae's baby shampoo and little-kid summer sweat in Taka's nose, her weight and warmth in his arms, the medals on Bruten's chest had caught the kitchen lights and hurt his eyes, they shone so bright. Bruten wasn't just some misty ghost, he was Bruten, the same fierce pride he'd exhibited at cadet graduations radiating from him.

"Nothing. We saw nothing until you picked her up. And she wasn't all there until you reached Andrea." Wind on the receiver and then the sound of traffic on the street. "I still can't..."

Taka waited for the rest of what Jimmy might say. It'd been over a month, but he still couldn't either. Couldn't believe in ghosts. Couldn't believe he'd been trussed up and incapacitated so thoroughly by such a loser. Couldn't believe he and his ex, Dewey, had survived.

Thank God Dewey was smarter than half of West Virginia's population combined.

Maybe too smart for his own good.

Taka was pretty sure that Dewey had arranged payback for the role his father, Senator Dante Sanderson, former Speaker of the House, played in the whole screw-up by staging a "carjacking" during which his father, was "tragically" killed along with Dewey's own bodyguard to make it look good.

And what would Taka do if he managed to link any of the traffic cam and CCTV footage he was sneak-surveilling to that investigation? Protect Dewey or give it to the man on the other end of the line, the state's liaison on the federal investigation into the senator's murder, the unknown now embedded in Andrea's life?

A man he was grateful to but wasn't sure he could trust.

At least he knew for sure he couldn't trust Dewey.

"You still there?" Jimmy said.

"It's not that I'm too proud to 'reverse my stance,'" Taka said, emphasizing the words. "I just don't want to..."

Jimmy let Taka's pause draw out for a long moment before he said, "You just don't want to."

"Damn it!"

Karl, at the desk across the aisle, turned his head sharply. Taka lowered his head and his voice and spun his chair to face the window next to him. He blew out a hard breath. Talking had become so damn hard this month. He just didn't want to get irreversibly caught up in anything related to... "We're talking fucking ghosts here," he hiss-whispered. "How is everyone just overlooking that?"

"We're just being pragmatic."

"How is that being pragmatic? Aaron's dead. Not just dead but long-ago dead. What can Andrea do to help him?"

"We won't know unless you help her."

Shit. "Fine."

"Fine?" Jimmy spit, letting his control slip. Anger seeped into the rest of his words. "Does that mean you'll help her?"

"I would never not help her."

"It hasn't seemed that way lately."

"Lately, I've needed time to process."

"Time's up."

"I got that." Taka let his tone sour further. "Thanks."

"You're welcome," Jimmy said and hung up.

STANDING under a tree at Quarrier and Court Street, Jimmy shoved his phone in his back pocket. He liked Andrea more than anyone he'd dated in the past five years. More than anyone he'd dated since he'd gotten tired of dating and wanted more. Someone to make a home with, maybe a family.

But, besides the sheer, undeniable proof of life after death that night in Andrea's kitchen, the memory that kept him up at night was the way that Andrea and Taka came together in the middle of the kitchen that stuck with him.

Closing his eyes, Jimmy turned his face up to the bare branches and grey sky and let the cold morning breeze off the river carry the memories away. Having to lie to both of them was getting more complicated. He'd been doing background on Dewey Sanderson for going on two years, and a full-out sanctioned investigation for more than five months.

Scott, an Undercover Investigator borrowed from North Carolina's State Bureau of Investigation, joined the op three months ago. And clicked with Taka over beers at Dewey's nightclub right away.

After October's shit-show and learning about their long-buried connection to Dewey, Jimmy now knew more about both Andrea and Taka than they had revealed to him themselves. Keeping it all straight while having a natural conversation was harder than he'd ever imagined it would be. But he thought—he'd been certain—that he could handle it. And he'd been so mad at Scotty for crossing the line with Taka, but now here he was right next to him.

He checked his watch. Eleven o'clock. Twenty minutes to go.

Ever since Scotty transitioned from Dewey Sanderson's bartender at the Coliseum to one of his bodyguards, it'd become a lot harder to arrange meetings. They'd set up a dead drop for new burners and exchanges of flash drives for reports. Probably overkill, but no one knew whether Dewey Sanderson just looked suspicious as hell or if he really was dealing illegal arms, transporting drugs, and involved in multiple counts of homicide-arson affecting both competitors and law enforcement.

There was Andrea's FX, coming down Quarrier. It'd been a guess that he might catch her on the right route to work from Louie's. And he had to be here anyway to meet Scotty, but his heart still lifted. The tree wasn't much cover, but she wouldn't be looking for him. He stood still with his hands in his pockets as she pulled up behind a Honda and a dry cleaner's van waiting at the intersection.

She wasn't a talker. She didn't dwell on her past or share much of her thoughts, though he knew from her passionate stories about her work that she thought deeply. She had a reckless older brother, but she hadn't mentioned him. Her father abandoned his family when Andrea was five and now lived an impoverished life on a decrepit farm outside Tulsa, but he had no idea if she knew that. Her mother worked for the city and died a long, slow death of breast cancer that spread to her lungs and bones, but she'd never told him more than the single fact that she died of cancer. Her maternal aunt in Huntington became her legal guardian for all of eight months after her mother died, but never actually supported her.

That didn't keep her from claiming Andrea as a dependent on her taxes until Andrea graduated from Marshall with her master's. Jimmy had a guy who had a guy checking to see if it was too late for the IRS to discover that little discrepancy.

Her long, dark hair, loose earlier, was now twisted up and knotted at the back of her neck. Her sharp profile and long, straight nose fit her height and personality. She stood eye to eye with him. In heels, she'd be taller. He hoped their relationship survived long enough he'd get to see her in a pair someday. Andrea turned left, headed to the river and Waltham-Young, swallowed up in the traffic passing by City Hall and the Courthouse.

Jimmy crossed the street and strolled past the Tidewater Grill's outside tables to the mall's entrance. The mall was late-morning busy. He joined several people in line at Starbucks. A few minutes later, Scott strode by without looking over. The barista called Jimmy's name. He thanked her and picked up his Americano.

In Price's Fine Jewelers, two of the sales staff were huddled over their display cabinets with customers. The sales manager, Jennifer, came to greet him and took him through a curtain into the back. Scott sat waiting for him in one of several private consultation rooms. Two small red Price's bags and Scott's cell phone sat on the tiny round table. Jennifer shut the door behind him.

"Hey, you made it," Scott said. "Thought maybe you'd be at Louie's."

"Word's out already?"

Scott nodded, leaning into his elbows on the table. "Cop cars on Quarrier and Hale? Hell to the yes."

"Andrea was there, so I swung by."

"Sit down, man, no one followed me. Dewey's still at the house."

Jimmy pulled a chair out and then sat, scruffed his hands back through his hair.

"You look tired."

"Can't sleep."

"Neither can Taka. I just can't actually imagine it." Scott flipped his cell over and over in both hands. "The torture he experienced."

"Why are you so nervous?"

"Dewey's prepping for a meeting. He's been locked up in his office on the phone for two days. We're going to Kirkby this afternoon. Dinner there tomorrow."

Kirkby was the warehouse, previously Kirkby Tire, where Dewey housed his wholesale weapons inventory, but Scott had been there before. That wasn't what was rattling him. Jimmy waited.

"He asked me if I'd ever shot an Mk21 or an FN SPR."

"Sniper rifles."

"Yeah. Might finally get something usable on him. So far, he's just mean." His hands stilled and he met Jimmy's eyes. "Ruthless in business."

"Anything that'll get us warrants is good. I don't care if it's stealing mail. You don't know who he's meeting?"

"Some business partner of his dad's. Haven't heard a name yet." He shoved the phone away and sat back. "The senator owed him money."

And there it was. Every case boiled down to either love or money. Suddenly aware of his own taut muscles, Jimmy relaxed. The room was warm after being outside a good part of the morning. "Probate was filed a couple of days ago, right before the deadline. I take it this guy doesn't want to wait to register his claim."

Scott shrugged. "We can only hope he's not legit."

"No access to Dewey's digital files yet?"

"How long will they let you run this op?"

The higher-ups were grumbling, but not yelling for results just yet, not after October. Proof that there was any reason to keep pursuing an investigation into Dewey Sanderson's activities would quiet them back down. "I can stall a while yet." Everybody knew the senator's death might hand them their best opportunity to flush Dewey into the open.

"Listen," Scott said, hesitant. "Taka wants me to meet Andrea."

Taka knew Andrea and Jimmy were moving their relationship forward. Andrea only knew Taka was seeing someone, a guy. She didn't even know Scott's name yet. "That could get awkward."

"I didn't know, you know, that Taka would get tangled up in the case."

"I know that, but you knew he was a cop who frequented Dewey's bar. That made him part of the investigation, no matter how clean we thought he was at first."

Turning his head to the room's blank grey wall, Scott looked away.

"I've gotten close to Andrea on purpose," Jimmy soothed. "We'll spin your involvement with Taka the same way. A friendship, nothing more, built to serve the case." No need to remind Scott that his undercover life was closely monitored, the number of overnights he spent at Taka's already noted. Jimmy's weekly reports to the federal task force were no more than updates. He could scrub almost anything from the final report if it became irrelevant for prosecution. And no need for him to know that Jimmy had obliterated his own professionalism with Andrea.

"What if—"

What if they needed either Taka or Andrea or both in the end to get Dewey behind bars. "We'll cross that bridge if we have to." He cleared his throat, to help him cough up the words stuck in his throat. "We'll do it honestly and take what comes because we got the job done."

Scott didn't move. Only his gaze shifted back to Jimmy. He'd noticed the "we." Jimmy waited for him to ask, but Scott only studied him for a long moment and then let it go. "So, dinner."

Taka wasn't stupid and Andrea knew BCI still had eyes on Dewey. "Stick to the cover."

"Friends from back home." Getting up, Scott pocketed his phone. He grabbed one of the two jeweler's bags.

Jimmy held himself still and tried for casual. "Taka been talking to Dewey?"

Scott eyes narrowed though, his brow pinching. Paranoia bred paranoia and while ideally he should trust Jimmy completely, Scott knew his job was already on the line, and more so if he didn't deliver.

"Twice. At the club. Both contacts were included in my last report. You know something I don't?"

Jimmy held his hands up, palms out. "Just asking." He and the big boss, Maddox, had already decided not to tell Scott that Dewey and Taka were talking nearly every other day since Dewey's dad died. As Jimmy was rapidly discovering himself, it was a further hardship on a UI to know and hide more than they'd seen from the suspect under surveillance. And they needed his responses to any consequences of that unknown knowledge to remain natural to the undercover situation.

"Jimmy, are they talking on the phone?"

"No. There's no evidence of that. I was just wondering if they'd had any more contact."

Another long, studied moment passed before Scotty let it go. "See you at dinner."

"That'll be fun," Jimmy murmured.

Scott shook his head and let himself out.

Jimmy waited five minutes, grabbed his own excuse bag and made his way back through the mall.

3

Sweeping through the big double doors of Waltham-Young, Andrea waved at Marji on the reception desk, who had a phone to her ear. She walked through the three-story-high, sunlight-filled lobby and past the massive modern art that filled it, very conscious of the beauty and privilege in her life. Very conscious that she had a life and that the dead woman no longer did.

Up the wide staircase, through another set of double doors, left past the conference rooms then onto the hallway that led to her office. On one side were floor-to-ceiling windows that looked out on the century oak and the peaceful, spiral stone path of the courtyard that surrounded it. The other side of the hallway, a series of office studios with sliding-glass doors. At the fourth door, she swiped her secure ID card and entered her workspace.

At the back of the studio, floor-to-ceiling cabinets held all her supplies. A long counter along the back wall allowed her to spread out files and documents, and below it, open shelves accommodated all the various sizes of books she used. She owned roughly half the current books and the other half rotated on loan, coming in and out of libraries all over the world.

She slung her backpack onto the floor near her desk. To her right, a small, faded photo caught her eye. Caught catty-corner under a newer photo of her and her brother, both were almost buried beneath the bits and pieces of her life she had tacked on her cork wall. She freed the photo and studied it. Dad wore his uniform. Her mom, in a sundress, leaned into him, both facing the camera, the sun in their eyes. They'd married at eighteen and nineteen, respectively, after he came back from Parris Island. The image of Aaron standing at attention came back to her. She studied her dad's uniform pants.

Over the last few weeks, she'd gotten a better look at Aaron. The blue chambray shirt was rough-woven. The pants were worn twill, a mix of cotton and wool, common among the foot soldiers of the Confederate Army in the War Between the States. This morning, they were tattered and bore faded vertical stripes. His feet were bare. Aaron would've been about twenty-four at the start of the war, around twenty-eight at the end of it.

Slaves had served as labor for the Army, ditch diggers and camp builders, cooks, blacksmiths, medical assistants. And as men's servants, personal valets for those who could afford to bring them along. Wealthy white Southerners clung stubbornly to the belief that their slaves were loyal, faithful servants despite the fact that many of them defected at the first chance to do so, especially after Lincoln's Emancipation Proclamation.

Those slaves with less to lose stole their masters' belongings and sometimes even his spare horses while the master was occupied in battle. Those with families they couldn't risk or bound by other considerations stuck by their masters, feeding into the myth. Many of them honored their masters with marked burials and took their belongings and messages back home as camp followers as soon as they could. Others crossed the lines and then returned to act as Union spies.

Could Aaron have gone to war as a slave?

It seemed plausible, even likely, now that she'd thought of it. Her expertise lay more in the physical regarding slave plantations. Locations, architecture, layout, design, operational efficiency, and how those factors developed through the lenses of human and geologic development, economy, society, and culture. Tracking down the records related to slave sales, changes in ownership, and the details of any one life involved in the process, not so much.

But with yes and no answers not possible, she'd spent the past month working backwards from this building and the businesses that had occupied it, then the business district, looking for recorded deaths of Black men under the age of thirty-five in law enforcement, hospital, and newspaper archives. There'd been plenty of deaths, but only thirteen possible matches and she'd eliminated nine of those through genealogy searches from details gleaned in the accounts.

She'd not gotten into the possible granular data recorded in journals and contemporary accounts of the past century. But her secondary line of research, under the assumption Aaron and Louie were related, had turned up a fifteen-year-old slave named Aaron sold by Live Oak, the plantation in South Carolina where most of Louie's family lived after his one of forefathers was purchased at the slave market in Charleston, South Carolina, and bred to his plantation born foremother.

But she had yet to figure out where Aaron had ended up. It'd be a massive, unlikely coincidence if he'd died here in Charleston, West Virginia, where Louie's family later established themselves. Still. The ring was almost certainly his connection to Louie and the reason he appeared here.

Talisha Roberts would be able to point her in the right direction, though. She'd developed her reputation for thoroughness, persistence, and a knack for connecting unlikely resources while she was still in school, a couple of years below Andrea. Andrea had been thrilled to find Talisha already working at Waltham-Young when she'd come onboard. She tried Talisha's office, then texted her cell, without luck. To the documents room, then, where Talisha spent half her days. She claimed the cold, dry room had stopped her aging process.

After carding in, Andrea found several staffers spread out among the massive tables. Looking for Talisha down the rows of document cabinets, she found Randy instead, rifling through one of the deep double-stacked drawers devoted to biographical files. Roughly the 'L' section. With the Civil War on her brain, she quipped, "Stripping General Lee to his bones?"

"Trying to see if we can strip a piece off his bones, for DNA testing."

That stopped her. "Really?"

"Really. A group in Charlotte's funding it and they've already gotten a research grant from the Randall Corporation."

"Corporate? For profit?"

He just grinned at her. Lordy. Double-checking General Lee's heritage or wanting to clone him to lead the South into secession from Federal tyranny once again? She shuddered. Probably both. "Have you seen Talisha?"

Randy pulled a thin file labeled 'Lee Chapel.' Lee's burial place. "Heard you have a ghost story to tell."

"From Ben, I'll bet."

"Tall, dark, and chatty?"

"Ha!" Ben was the opposite of chatty, but he and scruffy, blonde Randy came as a pair of mismatched hillbilly bookends. "You know Karie has ghost stories from Berrylane Plantation."

Randy gave her an assessing glance. "I'd rather hear yours."

"You'll have to wait a month of Sundays."

"I can do that." He waved the file at her. "Did you know Lee's retreat from Gettysburg took him within spitting distance of Berrylane?"

"Did you know there's six executed deserters and several unmarked graves there? Maybe the Randall Corporation could balance their profit sheets with some non-Lee DNA testing in the name of historical knowledge."

Randy's eyes glazed over, gaze drifting off over her shoulder. "I wonder if they would." Andrea laughed, waking him up. He grinned at her. "Couldn't hurt to ask, right?"

"I won't hold my breath."

He widened his eyes, cheeks blown out, then unsealed his lips with a soft pop of breath. "But I could ask. Talisha's in the vault."

"Thanks."

The book vault adjoined the documents and research rooms. Behind glass walls, thirty-five hundred square feet of space housed bay upon bay of moveable shelving, each eighteen feet tall and thirty feet long. Half the bays stored barcoded books by size for higher density and half stored rare and antique collectibles in archival storage boxes.

Another staffer sent her to Bay Eighteen where she spotted the top of Talisha's head poking up from a custom-built workstation on an electric scaffold, which was suspended halfway up the bay.

"Talisha," Andrea called.

"Here!" She popped up, shaking the scaffold, to peer down at Andrea.

"Sorry to interrupt. I need help tracking the life of a slave born on a South Carolina plantation and sold in Charleston. I'm not sure what direction to go in. An old photo"—she lied, which was becoming scarily easy to do—"indicates he was in service with the Confederate Army."

Andrea watched Talisha change mental gears.

She lifted her arms above her head and stretched. "Do you know his name and approximate age?"

"Aaron. He was fifteen when he was sold in 1851. It's taken me a month just to get that far."

She let her arms relax, her hands coming to rest on her head, thoughtful expression softening the tension her intense focus on her work had left in her face. "Investigate the buyer if you can nail him down. If Aaron was important, or freed, or impressed by the military during the Civil War, or if he became a paid employee after the war, there might be a notation in the owner's records or letters, if any exist. The Army didn't record anything about the slaves that accompanied their owners, but sometimes they wrote debt notes to owners for a daily rate for use of their impressed slaves."

"The sales notation was for a plantation name. But it was abbreviated."

Staring off across the room, Talisha said. "Was it a market record or a recorded sales deed?"

"A notation on the seller's plantation account. Live Oak, if you know it?"

Her face lit up and she leaned forward, gripping the picker's safety rail. "I do! We've got several copies of Live Oak's records from Charleston County. Have you seen the photo of the house at Louie's?"

The dead woman's face flashed in front of Andrea's eyes at the mention of Louie's, but yes, she knew the photo. Despite and because of its history as a slave plantation, the photo of Live Oak hung in a place of pride on the back wall of the bar. A group of Live Oak's slaves, some of them Louie's ancestors, posed to one side, on foot and on horseback, being shown off as surely as the grand house. "Yes, I think Aaron was related to Louie's family. It'd be nice to get confirmation."

"There might be an annual inventory or a birth record. By the time Aaron was born, most of the slave population was native. Babies were profit."

Although the concept wasn't new to her, Andrea couldn't help shaking her head at the thought once again.

Talisha didn't notice. "He'd be listed on the 1840 census by age and gender, but probably not name. He was gone by 1860. What was the abbreviated buyer name?"

"S.H."

"H could be Hill or Hall, if other plantation names are any indication or if it's even a plantation name for sure. If you find the buyer's name, you'll know which state to be searching in. Or if SH is associated with Live Oak, there may be other notes." She rested her elbows on the rails to look down at Andrea. "I'd start with everything you can get related to Live Oak and the bills of sale in South Carolina's Miscellaneous Records for 1843 through 1872. I think it's series number 'S' two one three zero five zero. We've got transcripts in the research room."

She was referring to records collected by South Carolina's Department of Archives and History, a system Andrea was very familiar with related to plantation operations. Andrea finished writing the number on the folder in her hand. "Gotcha."

"Just a warning, you probably won't find much," she said, her tone turning serious. "I don't want Louie to be too disappointed. Tracking a slave family's genealogy isn't the rousing adventure Alex Haley made it seem. Slaves were property that ostensibly took care if its own needs. Although they were sometimes bred, they weren't weighed, their health and diet weren't tracked with any regularity, they weren't inspected unless there was a reason, like illness or sale. The life of a single cow on a plantation or a certain year's crop of tobacco, rice, or sugar cane is arguably more documented than any one slave."

"So finding his grave?"

"Is that what you're looking for?"

Andrea glanced down at the ring on her finger. "Yes?"

"You think he was in service to the Confederacy? Does Louie know if he was killed in the war?"

Louie didn't even know if Aaron was family, just that the ring Aaron somehow managed to manipulate was family-made. "No. That photo and the single name on the back is where the story begins and ends."

"Slave have to be super important to get his own grave, let alone marked. You're on a wild goose chase, but I hope you catch it because that would be remarkable from a single photograph. If it's even possible." She nodded. "That'd be something else. Maybe he lived. Maybe he's lying in Texas somewhere or Mississippi, with a full name on his grave."

Andrea doubted that, but her previous experience of how ghosts presented themselves was limited to a study of two, so... "Maybe?"

"Hey. I'm not dismissing you. If you can eventually find any trail, more power to you. You just need to know it'd be a long road and one that might not even exist. It's just the way it is for families with slaves in their ancestry. And not just African slaves, all of them." Talisha stood up straight, the cloak of research focus she'd cast aside for a few minutes already falling back over her. "Find his buyer. Then you'll have a place to really start. And I can point you at other resources."

Andrea nodded. "Thank you." She narrowed her eyes and lowered her voice. "I'll be back."

Talisha laughed and waved her off.

In the documents room, Andrea pulled the copies of the extensive documents in the Live Oak inventory, leaving any originals untouched, and signed them out with her digital marker on the room's system. After hiking over to the research room and exchanging nods and waves with the various staffers that caught her eye, she located the transcripts of the Miscellaneous Records she needed and booked it back to her office.

Karie sat tucked in the back corner on Andrea's comfy reading chair, where Taka insisted on dragging it every time he visited, making notes on a sheaf of paper. "I'm gonna move my chair to the back of my office, too. I like seeing out into the hall."

Andrea rolled her eyes. "You and Taka both."

"Did you talk to him?"

"Yeah." Andrea pulled out her Current projects file drawer and added the copies in her hand to the slim Live Oak folder. "He wants me to find a medium to help."

"Did you tell him he *is* a medium?"

Labeling a new folder for the SC Archive transcripts, Andrea stopped midword. "I hadn't thought of him that way. I thought mediums talk to the dead. Except, y'know, not like I do."

"I don't know of any who even pretend to talk to them like you do!" Karie shifted, drawing one leg up in the chair and getting comfortable. "Some would argue the definition, but there are many types of mediums and, in essence, Taka channels spirits and amplifies their presence whether he wants to or not. So, yeah, we could call him a medium and mean like an artist's medium that you work through psychically whenever you connect to a spirit. Or call him a medium that channels spirit but doesn't interpret it."

"I don't think calling him a medium is going to make him any more willing than he is now. Maybe less so."

"Then call him a channeler. Or an amplifier. Or a conduit, like I've been saying. Just call him back and tell him—I don't know."

Andrea finished labeling her folder. "Can I use a medium?"

"Do you want to try? It's a pretty small world. You might get outed."

Andrea caught herself mid-Taka scrum, that sound he made when he was caught between options. She shoved the new folder in the drawer and shut it. "I can't stop thinking about her."

"That's why I'm here and not my office. Do you think Aaron saw her die?"

Andrea pulled her rolling chair around to face Karie and collapsed into it. "I think I saw her die."

Karie sat straight up. "What?"

"I don't know." She propped her elbows on her knees. "I saw

something like white mist rise from her body. But she was cold when I touched her."

"It was cold out."

Andrea nodded. "So maybe she was cold and not dead, until right then. Or maybe it was just steam or fog or something. Maybe we should've tried to resuscitate her."

"Was her skin soft?"

Andrea shook her head. It had been stiff and cold, like Sam, the outside cat they had when she was little. She'd reached out to pet him as he slept in a cozy ball on the woodpile by the backyard shed and jumped out of her skin when her fingertips landed on hard and cold instead of soft and warm like she expected.

"Andrea, the first responders didn't try, either. She was dead. Do you think Aaron knows how she got there?"

"Maybe?"

They both fell quiet, lost in thought. Andrea kept picturing the way the dead woman's mascara had run in trails across her upper cheeks, the shadowy smudge of her eyeliner across her temples, her glazed brown eyes. Karie's triumphant voice startled her.

"Ava Kim might help. She'd be discreet. She lives in Roanoke."

"Does she talk to ghosts?"

"She channels spirit. It's different from what you do, but she'd be useful. We can even do an unofficial double-blind. See if she can sense Aaron and matches up with your information."

"She wouldn't be able to see him, though?"

"Not in the way that you do. She's connected her own symbols that represent the emotions she picks up and sometimes she can pick up mental images of a specific nature. Say she channels a granddad. She might see her symbols of a spray of roses that represents love and a baseball mitt that represents the feel of fatherhood, and a vision of a number two for two kids. But then she might also see a battered brown wallet being tucked into a pocket and she could ask the person she's with if they have their dad's or granddad's wallet."

"I kinda wish I could just hand seeing ghosts over to someone who wants to see them. I helped Billie Mae, I think, but I don't know how to help Aaron."

"You definitely helped Billie Mae. I was there. Never doubt that. You'll help Aaron, too. He was probably around before, right? He's probably been around a lot longer than you were aware of him. Or than he was aware of you."

Andrea's heart sank even further, which hadn't seemed possible a second ago. She raised her head to stare at Karie. "Oh, god, I hadn't thought of that. That ghosts could become aware of me. What if more show up? I saw—" There'd been an older lady standing on the corner of the intersection near her house. She wore a blue dress with tiny pink flowers on it, one of those see-through raincoats draped over it, thick hose on her legs, and a white scarf over her hair. Although the morning was clear, drops of water clung to the raincoat, confusing Andrea's eye and for just a moment . . . "I think I saw one this morning. Near the One Stop. An older woman."

Karie stood up, cell phone already in her hand. "I'll call Ava." Leaving her notes on the chair, she stepped out into the hall.

Andrea shook herself and straightened up. She needed to finish up a client report on a historical cabin on a Roane County farm to be sent today and get started on the private project she'd accepted for the site of an old farmstead called Ivystone in Falling Waters near Berrylane. But then she'd take her notes from the past month and file an official Charleston preservation project memo on Louie's, which would include historical background on Louie's family and the influences that brought them to Charleston. As a nonpaying project, it would take lower precedent and maybe two years to complete but would give her some leeway in her research on Aaron and add to the community's long-term knowledge of established Black-owned businesses.

She'd just gotten started when Karie bounced back in. "You'll never believe this, but she's on I-77 already. She said she knew she needed to be in Charleston, but she didn't know why until I called her."

4

"Hi, ladies, come right in," Louie said, pushing the front door open just before eight. A hand-lettered sign announced his involuntary closure for the evening. He appeared a little worn around the edges.

Andrea grabbed the handle and pulled the door open all the way, ushering Karie inside ahead of her. "I'm so sorry to disturb you, Louie. You've had a day."

"That I have. I've left the key in the lock there," he said, pointing at the inside doorknob. "You use that for now. You come and go as you please until you get that boy straightened out."

"You talkin' about Taka or the ghost?" Karie drawled.

Louie winked at her. "I'll be in the back awhile yet. I'm making coffee for the officers out back."

"They're still here?"

"Just two, at either end of the alley. Been a lot of people coming by to take a look."

Andrea set her backpack on the same low-backed barstool she'd used for that purpose this morning. "I'm sorry you had to close. I wish I hadn't gone out back."

"Not your fault, missy. They shut us all down, between our fire doors being blocked and not wanting us to trample anything out there, so no matter. Besides—"

"There was a dead woman out there," Andrea finished for him.

He dipped his chin. "Death commands a certain respect."

"Did they figure out who she is?" Karie asked.

He raised his brows at Andrea. "I've not been informed if they have."

"I haven't heard anything from Taka."

"You lock that door now until your friend comes," Louie said, turning to the kitchen. "I'll go out the back."

"Good night, Louie," Andrea said, Karie echoing her.

He raised a hand in acknowledgement and continued on his way around the bar.

A light tapping on the door drew them both around as it opened.

Karie's voice burst with joy. "Ava!"

"Karie," the older woman said, "it's such a pleasure."

She wasn't anything like Andrea expected. She'd been stereotyping, she could see now, imagining a chic dark-haired Korean beauty about the same age as she and Karie, but Ava Kim was instead a willowy, Black senior, well past seventy, if Andrea's next guess wasn't wrong. She stuck out her hand. "Andrea Kelley, Ms. Kim. I'm so glad you're here."

Ava's skin was warm, her handshake firm. "Just Ava, please, and I'm happy to help. I had an annoying itch at the back of my neck until I gave up and got in the car. Good thing I'm retired, these spirits got me running all over the South. I was in Tennessee last week, if you can believe that, just to make sure a widow found the bundle of silver certificates her husband put under the floorboard before he died. Trouble was, she died herself, sixty years ago." She twisted her lips and widened her eyes. "These spirits, sometimes they be so confused. Their great-great-granddaughter was happy to have them though. She's a young mom, you know how that is." She eyed Andrea and then Karie. "Or maybe you don't. I know you don't, actually. You two, hmm." She shook her head. "Don't got the sense God gave you."

Karie laughed. "Don't get started, Ava."

"Only thing we should be starting is reading this ghost here."

Andrea turned to check, but there was no Aaron at the bar or anywhere nearby.

Brushing by them, Miss Ava plopped her yellow leather shoulder bag down on the round table nearest the door. "Shall we sit?"

They took seats around the four-top. From her bag, Miss Ava produced a notebook, two pens, and a voice recorder. "I'll send you the recording by email, Karie, that all right?"

"Yes, ma'am."

"I'm getting two spirits. One's a mother figure. Your mom's passed, Andrea?"

Everything in Andrea stilled, including her heart. "What?"

"Your mom, she's gone?"

"She died almost fifteen years ago." Somehow it hadn't occurred to her that her mom would be a ghost. "She's not...I've never seen her. She's at rest."

Miss Ava laughed and stretched her hand out to pat Andrea's, clasped together on the table in front of her. "Yes, darlin'. She's at rest. Doesn't mean she's not checkin' in on you and that rapscallion brother of yours."

Miss Ava knew about her brother? They weren't even Facebook friends. She threw a darting glance at Karie, who met her eyes and said, "Ava's the real deal."

"But you said you're a skeptic."

"I am, and Ava's a psychic."

"What she's trying to say without saying it," Miss Ava said, amusement coloring her tone, "is that I might be reading you, not an actual separate entity that used to be your mom."

Addressing Karie, Andrea said, "So you believe in psychics, but not ghosts?"

"Well, after last month, I'm only skeptical of people who say they see ghosts, not the ghosts themselves."

"Oh, darlin'," Miss Ava crowed. "You've been holding out on me!"

"I'm relying on your discretion, Ava. Andrea doesn't want to be outed."

Miss Ava lifted a hand. "Hold up now. Let me do my thing first and then I expect the whole story in return for my silence."

"Deal."

Andrea wanted to object to any form of blackmail, but the woman was four hours from home on intuition and an itchy neck, so that seemed ungrateful. Hopefully, she could be trusted.

"That's really all your mom wanted you to know, that she's checking in, that she loves you. Oh! She's showing me a medal. For me, that means she's proud of you. But she's also—I've only seen this once before." Miss Ava squinched her eyes in concentration. "Did you kill someone? A man. Not old. There's water." Her eyes popped open, her gaze landing directly on Andrea. "And you set a cop on fire?"

The intensity of her stare made Andrea's face burn, but she didn't look away. She relaxed her throat so her voice would be clear. "No, the man I killed did."

"Well, your momma says that he can't hurt you anymore, you stop worrying about him. And she's proud of you."

She'd told no one of her nightmares, or how sometimes in the middle of the night she was afraid she'd open her eyes and see his ghost standing by her bed, ready to take revenge on her. Every time her thoughts circled back around to that most terrible and most miraculous of mornings, she either focused on how Billie Mae felt in her arms, the light that surrounded her and Bruten Wilder at the end, or on something else altogether, some physical task or problem at work, or making a research list for Aaron.

"Yeah, darlin', you forget about him. He's being dealt with."

Tears sprung up in the corners of her eyes.

Miss Ava nodded, her gaze softening. "Now she's pulling back."

Andrea turned her head, scanning the restaurant, just to see if her mom was there somewhere, visible to her. Aaron stood to her right in his white shirt and twill trousers, the white apron neatly folded and tied at his waist. She could see the tables behind him through his body. Her mom wasn't visible. She wiped the tears off her cheeks.

Miss Ava focused inward, still looking at Andrea, but not seeing her anymore. "Oop, who is this? Karie, I've got a mother figure stepping in, a grandmother. She's showing me coneflowers, a whole colorful bouquet."

Karie raised both hands to her face.

"And lots of hearts," Miss Ava said, slowly shifting her thousand-yard stare Karie's way. "You're very loved from the other side. She's showing me a whole crowd of people standing behind her. She's making me feel like 'you go, girl' and rolling her fist, like, whoop, whoop. And the coneflowers again, a whole field of them. On a slope. She's pulling back now."

"Grandma Joan."

"And the flowers?"

"A project I'm working on."

"Well, you go, girl." Miss Ava flashed a grin and then sobered again. She looked past Andrea, into the dark corner of the restaurant near the bar. "Okay, the man standing behind you, Andrea. He feels old, but he's indicating he's a young man. A soldier. No, not a soldier. he's showing me boot black, boot polishing. A soldier's man. Like a valet. An 'A' name, Adam, Ar...Aaron, maybe, spelled like Hank Aaron." She laughed. "He's showing me a baseball bat. Maybe he had something to do with baseball.

"No. He's showing me . . . I don't know what that is, chains? Chains. He was trapped in a situation not of his own making. Is this a friend who's passed? He'd have passed some time ago." She was quiet a moment. "But no, he couldn't be an American plantation slave, that's too far in the past to be connecting through you. I feel like there's been a journey. I'm getting luggage, which means a long journey to me."

As a ghost, Aaron had been on a long journey of sorts. "You could say that."

"He's bringing a young woman forward. She's shy, but hmm. It's an odd combination. She's hiding herself, but at the same time, I can feel her amazing strength. She's practical. She's only just passed. A, uh, quiet death? But violent. Or violence before a quiet death. She wanted it." Miss Ava straightened up and came back to herself. "Any of that make sense? She didn't kill herself. Adam or Aaron is showing me my symbol for murder, but it wasn't unwelcome." She patted her heart. "She broke. I want to say her heart, but that's not quite it. All I'm getting is shards of broken glass. And a twist of hard candy. Sour candy. Is she connected to... she's connected to Aaron. And to you, Andrea. She's connected to you?"

Watching Aaron, Andrea shrugged.

"Andrea," Miss Ava said, her voice pitched low as if calming a scared pet. "Are you sensing someone?"

"Seeing," Karie said, copying Miss Ava's pitch. "She's seeing someone."

"It's Aaron," Andrea said. "I can see Aaron, standing just there, ten feet from us."

"Is the woman there?" Miss Ava asked.

Andrea shook her head. "He's trying to talk to me, but I can't hear him."

"Does he know her name? She's giving me a 'K' sound. She's also showing me my symbol for the military. I might be cross-reading them. I can't say now which information applies to each of them. You can really see him? Can you read his lips at all?"

"I can't. He's very transparent."

"You're seeing him with your eyes, he's not a mental image?"

"We were hoping that you would be able to strengthen her ability to hear him," Karie said, still in a hushed voice. "He led Andrea to a woman's body this morning. In the alley out back."

The entire time Karie was speaking, Aaron grew brighter, filling the space he stood in.

"This woman?"

"I don't know," Karie said. "Can you tell if she died today?"

There was still no woman visible, but Aaron walked closer to Andrea, in his drabs and knee boots, solid enough to touch.

"She's passed recently, but she could be anyone connected to Aaron or Andrea in some way. There's definitely some sort of connection."

"Tell him Aaron needs to clear a few things up," Aaron said.

Andrea stood up, her chair sliding out behind her. "I can hear him."

"It's working," Karie yelled, jumping up.

Miss Ava stood, too. "With your ears?"

"What, Aaron," Andrea said. "What do you need to clear up?"

"We're in the wrong place. Ned's in the wrong place. Ask Sally."

"I need more details, Aaron. Where are you?"

"In the wrong place." He tapped his ring finger and pointed at Louie's ring on hers. "Find Ned. Ask Sally." And although he looked calm, his voice was loud all of a sudden, like his sound had been turned up.

"Sally," Miss Ava said. "Her name is Sally."

Aaron looked at Miss Ava and shook his head. "She was in the wrong place, too," he boomed.

"How will the ring—" But Aaron was gone like he'd never been there. Andrea sank.

"Your chair," Karie said, rushing around the table.

Andrea straightened her knees and let Karie slide the chair forward then guide her down into it. A draft of cold air rushed over her and then a man stood silhouetted in the doorway. Miss Ava and Karie turned in alarm. They'd forgotten to lock the door.

"Taka," Andrea breathed.

"Well, damn," Taka said.

"You saw?"

"You talking to thin air? Yeah. I saw."

"It really is you," Karie said.

Miss Ava put her hands on her hips. "What the hell is going on?"

5

"Lock the door, please," Karie said.

Taka locked it and then set the key on the table. Andrea was pale. She didn't look at him, just sat studying the ring on her finger. Karie introduced him to Ava, a psychic medium from Roanoke.

Ava held onto his hand after he met her offered hand for shaking. "I see," she said.

"What?"

She patted his hand. "It was the right thing, you coming here, for however much you don't want to be here. You're a good man."

"I really, really don't want to be here."

"But you are. Now," she looked around at the three of them. "Who's going to tell me what you've got yourselves into here?"

Andrea remained lost in thought.

Taka's glance went to Karie, who shrugged.

"You tell her," Taka decided. "I smell coffee."

He swung another chair over to their table, took his jacket off and dropped it over the back, and took himself behind the bar. He ducked his head through the doors to the kitchen. Only the night lights were on. Although the scent hung in the air, the coffee pot was empty and clean, but the warped "Chock Full O'Beans" can that Louie filled with fresh-ground coffee every morning was sitting next to it, along with four mugs, spoons, a small stainless cup of cream covered with cling wrap, and a Tupperware of sugar on a serving tray. Four, because Taka had called Louie about his security and found out Andrea was planning to be in the restaurant tonight. Louie was the best.

After firing the pot up, he did not go peek out the back to check on the uniforms he knew were still on the alley. He stood at the counter waiting for the coffee to brew and then some, frittering around fixing Andrea's coffee just the way he knew she liked it, then searching Louie's shelves until he found the honey stash for Karie. He dolloped a couple of spoonfuls into a small bowl and added it to the tray. Surely they'd managed to tell the medium the whole sordid tale by now, including his own humiliation.

Picking up the tray, he carried it through to the restaurant. The women fell silent when he pushed through the kitchen's swinging half-doors. "You get the story?" he asked.

"The incredible story?" the medium, Ava, said. "The amazing, miraculous proof of life after death story? Loud and clear."

"Too bad we're still at witness stage though. I don't think the universe wants scientific proof." Karie had been lamenting the loss of the camera footage from the get-go.

Ava laughed and reached for the mug Taka set in front of her. "God works in mysterious ways."

"Let it go already," Taka mumbled to Karie. "I brought you honey."

"Thanks, Taka."

"Thanks, Taka," Andrea echoed after sipping from her mug.

He placed the empty tray on the next table over and sat. No one spoke while he and Ava mixed their coffees, using almost the same amounts of cream and sugar. Taka tipped the last bit of sugar left in the spoon back in the bowl when he realized, just to be contrary.

Ava cleared her throat. "You had no control over that situation, and you shouldn't let what those cops say bother you. They're wrong."

"What," Andrea said. "What are they saying, Taka?"

Taka stared into his coffee, willing himself blank as his chest and throat tightened and the corners of his eyes burned. Goddamn it.

Ghosts and mind readers. What the fuck ever. He shook his head slightly, warning Andrea off.

"They're just men being men, thinking they could've done it differently, escaped or not been taken in the first place. You know what that is? It's tugging on the Devil's tail, tearing holes in the wind because it scares them, to think they'd ever be in the same position and not able to help themselves. And you did, right, help yourself? You got out. Escaped death in—" Ava closed her eyes for a moment. "Oh, my. Many ways. Know that your brother was with you."

Fuck no. Taka took a deep breath, a sip of coffee, and stood up. "Can I take you home, Andrea?"

She looked at him and nodded and pushed her own chair back.

"We'll clean up," Karie said. "I'll bring you the key tomorrow."

HE HAD PARKED near her FX in The Huntington Bank garage. Their footsteps echoed in the quiet. A car started a level below them. She grabbed her laptop bag and locked the car back up. She wanted to ask, but he was in a mood and long experience had taught her pushing would just lead to a fight.

They were halfway home and stopped at an intersection before he spoke. "Why were you crying when I showed up?"

"Was I?" And then she remembered wiping her wet cheeks. "Miss Ava said my mom was there, with us, that she wanted me to know that he couldn't hurt me. That he wouldn't be coming around."

Taka's shoulders dropped an inch, the movement itself seeming to allow him a huge breath in, like he was emerging from underwater. The red light turned green, lighting up his face in the dark. Andrea settled back in the Yukon's seat, suddenly feeling the day catch up to her in the heaviness of her body, the lax weight of every muscle pulling on her bones.

"They all think I'm an idiot," Taka said into the dark. "For letting a dense asshole not only get ahold of me, but keep me so long, too. None of them would have ever let him get the drop on them, let alone drug them. And if somehow, through some freak occurrence, he did get them, there's no way he'd keep them for more than a few hours while the drugs wore off. Definitely not for days."

"All of them?"

"Not Horton. Horton gets it."

"Are they saying this out loud or is it what you think they're saying to each other?"

He shrugged.

She waited.

"They're definitely thinking it. Everyone stops talking every time I walk into a room and then they start talking too loud about nothing."

But Andrea had heard differently from their friend Carson, Taka's lawyer. Sure, there were probably a couple of loudmouths, but the ones who counted were in awe at Taka's survival. Just that he survived. That he got out of that burning house even though he'd been half-drowned and shot and was still in handcuffs. "Do you remember what Officer Mendel told you?"

"Mendel?"

"The patrol officer who stopped when your Yukon was—"

"On ghost fire. Yeah."

"You remember?"

Taka ran his hand back over his head.

"He said you're legendary."

That got a bark of laughter from him. "That is so not what he said."

"It's what he meant. You're a very young legend at CPD. All those guys who stop talking when you walk in? Who aren't sure what to say to you? They can't believe you're still alive. They're not sure they would be in your place and that's why they've spent a good amount of time imagining how they might have got out sooner. Because they wouldn't have been so relentless enough to still be breathing."

"Don't forget heartless."

Andrea swung her arm out and slapped his arm with the back of her hand. "Mendel was wrong. If you were heartless, you'd have left Dewey to burn."

Taka's grin faltered. "I wouldn't have gotten out without him."

"I know."

"I've been talking to him."

That was news.

The events of October swept over her.

They'd saved each other. She'd thought a lot about that. Dewey had saved Taka despite all the anger between them over the years. It was perhaps the only thing she and Dewey had in common, that they both loved William Taka.

Andrea cleared her throat. "You've been talking?"

"Yeah."

"About?"

Taka shifted his hands on the wheel. "Nothing in particular."

"Taka."

He hit the right blinker and slowed to turn on Timber Way, which would take them to her street. "Dewey says he barely knew the guy. He's been sorting through his dad's payroll, but he hasn't gotten all the records yet."

"They have multiple businesses, right?"

"More than Dewey knew about."

"Really?"

"He agreed to two corporate partnerships, but his name is on the paperwork for a dozen different companies."

"Sounds complicated." Did he know that the state had surveillance on Dewey while Taka had been missing? That they'd been hoping one of them would give them an opening to investigate Dewey more fully? "You could ask Jimmy what he might share. From the little he said when you were missing, they have some interest in Dewey."

Taka snort-chuckled and Andrea's heart twisted. Man, how she'd missed him this past month. "They always have."

"Is it warranted?"

He shrugged and turned onto her street.

"Will you come get me in the morning?"

"Jimmy not here?"

"We're just talking, Taka, not like he's moved in."

"You aren't seeing him a lot?"

"Dinner occasionally. We went out to Kanawha Forest one Saturday."

He pulled into her driveway and turned the car off rather than just leaving it to idle while she gathered her things. "He seems just your type. What's wrong with him?"

Jimmy was her type. And she liked him. She didn't know why she was hesitating to embrace him fully. "Nothing. He's just...a friend. Right now." She glanced sideways at him. He'd turned sideways in his seat to look at her. He raised his brows. "I like his lips."

He grinned. "He does have very nice lips."

"Oh my god," she said on a laugh.

"But."

"Just but. I don't know."

His gaze wandered her face and then he glanced at the house. "Can I stay here tonight?"

He'd not stayed since that night and only come by the house a handful of times. A lunch here, a late drink there. "Trouble in paradise?" she asked, striving for lightness in her tone and failing badly.

Taka shook his head and turned back to the house. He ran his hands over the steering wheel. "I want you to meet Scott."

Immediately, she heard Scott's voice on Taka's voicemail while he was missing. Something about a book. She'd known, of course. He'd told her he was seeing someone, a guy. That was why he ghosted Melissa. But a niggling streak of hurt that this was the first time she was hearing his name from Taka's mouth made her say, "Scott?"

"I know." His hands met at the top and slid back down on either side. "It's not like I was keeping him a secret. We've just mostly had other things to talk about. Like me not helping you with Aaron."

And okay, she'd been a bit of a broken record. "It's been frustrating to watch his not-quite-there lips move. I'm sorry."

Taka held up his hand. "I'm sorry. You're my person and it was mean of me to shut you out. But I want you to meet him." He closed his eyes and drew in a big breath before his sideways look found her eyes again. "He makes me feel safe."

"I get that, Taka. You make me feel safe."

He sighed. "Except—"

"No except. You always make me feel safe when I'm with you."

"Andrea, you had to kill a man," he said, holding her gaze. "Because of me."

Andrea tried again to feel remorse for that, but nothing came.
Nothing.

Not satisfaction.

Not horror.

Nothing.

Not even fear now that she knew he wouldn't be showing up to haunt her. It was just something she did to protect Taka. To—to keep him safe. She could say that, but he'd pretty much just admitted he didn't feel safe with her. "I like having you around."

"But I haven't been around much lately."

"But you are right now."

He dredged up some spit and swallowed hard.

Andrea grabbed his hand, grateful when he squeezed hers hard. "Stay."

He nodded again and she let go of his hand so they could get out and go inside.

They left their shoes and coats in the mudroom.

"Oreos?" Andrea asked.

"Fresh milk?"

She pulled out the Oreos and then went to the fridge before she realized what Taka was doing. "They ID'ed another one?"

"Paul Summers, seven, from Virginia." Taka finished writing the boy's name on the lined paper torn from an old spiral notebook, folded it back into thirds, and tucked it back into the leather address book that lived next to her cookbooks.

His own victim list from October was written in tidy, tiny print on a folded Post-it note. He slid it out from under the large rubber band acting as his money clip, added Paul's name, and snapped the band back over it. "The Superball."

He turned on his heel, shaking off the moment. "I'll bet Paul loved Oreos."

Andrea held up the milk jug and package of cookies. "To Paul."

They sat and dipped their cookies in milk in companionable silence. Between the reassurance from her mom, Taka's presence, and the comfortable, dim glow of the LED from the stove hood, Andrea's tension gradually seeped away. She yawned.

Taka stacked her near empty glass into his. "DEFCON five on standby?"

"Yellow alert is way more conducive to sleep."

"I'll get you pillows and a blanket."

"I can sleep in the guest room," Taka said.

The scent of baby shampoo filled Andrea's nose even as her mind's eye gave her the blood mist and the boom of the guns echoed in her head. Everything between them had changed in the moment. "Okay," she said. "No Billie Mae, right?"

"Right. Shouldn't be creepy in there anymore."

"It never was, Taka, that was your imagination."

He rolled his eyes and got up, taking the glasses with him to the sink. Grabbing the small stack of his clothes that had been sitting on her dryer the past month, he went upstairs to shower first.

Andrea washed up and went through her mail from the past few days.

Upstairs, the guest room door was closed, the familiar rhythms of a football game filtering through it from the small TV.

6

Grumpy Taka was at least familiar Taka. He obviously hadn't slept well. Standing next to him at the counter in the morning, Andrea poured milk in both their coffees and slid his mug to him. "Guest room not creepy anymore?"

He tried to conceal the shudder that rippled through him, but she saw it.

"No."

Andrea side-eyed him while he buttered his toasted strawberry Pop-Tart.

He picked one up and ate half in one massive bite while sliding the small plate with the second on it her way. It wasn't what she'd normally eat, and he knew it, but it felt like a compromise. She picked it up and he whipped the plate up and set it softly in the sink.

He quaffed most of his coffee before picking up the other half of his tart. "How was your run?"

"Cold. Wet."

He turned all the way around to fully consider the grey fog pressing wet fingers of condensation against her large kitchen window like he hadn't noticed it before. He wrinkled his nose. "Is it raining?"

"No, just wet." She parked her butt against the counter, Pop-Tart in one hand, coffee in the other.

They watched the fog and ate and then gathered their things and went out into the wet cold.

Traffic was snarled. They inched along Greenbrier until Taka could take a turnoff that took them along the river, but half the inbound drivers did the same, so it was still slow. Andrea could barely make out the swift churn of the dark water. Taka's wipers slid across the windshield every three seconds with a quiet squeak.

Eventually Taka rolled to a dead stop several cars back from the Y-intersection that would put them onto the downtown connector. They moved up two places before he said, "Can you try again? With the psychic? If she really can't help you, I'll give it a go."

Andrea just managed not to roll her eyes. If last night was any indication, there was no question that Taka, so far, was the only one who could actually help her. "If she hasn't left yet, I'll ask," she said, already tugging her phone out of the side pocket of her backpack.

She texted Karie, getting an immediate reply, and by the time Taka reached the intersection another meeting was set up. "She can stay. If Louie's in this morning, I'll clear it with him." And then she remembered. "Both Aaron and Miss Ava said the murdered woman's name was Sally."

"We don't know that she was murdered."

"Still, maybe that would help?"

"I don't know how to pass that on. I can't exactly walk in and tell Pete Tamarin that he needs to plug 'Sally' into NamUs because a psychic and a ghost said so."

NamUs was the National Missing and Unidentified Persons System. If he hadn't already located her locally, eventually Pete or his partner would put all the info he gathered along with everything the coroner gave him into a new database file and see if it matched up to any existing reports of a missing person nationwide.

"Maybe . . ." Andrea's mind was spinning on possibilities. She could say she overheard kitchen staff mention her name, but then Pete would want to question them. Or that she'd asked around, but he'd want specifics. Or that she just remembered she'd bumped into her one day in the parking garage and they'd introduced themselves. "No."

"What?"

"I don't know how'd you do that. Maybe tell him I'm interviewing a psychic today and can bring her around to meet him?"

"It's been one day, Andrea."

And the investigation was barely off the ground. If Taka had trouble now, it'd be twice as bad if she tried to force a psychic into the case at this stage. "I know. Just keep it in mind."

"It's not my case."

"But you can still keep an eye on it."

He shook his head, but said, "Maybe."

ON THE SIDEWALK in front of Louie's, Andrea swung the Yukon's door shut and threw a wave over her shoulder at Taka before she remembered that Karie still had the key. She knocked as hard as she could on the wooden frame of the double glass-paned door, then shook her fingers out. Although she could see lights on in the kitchen, no one answered. She didn't have the sous chef's number and didn't want to text Louie. He'd earned his late mornings. The bakery next door was already in full swing, though. A woman pushed out through the door with two bags in one hand and a long baguette in the other.

Movement behind the bar in Louie's drew her attention back inside. She knocked again before cupping her eyes to the glass of the door to peer in. The shadowy figure of a woman with her hair piled atop her head pulled transparent items off nonexistent shelves. Before Andrea could register what she was seeing, the woman turned, her features becoming clearer, and spoke to someone, gesturing towards Andrea and the door. A head popped up in front of the glass door.

Andrea jerked away, a scream trapped in her throat, her hand going to her chest. A white boy, a teenager, grinned back at her through the door and reached for the knob. Andrea heaved in air, feeling stupid. But the door didn't open. The boy stepped back, waving no one in, through a still-closed door. He wore a long-sleeved white shirt and dark pants, the cut from a former century. Acne. His hair swept straight back. He turned away, ushering his unseen guest in front of him.

The woman behind the bar was gone. Andrea stood stock-still, breath held. The teenager glanced back and winked at her, then he was gone, too. Andrea wanted to bend over and breathe but she didn't want to look away, so she just stood there huffing with her hand on her chest, suddenly aware of a car passing behind her. Two men walked down the sidewalk towards her, talking to each other, swinging briefcases in one hand and holding coffee in the other. A woman pulling open the door of the bakery called out to her, "Are you okay there?"

Andrea raised her hand off her chest in a wave. "I'm fine. A reflection in the glass gave me a scare."

"I don't think they open until after eleven," the woman said. Throwing glances their way, another customer sidled through the door the woman continued to hold open as she spoke. "I'd just call and leave a message if you need a reservation."

"I'll do that," Andrea said. "Thank you."

The woman nodded firmly, gave Andrea a brilliant smile and finally went inside.

Andrea didn't dare look back at Louie's door. She spun on her heel only to find Taka still sitting at the curb, watching her, and talking to his Bluetooth. A rush of relief and rage and she didn't know what all weakened her knees but burned her chest and cheeks. With clenched fists, she stalked back to his passenger window on numb legs.

He rolled the window down. "Yeah, got it, Fields," he said, not hiding his irritation.

From the other end, Field's voice, "Better than the desk, Taka," and then the line clicked closed.

"What's wrong?"

"You," Andrea snapped.

"What did I do?"

She waved her hand at Louie's, but two legging-wearing moms were coming down the sidewalk, pushing baby joggers ahead of them. She shook her head. Taka raised his brows, then said, "I gotta go," into her pissed-off silence.

"Then go already."

He chewed at the inside of his lower lip, staring at her, then gave her a firm nod, put the truck in gear and pulled away from the curb without looking. A blue Honda braked hard to avoid hitting him and a second later the driver found her horn.

Andrea deflated. She turned on her heel and headed to the garage to get her FX. What was she doing? One second asking Taka to come help her with Aaron and the next mad at him for unintentionally channeling more ghosts than she wanted to know about. No, mad because he still didn't really believe he could do that.

She still couldn't believe he could do that. Maybe he was right to stay away. She wanted to help Aaron. She was already involved, and he was part of Louie's family, she was sure of it. But she didn't want to be seeing ghosts everywhere.

She hadn't seen any others in all the months of Billie Mae talking to her before the little girl started pushing her energy out into a real haunting that even Taka couldn't deny. But then the state trooper's ghost had shown up and really stirred the pot.

How long had Aaron haunted Louie's?

Had he tried to get her attention before or was Karie right? Had she been hidden among the living, invisible to the spirit world, just another breath and heartbeat ignoring them, until Billie Mae turned on the ghost light inside of her, drawing the attention of those needing something from the living?

And Taka? He was what? Her dimmer switch? His presence turning her up to searchlight bright?

She slammed the FX's door harder than she meant to, annoyed all over again.

Here Taka was, finally coming back around. His absence more days than not had been harder than she'd let herself feel until last night. But getting the crap scared out of her by pop-up ghosts while he was around hadn't occurred to her as a possibility.

That was going to take some adjustment if it wasn't just a fluke. And God, please be a fluke. Just getting used to the fact that ghosts existed, whether they were souls or remnants and whether or not they persisted after they got what they were after—and God, had Miss Ava really channeled her mom? Or just picked her brain? Psychics? Really?

She jumped at the tapping on her window and registered the bar of the parking garage blocking her exit at the same time. The attendant smiled at her while she rolled her window down. "Sorry, sorry."

"No trouble. You were thinking so hard, your windows were fogging up. Got your ticket?"

"Of course, yes." She fished it out of the cup holder and handed it over.

Pulling out onto the street a few minutes later, she concentrated on the accelerator under her foot and the pattern of the leather steering wheel cover against her palms, and the road and cars around her. Not looking for ghosts. Yeah.

TAKA HAD to go to Clay, a tiny town only known for some political gaff that got its mayor run out of town. Was running down the registered driver of a stolen Enterprise van parked down the street from Louie's alley yesterday morning better than sitting at his desk all day staring at surveillance footage? Maybe, except it meant losing time on his own private investigation into Dewey.

And once he got locked into the role of "floater"—sent out to do grunt detective work without the prospect of a badge and gun and his own cases again—that was a hard hole to climb out of without a ladder. Taka couldn't see any ladders coming his way anytime soon, just getting his hair muddy under the hard tread of field boots as other guys stepped on his head on the way to their cases.

Brake lights.

He slowed to a stop. When the light turned, he crept forward, this close to spinning the wheel and heading over to the Coliseum to see if Scott's car was in the lot. "Fuck," he shouted. He slapped the blinker up, squeezed the Yukon over to make the turn that would take him to Clay.

Twenty minutes into the hour drive, Dewey rang his phone. He hit answer and waited.

"You there?" Dewey asked.

"Driving." The hills around Charleston meant everyone was used to the spotty cell reception. You could lose signal for a couple of minutes at a time downhill and then on the uphill, if the caller hung on that long, their voice would come stuttering back in.

"So. You coming?"

Dewey wanted Taka as extra, invisible security for a late business dinner, parked in shadow with a rifle. Scott was going. They'd agreed on a don't ask, don't tell policy on Dewey, but he'd spill anyway. Tell Taka about the meeting as they lay in the dark on Taka's bed. Give Taka more for his private investigation. He'd take it to Horton if there was anything CPD could use.

"You know I can't without more details." Knowing a record of his calls to and from Dewey could be pulled into an official investigation, even knowing that Dewey's phone might be tapped if the state was as curious about him as CPD, was one thing. Participating in questionable activity beyond a high-visibility drink at Dewey's table in the club was another.

"You're done at CPD. Come work for me."

It'd become an old refrain in just a month. Higher pay, better benefits. A complete one-eighty from wanting Taka's head on a platter.

"Still a cop, Dewey."

"They're never going to let you off that desk, William."

Dewey only used his first name when he wanted to remind Taka they'd once been something more than wary frenemies.

"I wouldn't mind admin."

Dewey laughed, that big boom of his echoing into the Yukon. He said, "I'll try again after you've worked admin for a year and you're ready to slit your own throat."

The tight muscles in Taka's neck loosened in response. Dewey didn't know yet about Taka's relationship with Scott or he'd be pushing Taka harder, playing up the danger and Scott's newbie status in security. He rolled his neck while he talked, loosened his grip on the wheel.

Scott was a big guy with defensive skills. Taka wasn't worried about him. He could do better than work for Dewey, but Taka couldn't exactly ask him to leave. They'd met while Scott was bartending at the club. Convincing Scott to bail would just put him back on the wrong foot with Dewey. And Scott wanted the security detail, was eager for the experience.

Whether or not Dewey had set up his dad's murder, it wasn't like Dewey's business meetings had ever involved open warfare. Mostly people that got on Dewey's bad side got disappeared and found months later, living far, far away just because they had "needed a change."

"What are you doing that's got you so paranoid?"

"I sell guns for a living, Taka. Trevor used to watch my back. It's just bodyguarding so I can woo my client over dinner without worrying about some anti-gun nutjob shooting me while I eat."

Dewey's irritation with Taka for making him pick at the scab that covered the trauma of losing Trevor might not be fake, but it also wasn't the real issue. Something about this meeting was crawling under Dewey's skin.

"Lots of cops moonlight," Dewey added.

"Call me later if there's anything I can actually help with, okay?"

"I'll do that."

And he would. Over the past month, it was almost like they'd never stopped being friends.

Almost.

The steep hills rising from the road should have been pretty, but they looked predatory. The occasional run of houses crouched at their feet like cowed prey waiting to be eaten. Heck. Half of them were already being devoured by kudzu and overgrown trees.

Taka caught his scowl in the rearview and tried to shake off the dark mood that had been creeping over him since he woke up in the spare room and wouldn't let himself claim his half of Andrea's massive bed. There might not be a ghost left in that room, but it still creeped him out. And the mattress was better than his. But the mattress in Andrea's room put the spare room's to shame. It'd been worth the wrestle to get it up the staircase. And a deal was a deal.

But he'd stayed put and stared at the strip of moonlight traveling the wall until it faded into the dawn. It was innocent between them, a good night's sleep next to a warm-bodied friend. But the thought of wrapping his arms around Andrea and falling into the deep sleep he'd only got in recent years when he was with her felt disloyal to Scott.

He was just so damn tired. Every minute of the last month took a year to crawl through, except when Scott lay next to him. Scott could make him forget for a while. Andrea brought it all roaring back in full living color.

Except.

Last night he'd been okay with that.

It was there, exploding again in his brain, water filling his mouth, heat singing the hair on his arms to frizzing crisps that crumbled when he touched them, the short hitch of his breath, blood on his face, and the boom of shots fired deafening him so that he couldn't hear the cars around them. But that was okay. It didn't get caught in his chest or dredge up that bottomless rage that scared him.

He'd recognized the slight detachment the eye movement desensitization therapy provoked in him during sessions. And he'd finally been able to open his mouth and ask, "Why were you crying?" And despite the out-of-control sensation that floated in his belly every time the subject of ghosts came up between them, the thought that that asshole wouldn't be showing up, even if it was based on the word of a psychic, helped.

He'd found his voice. Found Andrea again in the dark.

But laying there in the spare bedroom alone and missing her all over again after that brief flare of reconnection, he froze. If he traipsed over to the comfort of familiarity, it'd all be gone. The image was so strong. The dim room, the empty bed, dust on the furniture. The killer had gotten her. And even though he knew that wasn't true, it felt true. He couldn't get up to reassure himself just to find out the lie was that everything had ended well. Or that maybe he was the ghost.

Taka shook his head, hoping to shake the crazy thoughts right out of it.

This was why he couldn't sleep.

Ghosts were real.

7

Clay wasn't big enough to take up Taka's whole day. It sat ungracefully on the shoulders of the Elk River. Even the new structures built after the last flood looked tired. The address Fields gave him was on the west end of town, a ramshackle cabin with a front porch trying to collapse and about forty steep concrete steps up from the gravel patch a car's width off the state road.

A tall guy with zero body fat and no muscle or shirt to hide his bones answered the door. Taka doubted he was forty. Military tats. "You serve?"

The guy nodded, his eyes glazed over.

No sense bonding up. "Thanks for your service. Your name Conlon?"

He shook his head.

"Does Cash Conlon live here?"

Headshake no.

"I'm Detective William Taka, Charleston PD. I'm looking for Cash Conlon."

Patient stare. Had the guy even blinked yet? "Is there anyone here with you?"

Headshake.

"Mind if I take a look?"

The guy stepped back.

Taka hitched up his hip holster on reflex and went in wary, but the place was small and startlingly neat. One bedroom, door open, bed made with military corners. He pushed open the second door with his fingertips, bathroom, clean. Tiny kitchen. Clean. A rifle stood propped in the corner. A backpack hung on a hook next to it. Two gleaming knives, one in a sheath on the counter. A cluster of amber prescription bottles. A handful of oxy in a Ziploc bag.

Photos behind the couch. The guy with two women and a man, siblings by the chin and eyes. With an older couple. With his unit. In dress whites with a blonde woman in a blue dress, a bouquet in her hands. With a buddy, both in camo, loaded down with gear and tactical rifles. A dog in a vest and lift harness sat at their feet, tongue lolling out. Special forces.

Taka had never had the drive for it. He'd gone Infantry and then West Virginia National Guard, which sent him on his second deployment with a recon unit. Kept his head down, did his duty, but he'd never wanted more than to feel he'd contributed and get back home to Charleston. Not Charleston so much as just back home to the hills. Though he'd never tried to move anywhere else once he got back and then Andrea joined Waltham-Young.

"You got ID?"

The guy's eyes went to the raw wood table just inside the door. The only lamp in the room and a wallet sat on it. Taka eased over and lifted it. Driver's license and military ID with a photo match. Navy. Not Cash Conlon.

"You rent a van for someone?"

Headshake.

"Didn't do someone a quiet favor, pay off a debt?"

"Got no debts," the Lieutenant Commander said, voice surprisingly clear and firm.

Taka slid a business card out of his cell phone case and laid it on the table next to the wallet. "In case Cash comes around."

Thousand-yard stare. Maybe the slight twitch at the corner of the guy's mouth was just Taka's imagination. His back felt exposed all the way back down the steps and he was glad to get in the car and see the door above was shut, neither the commander nor the rifle in sight.

Clay was the county seat and he'd passed the courthouse on the way in.

As she had most days over the last month, Andrea set aside her paying work at lunch. Over takeout Pad Thai at her desk, she dove straight into her research on Aaron, flipping through the pages she'd copied from the SC records. While she scanned for relevant dates and plantation names, her mind wandered to Miss Ava and the reading at Louie's.

She marked her spot and picked up her cell, knowing her call would go straight to voicemail during lunch. Louie picked up right away, greeting her in his gracious drawl. The clatter and clank and murmur of voices placed him in his pub kitchen.

"Louie! Is everything all right?"

"As rain. Letting one of the young'uns play boss today while I taste test."

"Quality control?"

"That's me. What can I do for you, Miss Andrea?"

Right. She'd called without a plan except to ask him to call back. "Do you know a Sally?"

"Several." He raised his voice, "Grab a clean bar rag there, and wipe that rim again."

"In your family, maybe? Aaron said he and Ned are in the wrong place. To ask Sally."

Running water. A distant female voice, calling out a list of diners' orders. "Ned," Louie finally said. "It seems like . . . no. Great-Aunt Sally, though. She might help. She's still got the family bible. When do you think—you know."

Andrea didn't.

The kitchen sounds receded, and a door clunked shut. "How long ago did Aaron live?"

Or when did he die. "I don't know yet, Louie. I have a few more recent deaths to follow-up, but last week I found a slave from Live Oak named Aaron. It's not an uncommon name."

"What's he doing here in Charleston then?"

"If that's the right Aaron, it's gotta be the ring, right?"

"My sister'll send you Aunt Sally's info. She's ninety-seven, but she holds her own. I didn't mind, before, the place being haunted." The kitchen noise came rushing back down the line. He'd opened his office door. "But now—Well, I don't like folks thinking I've overlooked them."

It's why he'd become so successful. Keeping Louie's in the location where it started limited the number of diners he could host and assured he could give a little personal attention to each of them. Even those who just came in for a drink got a Louie one-liner and a pat on the shoulder.

She resolved not to tell him Aaron wasn't alone in occupying Louie's. "Aaron knows that."

Andrea let him go to work after confirming that she'd be in after the dining room closed and then checked the time. She'd try to get answers from Aaron with Miss Ava, and then Taka, if need be, if he kept his word to cooperate. But if all else failed, she needed more info to decide whether chasing Aaron down in military records, if it was possible, was worth the effort.

First, she needed to verify if his pants really matched the historic record for Confederate wear. And if so, whether that was a good indicator he'd be recorded as impressed by the Confederacy or accompanying an owner. She pulled open one of the deep drawers under the work counter running beneath her cork wall and rifled for her stack of directories. Waltham-Young gave them new ones every three months, listing the contacts used on every project to date and their role.

There was a guy who was a reenactor's reenactor and lived locally, in South Charleston. He'd become something of a legend regarding anything to do with kitting out men and horses for Civil War battle reenactments and living history museums. And the historians at Tulane's Amistad Research Center, who oversaw the nation's largest collection of African American and ethnic minority historical records, could definitely help her pinpoint where in the records to search if she needed to pursue that angle. She scribbled down the reenactor's number and called him.

Glenn Caulkey's response to her inquiry about uniform pants was way more enthusiastic than she expected. Calculating her time and resolving to work late, Andrea agreed to meet him at the VA in a couple of hours.

CASH CONLON DID NOT EXIST. At least not in Clay or Clay County. Clay County clerical assistant Chris helped him search car tags, property records, and criminal records. Eventually Taka had an address for a Linda Conlon in Summersville and another for an Alexander Conlon in Hico, in nearby Fayette County, who owned property in Clay. Not far from each other and probably related. Fortunately, both lived off Highway 19, which would loop him back onto Highway 64 southeast of Charleston. A quick Google search proved there were a lot of Conlons in West Virginia, so if proximity wasn't the key, it would take weeks of low priority checking to find out if any of them had relevant information on the stolen van.

An hour on the phone turned up the addresses and driver's licenses for five Cash Conlons statewide, none of them near Clay. When he'd finished digging with the DMV, he checked to see who'd beeped through twice. Fields. No voicemail. He called in to report his progress.

Twenty minutes later, he'd finished up his notes and logged his activities. He claimed the stack of photocopies Chris had made him and then shook his hand. "Thanks for your help."

"Anytime."

Taka pushed through the double office doors and trotted down the interior staircase past the vacant-eyed folks headed up to whatever document hell they were staring down. Out through the exterior double doors and into the late afternoon cold that bit through his jacket and cooled his overheated pits from the hours he'd spent in the too-warm county building. Wood smoke tickled his nose, raising the hairs on his neck.

He scanned the nearly deserted main street, looking for the source.

Smoke climbed in a lazy spiral from the chimney of a house set back behind a row of connected storefronts. Someone had built a fire in prep for whatever evening they had planned. As he continued down the outside steps, headed for his car, he took a breath, held it three seconds and then let it out slow. The burble of anxiety in his chest subsided.

ANDREA STOOD in the dim light just inside the door of the VFW in South Charleston. Several men sat in pairs and threes at small round tables, talking or playing cards. Three women had piles of papers scattered on a table near the back. One of them was flipping through one of those paper manuals four times as thick as any of the forms they must be filling out. Various flags on poles stood clustered in one corner. A large banner announcing the post and commanders hung above a long counter opening into a large kitchen. Plaques and photos covered every available inch of the walls.

While a couple of the men had longneck bottles in front of them, the community center vibe wasn't what she'd expected. A sturdy white man around sixty with a weathered face and a ring of grey hair came in behind her. "Andrea?"

She shook Glenn's hand. "I thought VFWs were bars."

He chuckled. "A lot of them are. We have a canteen of sorts, but it's mostly soda and snacks these days. The kitchen's for fundraising dinners and hall rentals. Let me show you what I've got."

They settled at a table near the women and Glenn unpacked the wheeled case he'd brought with him. He laid out squares of fabric samples, explaining the quality of each and the circumstances under which they'd have been made or purchased.

On the pants, he pointed out the stitching and how it varied from the real deal and how the reenactors replicated the sometimes flamboyant and ragtag quality of the enlisted infantry, who couldn't afford the frocks, overcoats, and shell jackets of the calvary units and higher-ranked field officers. He pulled out several notebooks of drawings and photos, rapidly flipping to show her various specifics. Both the fabrics Andrea had seen Aaron wear were there.

"What about slaves?"

Glenn sat back. "That's mostly a myth. There were no official Black Confederate soldiers. The occasional slave may have fired a dropped gun during the chaos of a Southern retreat, but who they were shooting at is anyone's guess."

Andrea was nodding. "I meant those accompanying owners or as manual laborers pressed into service. How often did they wear recognizable Confederate uniforms? Was it common?"

He rubbed a hand across his chin. "In my experience? After looking through thousands of photos and documents? At the start of the war, when enthusiasm was high, and owners still wealthy, yes, there's evidence that a handful dressed their valets in Confederate broadcloth and caps, usually without the full adornment. Plain bone or wood buttons, no fancy embroidery. The rest, impressed into service as cooks and ditch diggers and camp labor got by on very meager means, which included dressing in cast-offs to replace whatever worn clothing couldn't be mended or cleaned. The war was . . ."

Glenn slid the samples aside and leaned forward, resting his elbows on the table. "It was terrible. There's some who think reenactors glorify the war, that those who act as the Confederate units have an underlying wish the Confederacy had won, that they're racist, even white supremacists. But the vast majority aren't. If people do come in under those banners, they're exposed pretty fast."

He gathered his thoughts, gaze roaming over his samples. "We do it so the history isn't lost, which, I know, some would love it to all be lost and buried and never brought up again. There's lots of Americans, not just Southerners, who grew up watching TV and movies that romanticized the war. You know, the lost cause and the barefoot rebel. I haven't re-watched that stuff. *The Blue and the Gray* and all that.

"I doubt it holds up well. But there's plenty of born and bred Northerners, heck, Europeans, who exclusively play Confederates just because of those. Some admire Lee's strategy. You'd be surprised at the number of Black reenactors, too, playing both sides. It captures the imagination. Brother against brother."

Andrea waited a polite moment to see if he was done and then said,

"So slaves might wear Confederate pants whether or not they were accompanying their owners?"

"Confederate or Union pants, salvaged from the field if they needed pants, sure. Any of it. Homespun or manufactured. Drabs. Butternut. They weren't getting mail packages from home, that's for sure."

"I wasn't allowed to make a copy of the photo, but the subject is clearly a slave wearing—" Photos would be black-and-white. She laid her finger on the sample that most closely matched Aaron's latest version of his uniform pants. "Darker pants, maybe this color, with a light stripe."

"That'd be Confederate. Light stripe would be artillery."

"But if they were salvaged or cast off, or given to him—"

"No way to track him by association. Nope."

"Would the fact he's wearing them at all make a military record search worthwhile?"

"Who else is in the photo?"

"Just him."

"That's unusual. No wonder you weren't allowed to copy it. What's the setting of the photo? Farm? House? Camp? Battlefield?"

She should have thought this out better. "It's, uh, nondescript."

"Studio photo? Tintype? Glass?"

"It might be a studio," she hedged. Why did she go down this road? "It's a tintype."

"If someone thought enough of him to pay for a photo, and since you have a name, and age, then yes"—he held up one finger and shook it —"if you find out who owned him, even just the plantation name, then yes, it's worth the time to wade into the impressment records. It's not impossible, but certainly unlikely, that if he weren't involved in the war effort, he'd be wearing those pants. Now if he were just a valet, hauled along to cook and clean and keep camp for his owner, don't expect to find him anywhere in the record."

"Thank you." If she couldn't find out over the next month or so who bought him from Live Oak and if that buyer still owned him after the war started, she could sic an intern on the impressment records, looking for any slave of the right name and age owned by any plantation or master with the initials SH and work backwards from there. Another could check artillery officers' names throughout the Army. "I truly appreciate your time. You have a remarkable collection here."

"I'm the go-to-guy in this region."

"I'm not wondering why," she said.

She helped him pack the samples and notebooks up. He asked if she wanted a coke and when she declined walked her to the door. On the wall beside it were rows of photos in frames. Headshots of the local veteran members. She couldn't just leave without paying them the respect they deserved. She veered over to admire them. Glenn seemed pleasantly surprised by her interest. He pointed out a couple of the more notable men among them. But Andrea's eye fell on one of the few women.

She was Hispanic, with curly dark hair and sparkling eyes. But the shape of her face, her high cheekbones, her nose, and broad chin were burned forever into Andrea's brain. She wasn't ash grey in this photo. A gasp escaped her.

"What?" Glenn said, alarmed.

She pointed at the photo. "Who is that?"

8

"That's a sad story," Glenn said. "Lucy Garcia. She did okay for a while after she got home. But then she got laid off. Got in with the wrong guy and came around a couple of times high. Then she was gone. Haven't seen her now in nine, maybe ten months?"

"I think she's dead," she said before she could stop herself.

"What? How?"

"Did you see the news this morning? The woman found in an alley off Quarrier?"

A couple of the men nearby had come over. One of them called over to the women. "Doreen, this woman says Lucy's dead. That woman in the alley downtown."

"Oh, no!"

The other men in the room put aside their cards and books as all three women pushed their chairs back and came crowding over. "How'd she die?" Doreen cried.

"I don't know," Andrea said, regretting having said anything at all. "Maybe it's not her."

A younger guy at one of the tables held up his phone. "There's no picture with this article. What makes you think it's her?"

"I was there when she was found. I'm sorry. It might not be her. It was just a shock, seeing someone so similar. May I take a photo?"

"Sure," Glenn said.

"I have the detective's card. I can send it to him, just in case. Maybe they've already found out who she is. I can call Glenn after I talk to him."

She got her cell open and took the photo as Doreen said, "It's not her. She left town, isn't that what you heard, Sharon?"

"I saw that Candy guy down on D Street," another of the men interrupted. "And he said she'd got a job in Huntington."

"That's not so far, though," Glenn said.

Sharon shook her head. "Can't be her. She texted me before she left. Said she was going to Pittsburgh with him."

"I know who to ask," Glenn said.

The bull of a man who'd spoken before said, "And I know where to find him."

"Tripp and I'll go find out," Glenn said, command in his voice. "Y'all stay here and for god's sake, don't be alerting the phone tree. This might not have anything to do with Lucy at all." He turned to Andrea. "Right?"

"I'm not at all sure now," Andrea cringing at Pete's voice in her head, telling her again how different people look dead. But that hair. And those cheekbones. "I'm sorry for upsetting everyone."

"That's all right," Glenn said. "Lots of us in here have seen ghosts when we came home, ain't that right, boys?"

Nods all around. An eye roll from Doreen.

"No offense, Doreen," Glenn said, and to Andrea. "Doreen has more foreign service time than the rest of us put together."

The bull, Tripp, was maybe thirty with a paunch and the air of a guy who hadn't shaken off the thought he might re-enlist one day. He opened the door and swept Andrea and Glenn out ahead of him.

"Candy's stepdaddy owns the smoke shop on D Street," Tripp said. "You want to go with us?"

"Or I can call you later," Glenn said. "Tell you what we find out."

If Lucy Garcia was alive and well, Andrea wouldn't need to contact Pete at all. "I'll go."

Tripp pointed his key fob at a big black pickup truck, and it beeped. "You can ride with us."

"No," she said automatically. "I'll follow you over."

"Suit yourself," he said in the way of men everywhere who never questioned their safety and thought women were making a choice.

THE DRIVE to Summersville was uneventful. Taka recognized sixty-two-year-old Linda Conlon from her DMV photo.

He introduced himself. "I'm wondering if you might know a Cash Conlon?"

"No, but my husband is the Conlon."

She walked Taka through the house—upper-middle class furnishings, charity award plaques on the wall—to the bedside of her husband, Henry, who, she informed him, was dying of lung cancer. Without looking away from the muted TV he'd been staring at, Henry tapped the long ash of his forgotten cigarette into the pickle jar lid resting on his swollen belly. "I swan, every time I get to this part, someone comes waltzin' in. Who are you now?"

His wife took the lid from him, dumped it in the matching jar on the bedside table and set it back on his belly.

"Detective William Taka, sir, sorry for the bother. I'm tracking down the driver of a rental van involved in an incident in Charleston yesterday."

"Hit and run?"

Taka didn't actually know, but since Fields had been tapped by Tamarin, he was assuming it had to do with the dead woman Andrea found. "No, sir, just needing to speak with possible witnesses to a crime. They might not even know they saw anything."

"I h'ain't been anywhere but the hospital in months."

"Were you there yesterday?"

Linda Conlon snorted softly and took herself off.

"No, siree, not me. It's been a while. Don't walk so well anymore. Didn't care to go when I could."

Taka considered the hospital bed the man lay in, the big green oxygen tank, and the tube looped around his head to the cannula in his nose. The same setup as Andrea's mom when she lay dying at home. "To the hospital? Or to Charleston?"

"Take your pick."

"You know a Cash Conlon?"

Henry might've been thinking about it, or just watching the old war movie.

The babble of a talk show on the living room TV filled the silence.

"Sir?"

"None of mine. Don't know names of a couple of the younger ones, the cousins' kids. Might be driving now, but it don't ring a bell."

"Rent a van lately?"

For the first time, Henry rolled his head to pin Taka with his watery, blue eyes.

"Know anyone living in Clay?"

"A nephew, ten year back."

"He's not still in Clay?"

Henry turned back to the silent explosion taking place on the screen, soldiers flying. "Afghanistan. Died there."

"Sorry for your loss, sir. And I'm sorry I disturbed your show."

Henry lifted the cigarette for a deep drag. He let the smoke out slow. "No bother. Gotta do your job, no?"

"Yes, sir. I'll see myself out."

ON D STREET, Tripp slid his pickup truck into a slantwise space about midway along the street's retail walking district. Andrea found one a hundred yards down. By the time she caught up to the men, Glenn was pulling the door of the smoke shop open. A bell hanging at the top of the door dinged. The scent of pipe tobacco wafted out. An antique wooden Indian stood to the right, just inside. The shop itself was all dark woods, and glass display counters and the bright colors of a hundred different brands of tobacco and smokes and all the accessories plus vape pens, glass and wooden pipes, CBD. There were books and magazines, and a walk-in humidor, from which a man emerged.

"Hey, Tripp," he said. "What's up?" He was in his mid-fifties, more than six-foot, seeming like a hulk within the confines of the product-crowded shop. Tattoos disappeared under his rolled-up sleeves on both arms and appeared from under his collar to climb his neck. A beautifully detailed Jesus hung from the hinges of his jaws, head bowed beneath his beard and feet tucked into the hollow between his collarbones. He wore gauges in both ears.

"Skinny around?"

"Who wants to know?"

"We got a question about Lucy for Candy," Tripp said, ice coating his words.

"I wouldn't know anything about that."

"We know," Glenn soothed. "That's why we need to talk to Skinny."

A scowling, dark-haired thirty-something emerged from a door into the rear of the shop. "Talk to me."

"Candy," Glenn said.

"Heard you were over in Louisville," Tripp said.

"I came back," he bit out.

"Where's Lucy?"

"How would I know?"

"Y'all were inseparable," Tripp said.

Candy's black eyes held steady on Tripp. A wide shallow scar cupped his right eye, top end tipping through the edge of his brow "And then the bitch left."

"You told me she went to Huntington, but her friend said she went to Philly with you."

"We did. She took off."

"What about Huntington?"

Candy shrugged. The shop employee looked wary, gaze darting between Candy and Tripp.

Tripp hooked a thumb at Andrea. "This one says she's dead."

Candy's stare shifted to her. She held her hands up. "I don't know that it was her. These gentlemen thought you might know where she is so we can check on her."

"Haven't heard from her."

The bell rang, the opening shop door allowing a draft of cold air in and forcing Glenn to step up against Andrea's back. The men in front of them didn't move to let them further into the store. "Excuse me," a familiar voice said. Andrea peered back at Dewey Sanderson as Candy said, "Mr. Sanderson," with disdain.

"Looking for Skinny," Dewey said. "Rent's more than a bit overdue. And I need cigars."

Candy clenched his teeth together, making his jaw muscles jump.

Tattoo guy's hand moved to his back pocket. "Aht," Dewey said as the tall man behind him said, "Don't," and shouldered past Dewey. Tripp shifted closer to the display case and the man brushed by him. Both tattoo guy and Candy stepped back.

Dewey and a third man came all the way into the shop and closed the door, shutting out the cold. "That's better," Dewey said, looking around. "Andrea, this is unexpected."

"Dewey," she said, and shut her mouth. He and Taka might be best buddies again, but she couldn't forgive him for breaking Taka's heart.

The tall guy, all chiseled good looks and bouncer attitude, stole a quick glance at her. He seemed familiar, but she didn't recognize him. The third guy was one of Dewey's bodyguards. She'd seen him at the Coliseum last month and in the numerous photos of Dewey that she and Karie had dredged up online when searching for Taka.

Candy sneered at tall guy. "Step up from bartending?"

Flash of a bright smile, Jimmy leaning over to shout, *the bartender's a friend of mine from back home.* Tall guy lifted his arms and stamped one foot forward. Both tattoo guy and Candy flinched away.

"Scott," Dewey said mildly.

Scott, apparently, moved over next to Tripp, who stared at him like Scott might attack him at any second.

The voice of reason, Glenn said, "We came in to ascertain the location of a woman Candy was dating. She disappeared on his watch, sometime ago. Andrea thought she recognized her as the woman the police found in the alley downtown yesterday."

"I don't know if it was her," Andrea protested. "She just looked like this woman in a photo at the VFW."

"Jodie?" Dewey said.

Candy's actual name, apparently, was Jodie. It had to be rough growing up a boy in West Virginia with that name. "Last I knew she was in Philly."

"He came home without her," Tripp muttered.

Dewey raised his brows.

"We went clubbing. She left with some guy, so I left her ass in Philly."

Dewey looked at Tripp, Tripp looked at Glenn. Glenn said, "She was having some issues. Drugs."

"All sorted then," Dewey said, with an air of finality. "Your dad, Candy. Please."

Candy morphed from stony to sullen at the use of his chosen name. Andrea inched over, ready to go. Glenn moved with her, but Dewey and his hired thug continued to block the door. Candy fished his cell phone out, rolled his thumb across it, and it rang on speaker.

Skinny, presumably, eventually answered with a croaky "I told you not to bother me."

"I'm in need of three months' back rent and two boxes of Ramón Allones, the Superiores, this time, in interest."

"Well, fuck, ain't this just the ass canker my day needed," Skinny said without heat. "Write him a check, Candy, and give him the goddamned cigars."

"I'll be needing cash, Skinny. And the next three months in advance."

"Fuck me, Sanderson, I don't have that lying around."

"I assume you'll be moved out and the store swept clean by midnight then."

"You can't do that, Sanderson," he said, voice like gravel and louder. "We have a fucking written lease."

"That we do. I have it with me. I'm exercising the clause that requires..." He drew a triple folded sheaf of papers out of his inner coat pocket and unfolded it. "Here, Andrea, could you read 4C out loud so we can all hear it?"

Behind the counter, the neon cigarette box clock was ticking. Cars passed outside. No one moved. Andrea finally stretched out her arm and took the paper. She read the clause stating that a delinquency could result in the landlord lessee requiring the back rent plus all remaining rent on the contract, or any portion thereof, upfront upon written notice or verbal notice with witnesses.

"I got seven witnesses here, Skinny," Dewey said

Skinny made an inarticulate sound of frustration. "Give it to him, Candy," he yelled, words scraping up out of his tortured throat. "I don't have fucking time for this today," and the line snicked close. There was no satisfaction in the end of a cell call, not like slamming down a landline phone.

Andrea held the contract out. Dewey took it. Candy nodded at tattoo guy, who went skating into the back of the store while Candy dove into the humidor. The thug opened the shop door and stepped outside. Glenn left and Dewey stepped sideways to let Tripp by.

Through the window of the humidor, Candy held up a box of cigars. Dewey nodded his approval.

Andrea lifted her chin at Scott. "You know Jimmy Hoyle?"

He tensed, his eyes narrowing. "Friend of mine from back home."

Dewey clapped him on the back, in a good mood now that he had what he wanted. "Not a good friend from that tone."

"We took different paths," Scott allowed.

"You done something I should know about?" Dewey said, but his words were light.

Scott kept his mouth shut.

Dewey frowned, turning serious. "You don't think I knew about your connection to Hoyle? I'm disappointed in you, Scott. My dad was a senator. Trevor learned the fine art of background checks from the best. Chet's following in his footsteps."

Once again, Andrea regretted opening her mouth. What was with her today?

Hearing his name, the big guy outside ducked back in to see why Andrea hadn't left yet.

"You knowing a state cop from grade school was one of the reasons I added you to the team. Not just a state cop, *the* state cop keeping me on his personal radar."

"The only times I've seen him since high school are in the Coliseum, sir, after he found out I'd moved here."

"Charleston's a small town, Scott, as you'll find out. Andrea here doesn't care much for me at all, but we cross paths all the time. I wouldn't mind you getting reacquainted. Maybe you can convince him I'm an honest businessman."

"Yes, sir."

"Relax, Scott, we're all friends here."

"Yes, sir," Scott said, not looking any more relaxed.

Candy came out with the cigars, Dewey's face lit up in delight, and Andrea took the opportunity to leave.

"Tell William I said hi," Dewey called after her. "Don't be a stranger!"

To their credit, Glenn and Tripp were waiting down the block by her car.

"I've never spoken with Dewey Sanderson before," Glenn said when she reached them. "You know him?"

Tripp kept looking at the shop over her shoulder.

She owed Dewey her profession. The research bug bit her hard while investigating him after he stole Taka's heart. He inspired her early love for internet forums. "Yes. We're acquaintances through a mutual friend." Which galled her to say. Taka was a bigger person than she.

"None of this is right," Tripp said. "She smoked some pot, but she and Candy got along great guns. She was talking about marrying him. She was living with him before she left."

"Tripp," Glenn said. "She was with him because she lost her apartment."

"What?" Tripp said, tearing his attention away from the shop. "I didn't know that."

"She went to Sharon, asked to crash with her, but she was high. And it was more than just some pot."

"Oh," Tripp said, deflating. "Oh. She seemed so confident. And practical. And strong."

"Strength of spirit can be a curse sometimes," Glenn said, clearly speaking from experience. "Makes it hard to change course."

"I'm sorry," Andrea said. "I shouldn't have said anything. It's been a long couple of days. I'm probably imagining the resemblance." She pulled her car key out of her jeans pocket.

"You'll still send the photo to the detective?" Glenn asked. "Just in case?"

She nodded. "Just in case."

"You'll let me know what he says?"

"I will. And thank you again for sharing your expertise with me."

They waited while she got in and started her car and locked her doors before they headed to the truck. The midafternoon traffic was picking up. Kids were appearing on the sidewalk in ballet leotards and karate outfits. Dewey came out of the shop just as she was passing by, Scott and the thug right behind him. He waved. Pretending not to see him, she looked straight ahead. Glenn and Tripp were climbing into the pickup truck. Glenn looked five years older than when she walked into the VFW.

She didn't want to pull over to send the photo. She just wanted to get back to her office. She'd text Pete, shoot him the photo and name, file her notes, write out her plan for searching the Confederate military records for Aaron, if need be, and get back into the Ivystone Farm project. She needed to schedule a second call with the property owner, which went beyond the project-request basics with a thorough interview of the known facts, verified historical record, and more detailed future plans for the property beyond "B and B."

God, was it Lucy? Had she come back to Charleston without contacting any of the people who had tried to support her when she lived here? Where was her family? Or was she really still in Philly? Maybe she'd found the help there that she couldn't seem to manage here. Please let her be in Philly. Though that left the poor woman in the alley still unknown. Unless CPD had already ID'ed her. And then some other family was missing their daughter, sister, aunt, mom. Miss Ava had sensed her. She said—that her name started with a 'K' sound.

Andrea slumped in her seat in relief. Miss Ava said her name started with a 'K.' She may have been military and practical and strong, too, but she wasn't Lucy. Except . . .

That hair. Those cheekbones. That nose and chin.

9

W alking down the hall to her office, Andrea's cell rang. An unknown Charleston number. She answered with her full name and a deep, honeyed female voice spilled into the cup of her ear. "I'm Savannah. My brother Louie texted me your name and number and told me to put you in touch with Aunt Sally. She's not the woman she used to be, and I don't like to bother her unnecessarily. Why do you need her?"

"That's a brother for you," Andrea said once her brain caught up to the woman's sweet voice versus brusque wording. "Always telling instead of asking."

Andrea slid the door to her office open.

The woman, Savannah, surprised her with a melodious laugh. "Louie always thinks he's too busy to explain until sometime later."

A new side to Louie. A brother side instead of the accommodating restaurateur she'd known for years, or the developing friendship forged over the past month. Although . . . "You know, he never explains his new dishes to us long-term customers, just plops them down and waits to see what we say." She dropped her shoulder bag by her desk.

"And you just eat them without asking?"

Andrea let her grin color her voice. "We do. They're always great!"

She pulled her chair out and sat down.

"You know he puts weird not-mushrooms fungus and strange rooty things and tongue and, and . . . chicken feet in his food, right?" Savannah sounded appalled, but her version of the Charleston accent that Andrea was normally deaf to drew her words out a titch slower and gave every syllable a smoky bourbon-smooth curve that Andrea could listen to all day.

"I don't want to know, so I don't ask. But I do want to ask your Aunt Sally a couple of questions about your family. I work for Waltham-Young and I'm collecting background for a nonprofit preservation project for the pub, which includes historical background on your family and the influences that brought them to Charleston."

Silence. Then, "You mean the building the pub is in?"

"That'd make sense, right? But in Waltham-Young terms, a preservation project preserves knowledge. We're adding to the community knowledge of Black-owned businesses for historical purposes."

"And you want to know about our family?"

"Yes. Part of the process is tracing the cultural and ancestral influences that led to the establishment of African and Black American families as a vital part of Charleston's early history."

"Well, we didn't come from Malden, I can tell you that. We're latecomers."

West Virginia didn't gain statehood until 1863, and therefore generations were taught that slavery on the part of white Americans wasn't a part of the state's history. That whitewashing of local history was still widely accepted as fact. Schools taught the colonization history of the area, including how European women and their families were kidnapped by Native Americans to work the local salt mines. But Andrea had her master's and was working her third historical restoration before she learned that for the following 150 years, tens of thousands of owned and leased African and Caribbean slaves labored and died in the salt and coal mines near Charleston under brutal conditions.

But the Black community had never forgotten. They were the ones who gave Kanawha Salines its new name as they passed down remembrance of the slaves who received a mauling, or a 'maulden,' at the town's whipping post. But Louie's family wasn't from Malden.

"Actually, that's why I'd like to speak with your great-aunt. To see if she can tell me more about Live Oak Plantation in South Carolina. Whatever family history or stories I can confirm through existing records, I'll share the information."

A shadow fell across Andrea's desk.

"She does love to talk about the family," Savannah said.

Andrea spun her chair to see who had stopped in her doorway.

"And I'd love to know what's true. I tell you what, I'll find out her schedule and we can all sit down together."

Head of Security, Tim. Over his shoulder, a uniformed CPD officer regarded her without smiling.

"That sounds like a plan," she said to Savannah.

They traded contact info.

Andrea thumbed her phone off. "Can I help you?"

With a pained look on his face, Tim said, "Sorry, Ms. Kelley, Officer Rogers was sent to accompany you to CPD for an interview regarding a statement you made earlier this week? I did verify him with CPD. A Detective Tamarin sent him."

Andrea automatically looked at the phone in her hand. Did Pete not call her? She opened it again and tapped on her phone icon.

"Ma'am," the officer said.

She held up her finger. No call from Pete. No heads up from Taka, either.

"Did they identify her?"

"Identify who, ma'am?"

"The woman who was murdered."

"I don't know anything about that, ma'am," the officer said. "I was assigned to drive you over to HQ to speak with Detective Tamarin."

Tim shifted his bulk. "You don't have to go with him, Ms. Kelley."

"Is that true?" she asked the officer.

"I'm not authorized to answer any questions, ma'am. I'm just here to drive you over to HQ so that Detective Tamarin can speak to you regarding an ongoing investigation."

Andrea thumbed her phone again and found HQ's main number in her directory.

"Charleston Police. How may I direct your call?

"Detective Pete Tamarin, please."

Three rings and then a flat, male voice barked, "Investigations."

She asked for Pete. "He's not available. Can I help you?"

"This is Andrea Kelley. Detective Tamarin sent an officer to bring me in for an interview?"

"Didn't I just talk to someone about this?" Paper shuffling. "A security guard at Waltham-Young, right? Is Rogers standing there?"

"Yes, he's here."

"He's there to pick you up," he said, voice fading and then coming back again, attention elsewhere. "Tamarin wants a word before he files your statement."

"Can it wait until tomorrow morning? I have obligations this afternoon."

"Andrea," the guy said absently. "Aren't you Taka's girl?"

She bit her tongue on the leap of instant irritation. "No. I'm a woman. And his friend."

"Look," the guy said, his tone sharp, suddenly present on the other end of the line. "Rogers is there as a courtesy. Come with him or don't. You know how these things work. Murder investigations are time-sensitive."

"Why didn't Pete just call me?"

"Ask him yourself. Probably trying to dot his i's and cross his t's since you're a friend of the family."

It took her a second to catch his meaning. Because she knew half the staff investigating the murder.

"You found the body, yeah?"

"Yes."

"Do Pete a solid and ride in with Rogers. Looks cleaner later when it goes to trial."

Optics. Is that what this was about?

"Has Pete got a suspect?"

"I don't know. I just got stuck answering the main line 'cause Annika's out."

She became aware of the voices on his end, someone's blaring cell tone quickly cut off, the usual hubbub of the squad room. "Okay. Thank you."

"Yeah," he said and hung up.

Andrea sighed. "I have a gun on me, can you secure that here, Tim?"

The officer stiffened.

Tim just smiled. "I can."

"Give me a minute." Still uneasy, she turned back to her desk. Very aware of the men waiting on her, Andrea scribbled down the plan she'd decided on regarding Aaron's possible military connection, sorted and organized the Ivystone notes she'd left out, filing part of them and dropping the rest back into her open projects folder. She stuffed it into her backpack along with her laptop and picked up her bag again. She didn't have to go. She knew that.

But now she was curious. And if Pete had an ID, she wanted to know who she was, while hoping she wasn't Lucy Garcia, before her meeting with Karie and Miss Ava at Louie's later. Maybe knowing her name would help make sure she could move on wherever it was souls went when they weren't haunting people.

In Hico, Taka followed a crooked post-and-barbed-wire fence along a narrow field at the base of a steep hillside for maybe half a mile before finding the house he needed. He clattered over a steel-pipe ditch crossing from the road into a narrow gravel yard. Two thin hounds bayed at him, but no one came out to greet him.

The house mirrored the land, a long, low ranch-style with a new tin roof. A beat-up Honda Accord and a new Chevy truck were parked out front. A rusted Eldorado sat up on blocks near a cow barn in serviceable shape.

His phone vibrated. Andrea. Again. He thumbed the call off.

An outer glass door stood open on the porch. A boy of maybe twelve opened half the double front door in answer to Taka's press of the doorbell. "Tee," the boy yelled back into the house. The wood floors of the entry hall gleamed. Taka could see the house opened into a great room at the back with a large L-shaped couch, a huge TV, and sliding doors onto a massive patio with a firepit and lots of seating. Fancy.

A mousy woman came from somewhere to the left into the front hall. The boy didn't move. Taka introduced himself and asked for Alexander Conlon.

"Xander's not here. He won't be back until next week."

"And you're his wife?"

She shook her head.

"Could I have your name?"

"Tina. I just keep house and look after the boy."

"And your name is," Taka asked the boy.

"I don't talk to cops," he hissed. "I'm unknockable."

"Hush," Tina said.

Turning on her, the boy half-yelled, "I'm going to tell Skinny on you!"

She flinched from his half-raised fist. Taka knew better than to lay hands on him, but he stepped inside, knocking the boy forward, so he had to move past Tina or fall. "Sorry," Taka said, "I tripped."

The boy glared at him.

Taka almost asked about the van, but at the last second asked "Who's Skinny?" instead.

"Xander's uncle."

"You know a Cash Conlon?"

Tina hesitated, her gaze darting away, but then shook her head.

Taka handed her his card. "Could you ask Xander to call me?"

"I'll tell him you came by."

He looked at the boy and then back at Tina. "Feel free to call if you need anything at all."

The boy stuck his tongue out at him.

Taka smiled in response and the boy turned and ran.

He lowered his voice. "You need my help, Tina?"

She looked past him to the road before meeting his eyes and shaking her head again.

"You sure? We can go right now."

"I'm fine," she said, with a small, and to his mind, fake smile. "Xander treats me just fine. And the boy, he's just being a boy."

He held out a second card. "You hide this somewhere. You ever need to use it, don't hesitate. There's a good women's shelter in Charleston."

"You've got the wrong impression," she said firmly, refusing to take it. "Xander's a good man." She took hold of the door. "I'll tell him you came around."

"I appreciate that." He turned to go. The door closed with a solid clunk before he reached the porch steps.

10

The chair was one of those hard plastic ones with a too-small deep curve to the seat. It was one in a line of four in a dark, too-small hallway deep in the police department's portion of City Hall. A busy, too-small, dark hallway, so Jimmy couldn't stand without being in the way of everyone needing to get by. Two of the rooms staggered along this hall were interrogation rooms. Four more were around the corner in the next hallway.

Why he couldn't have just met Pete Tamarin in one of the briefing rooms downstairs was beyond him. He wiggled in the seat again, trying to keep his butt from going numb. This was ridiculous. He had data on his desk, and a report due to Maddox. He stood up to walk out, phone already in his hand to call work, tell them he was headed back.

Andrea came around the corner with a uniform escort. "Jimmy, what are you doing here?"

Tamarin came from the opposite direction of Andrea, stopping in the intersection of the halls. "Jimmy," he said. "Sorry for the wait."

"Apparently I was waiting to see you. Why are you here?"

"Lieutenant," Tamarin said.

Jimmy ignored him. "Are you coming or going?"

"Going," Andrea said.

"Hoyle, now," Pete barked.

At least she was leaving, that was good. "I'll call you."

She threw a bewildered look over her shoulder as the uniform crowded her on down the hall.

Jimmy glared at Tamarin. "What's going on?"

"A murder investigation." Tamarin held an arm up, directing Jimmy to the left. "Come on."

The interrogation room was plain, but not unpleasant. There was a barred window letting some light in, a scarred wooden table from some long-ago science class with four padded folding chairs around it. A stack of folders sat on the table. No observation window, but there were two cameras in the room. Jimmy assumed they were running.

"Relax, Jimmy, we're just following up."

"My friends call me Jimmy, Tamarin. I just met you."

Tamarin held up both hands, palms out. "Lieutenant, we've got lots going on. We've got a Town Hall meeting coming up and lots of security meetings going on, not to mention legislators deciding they should meet with city government in advance to make it look like they care about something other than their chances of making it to Washington one day. Sorry about the room, but this is what they gave me."

"You sent a formal request through my supervisor. You could've just called me."

"What did I just tell you? We got eyes on everything right now. On top of that, after that little shootout you and Andrea staged last month, I've got marching orders from PSD to document everything. Every exchange."

The Professional Standards Division, Charleston PD's version of Internal Affairs. "Inter-bureau communications count as official exchanges. You could've just phoned me and documented the call."

"Let me make myself clear, Lieutenant Hoyle. This is a murder investigation. You were at the scene of the crime before law enforcement was notified. With your girlfriend who discovered the body."

"I gave you all that in my original statement."

"Correct. Now, I don't know how you state boys handle an investigation, but I'm pretty sure you sometimes bring witnesses back in to ask them follow-up questions. If my doing so bothers you, you're welcome to leave and come back with your lawyer."

Exactly the catch-22 play-by-play Jimmy would use and that he'd seen coming. It felt different on this end. PSD had no direct jurisdiction over Jimmy, but they could make his life difficult. He rubbed his hands through his hair and relaxed. All he could do now was play the guy right back. "I'm in the middle of a time-sensitive investigation myself, Tamarin. Could we just move this along, make your PSD happy?"

They went back through his statement and then Tamarin started pulling out security camera stills and placing them in rows on the table. Jimmy and Andrea entering Louie's. Andrea's car pulling out of the Huntington garage both early and late. Andrea and Karie entering Louie's with five different timestamps. In three of them, a dark-colored van was parked in different spots along the curb. No clear shot at the tag. "Both you and Andrea are frequent customers at Louie's. But we've noted both of you in the area outside business hours as well. Or early in the morning. Although those shots are mainly Andrea. Louie's isn't on the direct routes to work or other places you both frequent from your homes."

Jimmy shrugged. "Andrea's known Louie a long time. She's working on a Waltham project, documenting his business."

"When he's not there?"

"If you check with Waltham-Young, you'll find her work always includes the finest of physical details related to places she's documenting."

Tamarin nodded, conceding the point. "That means she's observant."

Not knowing where the man was going with the comment, Jimmy kept his expression neutral, and his mouth shut.

After a long moment, Tamarin said, "Would you agree?"

"She's detail oriented when focused. Observant isn't the same thing."

Tamarin lifted the flap on a new folder and slid more photos out, lying the 8x10s over top of the old ones. Andrea passing a dark-haired woman in the street. The same woman huddled into the doorway of the closed bakery, looking away from Andrea and Karie as they came out of

Louie's late one night. The same woman with a man, getting into the dark van with two other women early one morning, though Andrea wasn't in that shot. The street and sidewalk were deserted, the timestamp 5:13 a.m., a few days ago.

Jimmy lifted that one to study it. The faces weren't clear, only the bearded man, dressed in jeans and a black coat, looking towards the camera. Two of the women were white, blondes, long hair left down and dressed for the cold. The brown-skinned brunette, in a dress and coat that left her legs bare, had her hair twisted up, but a scarf covered her neck and most of her face. "You think this is your victim?"

Tamarin's hesitation before answering with an affirmative nod told Jimmy that no, they couldn't say for sure. "You got eyes out on this van?"

"What do you think?"

Jimmy thought if that van had anything to do with the murdered woman, no cop was ever going to lay eyes on it again. "I think I'd be checking the chop shops and auction houses. Maybe recent trade-ins at the dealerships." But it was Charleston. A quick detour off 77 or Corridor G and that van was gone forever into a barn with blowtorches.

"Did you ever see this van on the street?"

"No."

Tamarin tapped the photo. "This woman?"

"No."

"See suspicious activity while you were entering or leaving Louie's?"

"No."

Next folder.

More photos. The same or a very similar van on a different street. "This van was parked on Quarrier, near Hale. Thirty feet from the alley where Andrea found the victim. You remember seeing it that day?"

"No."

Tamarin rolled his eyes. "You drove right by it when Andrea called you."

Taka had called him. He and Andrea hadn't spoken until his arrival at Louie's. So CPD hadn't been able to pull his phone records yet. Taka would catch shit if they did. "She didn't call me. I knew she was going to be there and had an appointment nearby, so I stopped in to say good morning."

"Lucky you."

"Yeah, lucky me."

"You didn't see the van when you drove back past it?"

"Was it parked illegally? Were there guys with guns standing outside it or a drug deal going on through the window?"

Tamarin gave him a sour look.

"Then, no, I didn't see it."

"Where were you coming from when you decided to stop at Louie's?" Tamarin said.

"That's state police business."

"That early in the morning?"

He already knew Jimmy was driving the wrong direction to be coming from his apartment. He couldn't even blame Tamarin for accessing the license plate readers because he himself used them all the time to figure out suspects' usual routes and stopovers. And to keep an eye on Scott's whereabouts.

"Who'd you see later? You go straight there from Louie's?"

He wanted to say again, 'That's state police business.' But if they'd further tracked their cars and the van on whatever cams they could pull, they probably already had him watching Andrea go by and then heading into the mall. If they were truly interested in Jimmy's whereabouts after he left Louie's, or this mystery van's occupants had gone the same direction, they could or already had, pulled the mall's security cams. But there's no way they'd had time to watch them yet.

Scott would be known to them because of their own interest in Dewey's activities. It was conceivable they'd watch long enough to follow their separate entrances and exits from the jewelry store. There'd be several scenarios they might envision if they noticed that could foul up his investigation.

Being honest here might defuse the whole situation if they'd not got so far as the mall cameras yet or he could convince Tamarin it'd be a waste of time to watch the footage. He made a show of giving up the stonewall front, letting his gaze drift over Tamarin's shoulder and shaking his head. He'd been caught out. "I was out early. I really only stopped in at Louie's for coffee, but since I walked into a murder scene..." He spread his hands wide and then dropped them. "And for your ears only, I like Starbucks. I was worried about Andrea, so I drove over to the mall, waited until I saw her go by and I knew you were done with her, then went to Starbucks."

Tamarin watched him.

"The meeting was with a CI in South Charleston. I can't tell you about it."

"Fine." He raked the photos into a single pile. "That's all I needed."

Jimmy checked his watch and stood, sliding his chair back.

"You decide you remember that van around, or any working girls, you call me."

"I've never noticed the van. Or any women working Hale near Louie's." He tilted his head a little and let the corner of his mouth lift. "I have noticed the giggly ones bar-hopping before closing."

Another sour look from Tamarin, this one directed at the photos as he sorted them into the folders. "I wouldn't know. We don't get the hours you boys do."

"I can put in a word for you," Jimmy offered.

"Naw. I like actually accomplishing something in my day."

"Speaking of."

"Yeah, yeah. I'll call you if I need you back again."

"See that you do," Jimmy said, sharper than he intended. Tamarin stopped playing with the photos to squint up at him. "I don't care to be summoned like a schoolboy."

After squaring the folders away, Tamarin stood. "I'll make a note for PSD. Now get out of here before I find something else to ask you about."

Jimmy didn't like the knowing look in Tamarin's eyes.

In the hall, he jerked his phone out and called Maddox to explain what the request had entailed and see if he could find out anything about the van CPD was so interested in. Then he checked in with his team. He and Andy Detweiler traded off shifts but ran the team together so there was always someone on while Scott was under with Sanderson. Once he was in his car, he gathered himself and called Andrea.

"Jimmy."

"Are you okay?"

"They were asking about some van. He had photos of me, but I swear I don't remember if I ever saw that woman. Or if that was even her. It's not like the streets are deserted at the times I go. I'm not there at three a.m.," she protested. "There's the bakery staff and a couple of the restaurants down the block open at seven."

He'd only known her six weeks, but he doubted she'd ever sounded as upset as she did right now in her whole life, it was so unlike her. "It's okay. You have nothing to do with the van or the woman. You told them about your preservation project?"

"Yes."

"You didn't mention—"

"Stop. Or I may never forgive you."

"I didn't—"

"Don't talk like a man right now, Jimmy."

"But I am a—"

"Don't. Just don't."

Jimmy took the phone from his ear and looked at it. She blew a noisy breath out and it occurred to him she'd been on Bluetooth the whole time. The car was running, and he didn't remember turning it on. He set the phone down in his cup holder.

"He knew. He knew I wasn't telling him everything. He showed me mugshots. A bunch of guys with shaved heads and goatees."

There were so many things he could say here but only words she'd tell him not to say bubbled up on his tongue. He swallowed them all.

"Are you still there?"

"Yeah," he croaked. He cleared his throat. "It's okay. I'm sure you just came off as confused. He put you in an awkward position and he knows it. He may not know what you're not saying, but he knows you had nothing to do with that woman's death."

"He wouldn't tell me if they had an ID. I showed him a photo I found of a veteran at the VFW in South Charleston that looks a lot like her, at least what I remember, and gave him her name, but he didn't say anything, just wrote it down."

The chances that she'd discovered the victim's ID that randomly were nil. Witnesses weren't very reliable with recall, especially those who discovered the dead. "They probably don't have an ID yet, and no autopsy photos to compare to yet. I'll find out. Or Taka can. Have you talked to him?"

"He didn't pick up."

"Did they bring Karie in?"

"No. She's still here. We're supposed to go to Louie's tonight, late."

"You go just like you planned. Don't change anything. I've already got people on it. We'll sort what's happening. Can I come have breakfast with you tomorrow?"

He thought she'd say no when she didn't answer right away. He didn't push.

"Can you meet us tonight? At Louie's?"

His heart sped up. "What time?"

"Ten fifteen."

"Yeah. I—" Shit. It had almost rolled right off his tongue. But he already knew she didn't feel the same. "I'll be there."

"You don't have to."

"I want to. I'll be there. I need to see you."

"I want to see you, too."

And he knew, he knew she meant it but not the way he wanted it to. "Be safe, okay?"

"You, too."

The line clicked closed.

Before the car radio could kick on, he turned the sound off.

11

Andrea tried to lose herself in the minutiae of the Berrylane Plantation restoration but couldn't focus. Instead, she started the laborious task of building the research foundation of the Ivystone Farm project. Ivystone was older, a Federalist style house built in the 1750s on three-hundred odd acres, but it was only ten miles as the crow flies from Berrylane. She could review and copy historical location data from that project, and then format the abatement spreadsheet for the standard list of old-house woes until she collected more specific data.

She caught herself staring at the keyboard yet again, seeing herself on the video, walking in front of the dead woman where she huddled against the bakery door.

Was it her?

Scooping her cell up, Andrea leaned back in her chair, grateful for the stretch of her lower back. She'd been sitting tense and hunched over her work for more than an hour. Taka finally picked up the phone.

His voice caught in her heart and her throat closed, tears springing up in her eyes. "Hey," she said, the word a croak.

"What's wrong?" His voice was sharp, concerned.

She shook her head and pinched her nose, trying to tamp that wild surge down. "It's okay. I'm okay. I just needed to hear your voice." She sniffed the tears back and breathed shallow through her mouth.

His tone softened. "What happened?"

"Where have you been?"

"They chopped the chain on my desk. Fields sent me out snipe hunting like he's not the new kid on the block."

"Pete Tamarin sent a uniform to bring me in for questioning."

"What?"

"He had video of me passing that woman in the alley on the street a couple of times. In front of Louie's. He says it's her, but I don't know. I don't remember ever having seen her before."

"People look different when they die."

"I just—I guess I'm that person who ignores people who need help. She was right there, Taka, and I never saw her."

"Did she ever ask you for help?"

"No."

"Have you ever ignored someone who visibly needed help or was, I don't know, in a confrontation or something?"

"If I notice, I don't, but obviously I didn't notice. And I walk by panhandlers and the homeless all the time. They need help, don't they?"

He was driving. The regular rhythmic shush of the pavement and cars passing filled the silence between them.

"Most of them have help if they want it, Andrea," he said gently. "They do have to say they want it."

"Some don't get the help they need, though."

"Some don't," he agreed. "Did Pete say who she was?"

"No. But I showed him a picture I took of a veteran's photo at the VFW today on a research trip related to Aaron. Lucy Garcia. She's been missing, but she might be in Philly."

"Did you ask for a lawyer?"

"No, he just wanted to know why I said I'd never seen her before."

"And then you pop this veteran on him as a possible ID."

"I know. But I didn't have anything to hide, except—" her throat closed again.

"He started asking why you were at Louie's early and late. You told him—"

"Yes," she blurted. Geesh. "I told him about the project, but he knew I wasn't telling him everything. And if I stopped then—"

"He'd be even more suspicious."

"And then he started in on this van, which I also never noticed."

"A van?"

"It was parked down from Louie's a few times when I was there. It has something to do with her. She and another woman and a guy are in the photos. He had mugshots, asked if I knew any of the men."

"Okay," he said, shifting into cop voice. "Let me call Pete, find out what's up. I'll confirm you're just documenting Louie's, not taking inventory of parked vehicles. Find a lawyer, just in case he brings you back in."

"But—"

"No buts, Andrea. You should've called me in the first place."

"I did."

"Then you should've called a lawyer to meet you down there. I'm sure Waltham-Young has plenty in their Rolodex."

He sounded angry. "You're being mean," she said, and even as she did, she realized he was doing scared-Taka, not angry-Taka. "You're scared."

"Yeah, I'm scared! Pete's a bulldog, Andrea. Pete is CPD's bulldog. He's got his teeth into that half-truth you told him, and he's gonna want the rest unless I can coax him loose. I don't think telling him that you're trying to talk to a ghost is going to do it."

She had nothing to say to that.

"Please. Find a lawyer."

"I'll call Carson." Carson Lazar was Taka and half the rest of the department's lawyer, representing them against the inevitable lawsuits made against them by both their own and the occasional suit-happy citizen.

"He'll have conflict of interest, probably, but yeah, do that. He'll find you someone good. I'm gonna call Pete, okay? Or catch him at HQ. I'm headed back in anyway. Are you still meeting that psychic tonight?"

"Yes."

"Good luck," he said and obviously meant it.

He didn't want to come bail her out. With the words on the tip of her tongue, she realized what she was about to say and bit her tongue instead. It still stung a little, but she got it. They disconnected and she called Carson. He gave her the same frustrated reminder not to ever talk to the police, no matter how long you'd known them or how friendly they seemed, then walked her through the finding of the body and both her conversations with Pete before promising to connect her with a friend of his who, he said, could talk bees into handing over both their stingers and their honey. CPD knew him and would know they'd picked the wrong fight the second he darkened their door.

Karie knocked on her doorframe a couple of hours later. "Want to go for dinner with Ava before Louie's?"

"Yeah," Andrea said. But she'd had chicken thawed in the fridge for two days already. "I've got pasta and enough chicken, should we just go to mine?"

ANDREA POURED three short glasses of red from the bottle left in the fridge and tossed it in the glass bin. The clink reminded her of the two trash bags full of glass bottles still sitting in the carport closet. Someday she needed to drop them at UC, the University of Charleston, where the art students made good use of them. Just thinking about it made her tired.

"To new friends," Miss Ava said, holding up her glass.

"And old ones on the other side," Karie added.

Andrea clinked her glass to theirs. "May they stay there."

Miss Ava chuckled, the sound just like Andrea's Grandmom, and wow, it'd been so long since she'd thought of her. After her dad left, Grandmom hadn't come around much and the few times Andrea rode the bus over to Pikeville, Kentucky, to stay the weekend, the false front Grandmom put up was painful to be around. "Except when we need them."

"Why would we ever need them?" Karie said.

A smile settled on Miss Ava's lips. "You know that nudge of 'go ahead' when you've got a leg on either side of a decision?" Her gaze slid back to

Andrea. "Or when you're being tugged in a certain direction no matter how little sense it makes? That's them, putting their two cents in. Maybe they know best, maybe they don't, but they's opinionated, all the same."

For whatever reason, Andrea's thoughts shot straight to Jimmy and how despite the fact she liked him, she just wasn't feeling the romance so much. Although Taka had declared himself and she knew his attentions lay elsewhere, she still felt drawn to him. She always had. Chuck had been the only other guy she'd been able to trust as fully as she trusted Taka. But he'd died.

Miss Ava dipped her chin at her, her eyes soft. Then she set her wineglass down and clapped her hands together. "I'm starving. What can I do?"

PROPPED against the driver's-side door of his Yukon, Taka watched Jimmy turn into the dirt lot. Jimmy's headlights strafed the river and the flotilla of barges moored in the current before strobing over Taka as Jimmy pulled up beside him. Taka opened the BCI-issued Impala's passenger-side door and dropped into the car, rocking it on its frame.

Jimmy turned the car off.

They listened to the engine tick as it cooled in the cold night air.

Jimmy tapped his steering wheel. "You called me."

"You know anything about the van?"

"No. Zipped lips over at CPD right now."

"One of the officers canvassing for info related to the victim noticed a guy sleeping in it. Tried to wake him. But he'd been stabbed. Weapon at his feet."

Jimmy absorbed that, fingers tapping. "How'd they keep it so quiet?"

"It was parked near the mouth of the alley. They looped it into the crime scene and Taylor had already spoken to the media."

Taylor was CPD's spokesperson. "Taylor labeled her as homeless," Jimmy said, his tone thoughtful.

Which meant that without family and friends to keep her death visible, she'd be gone from the twenty-four-hour news cycle by the morning. She'd only resurface when CPD needed the public's help.

"ID on either yet?"

"All I know," Taka said, voice hardening. "That's when Pete Tamarin walked in and found out Fields had put me on the van."

Jimmy's relentless finger fidget stopped. He turned his head, meeting Taka's eyes before Taka went back to tracking the gleam of moonlight off the dark barges.

"I wondered," he finally said, "if they'd find out you called me."

Taka shook his head. "Not yet. But Pete knows how close Andrea and I are. He was pissed that it was me looking for the guy who rented the van and pissed I was by myself. Said the whole case could be compromised."

"Is the dead guy the renter?"

Taka shrugged. "Door got slammed in my face. I'll be back on desk duty tomorrow."

"You get anywhere with it?"

"No. Waste of my time. I can't decide if Pete was trying to get me out of the building before bringing Andrea in or if Fields really fucked up that bad."

"Or both," Jimmy said. "Told Fields to keep you busy and Fields got stupid."

"He's not a stupid guy." He froze, not aware until then that the car had been vibrating with the jiggling of his knee. Fields was a good guy, one of CPD's best up-and-comers. And he liked Andrea. And he and Taka worked a successful undercover op together when they were both Special Enforcement.

"Yeah?" Jimmy said.

Taka went back to shaking the car. "He's not a stupid guy," he said again. And Jimmy wasn't stupid either. "Listen, I know y'all probably have an interest in Dewey Sanderson the same as CPD does. You know his people?"

Once again, Jimmy considered the question before he spoke with deliberation. "I might. Why?"

"You know Scott Fergusson?"

"Tall blond guy. Bartender turned security."

"I'm seeing him." Taka couldn't tell from Jimmy's neutral expression if he already knew about them. Whatever eyes the state kept on Dewey might be focused only on Dewey's direct interactions, which meant they might have spotted Taka's occasional public drink with Dewey and that was that. "I want to bring him to dinner at Andrea's. She doesn't know much about him yet."

"Okay."

"I assume you'll be there, I just wanted to heads-up you in case it's an issue."

"If Andrea wants me there, I'm in. It's not like we're actively investigating Dewey. We keep tabs is all."

"Just didn't want to mess you up."

"Thanks for that."

Taka rubbed his damp palms on the thighs of his jeans. "We're not public, by the way. I'm trusting you not to say anything. CPD doesn't know I'm bi and I don't want them to."

Jimmy reached out and smacked Taka's chest with his open hand. "Dude. I'm happy for you. Thanks for trusting me." He leaned forward and started the car back up. "Duty calls. And then I'm meeting Andrea at Louie's for a little ghost hunting. You coming?"

"We talked." Enough said. Even if Andrea seemed to have Jimmy firmly in the friend-zone for right now, he didn't think Jimmy would appreciate that he often stayed overnight, let alone in the same bed. "She's going to try the psychic one more time."

"And then you'll help."

Taka opened his door, grateful for the sudden rush of cold air. "If she needs me."

JIMMY COULDN'T GET AWAY FAST ENOUGH. He was always prepared to lie, but for him, this investigation had never been meant as undercover work. He had no identity to be except himself, the lying, untrustworthy version, and he hated himself for it. He was starting to hope Dewey never made a mistake they could collar him on just so he wouldn't have to deal with the mess that first Scott had made and then he had trampled into that day in the woods with Andrea.

And now getting mixed up in a double-murder investigation. Maddox had already read him the riot act over opening his mouth to Pete Tamarin once it became clear he was being interrogated. Mentor after mentor had taught him to keep his mouth shut if that ever happened and yet, like all the horror stories, he'd done the same. After Andrea texted that she was connecting with a lawyer, he'd called Sweet Joe Babbington and discovered he'd just gotten her name from the CPD boys' Carson Lazar.

Sweet Joe had no issue rep'ping them both if they had need of him. He only carried one cell phone. Call him anytime, day or night. Jimmy hadn't even registered his anxiety level until it dropped. But then Taka called, and it ratcheted right back up again. Now he was riding the rollercoaster of adrenaline back down again. Fields had no more screwed up than Jimmy had ever grown a watermelon in his belly after swallowing a seed. Fields had given Taka, and Andrea, and unknowingly, Jimmy a way out of their forced involvement.

What was Pete Tamarin thinking? What would he be thinking if this were his case? Andrea said Tamarin showed her mugshots that he hadn't shown Jimmy. A van, two women, a man with a past criminal record. Doing the dirty in the van? A threesome hookup that went wrong? Was the van just a kink?

The dead woman loitering, early in the morning, late at night. He conjured her up in his head. Andrea said she'd had old ligature marks around her wrists. No obvious stab or gunshot wounds. She'd been beaten. Pete had implied they were thinking prostitution. A hooker who wanted out? With a van, you could drop more girls around town. Move them faster if you had rooms set up.

Women sometimes recruited teenage girls. Offered them money and makeup and a hot meal and boom, they were on their backs before they knew what hit them. Some of them not by choice, but by then the pimps owned them, by drugs or by threat. If the victim did happen to be this veteran Andrea discovered, did Tamarin think Andrea was working with her to recruit prostitutes? That made no sense.

He'd navigated over the river, two streets over from Dewey's place.

He got out and walked with short, swift strides into Danner Meadow Park and straight to the covered picnic tables. Although it was closed and long after dark, he expected to see teens, on the soccer fields, or maybe huddled together on the tables. The cold must've chased them off. He stuck his arm down in the trashcan furthest from the sidewalk and was relieved to find the bag Scotty had left there a couple of hours ago. It clinked when he hauled it out.

His phone vibrated in his back pocket. He ignored it.

Back at the car, he inspected it. Still sealed, with Scotty's short handwritten report and makeshift evidence form inside along with thirty or forty bullet casings of about four different sizes in marked sandwich bags. Personal guns, not choices from the Kirkby warehouse. Looked like they'd sharpened up on a full session at the range. Jimmy signed the form accepting chain of custody and stuffed the form back inside. It wouldn't hold up with the gap in time between drop and pickup, but it didn't really have to. If any of the casings proved connected to a crime, Scott would either get it to them as legal evidence under his protection as an "invitee" into the suspect's world and the implicit knowledge that anyone can betray another, or they'd seize the matching gun when they arrested Dewey and his crew for whatever they ended up getting him on.

This time when his phone rang, he picked it up.

"Boss," Nina said. "Rawlins is floating face down in a pool on Branchmead."

"Well, shit." Bud Rawlins was a state witness on a case coming to trial in January. The AG would be livid. "Text me the address."

He put the address in his GPS and then texted Andrea. *Got to work. I'm sorry.*

Don't apologize for your job, she replied. *Breakfast at mine if you're free. 8.*

He sent back a thumbs-up emoji and headed for the body.

12

Taka cruised past Louie's for no good reason, just seeing how the crowd was tonight. Good for a Tuesday. Most of the tables in the front room full, three-quarters of the barstools filled. He missed the casual slide of a Louie dinner special onto the bar. The momentary pause the next time he walked by, to see if Taka was picking through it (rare) or had inhaled it already (almost always).

He missed the student waiters deftly poking fun at him for being a cop, at Louie for his resolute accounting of every ingredient bought and every meal made on paper in the face of technology, at anyone else who would engage with them, the cool kids readying themselves to rush into the world and fix everything that came before.

He didn't know when he had crossed that threshold of actual adulthood. Maybe when his brother died, and his mom went from rarely going out to never going out. He'd been on his own a long time before that, but maybe that was when he knew in every part of him that there'd be no quarter given in life, no backsies to carefree Saturday nights tossing bits of stale hamburger buns to the dogs while Andrew tossed the bits of leftover meat, the dogs working themselves up until they were so excited their whole bodies were wriggling. He couldn't even really remember what carefree felt like anymore. Heck, what energized felt like.

Only he did, didn't he? That night before one bullet whined by his head and the next ricocheted into his vest, thumping that big ol' bruise into his back that still hadn't completely faded away. Before that moment, he'd been in the flow, living his best life. Doing what he knew he was meant to do. Serve and protect. Nothing had been right since and Andrea had blood on her hands because of it. The least he could do is help her.

Taka made the turn to the Coliseum, then went by it. Drove past the turn for Hansford and parked down a side street. He walked over to Dewey's unmarked warehouse, not bothering to hide himself. He wanted Scott to see him. As a wholesale supplier to large gun dealers and online retailers across the nation, Dewey had no local retail customers and no need to announce his presence. He had several such buildings scattered around. In the heart of a small, run-down industrial area near downtown and the railroad tracks, the Kirkby warehouse made an ideal meeting place late in the evenings with few residential neighbors to disturb and most of the surrounding businesses closed.

Light and the faint sound of music rose from the rear. Dewey had a very large, raised deck back there with a tin roof cover. Taka had never been invited to a catered dinner there, but he'd seen surveillance photos from a couple years back. This meeting would be smaller, but from Dewey's hints, it'd be white tablecloths and porterhouses with cigars and some fancy single malt to follow.

His phone vibrated. He tucked himself against a chain-link fence in the shadow between security lights. "Hey."

"What you doing here?"

Taka kept his voice low although he hadn't seen so much as a cat on the walk over. "Dewey invited me."

"You turned him down."

"You don't want company?"

For a minute, Taka didn't think Scott would answer him, but then he said, "Roof, southwest three-story. There's a fire escape in back."

Taka moseyed on down the street and doubled back in the shadows until he found an opening into the right gravel yard. He climbed up and found Scott belly-down on a wooden platform built into the front corner of the roof. A deer rifle balanced on a stand braced on the roof's short parapet. In black with a black ball cap turned backwards on his head and his eye to the long-distance scope, Scott screamed cop.

Without moving, Taka took a quick look around. If he stayed where he was near the rear fire escape, he couldn't be seen from the street or surrounding buildings. "You lied to me."

Scott stayed on target, though Taka saw the long slow breath he drew. "Marine Scout Sniper. One deployment. I swore I'd never talk about it again."

"Why Dewey?" Taka asked yet again. "Why not law enforcement?"

"Got busted on opiates. Dishonorable discharge."

"So, Charleston?"

"Just a place I was passing through." He lifted his head but continued to watch Kirkby. "Needed cash to get somewhere else. And then you walked in."

"You still hooked?"

"Once an addict always an addict." He turned his head to look at Taka over his shoulder. "But no, I don't drug anymore."— and, anticipating Taka's next question—"Drinking's not a gateway for me." His voice dropped on the last word.

Taka set his jaw against the denial building in his mouth and frowned at him. "Dewey said he needed standard protection, someone to notice any angry anti-gun types headed his way while he's distracted."

Scott dropped his eye back to the scope. "He told me to stay trained on—" He caught the rest of the sentence in his teeth and shut his mouth.

Taka didn't like anything about this conversation. Not one thing. "What happens between us stays between us."

He waited. After a minute he sat down on the rear parapet and threw one leg over onto the fire escape. It rattled.

"He's meeting a guy called Bulldog Bailey," Scott said.

Taka watched the back of his head, but Scott didn't come off the scope. Taka had gone to school with Bulldog Bailey. With less than thirty Black kids out of a class of 600, everybody knew Bulldog. Plus, in ninth grade, he'd supplied Sarah Mack with pot, and that's the only reason she made it to school at all that year. Everyone loved Sarah Mack. She was just that kind of girl. And after Bulldog made his first connections, high school became his business incubator.

"Told me to keep my rifle trained on him," Scott continued. "Said Bulldog's not above shooting his dinner companions and letting them rot."

"Nice." Bulldog Bailey was the same fixture on Kanawha County's drug crime radar as he'd been in school. Low-profile. Pot, speed, oxy. His groupies still took the short-term falls. But over the years, Bulldog had cultivated a more regular turnover. Lots of new faces and tight lips. He used his people as a shield and probably calculated customer loss due to overdose into his bottom line, but if he was shooting his business partners, Taka hadn't heard about it.

"Why the meet?"

"Said he had unfinished business with the senator."

It seemed highly unlikely that Bulldog had ever had business with the senator but claiming so could get him in with Dewey. It was also highly unlikely that Bulldog had nailed down enough concrete evidence regarding Dewey's activities that he could blackmail him on anything. Not at his level of the game. Taka's guess was Dewey was lying about Bulldog's excuse to meet or that Bulldog had decided to go fishing.

Either way, not his business. Except. "So you'd commit murder for Dewey if Bulldog, what, moves his arm too much under the table?"

"Give me some credit," Scott said, "I did enough killing. And Dewey doesn't know who I am."

"Apparently I don't either."

"It's embarrassing, Taka. I'm sorry I lied to you."

"Your dad?"

"All true." He wiggled a little and settled again. "Why are you here again?"

"I don't know anymore."

He went down the escape and then slid the ladder at the bottom up again as quietly as possible.

He thought he'd go home but drove to Andrea's instead and let himself into the dark house.

WHEN ANDREA ARRIVED at Louie's with Karie and Miss Ava, hostess Daisy took them through the bar to the dining room. One table remained, checks on the table and final drinks in their hands. Andrea eyed the group as she sat down. She really needed this day to be over. Karie sat down with her sling bag in her lap.

Miss Ava leaned forward to pull her jacket off. "I think I'll have an after-dinner drink, ladies. Care to join me?"

"I was just about to ask," Daisy said. "Anything you want, on the house."

Andrea ordered last. "Please tell Louie thank you," she added.

"It's so exciting that Louie's will be recorded in Charleston's history," Daisy gushed in her usual exuberant manner. "My great-grandbabies will be able to look up where I worked and see everything about it!"

"That's the plan," Andrea said.

"I'll be right back with your drinks!" She waltzed away. Andrea stared after her, positive she could see the sparkles of Daisy's privileged life trailing after her.

"I wish I could be that optimistic." Karie said, thumping the spirit box onto the table.

Andrea tore her gaze away. "Me, too."

Miss Ava laughed at them yet again. "The world has slapped her silly, ladies. She chooses to put on her happy cape every day. Reality is all in the perception."

"Glass half-full?" Karie said.

"Every day," Miss Ava agreed.

"I haven't seen Aaron since we walked in."

Miss Ava closed her eyes for a long moment, head tilted like she was listening.

Karie picked up the recorder she'd packed and turned it on.

"I feel him. Close but not right here with us." She opened her eyes, her gaze shooting across the room. "However, there is a brother energy over there."

They all looked at the other diners. All in their thirties or early forties, friends or colleagues. One of them noticed, with a curious glance in their direction. He swung his head back to his companions, said something, and then stood. His friends ignored him. Andrea had a bad feeling. She sat up straight.

As he came over, she glanced at Miss Ava and Karie and back at him, but then realized they were looking at her, not the guy approaching them. "What?"

"What's happening?" Karie asked.

Andrea frowned at her. "I don't know." She turned back to the man to see what he wanted, but his striped oxford had become a dirty white T-shirt. His jeans tattered at the knees as he approached. Long streaks of grease from where he'd wiped his hands on his thighs appeared. And he was fading. "Oh."

He said, " . . . ance . . . me?"

She couldn't read his lips. His image fluttered in some sort of spectral wind. "I'm sorry," she said.

Miss Ava stood.

The EMF meter in Karie's hand whined.

She had it turned low, but Andrea still jumped. Karie spun the volume all the way down.

The ghost turned his attention from the meter to Miss Ava and then seemed tugged along in her wake when she headed for the table. The group fell silent as she approached. "Excuse me, I'm sorry to bother you. I'm a psychic." She raised her hand and rubbed at her lips. "I often connect with spirit, those who have passed."

"We're not interested," the big guy at the end of the table said. Maybe in his late-thirties, he was stuck between used-to-be-ripped and encroaching-middle-age. His dark hair was military cut, a sprinkle of grey showing through. "Just having a meal."

"I have a brother energy here. Passed in the last couple of years." She patted her chest. "Crush injury."

Eyes going wide, one of the women raised her hands to her mouth.

"Brant," one of the men said.

The ghost raised his hands, ecstatic.

The big guy shook his head. "Look, I don't know . . ."

"He's showing me a tied scroll," Miss Ava continued. "Which is my symbol for insurance."

The woman stood up, her chair scraping across the floor.

"Lisa," the big guy said. "She's a con artist."

Miss Ava addressed the woman. "Do you have a coin? In your pocket? He's showing me a four-leaf clover. Maybe he used to carry it?"

Nodding furiously, a sob escaping her, she dug into her jeans pocket and extracted something Andrea couldn't see. She held her open palm out to Miss Ava. "Know that our loved ones are aware when our thoughts are on them. They continue to feel our love, but they are also moving on, and we should, too. Brant wants you to be happy. He wants you to love and be loved."

"Look," the big guy said.

"Be quiet, Ed," another woman said. "We want to know what she has to say even if you don't. You said something about insurance? Brant didn't have any. Left Lisa and their two girls strapped."

Miss Ava smiled. "He's showing me a binder."

Lisa shook her head. "I don't have one. The girls do. They have school binders."

"It's red," Miss Ava clarified. "He's showing me a red binder. He's stuffing the scroll inside it."

Ed cleared his throat. "You mean like one of them drugstore notebooks, y'know, ruled paper, for different subjects?"

"None of the girls' notebooks are red," Lisa cried.

"Brant had one," Ed said, voice choked. "In his locker at the mine."

"Oh, God," the second woman said. "Is it gone?"

"I have it," Ed said, his fists clenched. "I still have it. He scribbled in that thing all the time on breaks. It—I just wanted something—" His hands opened and closed again. "That was his, you know? I never opened it though. That was his, I don't know. His private thoughts. I figured I'd give it to Lisa one day, but...I haven't yet." He looked at Miss Ava. "He was my little brother." He nodded. "He was my little brother."

"He still is, Ed," Miss Ava said. "He wants you to know he doesn't blame you. It was just his time."

"It happened so fast. A car fell on him. The jacks collapsed."

"He loves you all. He's drawing his energy back now."

Ed wiped his cheeks.

The ghost, Brant, gained color and heft.

The woman named Lisa was still standing, tears streaming unchecked, arms wrapped around herself. "Bye, Brant. I love you."

"He's showing me a robin, my symbol for new beginnings. I'm going to let him go now."

The guy sitting beside Lisa tugged her down and she folded up against him, crying hard.

Brant could've been anyone, just another diner in Louie's. He walked around the table, bent over Lisa and kissed her head. His hand landed on the man's shoulder, and he squeezed it. He continued around to Ed and ruffled his hair, then left his hand there for a second. The big guy stilled, a look of wonder on his face. His lips moved. Andrea had no problem translating. "Love you, bro."

Karie grabbed her hand. Andrea closed hers around Karie's fingers.

"Oh, my," Daisy said, breaking the rapt silence. She held the tray with their drinks in one hand, her other pressed flat to her chest. "That was the most amazing thing I've ever seen!"

The barback, a white boy with slicked back hair and a fondness for saying "aight," stood in the doorway, his mouth open. He stepped back and swung the double doors shut. The frosted-glass panels gave them a small modicum of privacy.

In the corner of Andrea's eye, Brant brightened. She raised her hand to block the light but couldn't look away. He went supernova, nearly blinding her, and blinked out.

No one else noticed.

Miss Ava pointed at Ed. "You look in that notebook now, you hear?"

He nodded. "Yes, ma'am, I will. I hope you're right."

"I am. I'm sorry to disturb you."

He ran his hand back over his head. "That's quite all right."

"You just take your time," Daisy said to the table, even as she headed over to Andrea and Karie. "Gather yourselves together before you head out."

Karie set her phone down.

Andrea shot her a glance and she nodded.

Daisy placed their drinks in front of them as Miss Ava slipped into her seat. Daisy handed her bourbon rocks to her. "That was amazing, ma'am. I missed the first part, but I saw enough. It's comforting, isn't it? Knowing life goes on?"

Miss Ava swallowed the big gulp of whiskey she'd taken. "I suppose it is."

"You're so matter of fact about it," Andrea said. "Like it doesn't bother you that people don't believe you. He called you a con artist."

Miss Ava lifted her bony shoulders in a delicate shrug. "It doesn't always end that well, but I know what I know, so why should I care what other people think?"

"You don't worry about your safety? Or people coming to your house at all hours?"

"I set clear boundaries. I have a security system." She leaned back, grinning. "And a great big ol' dog. I left him with my granddaughter since I wasn't sure what to expect when I got here."

"I can't imagine everyone"—crap, Daisy—"knowing." Andrea managed to twist her tone at the last second, so it sounded like that was all she meant to say.

"Me, either!" Daisy exclaimed.

Karie jutted her chin out at the other table. "They're getting up."

"Just yell if you need anything!" Tray tucked under her arm, Daisy bounced over to see the group out, visibly adjusting to a more somber tone by the time she reached them.

"It's a little different than what you do, Andrea," Miss Ava said after another big sip of her drink. "What you do, well, Karie's right. You have a very rare gift. What you need to do is feel out your boundaries and figure out the limits of your ability. Learn how to shield yourself so you aren't constantly being bombarded by spirit."

"You don't want every ghost on the sidewalk asking for help," Karie said, checking the EMF meter again. "I think I got the drop when he left on video."

Daisy herded the disheveled group out and shut the doors behind her, leaving them alone.

"He couldn't," Andrea said.

Karie raised her brows. "He couldn't?"

"Brant. He couldn't ask for help. I thought he was real. But when he came over, he faded almost transparent. He was wavering, too. Like a flag in high wind. I could hear him trying to speak, but I couldn't make out any of the words."

"You didn't recognize him as a spirit before he came towards us?" Miss Ava said.

"No. And I think I've seen others. Maybe."

Karie contemplated the ceiling. Miss Ava studied the shifting ice in her drink. The low music spilling from the dining room speakers cut out. It still trickled in through the closed doors from the bar, along with snatches of laughter and the hum of the bar crowd that would remain until Louie shut down at midnight.

Karie stirred and took a sip. "You've only talked to three ghosts. Actually talked."

Andrea nodded. Karie checked to see that the recorder was still on.

"One was living—well, we can't say that can we? We don't know where they go when they aren't around. Billie Mae was appearing in and connected to the house you live in. Wilder was connected to her and to Taka through their shared trauma." She sipped. "Aaron is here, a place, from what you've said, I suspect you sometimes frequent more often than your own kitchen. And he's connected to Louie, who, if I'm not mistaken, is quite fond of you and Taka."

"And?"

"I see where you're going," Miss Ava said. "Brant was here because his family was here, not because he had some connection to Andrea. And he couldn't approach her."

Picking up her phone from the table, Karie started punching away with both thumbs.

"Isn't that just because Taka's not here to play amplifier?"

"I don't know," Karie said absently. "We'll have to test our theory."

Miss Ava rattled her ice cubes. "We need some of those bones my grandmother use to throw. Call your spirit in to talk to us."

"Can you still feel him?"

"He's close to the veil all right, but not close enough to read."

Karie looked up. "This is your ninth or tenth visit with Aaron?"

"Tenth," Andrea said.

"And he hasn't shown . . ."

"This is the third time. Are you—"

"I've been documenting separately but I want to get my thoughts down and the details from tonight. I'll double-check the number later. Ava, is your release still good?"

"As long as you don't use my actual name."

"Of course. And only single initials for our unwitting participants."

"You can't use the video," Miss Ava said gently.

"Internal use only. If there's nothing paranormal on it, I'll delete it."

"Let's turn these lights down," Miss Ava said. "And try reaching out. Is that spirit box on?"

13

An hour later, the hair on the nape of Andrea's neck hurt from standing up so long. They had one perfect EVP with the quiet hum of the bar outside the dining room's doors in the distant background and then a woman saying, "Well, I'm a girl, aren't I?" And a cell phone photo of a sizable blue orb hovering to Miss Ava's left, a smaller white one caught just beside the edge of the frame. The recorder had also picked up their excitement when Ava's glass slid from in front of her to the center of the table, hitting the EMF meter, which was pegged out all the way to the top. But no Aaron.

"He's nearby," Miss Ava said again as they gathered their things. "He's focused elsewhere. I feel it."

Andrea felt nothing. No connection. But her chest ached with the need to be home. She wanted so bad to be anywhere but here that she was afraid she might burst into tears at any minute. She'd rarely cried, but right now, she needed to. She hadn't felt like this since Chuck died in Germany two weeks before coming home. Taka had been there when Chuck's dad called. She wished he were here now. She needed his big hug, the one that swallowed her up and let her hide from herself for a few minutes.

All she could think about was that little wisp of soul rising from the dead girl's body, the wavering smoke of her presence near Aaron last night in comparison to the white burst that Brant became. Shouldn't everyone leave like that? With . . . joy? Was that it for the girl? A whimper of spirit into the universe? Or was she still here? Waiting for justice?

They went out into the bar, closing the dining room doors behind them. A handful of tables were all that remained of the earlier crowd. The music was mellower and the lights lower, Louie easing his patrons into the night. Behind the bar, Aight raised his hand. Louie came through the kitchen half-doors to see them out.

Andrea caught Karie's elbow. "I'll update Louie. I should tell him about the police, too."

"Miss Ava," Andrea said.

Miss Ava turned. "Oh, darlin'. No need for thank yous or goodbyes. We'll be seeing each other again. You call me. Anytime."

"Thank you, Miss Ava, I will."

Andrea waved them off and turned to Louie. "He didn't show."

"He's not gone far."

Andrea smiled. "Miss Ava said the same. I think you're holding out on me, Louie Orengo."

"I may have been aware awhile the place isn't exactly empty."

"Savannah called me. She's going to set up a meeting with your Aunt Sally. I might get her to tell tales on you, too."

"You can try, missy, you can try."

"Look, the police brought me back in for questioning today. They might want to talk to you again, too."

"That Detective Tamarin, he was here today. Asking me about my customers, did I have security cameras, about a van out on the street. I told him I'm minding my store and my meals, not watching who's doing what out on the street. He invited me down to CPD. I told him no. Jesus backed me up. Handed over my lawyer's number, neat as you please. The detective didn't take it, but his words dried up." Louie's expressive face couldn't hide his satisfaction. He folded his arms. "He left without his lunch. Jesus gave it to the cats out back."

"He's lucky you didn't pull your grandfather's hunting whip off the wall to send him on his way." Andrea had witnessed Louie's ability to make the whip do his talking with a simple twist of his wrist.

He reached out and patted Andrea's arm. "Now don't you worry, Miss Andrea, I know the game better than you'd think. I'm a Black man living in a white man's world. This isn't the first time cops have come around thinking I'd know more than them about the Charleston underground."

She gave him a long look, daring him to tell her that he did. He just looked back at her with his depthless eyes, giving nothing away. "You'd never seen that woman before she died."

"I'm sad to say no, Miss Andrea." He waved a hand towards the big plate-glass window. "I really *don't* pay any attention to what's going on out there, so long's the sidewalk's clear and the glass is clean. She wasn't a customer."

"I walked right by her, Louie, more than once, and never saw her."

"You and I can both practice better manners in the future." He looked past her, raised his hand with a finger indicating just a moment more. "You'll let me know when you're meeting Aunt Sally?"

"Of course."

"Should I tell Jesus next Tuesday morning for Aaron?"

"Same bat time, same bat place."

He pulled the door open for her. "You get a good night's sleep, Miss Andrea. Things'll be brighter in the morning."

"Thank you, Louie. You, too. Bye now."

"Good night."

The bell tinkled as he shut the door behind her. It carried on the cold, crisp air. It sounded lonely.

Andrea swallowed her sadness. Twenty minutes home and a hot shower and a good cry. She'd be fine. She took a good hard look around. At this time of night, there were still diners strolling under the white lights decorating many of the storefronts along the historic street. The bars were shut against the weather but doing a brisk business inside. A bluegrass band was still swinging. It wasn't as busy as Capitol Street a block over, but it wasn't deserted. She walked in the direction of the garage entrance. No one was sheltering in the doorway of the bakery or the trendy outdoor shop. There were no vans.

But Aaron stood, solid as any man, just outside the art gallery. Again, his pants bore stripes that disappeared into his knee boots. Andrea stood still on the sidewalk. The only other people were behind her, crossing Quarrier. When Aaron was sure she'd seen him, he turned to look inside. Andrea eased over beside him, staying out of view of the window. That ache she'd been carrying blossomed into a painful anxiety. She couldn't seem to get the air she needed.

A woman in a power suit and peacoat came off the bottom of the stairs inside the lobby that held the art gallery. Her long, straight blonde hair hung down over her shoulders. Most of the buildings had back stairways up to second- and third-floor offices or apartments, some were tucked inside. Two girls in dresses and knee-length coats trailed after her, one a sullen older teenager, the other a tween. The tween had been crying, her cheeks splotchy and red. She clutched a blue backpack to her chest. Her eyes were wide and blank.

As she reached for the lobby door, the woman met Andrea's gaze. Andrea looked away, turning her head to consider the gangly metal man standing on the window's display shelf. A large modern primitive painted in thick layers hung behind him. Andrea was certain the woman was one of the blondes in the photo Pete showed her.

She turned towards Andrea, walking right through Aaron. The girls followed, though the tween veered over, avoiding Aaron, though she neither acknowledged him or Andrea as she passed. This late, they'd only be leaving if they'd been visiting someone. If the woman lived here, Pete would have discovered that and just gone knocking on her door.

Aaron watched them go down the street. He vanished in the sweep of a car's headlights as it came down Hale. Andrea wanted to see what car the woman and girls got into but worried the woman would glance back. She scurried past the gallery doors into the shadow of the awning of the dark clothing shop next door before she turned around. But their car wasn't on the street. They turned right at the end of the block and disappeared.

Before she could follow, the sound of muffled laughter erupted from the gallery. Three men in jeans and leather jackets burst through the doors, laughing and shoving at each other, drunk or high, smelling of cologne and that sweaty musk she associated with horny guys and dark clubs. "Derek knows how to throw a party," one of them crowed.

Aaron followed them out, bare chested. The manacles she'd seen the night before dangled from his wrists. Blood streaked down from a gaping hole in his chest and soaked into his apron. His striped pants were caked in mud, legs torn at the ankles of his bare, swollen, and bruised feet. Welts and flayed skin wrapped around his ribs from his back.

"I can't believe we did that," another said, as they jaywalked across Hale to the garage. "I'm never going back."

Aaron stopped in the middle of the street.

"I am," the third said.

"No, I meant no more bitchy online hookups for me. I got her number."

"You got that, bud," the first said over his shoulder. "High-five." He spun and jumped, hand out, and the other two were quick enough to meet him, slaps echoing off the concrete wall. He said something else, and they all laughed, but they were too far away for her to hear anything else clearly.

She started to go to Aaron but sunk back into the shadows when the lobby doors again swung open. Two men in suits came out together, one of them just lighting up a cigarette. Aaron glared at them, fists clenched.

The smoker pocketed his lighter and took a deep drag. "I have to admit, I didn't think you'd get me what I needed. I'm glad I trusted you."

The parking garage entrance lit up. Karie's car rolled to the exit. She'd be coming this way. Andrea slid sideways to the clothing shop door and turned to face it, her hands on the knob by the time Karie's headlights hit her. She hurried towards the street, headlights from the opposite direction now washing over her as well. An SUV passed Karie as she slowed down. She braked a couple of yards past Andrea and Miss Ava poked her head out of the window. "Andrea, darlin', are you okay?"

"Just locking up," Andrea called out. She glanced over at the men, who wore identical expressions of wariness as they looked back.

"Do you need a ride to your car?"

Andrea tugged on the back door, grateful when it opened right away. "Yes, please."

She slid into the back seat and slammed the door.

Karie hit the accelerator. Andrea scrambled around to see the men.

They were walking away. Aaron still stood in the road.

When they stepped off the sidewalk, Aaron expanded and rose, a darker-than-the-night shadow that flapped down on them like the closing of a deformed crow's wings before it exploded into nothing.

The men walked on.

The orange tip of the smoker's cigarette between his fingers bobbed as he talked.

Andrea flopped back around, her eyes closed, and tried to breathe. Could you have a heart attack from anxiety? People died from being scared, didn't they?

Karie spun the wheel right at the corner. "What happened? Are you okay?"

Andrea sat up, scanning the street for the woman and the two girls, but she didn't see them. "I don't know. Slow down! Aaron was standing right there on Hale, in chains, all bloody and his chest"—she splayed her hand open—"and he was so scared and so angry. I could feel him. Slow down, I need—they're not here. Where did they go?"

"Who, Andrea?" Miss Ava asked.

"One of the women, from the photos, and two girls." She whipped her head left to see down the next block. "Where did they go?"

"Was the woman blonde?" Karie said. "There was a family in the SUV that passed us on Hale. The passenger was blonde, and there were girls in the back."

"I don't know. It was just the three of them."

"Do you want me to go back around again?"

Andrea slumped back in the seat, her arms and legs going heavy. "No. They're gone."

Karie caught her eye in the rearview mirror. "What did you mean, you could feel him?"

"All night, I just thought I was anxious, though I don't really get anxious normally. I just wanted to go home and cry."

"That happens to me," Karie said. "It's been a stressful day."

"It was more than that." But she didn't know how to explain it. "I'm not a very emotional person, I pretty much go with the flow."

"People who shake grief's hand early in life cry themselves out young," Miss Ava said. "They learn emotional balance."

Andrea had never thought of it like that, but yes, exactly. And perspective. She'd gotten a lot of serious reality checks before she'd even finished high school. And it had led to her being accused more than once of being too even keeled in any given situation. Promotion? Why aren't you happier? Funeral? Why aren't you more upset?

"Or they die," Miss Ava added.

The memory of her brother throwing himself off the New River bridge on a frayed bungee cord bled across her mind's eye. She so did not need to think about her reckless, trying-to-kill himself brother right now. "Anyway," she said. "I think my anxiety was Aaron. It's gone now, but no. Just no. Do not want."

"Did you feel anything like that before, with the others?"

"Now that I realize, yes. I just kept shoving it down instead of letting it in. But Aaron, he's different."

"I'll send you some exercises," Miss Ava said. "You can build a psychic shield, but you need to be in the presence of spirits to practice."

"What do you think he was doing?" Karie asked.

"Trying to show me something."

"Do you think his change of appearance meant anything?" Karie asked.

"How am I supposed to know, Karie?" Andrea wailed, and then cringed when she heard herself.

"I'm sorry," she said at the same time as Karie said, "I didn't mean—"

Miss Ava broke the resulting silence. "I don't see them like you do, but based on my years of experience, I'd say it may or may not mean anything." She forced a dry chuckle. "That's helpful, isn't it?"

Karie stopped at a red light. "We documented a lot last time, but we didn't really analyze your experience with Billie Mae before I met you down to the details. Like when she came to you exactly, and her different appearances when she did. How she acted when you said one thing versus another. How her clothing and demeanor differed after those kids were found in the lake. Maybe doing that would help you make more sense of Aaron."

"You think there are rules to this?" And yes, it sounded more bitter than Andrea intended.

The light changed, but Karie didn't move the car. She sat still, with that particular tilt to her head while she processed. A car honked behind her. "I do." She made the left turn. The horn blared again as the car blasted past on the straight-ahead. "There are rules for science. For physics. These hauntings are just a natural process that we have no way to measure or quantify or understand yet."

"It's true," Miss Ava said, "that my peers and I can teach each other different methods of listening and experience many of the same sensations. I'd bet that Karie's right. If not rules, then there will at least be patterns that could be helpful for deciphering spirit's intent." She sighed as the sign for her hotel came into view. "I wish I could stay but needs must."

"I'm glad you came. It's nice to know I'm not alone."

"Ah," Karie said. "But now we know we're never alone."

"You don't want to think too hard about that, darlin'."

"I guess I don't," Karie said, her tone rueful, and then she laughed.

Andrea's mood lightened just a bit as the consequences dawned on her.

"I'm just teasing," Miss Ava said. "I've been assured they have their own work on the other side to keep 'em busy."

The portico of the hotel filled the car with a warm amber light. Karie rolled to a stop. "Good to know. Can we call you if we run into trouble?"

Miss Ava reached out and patted Karie's hand. "Anytime, Karie. Drive careful."

"You, too."

Andrea levered herself out of the back seat, so tired she could hardly think.

Miss Ava was waiting for her. She closed her hard, thin fingers around Andrea's biceps. "You take care, you hear? I hope your man comes through for you."

"He's not my man, but I hope so, too."

Miss Ava's eyes narrowed, and she pressed her lips tight together. "Mmm-hmm. Don't let that detective brush you off now."

"I'm going to call him right now."

"Be persistent. I'm not sure why, but spirit's saying it's important."

"I will."

Karie waited until Miss Ava was safely inside, then pulled around into the parking lot while Andrea found Pete Tamarin's card. She dialed his cell phone.

"Yeah," he said, sounding wide awake.

"It's Andrea Kelley. I saw one of the blonde women in the photos outside Louie's less than ten minutes ago. She was coming out of the building with the art gallery and had two young girls with her."

"Okay."

"I thought you'd want to know. Three men came out and said there was a party at Derek's. If that helps."

"Were they together?"

"The woman and the men? No."

"Okay. Thanks."

"Is that all?"

"Was she doing something illegal?"

"No."

"Then yeah, that's all."

"Okay. And if I see her again?"

"We're handling our case, Andrea. You just go on about your life."

"You made her part of my life."

"All I did was show you photos of you with the victim, even though you said you never saw her before. You said you never saw any of the other people in the photos either. Do you really think you'd be able to recognize one of them now after seeing one photo when you've probably already been walking by them for weeks?"

"It was her. She was one of the blonde women in that photo with the victim and the two men." The word "victim" made her mouth taste sour. "It looked like she knew her, the victim."

"We're aware," he said. "We showed you the photos, not the other way around."

How could he not think this was important? "Was I right about the victim's ID?"

"We're handling it, Andrea. Don't go harassing a woman you don't know."

She started to say she'd never do that, but the thought had just crossed her mind to find out if a Derek lived in the building. "Have you already talked to a Derek in that building? The windows look out over the alley."

"We know how to do our jobs, thank you very much," he said, making sure she knew she had offended him. "Good night."

"I'm sorry for bothering you."

"I only picked up the phone because it was you, Andrea, but seriously, we got this. I'll let you know if we need your help."

"Okay, Pete."

He hung up. Andrea thumbed her phone closed.

"What'd he say?"

Andrea shook her head. "Thanks, and goodbye."

"I guess she could be just like you, living her own life."

"I think Aaron knows more than Pete does."

"Do you think she needs help?"

"I do. And now that I've seen her, I'm not going to ignore another woman who needs help."

"You want to call Jimmy?"

"Let him sleep. He's coming for breakfast."

"So . . ."

"Can you take me home? I'll get my car tomorrow."

Karie started the car, turned her country playlist back up, and let Andrea gather her thoughts. The traffic was light, but it seemed like there were more people out on the streets than normal. A few walking, but her brain seemed intent on picking out the people it usually let her skim over. Two men sleeping under tarps next to a full shopping cart. An old woman wrapped in blankets and huddled in a doorway. A dog lay passed out across the heap of her belongings in a child's wagon. Two hookers strolled towards her from a side street as Karie rolled through a yellow light. A group of teens smoking and walking in the middle of the road, dribbling a basketball between them.

On the highway, all the lights blurred together.

Her exit was dark except for the One Stop station. Her street was asleep.

But Taka's Yukon sat under her carport.

Why? Why tonight?

"Well," Karie said. "Your morning might be interesting."

14

Andrea woke to male voices in her kitchen. She fumbled with her phone. Jimmy was early. Very early. Taka must've let him in. She yawned and stretched and then fell limp again. Just before she fell back asleep, she made herself get up.

She blazed through her morning routine, slightly worried about what they could possibly be discussing down there. Pulled on jeans and a Henley and her favorite black sweater. Tucked her gun into her SuperSlide holster. Pelted down the stairs but made a point of slowing down in the hall so she could listen for a minute. They sounded... companionable. She meandered into the kitchen.

Jimmy and Taka were devouring a huge stack of toast and a mountain of scrambled eggs. They'd set a plate and a mug out for her. There was butter, two kinds of jelly, and ketchup on the table. Engrossed in a discussion about spiders and—egg sacs in space?—they didn't even look up when she snagged her mug off the table.

She poured her coffee, still hot, thank God, and watched them plow through the food, talking with their mouths full. They wandered from egg sacs to some new trigger guard they agreed was stupid to whether or not this year would be the year that the developer who built Lake

Vickers would go broke and how long it'd take for the muskrats to drain the lake if no one kept repairing the earthen dam at the south end.

"Five years tops, before you can't tell it ever existed," Jimmy said.

Taka scooped half the remaining eggs onto her plate and half on his. "Archeologists are always discovering ancient lakebeds."

Jimmy matched him by giving her the second-to-last piece of toast before slathering butter on the last one. "True, but Lake Vickers has only been in existence three years. You think it's made a lasting impression?" He was still slapping jelly on when she pulled her chair out and sat down.

"Haven't the foggiest." Taka slid all the condiments in her direction without missing a beat.

"Where's your car?" Jimmy asked.

Andrea assumed that one was directed at her. "Louie's."

"She got in late," Taka muttered.

"Yeah?" Jimmy said. "Does that mean Aaron finally spoke up?"

Andrea swallowed her first mouthful of egg and snagged the butter knife. "Not the way you mean."

As she ate, she told them everything up until she got in Karie's car.

"Hmmm," Jimmy said when she was done.

Taka had closed up the jars and capped the butter dish while she talked. "So, the young guys." He tapped the end of the knife he'd been absently holding on the table and then laid it down on his plate. "They said they couldn't believe they did that, and they were never going back to online dating. Did they mean they went to a party and met girls in person?"

"They were closer to thirty than twenty. Surely they've met women in person before."

"Could've been anything," Jimmy said. "Maybe they meant the way they got to the party. Talked to someone they wouldn't normally have, accepted a blind invite."

Andrea pushed her empty plate away and picked her mug up in both hands. "The thing is? They were talking about sex."

"And you want to connect the girls to them because of Aaron."

"Hard not to," Taka said, "with Aaron in manacles and whipped."

"Human trafficking?" Jimmy shook his head.

"Modern-day slavery," Taka said.

Andrea looked back and forth between them. Human trafficking wasn't what she was thinking. "I was thinking maybe the girls saw something they shouldn't have. Something upsetting. What do you know that I don't?"

Jimmy shook his head. "Nothing. I've just got a headful of dark and all those questions Pete Tamarin was asking yesterday."

"Ditto," Taka said, but he wasn't looking at her. He was pushing crumbs and leftover egg around his plate with the tip of the jam knife.

"Does human trafficking even happen here?"

"Sure," Jimmy said. "We had a group trolling the college campuses last year."

"You can get abducted on campus? How is that even possible?"

Taka scrummed down in his throat. That's what they called it, scrumming. It was a peculiar burr of sound he'd picked up somewhere that meant something and nothing all at once.

Jimmy gave him the side-eye from across the table and said, "Abductions happen, but usually the entry is through grooming."

"Like how sexual predators groom little kids?"

"It's different, but yeah. Guys court girls, romance them, take them out, buy them gifts. Eventually they encourage drug use, just a little, come on, it's fun. Then it's hey, meet my friend, do me a favor and sleep with him. And when the girls back off, I'm going to leave you, or hurt you, or threaten your family, come on, it's no big deal, you sleep with me, I like to share. They're in it before they know it."

"Or," Taka said, glancing up and back down at his plate again. "The boyfriend who's managed to separate her, or him, from family and friends with the hard-court press says let's get away for the weekend. Roofies the victim during a nice dinner. Victim wakes up the next morning to no clothes, no shoes, no cell phone. By the next day, victim's been sold repeatedly to drive home his control. Or he's just sold her, period, and she's gone. We had a girl that happened to last year. It took her eight months to escape. The hospital called us. She was from Idaho."

Andrea's stomach rolled, the eggs not agreeing with the thought of that blank eyed tween last night. The sullen teen.

"But most of the time, they don't even try to escape. They're basically either exchanging protection, food, and shelter, brainwashed into thinking the trafficker loves them and is taking care of them, or are silenced by threats to their family and physical violence."

"How am I unaware of all this? I mean, I've seen news articles on human trafficking, but it's American tourists acting badly in Bangkok or Indonesians in Saudi Arabia, not college kids in West Virginia."

"It's high school and college students across the nation," Jimmy said. "Boys, too, like Taka said, not just girls. Even middle-schoolers. Some of them stay in school and live at home. They get trafficked on the weekend by family friends or coaches. For sex. Some are sold as domestic labor."

"But if Aaron hadn't been there, hadn't looked the way he did," Jimmy said.

"We wouldn't be suspecting anything," Andrea finished for him.

Taka got up, reaching across the table to grab and stack their plates. "A lady and her unhappy kids who may have been doing anything, leaving divorced dad's place, dinner with the grandparents, a party they got dragged to where they were bored."

"Some guys leaving a party where one of them met a girl," Jimmy said, gathering the condiments and heading for the fridge.

Taka came back from the sink for the glasses. "A couple of suits having an after-dinner drink and talking about a deal they made."

"I called Pete last night."

That got Taka's full attention. "Why?"

"To tell him I saw one of the women from the photo he showed me. She knew the woman in the alley."

"Don't talk to him anymore," Jimmy said. He had the coffee pot in his hand.

"Did you get a lawyer?"

"I did."

"Sweet Joe," Jimmy said.

"Yes," Andrea said. Taka took her empty mug from her. "How'd you know?"

"He's good," Taka said.

Jimmy turned the water on and rinsed the pot. "I put him on retainer, too."

Andrea's insides hollowed out. "How worried do I need to be?"

Taka took over Jimmy's place at the sink. "Just don't talk to Pete again without him." He started loading the dishwasher.

Jimmy was emptying the coffee filter into the trash. "You had nothing to do with anything. Pete's probably already spoken to that lady, and if he hasn't, you can bet he has patrol down at that building right now, knocking on doors until they find out where she was last night and get her contact info."

"Those girls—"

"Fields is working with Pete," Taka said to the sink as he rinsed it. "I'll have a word. Tell him you saw her with kids and ask them to do a safety check."

"Okay." The shakiness from her spike of anxiety was already fading. It was so different from what radiated through her last night while Aaron raged. Why would Aaron do that unless he meant something by it, wanted her to take notice of those people?

Taka dried his hands, grabbed his keys, and dropped a kiss on her head. "Gotta go."

After the door slammed behind him, Jimmy said. "Got out before you could pin him down on Aaron."

"That he did."

Jimmy leaned back against the kitchen counter. "I should get going, too. I've got a lot of paperwork ahead of me today and not one, but two reports due."

"I thought Taka was a glutton for punishment getting a minor in English, but it's come in useful."

Jimmy's mouth twisted. "Double major. Social Sciences and English. My master's was in Criminal Justice."

Color her impressed. "Did you always want to be in law enforcement?"

"Third grade. My dad came in and talked about working admin in a coal mine. Trey's dad came in and talked about being a criminal investigator for the state police in Virginia before joining the FBI and getting stationed in Huntington."

"And that was that."

"He set up a mini crime scene. I was hooked."

"The FBI in your sights?"

Looking thoughtful, he crossed his arms. "No. I really like my job. I like my team. I like Charleston."

"And you like me?"

He did that whole-body-grin thing. "I do. Can I get a good morning kiss?"

She met him halfway. She loved the way he kissed, like he had all day and wanted nothing more. Every time she kissed him, she wanted to catch fire. He was thoughtful and pretty and she got him. He got her. But she was satisfied with a thorough kiss. Every time. And he never pushed for more. Because he was a good guy. She should want everything with him.

He broke the kiss, just when that delicious feeling was settling in, and she could hang out in his arms all day. "I wish I had time to carry you upstairs," he muttered against her lips. He kissed her again. "I'd like to, just so you know." Another kiss.

"Okay," she said.

"Okay," he breathed into her mouth.

Kissed her again and pulled away. "You need a ride?"

"Do you have time to drop me?"

"It's on my way. I'll start the car, make a couple calls. No rush."

She followed him to the kitchen door and kissed him again when he leaned back in.

She shut the door and leaned against it. Listened to the engine of his RAV4 kick over. The initial rattle of the idle smoothed out.

She thumped her head against the door. "Okay? That's all you could say?" She'd been dragging her feet on sex for six weeks for no real reason at all. She liked sex. She hadn't had any in a long time with anyone but herself. All the single women she knew complained about the expectation of third-date sex. No third-date sex seemed equivalent to a breakup note. Guys ghosted when it didn't happen or pushed too much, got a tense, obligatory ride on the fourth date, and ghosted anyway. What was wrong with her?

Ghosts.

That was what was wrong with her.

And now she had to worry if they were watching. She rolled her eyes at herself.

It was ten after eight. Everything she needed was right where she dropped it last night. She packed up the leftover chicken and pasta for lunch, filled her water jug from the cold water stored in the fridge, and headed out.

A light frost coated the grass and tops of the cars across the neighborhood. She had barely noticed it out the kitchen window, she's been so busy watching Taka and Jimmy together. But now, everywhere the sun touched sparkled. As always, she glanced over at Susan Pepper's house on her way out of the carport. All quiet. Mr. Huntley across the street had his outdoor lights up and a pair of reindeer on his lawn, just the deer, no sled or Santa. But the Larsens had taken care of that. An inflatable Santa with a sack of toys waved from the yard near the porch. His beard was blinding. His eyes how they twinkled. The McMullins had hung lights and a wreath.

She saw the police cruiser go by out on Timber Way but thought nothing of it. She could probably buy a wreath from the Boy Scouts' lot this weekend. She pulled open the rear passenger door of Jimmy's little RAV4 just as he was finishing his call.

"Ten. Yes. See you then."

She tossed her bags on the floorboard, slammed the door, and got in up front. "Want to go with me to buy a door wreath this weekend?"

"Sure. I'll buy two for my mom in exchange for pie."

"What kind?"

"Fruits of the Forest."

Her heart panged. "Sara Lee. My mom loved it."

Jimmy gave her the softest look, one she'd never seen from him before. "Made from scratch, but much the same, I'm sure."

Of course. She wasn't often self-conscious. She ducked her head, letting her hair block her burning cheeks. She'd lived for Spam and Sara Lee, once.

"Hey, now, who doesn't love Sara Lee? The pound cake! With Neapolitan ice cream." He leaned towards her. "I only ate the strawberry though."

She laughed. "I only ate the chocolate."

"Our moms were troopers getting stuck with the vanilla."

He threw the RAV4 in reverse. Red and blue light strobed through the car. "Well, shit," Jimmy said.

The cruiser sat at the end of the drive, blocking them in.

"Seriously?" Andrea breathed.

15

L ieutenant Ronnie Horton rapped his knuckles on Taka's desk.
Taka jumped up, his chair rolling away somewhere behind him, and ripped his earbuds out.

"Need a word with you. My office. Ten minutes."

"Yes, sir."

Horton strode out of the bullpen, leaving Taka staring after him, his heart pounding. He'd had his finger on the video fast-forward, completely focused on the fast-moving images on the street cam he was watching. Something yellow came flying at him. He tried to bat it down and missed. Karl's balled up fast-food wrapper hit him in the face at the same time the laughing donkey-ass brayed, and half the pen looked over.

Taka scooped the wrapper off his desk and pitched it back at Karl, nailing him in the shoulder. He paused the video, wrote down the timestamp, and closed it before maximizing the one he was supposed to be watching and doing the same. He gathered the sparse notes he had on the series of robbery videos he'd been handed to pull patterns and identify if they were connected, and if so, the physical characteristics of the suspects. He printed out the Administrative Inventory Priority Action report he hadn't completed yet and labeled a folder for it. Closed the screen, but left his computer running.

Uneasy, he patted his pockets. Keys, cards, cell in its case on his hip. He stuffed his earbuds in his front pocket. Grabbed his jacket. Without cases to organize, he'd been leaving his laptop at home. He'd been dismissed before and had the heebie-jeebies. Horton was Detective Chief and his boss, but Taka also considered him his mentor in the department and his silence had been deafening. But at least it wasn't Captain Cahill asking for his presence.

"Geesh, Taka," Karl said, "he just wants a chat. Stop packing up."

"Not taking anything for granted these days, Karl."

"Good luck, then. Call if you're not coming back."

"Shut up, Karl," Fields said from his own desk.

Taka took one last look to see if there was anything else he couldn't do without and left the bullpen. He trotted down the stairs rather than wait for the elevator. The hallway past the conference rooms was freshly painted, which made the carpet look worse. He knocked on the frame of Horton's office doorway as he came to it. Stacks of paper sat on every surface except the one chair in his office. That was ominous.

Horton waved him to the chair.

The pit of Taka's stomach yawned open then snapped closed. He resisted the bile that tried to rise in his throat. "I'm good."

"Sit down," Horton ordered. "And close the door."

Taka closed his eyes.

"Please," Horton said, which did nothing for Taka's nerves.

He sat, fingers clenched tight in his jacket.

"We know you called Lieutenant Hoyle two days ago after patrol was dispatched to Louie's. We understand the relationships. Hoyle lied when asked. We've reported that to his supervisor."

"Okay."

"Do not stand up, understand?"

No. "What?"

"What I'm going to say next. Stay seated. Do you understand?"

Taka's heart about stopped. "Yes, sir."

"Andrea's—"

He was on his feet before he knew it.

"Taka. She's fine. Sit down."

Taka's legs were numb anyway. He sat. Not gracefully.

"She's in holding."

Taka leaned forward and breathed. Okay. Better than the hospital. "Why?"

"She called Pete Tamarin last night about a woman—"

"She'd seen in the surveillance photos he showed her. Yeah."

"Carpool came for the kids this morning. Kids were a no-show. Mom went to the door, looked through the sidelight, saw a body in the foyer. Tamarin already had her on the radar, but not under surveillance. Fields talked to her yesterday morning."

"Why pull Andrea in?" He knew already, though. Last to see her. But Tamarin must not have liked her answers to whatever questions he asked.

"She gave Pete witnesses, but they can't corroborate her time between twelve-forty last night and seven this morning. Lieutenant Hoyle has proven untruthful."

"And that leaves me."

"She says you stayed over in the guest room, but she didn't see you when she came in at twelve-forty."

"Twelve-forty-three."

"But you didn't see her."

He didn't put his head between his knees, but he didn't sit up, either. "Not until this morning. But I heard her come in."

"Did she go out again?"

"She didn't have her car."

"Access to your keys? Or Hoyle's?"

"Hoyle didn't stay over."

"You sure? You were sleeping."

"I let him in at seven."

"Your keys?"

He looked up and met Horton's straightforward gaze head-on. "They were where I left them on the guest room dresser. The door sticks. I'd have woken up if she came in, let alone twice."

"Judge has already given us a search warrant."

"Andrea has nothing to hide."

"Sweet Joe's already been here. He's driving over to meet the team and unlock her door. Her car's been impounded."

"What about the kids? The two girls?"

"Gone. Double bunk beds in two bedrooms. Evidence of seven kids. The murder victim was neither a biological nor official foster mom. Forensics is still working the scene."

"Karie Wilson?"

"Questioned and released at her home. Her car was searched."

"There's nothing solid enough to warrant all this. What's going on?"

Horton dropped his gaze to the open file laid out on his desk. He pressed his lips together.

"C'mon, I've done everything CPD has ever asked of me. I'm losing my job here because I've done my job. Faithfully."

Horton didn't correct him. Taka's heart ached so much, he had trouble breathing.

"She ID'ed Luciana Rafaela Garcia before Tamarin and Fields did. It might've been months before she showed up in the database checks if they hadn't had her name to cross-reference. She was fingerprinted for a background check. ME already verified. We have a request into the FBI for confirmation against her military records."

Taka studied the greige industrial carpet between his boots. Was there any ventilation in this room at all? The stale air was suffocating.

"What are the chances, Taka?" Horton slapped the file closed, ran a hand through his hair, and fell back against his chair. He twirled the pen in his hand across his middle fingers. "She says she doesn't know the victim. Swears she never saw her. But we have photos showing them in close contact. Then she just *happens*"—Horton made air quotes with his fingers—"to see and recognize Garcia's VFW headshot based on what? A grainy still and a glimpse of Garcia's corpse?"

"I'm sure she had a legitimate reason to be at the VFW related to her current projects at Waltham-Young."

"Actually, no."

Taka sat up. "What do you mean, no?"

"She has seven active projects. The one that took her to the VFW is related to her community historic preservation project connected to Louie Orengo. Supposedly, her meeting was part of her discovery process to outline the possible time and effort it would take to trace an

Orengo slave ancestor from the plantation he was born to the location of his death. He was photographed in Confederate uniform pants. You know, related to the Civil War."

"Yes," Taka said drily. "I'm familiar with the Confederacy."

Horton waved his hand. "Sorry. History seems to have fallen by the wayside in my kids' school. They say I do too much"—air quotes again —"*dad-splaining*, but it's hard to help myself these days."

"Andrea?"

"Yeah. This VFW meeting was in regards to this photograph, but she didn't show it to guy she met with, had some explanation about not being allowed to document it visually, and she can't produce it. Refuses to give us the source because that person requested to remain anonymous. How she even knows it's a legitimate photo in that case, I don't know."

Andrea had talked about discovery for projects before. Sometimes projects weren't approved by either clients or Waltham-Young due to projected time requirements, difficulty in verifying facts, or expense. Of course, in this case, there was no photo. Taka was almost certain she had gone hunting info on Aaron based on her description of him. "It's discovery. If the source is one she's worked with before or she had good reason to believe the photo was legitimate, it would only be verified by third parties and the privacy issues resolved if the project's green-lighted."

"That's what she said."

"Her boss'll verify that if it helps."

"Tamarin has a call in. Bobby Waltham's out of the country."

Of course he was. He traveled a lot, researching one esoteric thing after another. Not Taka's cup of tea, for sure.

"She's mentioned board approval before."

"Project board, yeah," Horton agreed. "There's a call in to the current head. Apparently, leadership rotates through the various departments every few months."

"They'll back her up."

"I'm sure they will," Horton said, his tone carefully neutral.

Because that might end up being a point of tension as well.

Horton set the pen down and leaned forward again, linking his fingers together.

"It's okay," Taka said. "How long?"

"We just need you out of the office while she's under investigation."

"And if she's charged?"

Horton glanced over at the closed door. "You and I both know Andrea had nothing to do with this. But Tamarin can't ignore the only leads he has and Andrea's not helping herself any. Killers attend funerals, right? Insert themselves in investigations. The day after the first victim is discovered, she stumbles across the victim's ID? And then spots the second victim before she dies and calls Pete Tamarin?"

"Establishes time, attempts to draw Pete into a compromised position."

"I'm glad you understand. Fields followed you up. The small conference room. You can give him your official statement."

"Not without Carson Lazar."

Horton sighed, then rubbed his temples with his eyes closed and a contemplative air. "Probably for the best."

He flipped through a couple of files, scribbling his signature at the bottom of reports while Taka called Carson. When Taka hung up, he said, "Wait with Fields. And, Taka, stay out of it, okay? Whatever Andrea's doing. It'd best if you don't have any contact with her until Tamarin gets this sorted."

"She's just doing her job, Chief. The rest really is coincidence."

"You know the drill, your duty station is your home until further notice. Monday through Friday, you're there from eight to four. If you leave for any reason, call it in. I'll call you Monday."

"Yes, sir."

ANDREA SAT in the corner of the concrete bench in one of the holding cells. Two other women paced the floor. Sweet Joe said he was confident she'd be released later in the day, but she wasn't so sure.

The woman, Anna Lansing, was dead. Pete had a statement from her the day before stating she'd barely known Lucy Garcia, and not by that name. They'd partied together once. The uniforms sent to the art gallery building on Hale this morning found no one named Derek living in the building. Because it lay across the street from the garage, there weren't any security cameras directly across the street and the gallery's security cameras showed only the gallery entrance from the lobby, the gallery interior, and the back exit.

Someone would still review them to see if any portion of Lansing or the girls or the men were caught on video. The other businesses and the traffic camera may have captured them on the sidewalk or down on Quarrier when they went around the corner to whatever vehicle they left in. The parking garage had a camera over the exit, but it was broken. Had been broken for weeks, so they didn't have anything from it. But the credit card reader should give them something on subpoena. The men would be questioned as to if they knew Lansing or Lucy Garcia, and if they remembered Andrea. Pete had probably been being kind to share that information with Sweet Joe for her benefit.

Andrea didn't know how that could work in her favor except if one of them incriminated himself. In the meantime, she was freezing. She wrapped her arms around her bent knees. She was afraid to put her face down, afraid to lose sight of the women in the cell with her. The one muttered to herself as she stalked back and forth. She wore bib overalls and a T-shirt. Her hair was just long enough for two cockeyed pigtails. The other, in a midcalf knit dress and combat boots, kept quiet, following the first, step for step, wringing her hands. Maybe they were related.

On the next pass-by, though, Andrea noticed the blood on the second one's temple. She stretched her arm out. "You've got—"

The first woman whipped around, practically growling and snapped, "What, what is it now?"

The second woman whirled up and away like so much smoke. There one minute, gone the next.

Andrea had said nothing since she was deposited in the cell. She covered her open mouth with both hands.

"What? Cat got your tongue now? No more blah-blah-blah?"

If she were Miss Ava, she'd know what to say. But the ghost was gone, and Andrea didn't know what it had wanted from this woman anyway. The woman threw up her hands and resumed her march.

Andrea did hide her face then.

Why was she so stupid to have fallen from that ladder in the first place? Her brother took unnecessary risks constantly and just skated through life. She needed to know how the loft was nailed to the support beams in a midcentury barn and this was what she got. If Mark got a concussion, would he get ghosts, too? Or was it just lucky her? She hoped Karie was right and there were rules they could sort and write down. Document. Record.

She hoped Pete got whatever answers he needed and Sweet Joe came to pick her up before she had to spend the night at South Central out on Corridor G.

16

Jimmy sat chewing on his thumbnail.

"Stop," Nina said, reaching out to lay a hand on his jiggling knee. "You're making me seasick."

On top of watching Andrea leave in the back of the cruiser and meeting Sweet Joe at the station only to find himself shut out, he'd come into Nina and Bill hard at work already. Detweiler's morning report had Taka on the roof with Scotty during Dewey's meet with Bulldog Bailey. And by this morning, every alert the tech wizard at North Carolina's State Bureau of Investigation in Raleigh had set on Scott's cover identity had pinged.

Dewey's previous head of security had tripped a couple when Scott had been hired to bartend. A financial check, standard background, Facebook page. But someone had lit all of them up between midnight and eight-thirty a.m. from two separate IP addresses. Facebook, Instagram, GoodReads, Twitter, complete background, previous addresses, arrest record, AFIS, and NCIC. It had Taka written all over it.

Bill leaned back in his chair, hands paused over the keyboard he'd been massaging for what seemed like a long time already. "The AFIS and NCIC requests came from a small department outside Boise, Idaho."

Hadn't he just heard something about Idaho? The trafficked girl

Taka mentioned at breakfast. From Idaho. "I want to know if Detective Taka has a friend in Boise."

"That's gonna take time, Boss," Nina said.

"Bill?"

"On it."

"It's holding up, though, right?"

"Yeah, Boss."

This was bad at the agency and investigation levels, but terrible for Scott and Taka if Scott couldn't come clean before his cover broke. And Jimmy was pretty sure Andrea would never forgive him, either, whether or not he avoided the direct blast.

Then he'd had to sit through his ten o'clock with a lecturing Maddox regarding his "discussion" with Detective Tamarin until he cried mercy and the two of them could finally start calling favors in to find out what why Tamarin was going hard at Andrea.

What were the chances the blonde would be killed now?

Okay, maybe pretty good, considering the fate of Lucy Garcia and the fact they knew each other, but still. Not a good time for Andrea to have gotten eagle-eyed. Maddox had discovered the man in the surveillance stills was the dead man in the van. Three bodies and Andrea standing in the middle.

Nina reached out again, her hand warm on his knee. "Stop," she said.

OUT IN THE glare of the cold sun, Taka called Jimmy.

"Hey."

"What the fuck?" Taka exploded. "You couldn't text me?"

"And what, exactly, would you have done if I had?"

Taka spun in a helpless circle, then leaned back against his car, crossing his free arm over his chest.

"She's fine, Taka. Sweet Joe said she did great. Stayed calm. Explained her job. They didn't rattle her like they did the other day."

"Andrea doesn't rattle."

"It's been a hard six weeks."

And you haven't been around he didn't say, but Taka heard it all the same.

"They know I called you the other morning. Horton isn't writing me up on it because nobody asked me, but he said you lied."

"Not really. Tamarin assumed and I let him."

"Still, he had you in officially."

"I know."

"I'd have handled it."

"I know. Maddox can't avoid putting a warning of disciplinary action in my file."

"Can you tell me? What's going on?"

"Gotta go." Before Jimmy cut the line or Taka could protest, Taka heard him say, "Y'all want coffee?"

He crossed both arms and waited. The damp and wind of the river cut right through his jacket. He'd need to start carrying his bulkier black winter coat soon. During the summer, he longed for the cold, but once it got cold and wet for longer than a couple of weeks, he was already dreaming of warmth.

The cell vibrated in his hand. A number he didn't know. He answered it but didn't say anything.

"Had to come outside," Jimmy said.

"Burner?"

"I keep a couple in my car for informants."

Taka decided not to ask. Informants were usually given burners through the department at CPD, but Jimmy wouldn't be calling him on any state-issued burner. "I don't want to mess you up, man," Taka said. "I think my job may be toast already."

"You deserve to know. You're a cop. Just don't say I told you if anybody asks. If you can't do that, morally, tell me now."

"Tell me."

Jimmy related what he and Maddox had beat out of their connections.

Taka had thought he'd be relieved to know the details, but it really didn't help. "How'd they get the warrant?"

"Sweet Joe said he couldn't tell me, and we couldn't get it out of anyone else."

"That means it's pretty damning. Nobody wants leaks." He ran his hand back over his head and then covered his eyes. "From what she said this morning, you think Aaron could actually be useful?"

"I don't know. Bruten proved useful."

Taka's lungs closed, the water hitting his face. He dropped his hand and stood up, turning into the wind to watch the cars zipping through the light at Court and Kanawha to ground himself. "Okay."

"You'll help her then?"

"Yeah. I don't know what we can do with the info without getting Tamarin involved or tying all of us up in knots we'll never get out of, but yeah. I'm not risking Andrea's safety just to keep a job I don't think I'm going to have much longer."

"You know Tamarin'll get this sorted, right? He's a good cop. We don't know everything that he knows and he's working this like we would. Catnaps and an extra suit in his car."

"Three bodies is a lot, Jimmy." CPD got a couple a month and not even half were murders. Crime was higher than the national average but had been dropping for years and most of Taka's job was drug-related break-ins and theft. Detectives could go years on rotation without catching a murder. CPD assigned Tamarin or Tracy Manners as leads when they happened. They had the most training and experience. Depending on caseload, the responding detective worked under them to increase experience across the investigative division.

Until six weeks ago.

Now Tamarin was the only lead.

And three bodies was a lot.

"We'll figure it out. I'll text you Sweet Joe's number. I gave him yours. He knows you'll want to be notified when Andrea's released. What are you doing now?"

"If I show up at Andrea's while the search is still going, Horton will have my hide. I'm supposed to be home until four anyway."

"I'll meet you at the station later then, okay?"

"Yeah." Taka's voice cracked on the word. He lowered his cell and ended the call. He wiped the hot tears off his cheeks in two rough swipes. He climbed into the Yukon and stared at the phone in his hand.

He'd not talked to Scott since the roof. He couldn't remember his schedule. He dropped the phone in his cupholder, started the truck up, and drove home.

ANDREA STARTLED at the clink of the electronic door lock letting go. Somehow, she'd been dozing, curled upright between the back wall and the concrete bench after her cell mate had been removed. The officer was a new face. She verified Andrea's identity and then escorted her back through the hallways to the room where Pete Tamarin had questioned her before.

"Do you want coffee?" the officer asked.

"Sure. What time is it?"

"Almost ten."

"Thanks."

She left the door open. Andrea wasn't sure what that meant.

She was wide-awake, vibrating with tension and halfway through her second cup of coffee and a packet of peanut butter crackers before she heard familiar voices in the hall. Pete and Sweet Joe. They came in but didn't sit.

"Thank you for your cooperation," Pete said. "You're free to go. For now. Sweet Joe has a list of the items seized from your house and car."

She didn't know how angry she was until that moment. "I don't know what you could have possibly taken, I didn't—"

"Andrea," Sweet Joe muttered.

She shut up.

"C'mon, Andrea," Pete said. "I'm just doing my job. Let's go get your things."

She followed him back to the booking area. Her hand shook, her signature not the same at all as the one she signed on intake. The officer placed her purse, its contents, and her cell phone one by one on the counter in three separate evidence bags. She'd sort them later. She scooped all three up at once and held them against her chest.

Pete said, "You got a laptop?"

She opened her mouth, but Sweet Joe said, "You just searched her house, her car, and her workplace, Tamarin, did you see a laptop?"

Andrea's raised blood pressure dropped, leaving her stone cold in seconds. "You searched Waltham-Young?"

Pete squinted at Joe, his face sour. The dark circles under his eyes did him no favors.

"Just your office," Sweet Joe answered, still looking at Pete. "Well?"

"No."

Detective Fields came through the doorway, followed by a dark-haired white guy.

"So there's your answer," Joe said.

Fields smiled at her, which he hadn't done once this morning while Pete shot questions at her. "Headed out?"

So they were back to casual acquaintances now? Andrea nodded. He stepped to one side to let his charge step up to the counter. Candy from the smoke shop looked up and met her eyes. Skinny's son. Lucy Garcia's fleeting boyfriend. His lip curled up. "I don't know what you're up to, but you better stop messing with me. I've filed for a restraining order."

Her ears roared and her skin buzzed.

Somewhere far away, Sweet Joe said, "Let's go."

Someone took her arm, and then things shifted into fast-forward. People and rooms went by. They were out in the main lobby of CPD, and then the soaring foyer of City Hall, their footsteps echoing in the nearly empty space, then outside, in the freezing cold, going down the steps, and then someone blocked her path and big arms were wrapped around her and she was crying into Taka's shoulder, pressing her face into the familiar scent of his winter jacket.

17

The house wasn't ransacked, but it seemed like everything had been moved that much out of place. The whole house felt off. And grubby. The desk in her office looked violated, with the bare spot where her tower usually stood and the research sitting on it shuffled through. All her file drawers were standing open, some unknown number of her files gone, leaving gaping holes.

Andrea could just imagine what the techs and Pete would think about her search history and the articles she printed out, the files holding all the arcane and fascinating historical facts like the ingredients for the chinking between logs in slave cabins, how corn was fertilized in the 1840s, and the intricacies of outhouse construction.

She frequently deleted her browser history but knew one way or another that they'd probably still find a lot of her searches, forum passwords, and posts related to her serial killer hunt six weeks ago, along with a plethora of search strings including the paranormal and GPS trackers and arson and the senator and Dewey Sanderson. God knows what they'd make of that. She couldn't even look at the rest of the house.

When she started cleaning the kitchen, wiping everything down, Jimmy pitched in. Taka disappeared into the living room without a word but took her bottle of Orange-Glo from under the sink and an extra cloth wipe. She and Jimmy had moved onto the office when she heard Taka running water in the bathroom upstairs.

When the house felt better, Andrea made hot chocolate. She tried to ask a couple of questions, but both men said they didn't know anything. When it was done, she carried it over to the kitchen table where they were sitting and filled three waiting mugs. Taka tippled whiskey into them. Andrea sat down next to Jimmy.

Jimmy blew on his hot chocolate. After a careful sip, he said, "Sweet Joe said you were fine until Tamarin and Field's dog and pony show. Something about a restraining order that he's going to look into in the morning."

"His name is Jodie something, but everybody calls him Candy. He was Lucy Garcia's boyfriend. The guys from the VFW in South Charleston wanted to ask him if he knew where she was because he told one Huntington and told another Philadelphia. I was hoping to hear she was alive and fine somewhere and I'd made a mistake. His dad owns a smoke shop on D Street, so we went over there. It got a little heated and then Dewey walked in, looking for the rent." She glanced up from her hot chocolate at Taka. "He said to tell you hi."

"How did this Jodie learn who you are?"

"I don't know." She tapped her middle finger on the table. "Oh, I know. Dewey called me by name, but only Andrea."

Jimmy said, "Tamarin may have shown him your photo, or asked about you by your full name if he's connected you somehow."

"Are they watching Dewey?"

Taka shook his head. "CPD is always interested, but I don't know of anything active right now." He looked sideways at Jimmy.

"The state keeps an eye on him, but not twenty-four-seven."

They sat sipping their hot chocolate and thinking.

Andrea set her mug down. "Maybe Candy knew Anna Lansing, too?"

"Maybe," Jimmy said.

And then Andrea remembered the tension between Dewey and the bartender.

"Oh!" She grabbed Jimmy's forearm. "Candy knew that guy you know. The bartender. I guess he's one of Dewey's bodyguards now."

"Um," Taka said.

"I guess you might know him, too, Taka." She held her hand up above her head. "Tall. Blonde. Chiseled," she said and then turned back to Jimmy. "He said the same thing you did. Exactly. That you were his friend from back home."

Taka tensed up and Jimmy said, "How'd my name come up?"

How did his name come up? And then it dawned on her. Heat rose in her face. "I remembered where I knew him from. I asked if he knew you. But then Dewey said he knew you, too. Scott, that's his name, right?"

Jimmy nodded.

"Scott seemed . . . I don't know. He said the two of you took different paths. Dewey said Charleston's a small town, and one of the reasons he moved him into security was because he knew you. That he wouldn't mind Scott crossing paths with you and getting reacquainted, that maybe Scott could convince you he's an honest businessman."

Jimmy laughed. "Fat chance of that." He drained his hot chocolate.

Taka slid a sharp look her way and she frowned back. What was wrong with him?

When Jimmy set his mug down, licking his lips, Taka said, over-casually, "How long have you known Scott?" That put-on sincere look meant something, but Andrea was too tired to even think about how to go about unraveling his weird mood tonight.

"A long time," Jimmy said, picking up Taka's weirdness in three words and wrapping it around himself like a cloak.

"He told me one time that he served but he didn't say which branch."

"Did he? I wouldn't know. I hadn't talked to him since high school until I saw him at the Coliseum." He slid a glance at Andrea.

Scott had drawn Jimmy's beer before he'd ordered, and Andrea assumed he'd been in before, but that glance made her wonder.

Taka looked constipated.

"I'm wilting," she said, standing up. She gathered the mugs and took them to the sink. Well, shit. She turned around. Jimmy and Taka were holding a silent conversation in traded scowls and frowns. "Taka."

Both their heads whipped around. They couldn't be less alike except their eyes. Taka all close-cropped hair and brown skin and broad. Broad shoulders, broad hands, broad thighs. Jimmy bedhead blonde and redneck fair and V-shaped. His biceps and quads and calves rounding out from the rest of him. But their eyes. Their brown eyes, though. Those were just alike. As if from some shared ancestor a few centuries past.

"You okay?" Taka prompted.

She'd been staring too long.

"Yeah. I had your phone, remember? When you disappeared?"

His eyes narrowed, his lips flattening. He nodded.

"There were texts from a Scott. Wanting to return a book. Wanting to know where you were."

"Yeah."

Really? He wasn't just going to tell her. "Same Scott?"

"Yeah."

"Secret boyfriend Scott?"

"I told you I was seeing someone."

"Who you wouldn't tell me anything about. But Jimmy knew."

"Yeah."

Andrea considered Jimmy, sitting stiff in his chair. "Because of Dewey."

"Dewey doesn't know."

"Lordy, Taka!"

"I asked Scott to dinner." He patted the table. "Here. I was going to ask you to see when would be good. And Jimmy, too, but then everything happened."

He was telling the truth, that was at least something. But why hadn't Jimmy told her? He read her expression before she could ask.

"I just found out yesterday," he protested. "Taka wanted to make sure I knew in case our occasional surveillance would be compromised by me having dinner socially with one of Dewey's bodyguards."

"And he didn't tell me," Taka added, glaring at Jimmy, "that he knows Scott. Like actually knows him, not just knew him because of stalking Dewey."

"And Scott already knows who I am because y'all have been discussing this dinner for how long now?"

Taka chewed on the inside of his lip while he thought. Finally, he said, "Just a few days. I know I haven't been here for you the last few weeks, but I needed some time to sort things." He ran his hand over the table. Back and forth. "In my head. I wanted to make sure I didn't bring someone around who wasn't planning to stay for a while."

"I'm a big girl, Taka. I can handle you having a short-term relationship, even if I lose a friend." She'd hated his last girlfriend, Melinda. Disliked. Hated was a strong word. But she still missed Alison, whom he'd almost married.

"It wasn't about you. It's about what I need."

Andrea smiled. "I can't believe you just said that. I'm so proud of you."

Taka refrained from rolling his eyes, but barely.

"But I'm still mad you've hidden him for a month and then told Jimmy first."

Taka shrugged.

"If Dewey wants Scott to renew his acquaintance with Jimmy and he doesn't know you're in the mix, that could get complicated. Especially since you two are talking again."

Taka heaved a sigh, looking to Jimmy again.

"Good to know," Jimmy said.

Whoops.

JIMMY DIDN'T SEEM inclined to leave.

Without discussion, Taka went upstairs, used the bathroom and brushed his teeth, then grabbed the spare pillow and an extra blanket from the closet and dropped them on the couch.

"Guess I'll take the couch," Jimmy said.

Andrea gave him a hug.

Taka headed back up the stairs to the guest room.

"You don't have to stay," Andrea said.

"Stay," Taka called down. Not knowing what was going on and if this Candy guy was a danger to Andrea, he didn't mind Jimmy staying, but he couldn't stomach the thought of him in Andrea's bed. He knew that was wrong, hypocritical to the max, but there it was.

"Got a duffle bag in the car," Jimmy yelled back. Lowering his voice, he said to Andrea,

"I have to be at BCI for an eight o'clock meeting, I'll get more sleep if I just stay." Like Taka couldn't hear him anyway.

Taka listened to him go out the door. Andrea dragged up the stairs. Taka closed the guest room door as she crested the landing. A moment later, the bathroom door squeaked and closed behind her. She'd set out towels for both of them. Probably washcloths, too. Andrea liked washcloths.

He crossed the room and lifted a couple of the slats on the white blinds. The lights on Jimmy's RAV4 blinked in time to the beep-beep of its security alarm and Jimmy came back up the sidewalk to the front steps.

Taka dropped the blinds, backed into the bed, and sat with his phone in both hands. He shoved his shoes off with his toes, answering the text Scotty had sent half an hour ago with both thumbs. It read: *At yours, you at Andrea's?* Which was marginally better than Melinda, who never referred to Andrea as anything but *her* and *she*.

Andrea ws arrested. Search warrant on her hse and office. Took her cmptrs. Murder invstgtion. Released at 10pm.

Taka pulled his shirt out of his jeans and sat back against the headboard. He was rewarded by bubbles floating up in the text box.

That blows. We saw her ystday in s chrlstn. I ddn't get to tell u cause u ghosted. She was asking about a woman.

The first victim.

The first?

Long story.

Srry abt last nght. I shd've told u b4.

Not a txt conversation. You dn't tell me you know Jimmy Hoyle.

Is he Andrea's Jimmy? You nvr tld me his last name.

Did he never say Hoyle? Maybe not. It wasn't like Jimmy was a big topic of conversation between them except in relation to Andrea. He also avoided most everything related to law enforcement with both Scott and Dewey.

I told her about us tonight

Gd

Yeah?

Yeah

Wht's Jodie/Candy's last name? He took out a restraining order angst Andrea

Seriosly?IDK I can find out tmrrow

Thks. How lng hve u known Jimmy?

A long time.

How lng since you tlked to him before moving here?

Long time

That niggling in his back brain just wouldn't leave it alone, but he knew he couldn't push.

I just wndred if he knows – wht happened to u

He didn't think Scott was going to answer but then:

Yeah he knows

What that meant, Taka didn't know. Did Jimmy lie about not knowing anything about Scott to protect Scott? If he hadn't fessed up? Or were they both gaslighting him? Because his gut said gaslighting.

Gd, he texted back. *Tired of secrets. Hard to rember who kws wht @ work. Need trth @ home*

I hear you, man

And Taka could hear Scotty saying it, "I hear you, man." He wished he were at his place, with Scotty lying beside him. Sometimes they texted like that. Sometimes it was easier to talk that way. Then he could just turn over and kiss him and they'd be good again. Just like that.

Turning in, Scott sent.

Nght

He found a gif of the moon over mountains and sent it.

Scotty sent back a moon over a deserted beach, waves lapping over the sparkling sand.

JIMMY DIDN'T BOTHER with the half-bath. He went back into the kitchen and brushed his teeth and splashed water on his face. He changed into a T-shirt and gym shorts. When Andrea left the bathroom, he trotted up the stairs. He paused to see if Taka's door would open. But when it didn't, he made quick use of the bathroom and flipped the hallway light out on his way back down to the couch.

He lay down and got comfortable before he texted Scotty burner to burner. *Hey, you working?*

Home

You ran into a mutual friend

Yeah

Details later

Yeah

Jody Uk? Uk for Unknown. But it came across as United Kingdom mostly.

MKPI

That'd take him a minute to decipher. *Ha! Haven't seen that in 4ever!*

Gave T1 V2 last nght

Lolol he responded in acknowledgement. So Scotty told Taka version two of his cover story. He'd been a sniper, got addicted to opiates, and was dishonorably discharged. Probably had to on the roof.

You know

Well, crap. He'd told Taka he didn't know anything about Scott after high school. *I didn't*

It took Scotty a long time to decipher but then: *Fix at dinner*

Jimmy sent a thumbs up and erased the message thread. Then he typed the alphabet and Caesar code plus a shift of two in his Notes app. Jody's last name was King.

He switched to his own cell and texted Nina. Jody 'Candy' King, S Charleston, P1

Priority one would get her on King first thing in the morning.

18

Both Taka and Jimmy were gone by the time Andrea came downstairs at seven-thirty. The early morning light was weak. The day outside the large kitchen window grey. Even the trees looked cold. Her backpack was sitting on top of the kitchen table. She'd put it behind her seat, on the passenger floor of Jimmy's car with her purse. When the patrol officer asked for ID, Jimmy had only grabbed her purse and handed it to her. She unzipped the bag. Her laptop and all her project notes were undisturbed. She clutched the laptop to her chest. Thank God.

Jimmy had also torn a sheet off the notepad on the fridge and left her a note hoping her day was better than yesterday. Taka hadn't bothered to get his own sheet. Instead, he'd scrawled *home 8-4* on the bottom of Jimmy's.

So they'd taken him off light duty and sent him home again. Probably because of her. She sighed. She took toast and jam and a warmed-up cup of the coffee they'd left in the pot to the table and attacked her text and voicemail messages from the day before. Most of them were work texts and Karie trying to locate her.

Louie's sister, Savannah, had called saying Aunt Sally wanted to go to Louie's, the pub, not his home, she clarified in a little rush of breath, since it had been a while. They would be there for coffee at ten in the morning and would love Andrea to join them. Otherwise, Andrea could come to Aunt Sally's nursing home next Tuesday.

Bobby Waltham had left a message saying he thought it best if she took a few days off after the police presence two days in a row, that if she had anything pressing, she could work from home and bill those hours. Although it was a reasonable request, it still stung a little.

Her current intern had left increasingly frantic messages about the Ivystone Farm client showing up unexpectedly. Andrea punched her up on her cell. "Megan, I'm home now, what happened?"

"Mr. Pederson showed up with a carload of boxes for you."

"Of?"

"Documents related to Ivystone. Old journals, account logs, repair receipts, photos, drawings, field crop rotations, you name it."

"I told him anything like that would be useful, but I thought I'd go get it after we really got started."

"He brought twenty-six boxes."

"Twenty-six boxes!" The project was a documentation of the history of the site and restoration of as many of its original details as possible while accommodating modern-day conveniences. Pederson planned to live and farm there while hosting a sort of "back in the day" bed-and-breakfast program.

"I didn't know what to do. The police were taking things from your office, so I asked him to meet me around the side of the building at the storage bay? And we put all the boxes on a pallet. I taped a big note on that said "Pederson/Randy" in case the cops found it and then went and told Mr. Randy. He was fine with it."

"Thank you, Megan. I bet Randy thought that was a great idea."

"He did. He laughed."

"I'll ask Talisha to show you how to fill out the archival documentation forms. Then when you have time, you can start sorting through the boxes. Be sure to photograph or scan every page. She can show you how to do the journals." The interns were shared, but Andrea had dibs on Megan's time since Megan had expressed an interest in historical property preservation and restoration.

"Mr. Pederson said he cut circa-1900 wallpaper samples for you. Still on the canvas. Lincoln, the contractor at Berrylane told him to do that. He knows you want to see and document the house before he does anything to it but he's clearing the piles of obvious junk and setting aside anything he thinks you might be interested in."

He'd sent Andrea photos via Google Drive. The house had been occupied by squatters and while raided of much of the furniture, housed an impressive collection of old newspapers, clothes, and piles of indeterminate objects.

"And," Megan continued, "he wondered if you knew the curtain samples for Berrylane came from Ivystone. Apparently Lincoln was wondering if he was going to commission the same curtains."

"No, and no, we're focusing on a different time period. I'm confused. I confirmed the drapery fabric is Civil War era, but because of its history, and the photos I saw showing its turn-of-the-century embellishments, it's unlikely that Ivystone would be the source of those samples."

"I told him I didn't think you knew, because I labeled everything as Berrylane when we were working on them. He said the drapes were used as burial shrouds! When he bought the property two years ago, there was a major drainage issue around the footings under the sun porch and since they're the original stacked stone, the first thing he did was try and fix it. They found three bodies!"

"Civil War era, I take it?"

"Two were soldiers."

"Who handled the bodies?" A sprinkling of rain clattered like thrown pebbles against the kitchen window. The limbs on the trees in the back yard flapped, their leaves fluttering in a gusty swirl of wind.

"I should've asked, shouldn't of I?" Megan said, worried.

"Yes. Call him back. Tell him we'd like to document the circumstances. If he can't come back, get him on Zoom and record him telling the story of the discovery. Call whoever handled it, the sheriff's office, the funeral home. They may have had a forensic anthropologist. Probably the department in Charlotte. You find out. You call everyone involved. Get every report. Your own project, okay? It'll be good. Berrylane can do an exhibit on it. Mr. Pederson can use it on the Ivystone Farm website to draw overnight guests."

"Thank you! I won't let you down!"

"I'm sure you won't."

The doorbell rang. Andrea hung up with Megan and hurried to answer the door. Right before she opened it, she thought of Candy. And then Lucy. And Anna Lansing. And that little girl clutching her backpack to her just like Andrea herself had earlier. Her door had no peephole or sidelights.

"Who is it?" she called.

"Sheriff's Department, ma'am." A woman's voice.

She crept to the living room window and its white plastic plantation shutters. She always left the louvers partially open. She had to maneuver a bit to see, but standing on her top step was a woman in uniform and duty belt, her heavy jacket dotted with the spitting rain. Beyond her, the trees and bushes swayed. As Andrea watched, she knocked again. "Ma'am? Ms. Kelley?"

Get her name and badge number and call the Sheriff's Department? Or open the door so her neighbors didn't get another show? None had come out or texted her, so they probably didn't know what happened yesterday, but still.

The deputy knocked again.

A dark figure across the way resolved into Dr. Huntley coming across the street in a blue winter coat, galoshes, and a floppy rain hat. Andrea ducked back into the foyer, flipped off the deadbolt and hauled the door open. The cold and wet came rushing in.

"Andrea Kelley?"

"Yes?"

The deputy held out a manila envelope. Andrea took it on autopilot. "You've been served."

"What?"

The woman turned on her heel. A car Andrea couldn't see from her doorway started.

Dr. Huntley stopped at the curb fronting her yard. "You okay?"

"Yes." She held the envelope up so he could see it. "Just some paperwork. Thanks for checking, Dr. Huntley."

The patrol car backed out onto the street. The deputies lifted their hands and she and Huntley lifted a hand in return. Dr. Huntley took one more look to make sure she was set and traipsed away again. Andrea swung the door closed.

She opened the envelope. A hearing notice for the promised order of protection and the complaint, which accused her of verbally threatening and harassing Jodie King in relation to the death of Lucy Garcia. At least she knew his name now.

"JODIE, WITH AN 'IE,' August King. They call him Cotton Candy," Nina said.

"Not much of a gangster name," Jimmy said. He swung the chair he was sitting in, legs sprawled wide, in a half circle and then back again.

He'd placed himself in the middle of the unit's small case room so he could see both Bill's and Nina's computer screens while he contemplated the morning's whiteboard and what Detweiler's overnight team had added to Dewey's case.

"He's not much of a gangster. Two speeding tickets, a couple of possession charges, and a domestic. She hit him. Six stitches from a ring she was wearing."

"Jodie, Jodie, Jodie. What'd you do to piss off a woman so bad?"

Nina leaned back in her chair, head tipping over to gape at him.

"What?"

She shook her head. "Since it's a guy, nothing."

He thought about what he'd just said. Yeah, okay. "Victim blaming."

"Got it in one." She went back to her screen.

"I got Boise," Bill piped up. "Russell Smith, Violent Crimes Unit."

"Guess Taka didn't buy version two of Scotty's background story."

"Smith got ahold of the DD-214 that shows Scott's Other Than Honorable discharge for drug rehab failure."

"Good," Jimmy said. "Hopefully that'll put Taka off the scent. What are you thinking about Dewey's meeting with Bulldog Bailey?"

"Going through the audio today. There's some wind interference. And two of the bugs on the deck were cleared. We need to drop a couple more to Scott when we can."

"We've got more?"

"Five left before we have to go begging."

"Nina, thoughts on Bulldog?"

"None, Boss. Not yet. Wait and see. I've got more on the Candy King."

"Hit me."

"There's a permit and business license for a smoke shop in South Charleston under an LLC with Candy and Alexander Conlon listed as officers. Dewey Sanderson owns the building. Conlon owns an "entertainment" business as well. He does live events for private clients."

Jimmy swung in the chair. Andrea said Jodie's dad owned the shop. "Scott was there yesterday with Dewey for rent collection. It'll be in his report. Alexander Conlon, is that Candy's dad?"

"Candy's dad is deceased. His mother's last known address is an apartment in Charlotte. No social media presence."

"Conlon's the stepdad? Nickname Skinny?"

Nina skimmed through her notes. "He's only five years older."

"Scott's understanding was that King's dad owns the shop or at least rents the space, I suppose. Dewey talked to him about the late rent."

"And his name is Skinny?"

Jimmy smiled at her.

She sighed in exasperation. "I'll see what I can find."

"Thanks."

"I wasn't to the good part, yet."

"I'll bite."

"Alexander Conlon's dad, Harrison, and Senator Sanderson went to school together. They were part of a group that met once a week for years at one of their old classmates' estate properties in Louden Heights. Until a twenty-four-year-old with two arrests for solicitation died of a drug overdose after one of their get-togethers. Of course, none of the more influential members were in attendance that night."

"Of course not," Bill said.

"Harrison did three years way back for distribution."

"What's way back?"

"1972."

Bill whistled.

"He was twenty-two when he was released. They dropped a pimping charge. Fined for a DUI two years later and nothing since. After his driver's license expired, he never renewed it. No recorded investigative contact with Dewey Sanderson."

Parties with prostitutes. Distribution. Possible pimping. Not a smoking gun, but another interesting puzzle piece if Pete Tamarin was looking in that direction. Or if Sweet Joe needed help shaking Andrea free from whatever Cotton Candy was spinning. "Flag all three names. I want to know if any of them have any further contact with Dewey. Moving on. Maddox has a meeting with the AG later today. I need full case updates and task lists for everything we got burning. What'd we get on our floating witness from the ME?"

19

Andrea slammed the passenger door of Taka's Yukon shut. "Sweet Joe said it might be days before they release my car."

He threw his right arm back, hand landing on her headrest and winced. "Takes time to process."

The hard rain drummed along the roof and then sloshed over the windshield as he backed out of her carport.

"Your shoulder still hurt?"

"Twinges. Bruise is almost gone."

"You could use your backup camera."

"I could."

Apparently, the Johnsons had added more Christmas flair to the neighborhood yesterday. Several huge red and yellow and blue ball ornaments in the trees of their front yard swung in the stiff wind.

They reminded her that she'd hoped to get a wreath this weekend. "Did you take your mom her tree?"

"Not yet," he said, already defensive. "I will."

"I can go with you, do some cleaning and laundry so you can sit and talk with her."

The muscle in his jaw bulged at the thought, but then he said, "That'd be good. I'll let you know when."

It wasn't that the house was a total wreck. The small pack of interchangeable dogs lived outside and ate on the porch. She mostly kept up with the dishes and trash. But she didn't bother with the rest of the kitchen or dusting or cleaning the floors or changing the beds, though she insisted the empty rooms be made up. Except for when he was overseas, Taka went twice a year in April and October to do a deep clean and wash the windows while she flapped around in distress and then retreated to her room after it was clean and refreshed. But he'd missed this year.

"You talked to Karie?"

"I did. I invited her to join us at this future dinner we're having."

He didn't say anything to that. The wipers swished and the rain seemed set to stay a while.

After they were on the highway, she said, "They call him Candy on his social media pages."

"I knew you'd put that summons to good use. Those usually take a lot longer to go out."

"Sweet Joe says since I'm a person of interest in the murder investigations, it'll probably be granted. I don't know what Pete's thinking. Candy and Anna Lansing are Facebook friends. And he's in Lucy Garcia's Instagram posts. Our paths have never crossed."

Taka slid a side eye her way.

"Okay, they did, I guess, on a sidewalk. The point is, he knew her, and Lucy, too. So why do they think I had anything to do with killing them?"

"Want my honest guess?"

Did she? Taka had a darker view of the world than she did, though hers had dimmed considerably these last few weeks. "Yes?"

"You can't get mad, and you can't say anything to Pete."

She could do what she wanted, but she got his drift. "Okay."

"If I were him and I had just enough circumstantial evidence to get away with it, I'd use you to lull Candyass, or someone in his circle, into thinking that with a little bit of questioning and some paperwork, he's in the clear. Then I'd watch him."

Her jaw dropped on her instant outrage, and she snapped it shut. She reached out and slapped the heating vent closed. Taka spun the temperature down and the fan shut off. She adjusted her volume inside her head. "This could all be for nothing?"

"Lucy Garcia and Anna Lansing and those missing kids would probably disagree."

And now she felt like shit. "You make me sound like a terrible person," she grumbled. "It won't be for nothing only if Candyass has anything to do with any of it."

He shrugged. "Maybe Pete's got nothing and he's only stirring the pot."

"That'd be worse. Do you know how much Sweet Joe's charging me?"

"But if Pete's right . . ."

She nodded. "Cheap price to pay for a murderer. But why me?" In her mind's eye, the ghost in the holding cell swirled away again. She'd have never been going in and out at Louie's at odd hours except for Aaron. "I don't want to see ghosts."

He held his hand out and she took it for a moment.

A mile later as they came off the highway onto Pennsylvania, a family of four huddled on the wide grass verge, watching the traffic go by. Their winter jackets were all drab brown and old-fashioned. The mother and young girl were in dresses and stockings, their hair tucked under hats. How'd they get stuck there in the rain? There was no broken-down car. Going past them, Andrea craned her neck to see around Taka. Were those cardboard suitcases?

"What are you looking at?"

"That family." She was turned now, looking back the way they'd come. Those were cardboard. "That was weird, right?"

"There was no one there." Traffic was heavy and the rain was still rocketing down. He was wholly focused on the road ahead.

"On the grass, right when we got on Pennsylvania."

The lights were green. He didn't look over. "Andrea, there was no one there."

She turned all way around to sit properly in her seat and tried not to look at anything but the rain and the car ahead until they pulled into the Huntington Bank Garage. "They aren't the first I've randomly seen."

Taka parked before he spoke again. "I'm sorry this happened to you."

"At least the random ones have pretty much ignored me."

"Do you want me to come in now, or should we come back tonight?"

"Louie doesn't open until eleven-thirty. Do you mind having coffee with us? If Aaron shows, we can excuse ourselves or you can come back out here. Is that okay?"

"Yeah. I took a personal day since I didn't know how this was going to go."

"Thanks, Taka." She hoped he understood how much she meant it. "If it doesn't help me with him, then we'll know."

"I thought you'd be more certain after the other night."

"I am, I'm just trying to make you feel better."

He laughed and pushed his door open. "Do me a favor and don't do that anymore."

"I can't help it," she said, getting out.

She couldn't see him over the roof of the Yukon, so she closed her door and waited for him to come around. He hit his remote and the Yukon blinked its lights and choked on its horn.

She fell into step with him to the stairs. "You're my best friend. I'm always going to try and make you feel better. Especially when I know you're doing something you don't want to do."

"I'd rather have surgery without anesthetic than go help you talk to Aaron."

"I'm aware," she said. "It'll be fun."

He rolled his eyes and ran out into the rain.

SINCE KARIE still had their key to the pub, Andrea crowded in with Taka in the spot of dryness the building's roofline provided and knocked. She didn't look into the bar this time through the glass, instead focusing on the crooked "closed" sign. Jesus must've been close. He opened the door in seconds and ushered them in.

The woman shopkeeper stood arranging small glass bottles behind the end of the bar closest to the street. Andrea glanced at Taka. He seemed oblivious to the presence of a ghost. She didn't look up or seem to realize Andrea was watching her. Something Andrea's mom used to say to her came back in a rush. Be grateful for small mercies. And let them be.

Savannah and Great-Aunt Sally were seated in the back of the bar, close to the kitchen doors. Keeping Taka between herself and the ghost, Andrea followed him to the bar. They skinned their jackets off and put them over the low backs of two barstools to dry. Taka slicked his wet hair back, prompting Andrea to slide a hand over her own head and check the tightness of her ponytail.

Behind the bar with the ghost, Jesus climbed back up on a waiting stepladder to continue transferring Louie's family photos from wall to bar counter. Andrea and Taka picked up several of the framed photos and carried them over to the tables to introduce themselves. As they did, Louie came through from the kitchen carrying a tray of mugs and a large silver pot and all the fixings for coffee. The ghost was sashaying on a collision course. Andrea couldn't look away. Nothing happened. Of course. Passing through Louie, the ghost swirled and re-formed on the other side of the swinging doors. The pile of her hair faded before she was out of sight.

Taka and Savannah were moving the thick leather-bound bible, several small books, and a couple of photo albums stacked between Savannah and Aunt Sally to make room. Andrea sank into the closest chair under Aunt Sally's sharp gaze.

The second everyone was sitting with coffee in front of them, Aunt Sally raised her quivery, but strong voice in rebuke. "What's that ring you're wearing?"

Andrea straightened her fingers out, looking at the ring in question.

Louie, pouring creamer in his coffee, said. "It's mine. I let her borrow it while she's researching it."

"What's to research? Whay Orengo made only four."

"I'm using reverse image searches," Andrea explained. "And networking through various online forums to see if the design's been copied or any of the other original rings have surfaced. Louie said this is the only one of the four your family knows of?"

"Stanley Orengo, of Kitch's line, was buried with his. He refused to pass it to his daughters, who had only daughters."

"And you know that . . ."

"My father told me. Stanley was a cousin."

No way to confirm without an exhumation. "Could you tell me what you know of the rings? The family story?"

Sally patted the bible. "My grandfather was Thomas Yaffee Orengo. I heard the story from him many times growing up. It was *his* grandfather made that ring. His name was Whay and he was from Africa. He'd been stolen by another tribe while hunting with his father and used as a field slave on the coast before he was sold to white slavers.

"He was still a young man when he arrived here sometime before the Revolutionary War. He was caught as a runaway trying to get to the British front line. He was beaten and dragged by men on horseback and his leg was badly broken. He limped the rest of his life."

"Aunt Sally," Savannah interrupted. "Whay came here before the Revolutionary War? Daddy only ever told us that despite being an African, he became the huntsman for Live Oak. Not any of this other stuff."

"He was a slave in Africa?" Louie said.

"Your daddy never did listen up."

Taka leaned forward. "Why was he trying to get to the British front lines?"

"The British promised American slaves freedom and land if they came to fight for them," Aunt Sally said, like they should know.

Andrea did know, but only because of the research she'd put in on the history of the colonies leading to the Civil War as background for the properties she'd documented. Hearing it from Aunt Sally, though, a woman in her nineties, speaking about the story her grandfather told her? Andrea's inner archivist was leaping.

"But some slaves didn't believe them," Aunt Sally continued, "because they were already the property of British subjects, weren't they? And no one been offering them freedom. But the Declaration of

Independence, now. It said all men were created equal. It was read out loud all over the South and those slaves thought once America won her freedom, they would, too. So there were slaves on both sides of that war, not like the next one." She took in their rapt attention. "Do you children not read?"

"Was Whay already at Live Oak then?" Andrea asked.

"No, no. One of the Dunbars bought him cheap since he was no good for hard labor anymore." She tsked. "Like a broken-down old horse. Once he recovered, he must've looked fine, though. The Dunbars hired him out as a stockman. Do you know what a stockman is?"

Andrea bit her lip. The Dunbars were the Scots immigrants who had built up the land holding in Newberry County, South Carolina, they called Live Oak. While they mostly grew cotton, the Dunbars also grew tobacco, raised cattle, harvested and milled lumber, and supplied slaves to other plantations in the area.

"Live Oak raised cotton and cattle," Louie ventured.

Aunt Sally crossed her hands in front of her. "He wasn't that kind of stockman. The Dunbars leased him out as a human stud. He had plenty of children. Some he knew and most he didn't."

"We're from the ones he knew, though," Savannah said, uncertainly.

Aunt Sally reached out and Savannah took her hand. "He and Athena were a forced match, but they suited one another, and he always came back to her. Eventually the Dunbars retired him from *service*"—if she could have spit without tarnishing her elegance, Andrea believed she would have—"and he became Live Oak's huntsman."

"They said he could track boar in the pouring rain without a single hound," a deep, melodious voice said from the area of the bar. Andrea had only heard it clearly twice before, but she knew it was Aaron. She resisted turning to look at him. "I was a stockman, too."

"He made those rings when he was an old man," Aunt Sally said. "For his four remaining sons by Athena. Boway and Kitch were two of them."

"And the other two?"

Her mouth turned down. "People get old. Like me. He didn't remember their names, if he ever knew them."

"Seven sons," Aaron said.

Seven sons and four rings. Andrea finally moved for her phone. "Do you mind if I make notes?"

"You better," Aunt Sally said. "You're trying to find the others, aren't you?"

20

Andrea grinned, thumbs already flying over the keyboard. The names would be written in the Bible as they sounded.

"So, the ring is even older than you thought, Louie," Taka said.

"That whip I have, though," Louie said. "It's Papa James's, right?"

"My father's. Your great-grandfather. Yes."

"At least I got that straight."

"He was born free at Live Oak. All the Dunbar menfolk died in the war. Afterward, Mrs. Dunbar gave James's parents and my other grandparents five acres of land each and a contract for wages to remain on. Like all the Orengo men, James loved to hunt. He trained and sold hunting hounds for miles around."

"And the rings were handed down from Whay's four sons to each of their first sons?" Andrea asked.

"No," Aaron said.

"Oh, no, missy. Those times were hard. They were handed down to oldest remaining sons. Now Louie here, he has no children a'tall. That ring on your finger will go to Savannah's son, as she's the oldest daughter. So long as he's still here when Louie passes."

"You hush, Aunt Sally." Savannah tried to take her hand back, but

Aunt Sally kept hold of it with what looked like surprising strength for a woman in her nineties. "Don't tempt the devil."

"I see the news, hon."

"How about a slice of cake, to go with the coffee," Louie said, getting up with a sidelong glance at Taka.

Obviously relieved for the out on needing to reply, Taka said, "Cake's always good."

Andrea took the moment to shift around and look for Aaron. Her heart jumped. Aaron wasn't in evidence at all, but the boy ghost who'd scared her at the door was sitting on top of the bar, playing jacks. Beyond him, the rain beat at the window, casting a rippling light through the bar.

"I brought these photo albums, if you'd like to see them," Aunt Sally said to Andrea.

Andrea spun back around. "I would. Could I come see you next Tuesday so we can look at them? I'd like the story of how your family ended up here in Charleston and your memories of historical events, but I don't have much time this morning."

Taka cut a suspicious look at her and then back at the bar. She ignored him. The ball from the jacks thumped into the bar, sounding like distant thunder.

Aunt Sally smiled. "That sounds fine, missy. Might take a couple of visits."

"Or more." Great-Aunt Sally was a treasure trove of information. Visiting her would be no hardship. "Do you remember any mention of a family member named Aaron? Or Ned? I have a few of Live Oak's records just before the Civil War and I think a couple of the slaves sold then may have been related to you."

Why was the slide of the boy's hand so loud? She could hear the clanking of the metal jacks.

Aunt Sally dug in her bag for her reading glasses. She opened the Bible. As she flipped pages, she said, "Auntie June started the family Bible back in the 1870s with names and as many birth dates and death dates as she knew"—Andrea's heart soared—"but it burned in a fire."

Dang.

"Mama and Daddy did the best they could remembering names and ages." She ran her finger down one page. And then another. "I don't see any, but my eyes aren't good anymore. Do you have a camera on your phone?"

"I do." With Taka lending the flashlight from his phone, she photographed five pages of the family tree and notes in different hands.

"The cousins can look for those names, too," Savannah offered.

"Please," Andrea said.

"This seems an awful lot of trouble to go to, just to document a Black-owned business."

Louie brushed through the doors again, cake and plates in hand. "She's thorough," he said. "Aunt Sally, Savannah said you were thinking about donating Mrs. Dunbar's journals to Waltham-Young?"

Is that what the stack of small books were?

"I've been considering it." She eyed Andrea again. "Louie said you work there?"

"I do."

"Would they be useful to anyone?"

Andrea could barely keep herself from snatching them. "Yes. Very. We have other documents from Live Oak on file. We keep the records of many defunct and lost properties for future reference not only for Waltham-Young researchers, but researchers around the world. Other institutions, other centers of Black history, will have free access to them. Your name will be recorded as the donor."

"They're mostly recipes and gatherings," Aunt Sally said with hesitation.

Savannah set her coffee down. "They aren't ours, not really."

Louie placed a piece of the most decadent yellow cake she'd ever seen in front of her. There was a jack, like the ones the boy was playing with just under the lip of the plate. Louie smoothly palmed it. "There weren't any Dunbars left to take them when my family sold the land."

Aunt Sally sniffed. "An interstate cuts through it now."

"I-26," Louie clarified.

"I'd be happy to accept them on behalf of Waltham-Young."

Thirty minutes later, in the kitchen with Aaron still not around to speak with, and Louie wrapping Mrs. Dunbar's journals in plastic wrap to protect them from the rain, she couldn't put it off any longer. "I saw you pick up that jack from the table."

"Always picking up jacks here. Don't know where they come from."

"There's a boy. He plays jacks."

"Maybe you could tell him not to leave them all over?"

"I don't think he's aware of me. What do you do with them?"

For good measure, he placed the wrapped journals in a plastic bag and tied it off. "Come look," he said.

He took her in his office and opened one of the drawers in a sideboard acting as a bookshelf. It was filled to the brim with jacks. "Never overflows," he said. "Don't know where they go. Staff leaves me a pile on the order shelf every night."

They said their goodbyes and waved the ladies off, then she and Taka were back out in the wet. "Now, that wasn't so bad, was it?" she said, as they crossed the street.

Taka held the journals up. "I wonder if Mrs. Dunbar will be as fascinating?"

"Let's hope!"

"Where was Aaron?"

"He was there earlier, along with two companions."

Taka stopped dead, and she swung around to face him.

"You did your thing, Taka, and it didn't hurt at all."

He searched her face and then huffed a breath out into the cold air. "Okay."

They trotted up the curb and Taka yanked the door open to the garage stairs. Halfway up the last flight to the third-floor landing, Aaron said, "Andrea," right into her ear. She startled into Taka and grabbed his arm. Aaron stood, barely there, no more than a wisp, hint of his head, the outline of his shoulder, on the third-floor landing. He lifted a finger to his lips, the broken chain for the iron manacle around his wrist swinging in misty silhouette, then pointed to the propped open door onto the third floor where they were parked.

"Andrea," Taka said.

She repeated Aaron's gesture and they crept up to the landing.

Two men were talking, in low, furious exchanges. ". . . called him on

Eddie's phone. He didn't tell me, or I'd have never brought her back through here."

"He told you to send her to Cincinnati with Trey."

"I was! Trey was coming to get her! He didn't tell me! How was I supposed to know? He's having a fuckin' conniption over nothing."

"Eddie's dead!"

The men were walking closer, towards them. They'd probably come in the central entrance and taken the elevator up.

"You fuck 'em," the first man said. "You don't trust them. That's not my fault."

"Why were you here in the first place?"

"I already had a deal. Six parties, set-ups on the side. I told him that!"

Taka reached out and moved her against the wall inside the door.

"But she wasn't supposed to be here."

"No one told me that," the first man said again and stopped walking. "Trey was coming."

"How'd she get Eddie's phone?"

"What Eddie does isn't on me. I make the deals. He delivers the merchandise."

"Delivered. He's dead. Because of you."

"Yeah, yeah." All the hurt indignation had dropped out of the first man's tone. He sounded...bored.

"Skinny wants him buried."

Andrea's blood frosted over; her scalp tightened.

"No one knows who he is," the second man continued. "And Skinny doesn't want anyone finding out. Those girls, too, so deep no one ever finds them."

"They're gone already." A clunk. They were close, at a car.

"You wipe that apartment down?"

Another deep thump. "Yeah. I'm not an imbecile," the bored guy said, his voice moving.

"Kinda hard to tell these days, Derek."

Definitely a car door opening. It slammed. Taka leaned in close to her and poked his head around the door. An engine turned over. Taka drew back sharp, but then crouched a little and looked again, from middoor height.

"Fuck you!" the second guy yelled into the garage as Derek, presumably, drove away from them.

Taka eased back from the doorway and stood up against her, waiting. Footsteps, coming towards them. He grabbed her hand and they trotted down the stairs on cat feet. Second guy came onto the landing while they were still two stairs from the lower one. Taka practically scooped her off the steps, spun her around and threw her against the wall hard enough her breath huffed out onto his chest as he pressed up against her.

What the hell? She looked up and saw his plan written in his worried eyes and the set of his jaw. Second guy clattered down the stairs. What the hell. She might never get another chance to find out if he could properly kiss. Andrea threw her arms around his neck and met him halfway, Mrs. Dunbar's journals thumping onto his upper back.

Second guy's steps slowed on the stairs as he caught sight of them.

It wasn't awkward like it should've been. And it wasn't that fizzy excitement she shared with Jimmy. It was like they'd been kissing every day for twenty years. As familiar as everything else they did together. She didn't know who opened their mouth first, but that was only because for a few minutes there, she didn't know anything. Not which tongue was hers. Not whose skin burned against her palms, not whose heart beat in her chest.

They broke for breath, heads pressed together cheek to cheek, Taka's breath soft in her ear. He lifted his hands to brace them against the wall on either side of her.

"Oh," she breathed, when her shirt and jacket slid back into the cold hollow of her lower back. She took one of her own hands back from under his jacket, the other from its grip upon his neck.

He brushed a kiss against her ear and pulled away.

On the level below, a truck started up and then another car.

"Shit." He bolted down the stairs after the sound.

Vaguely, she remembered the fall of a heavy door shutting. The garage doors were all propped open, so it had to be the outside door onto Hale Street. She trotted down. Taka was striding out on the ground floor of the garage proper. A blue SUV cruised by him. Another engine idled nearby. She pushed out through the closed door onto the street.

No one to the right.

To the left, a couple was walking towards her on this side of the street sharing a huge red umbrella. Along the line of parked cars on the far side of Hale, a dark-haired man was lowering himself into an old gold Mercedes. Black jacket, jeans, average height. Flash of cowboy boot as he pulled his foot in. He looked back and their eyes met. The same guy she'd seen the other night outside the gallery. Even all the way across the street, she could see the frown when he recognized her, too.

Andrea nodded at him, trying to act normal.

He shut his door against the rain.

She flipped the hood back up on her jacket, let a car pass, and then crossed Hale herself. The car grumbled to life, lights flashing on and reflecting off the other cars and store windows in the gloom. Andrea threaded between two parked cars and bounced up onto the wet sidewalk where she came to a halt.

Aaron stood in front of the art gallery, in his manacles and tattered blue pants, glaring in the direction of the Mercedes with frightening intensity. Blood ran off his chest like the rain was actually hitting him, except it didn't wash away. It just kept flowing, streaming into nothing as it fell from him.

When she tore her gaze from him, she saw the car's exhaust still rising in the cold rain. She moved, walking fast past Aaron to the clothing shop door. She pulled it open and went inside, dripping on the large floor mat at the entrance.

A woman popped up from behind a circular display of folded jeans and sweaters. "It's wet out!"

"It is," Andrea agreed. She stepped around a freestanding coat rack onto the hardwood floor to peek out through the display window at the back end of the Mercedes. Because of the angle, she still couldn't see the license plate.

"You can hang your jacket there on the rack. So it drips on the mat?"

"I'm so sorry," Andrea said, but didn't move.

The brake lights on the Mercedes winked. The driver finally pulled away.

"Here," the woman said from next to Andrea's elbow. "Let me help—"

"I'm sorry," Andrea said again. "I'll come back. I just have to go."

"Okay," the woman said, raising her hands and backing away. "Anytime. Fifteen percent off lasts through the end of the month."

Through the door, she could see Aaron was gone. She went out on the sidewalk. Taka stood near the closed door for the garage stairs, looking up and down the street. She lunged off the curb, dodged around cars coming from either way, to grab the front of his jacket. Her hand closed on it, the fabric cold to the touch, a metal snap hard against the palm of her hand.

As Taka closed his arms around her, a shadow slid between them.

21

A shock of ice water hits her.
　　　A scream claws up her throat, bursts from her open mouth. Water fills it. She grabs for anything solid, finding the hard edges of a bathtub. A boot on her chest. Lungs burning, she strikes and kicks. So cold—

—SO COLD.

White blinding light.

She kicks for it, swimming up hard for the light.

Her head breaks the surface.

A gibbering blast of wind slaps her wet face and rips her streaming hair into a flail that punishes her face and shoulders, draws her bodily up from the dark of a raging river.

The booms of explosions batter her ears, flashes of fire that can only be cannon on the banks. Underneath, an undulating volley of sharp cracks and muzzle flash and unearthly wailing from both sides. From above, the river is barely a creek, water eddying over and around the dead and dying. A riderless horse gallops along the middle, plunging in and out of the deeper pools, the whites of its eyes gleaming, foam streaming from its lips and lathering its flanks.

She falls.

The scream ripped loose echoes in her ears.

There's a hard gag between her teeth and searing pain flaming in her leg.

Hands on her shoulders.

And as darkness takes her, the ceiling of a dirty tent, the cries of men staining the air—

—BECOMES A LANGUID STILLNESS.

Sun stripes on soft beige carpet.

Sun in her eyes, lids so heavy she can't lift them.

She stretches like a cat and curls back up.

Has she ever felt this content before?

She blinks at the fallen syringe, the spoon that ran away with the moon.

Why did she ever just say no when saying yes feels this good?

Can she see the moon from here?

She tilts her head back to find out, but there's no moon—

—AND THE UPSIDE-DOWN walls she sees instead are peeled logs, the floor dirt.

Her sister is crying. Pathetic whimpers and half-screams. Her breath is ragged and hard. She can barely see her; the white man is so large. They're standing. He's holding the back of her sister's head with one hand, pressing her face into the wall, trapping her between it and him. His other arm is wrapped around her waist to hold her steady for his hard thrusts.

She wishes her sister had already taken up with a man or the master had arranged a marriage. Her sister may have cried, but not like this. Her own upside-down view is shifting, her head lolling over the side of the low bed with every pump of the overseer's hips, the wood frame digging into her shoulders. His duties in bringing the man here to buy her sister's first time sure have inspired him.

She's trying not to care.

She's got her fourth child quickening inside already.

Her husband knows his duties, too.

Sweat drops onto her brow, alongside her nose. He stinks like white man. She closes her eyes—

—AND THE ROCKING of the shuttle bus down the long gravel driveway stops as they bump up onto a section of smooth concrete curving along the front of the massive white and red brick mansion.

They've arrived at the next gig.

Donny eyes them in the rearview mirror. "Ladies, it's a thousand-dollar quota tonight. Fucks are two-fifty. Sucks are eighty-five. They want candy, send 'em to Hal at the front of the house. They don't want a condom, charge 'em a hundred more and see me tomorrow."

For a Plan B. Pregnancies ruin the bottom line. STDs only dent it.

She unbraids her hair while the other girls get out, chattering among themselves. They preloaded on vodka and canned spritzers at the Airbnb, and Donny holds out the Tupperware so they can pick their high of choice. She didn't used to get either drunk or high, but she likes it now.

"Hey, Doll," Donny says when she climbs down last.

She bends over and shakes her hair out and then flips her head back up, so it settles in soft curls around her face and over her shoulders.

He shakes the Tupperware at her. She used to put meatloaf in one just like that. She's just drunk enough that she can let herself say her daughter's name. Elsa. Like in Frozen. Her heart crunches on the music that swoops through her brain and shuts off. She reaches into the bin and takes a green plastic wrap twist of oxy and X.

"You remember, right?"

She nods.

They collect cell phones from the clients at the door, but one guy had two last time and while she blew him, he made a call, some complicated business thing that involved a lot of cussing but seemed to make him happy in the end. Afterward, she offered him intercourse for free if she could make a call, but Hal called time and opened the door and caught her with the phone in her hand mid-dial.

Her eyes were still black, and they were turning her every fifteen minutes on twenty-five-dollar tricks when Donny threw the paper on the dirty bed. It was a printed screenshot from Facebook. Elsa, two years older than when Doll left for a girls' weekend in Atlantic City and never came home again. Elsa, out on the sidewalk of the house Doll used to live in with her used-to-be husband.

They say they can take Elsa anytime they want. She plays outside all the time. They can kill her husband during a break-in and the cops will never solve the case. Maybe they should kill him, they say, the TV alone would be worth more than Doll is.

She believes them.

Donny raises his brows. He wants her to say it out loud.

"Yes, I remember."

"Have a good roll," he says.

And then she's walking into the house on her stilettos—

—AND INTO A FIELD of cotton after dark.

Her muscles are weak and she's weary. There's a bag slung round her neck, and she's paused for much too long, coming back to herself from some dream she doesn't recall. The driver yells and rides her way on his big chestnut horse.

The whip whistles and cracks and she grabs at the cotton with both hands, plucking three or four bolls with each, dumping the cotton in alternate handfuls into the sack. But don't break the branch, don't break the branch.

She reaches out—

—AND IT'S DAYLIGHT, hot, sweat running down into her eyes, burning them.

She's plucking, plucking, plucking.

Someone, a man, except he sounds more like a beast, roars.

The driver gallops down the end row, every field slave stirring to the bad energy. Some crouching, others stretching to see. The whip cracks and cracks again. Another roar, a bellow of outrage, the new slave, out of his head.

Another of the drivers gallops by and then a third.

Now half the slaves are still picking, but the other half are watching the trouble gather in the rows.

She sees motion and turns her head.

Mary and that boy Yap, trotting past her.

Mary's eyes are wide and scared, and it looks like her legs are stealing her away against her will. Where she think she's going with that boy? She might get across the river, but she'll be in the workhouse before morning. And that is not never anyplace a slave wants to be.

The new slave is still roaring, the drivers are all yelling now and then one of them levels his shotgun and her ears vibrate with the harsh bark of the shot.

She ducks down in the row, but her hands are still working.

The field is silent.

Then the drivers start yelling again and a whip sings high, and the lash cracks, and she creeps two feet further down the row, her hands still plucking the fat bolls, skimming over the unripe—

—THE NEXT BOLL IS A BLANKET, and she jerks it over the dead girl's face.

They'll dump her in the woods somewhere and she'll never be found.

Unless some unlucky hiker taking an off-trail piss stumbles over her bones.

Then the cops'll ID her or not. Another Jane Doe.

Either way, her story won't ever be told. Just like her own when she's outlived her profit potential and becomes another liability that needs putting out with the trash.

She goes through the girl's stuff, but there's no stash.

Nothing.

Maybe she took it all at once and that's how she managed to escape this life.

But her own blood's jumping and her arms itch and she's jonesing and she doesn't want to be here, but she doesn't want to die and it's not like she deserves a real life anyway after falling so far into this hole. The boys feed her, and the sheets are mostly clean and it's not like she's having to pay rent. She just has to earn her keep.

When Eddie comes back to the hotel, he makes a call and then they load up in the van.

He drops three girls to meet their lookout and then notices she can't sit still.

"Sorry, baby, what you want? I got your back."

After he parks, he lets her snort, then hands her an X-ie to take after the initial buzz wears off so she can roll. He walks her up and goes for a smoke. On this job, he won't go far. After the client's done with her, she slides into the guy's bathroom. He's rolling a joint when she comes back out and offers her a hit, which she takes. It'll help slow her roll and bring her down. Maybe she'll even sleep.

Eddie knocks on the door at four. The client doesn't get out of bed, just points at the clean stack of cash under the fancy china lamp on the antique dresser. She pulls her dress over her head, grabs her clutch, and the cash, and on the way out, tiptoes into the kitchen and helps herself to a knife from the block she spotted on the way in.

Eddie hands her the thick blue hoodie he knows she loves. She pulls it on over her dress to brave the short, cold walk to the van. She gets in back. He slides into the driver's seat and never sees it coming.

Shaking, she fumbles for his cell. Her bloody hands slide over the touchscreen, and she has to wipe it off on her hoodie. She has to try three times before she remembers the right numbers.

"Yeah," he says.

"Candy," she says, but she chokes on the name, and then she's crying. "Candy, I'm here, I'm in Charleston. Come get me, come get me, I woke up and you were gone and these guys, they were—and I couldn't get away, they took everything, my money, my... my phone, come get me, come get me."

"Why should I come get you, bitch? I'm the one what's selling your ass."

"What?"

"You call your handler before I do, or you'll be flipping dime buys thirty a night."

"Candy, please."
The van falls out from under her—

—SHE GRABS FOR IT, she's Lucy, she's Lucy— spinning in freefall, belly sloshing, throat closing—

—SHE'S pressed shoulder to shoulder with the stockman, his arm around her.

A fire flickers from the other side of the tiny cabin, but it doesn't seem to throw any heat. Three women are sleeping curled together on a pallet of pine boards under two shared wool blankets. She's sitting on the dirt floor, her back to the cabin's plank wall.

Winter is sneaking through the crevices, tasting her neck, sliding into her bones. Wetness seeps from between her legs. She shivers and tucks her skirts down tighter between her knees. The stockman's young. He was raised down south. His accent is all soft edges.

That doesn't make it any better.

She wishes the master would give her a husband, but most of his slaves are women, now. The few men he has are married already.

"Shhh," he says. He turns his head, so his lips are against her temple. "This ain't forever."

"How many my babies gonna be sold away before it ain't forever anymore?" she whispers.

"Shhhh," he says. And he's there, so she lays her head on his chest—

—A LONG SIGH of Aaron's breath, "wife"—

—WATER CLOSES OVER HER HEAD, too cold, can't breathe, can't breathe, a cowboy boot on her chest, hard tub under her back, out, out, getup getupupupup—

Andrea gasped, air rushing into her starving lungs.

Taka caught her weight, following her down to the wet cement, keeping her head off the ground, leaning over her to keep the heavier rain off her face. "Andrea, Andrea."

Every ten drops brought ten more brought a hundred and then the sky really opened.

She opened her mouth, but nothing came out.

He looked away, up at someone. A couple of someones.

And the lady from the shop.

Then something black dropped over them so that she cringed closer to Taka. He sat flat down onto the puddled sidewalk and pulled her back against his chest and they stayed like that, deafened by the drumming of the rain on the umbrella, until the medics came.

22

Karie poked her head into the small cubicle in the ER. "Andrea?"

"Hi," Andrea croaked. She'd cried for two hours while everyone asked her what happened, and she couldn't explain. "I'm okay."

"The fluids would say otherwise," she said, pointing at the hanging bag and the line running into the back of Andrea's hand.

"I was a little dehydrated. And they gave me Valium. For a panic attack."

"Where's Taka?"

Although they'd put two warmed blankets on her, she was still cold. "He went to find us coffee."

"What happened?"

Andrea shrank further down in the bed and covered her eyes with one hand to try and stop the tears. Karie covered her in a hug, and the tears rolled down Andrea's cheeks anyway, so she hugged her back.

"You really are still cold." She let go and placed the bag in her hand on the bed. "I brought you dry clothes, and Taka a dry pair of jeans since they were sitting on your dryer."

Andrea sniffed and wiped her tears away, her eyes still welling over.

"It was Aaron. And Lucy. And a few others." She sniffed again, her nose starting to run in earnest, tears dripping off her chin. "And Taka."

"Taka?"

"He almost died in that bathtub, Karie. Maybe he did, for just a second, I'm sure that's why—"

"Why what?"

"Why I went *through* him." She covered her face and cried hard again.

Karie stroked her arm until she could catch her breath again, then ripped a bunch of tissues out of the box on the tray table and handed them over. Andrea wiped her eyes and blew her nose and heaved in a couple of deep breaths.

"So what do you mean, through him?"

"I think." Andrea wiped her eyes again. "I think I experienced what he experienced and then I was on a friggin' battlefield and it felt like . . . a memory. It was Aaron's. And then it was like, different women, slaves" —her breath hitched— "being raped, and a drug addict and a woman who'd been stolen, and Lucy. It was Lucy."

"The woman in the alley?"

Andrea nodded. "That van Pete Tamarin's been on about? She killed a man named Eddie in it."

"Oh, Andrea."

"And then." She wiped her nose, didn't bother with her wet cheeks. "Aaron. He was a stockman."

"What's that?"

"He was used for breeding more slaves."

"That was a thing?"

"In the upper South." Her breath caught again, then gave. "Cross-Atlantic import had been outlawed and cotton was exploding in the deep South. Huge numbers of slaves were sold domestically and force-migrated further south and west. That's probably why import was banned, to drive domestic prices up."

"So he was trafficked."

Andrea looked up, blinking hard, willed the painful hitch of her chest away. "They all were. We use these words, slavery, trafficking, involuntary sexworker, but it all amounts to being used as a thing, less than an animal, a throwaway commodity. There was a woman he . . . serviced. I think she was his wife, later. He said it wouldn't be forever, that she just had to get through it." Her chest tightened. He'd been so young. "Can you imagine? She just needed to get through being forced to give up her children as labor to be used and replaced when they broke. It wouldn't be forever. But it is, it is forever, for all of them! And then I was drowning and so cold and there was a foot on my chest, keeping me down and I couldn't breathe." She sipped air in little gasps and then finally got a deep breath. "I couldn't breathe. And then I was back on Hale, in the rain with Taka over me. I went through him into . . . I don't know."

Miss Ava used spirit as a noun, the same way Karie did. They talked about connection with spirit as a whole. About Andrea needing a shield so she wouldn't be bombarded by spirit. Andrea looked at Karie. "I went through him. And Aaron, too, into spirit. We're all connected in spirit, aren't we?"

"Yes," Karie said, her tone thoughtful. She rubbed Andrea's arm again. "Somehow you must be, right?"

STANDING in the hall outside the little hospital café, Taka tried Jimmy once more. No answer. He hadn't wanted to text but also didn't want to wait any longer. *Something happened with Aaron. Andrea in ER. Fine, but could probably hear from you.*

His phone rang. Scott.

Taking her home soon. He hit send and answered, "Hey."

"I'm surprised you picked up," Scott said.

"When have I ever been passive-aggressive?"

"That's fair. But I'm still happy you're talking to me."

Taka ran his hand over his lower jaw. He should've shaved this morning. "Now's not a good time. I'm in the ER with Andrea."

"Why?"

"Panic attack." Was his lying to Scott any worse than Scott's lying to him?

"She's in a scary situation."

Scott didn't know the half of it. His stomach rolled. He backed against the wall and leaned forward to breathe better. "Everything wash out okay with Bulldog Bailey?"

"It was something to do about a woman the senator was involved with. Left her high and dry, I guess. I don't know why Bulldog's involved. Or why she just doesn't go to the press. I can hear you breathing, are you okay?"

Taka stood up. "Yeah. See you tonight?"

"If you don't mind me coming in after two a.m."

"That's fine.

"Call me if anything else happens before then."

"I will. Bye." Taka thumbed the call off on Scott's, "See you."

He leaned his head back against the wall with his eyes closed.

"Hey," a rough male voice said. The guy cleared his throat.

Taka opened his eyes. Bony addict guy from Clay. Hell if Taka could remember his name. "Commander."

The corner of the guy's mouth twitched up. "Bowman. Luke."

"Taka."

"I remember." He pulled his T-shirt down at the collar. A big square of gauze and tape covered part of his collar bone, a loop of clear plastic tubing showing. "Just got another central line."

"Cancer?"

"Stubborn infection. Had sepsis a couple of months ago."

That explained a lot. Taka didn't know the aftereffects, but he knew people mostly died of sepsis. Watching him turn that over, the commander almost smiled. "Sorry," Taka said.

"Your van driver? Cash Conlon was a woman."

The police report from Enterprise said no copy of the driver's license had been made and included an affidavit from the employee who rented the van saying that the renter's description matched the license. All he remembered was the renter was a Caucasian male. "And how'd you come by that info?"

Commander Bowman shrugged. "I'm not a cop. I asked because it was my address used and Miss Emily shared that Cash Conlon was an older woman."

"And did Miss Emily say why they accepted the fake license?"

"Cash?"

"Cash Conlon." Taka rolled his eyes. "Was she the rental agent?"

"No. She doesn't work there anymore."

"Grapevine?"

"Grows thick in these parts."

"That it does." Taka held out his hand.

The commander shook it. "Grapevine says you're a good cop."

"Admin might not agree."

And for the first time, Taka could see the SEAL inside as the commander grinned. "Fuck Admin."

Taka laughed. "I might have to."

The commander clapped him on the shoulder and wandered off.

Taka checked his watch and called Fields to tell him about the former Enterprise employee named Emily and Cash Conlon.

"And where'd you come by this info?" Fields asked.

"Good police work. I left my card with the guy I questioned at the false address." He gave him the commander's name.

"Number?"

"I'm off the case, Fields, I'm just relaying follow-up. Do the legwork yourself."

He hung up and collected three coffees in a tray, including one for Karie, who might be here by now. He hated the hospital. He tried not to look at anyone, especially the patients on his way back to the ER. He hit the buzzer and gave his name and Andrea's. After a minute, the security door clunked and then swept open.

Andrea held both her hands out for her coffee. Her cheeks were dry. She looked better, a little color coming back into her face, though she still looked exhausted. When he handed Karie her coffee, she stepped in and hugged him. He hugged her back. Karie had never offered him a greeting hug before, proving how shaken she must be. They pulled the two chairs closer to the bed and sat down.

"I texted Jimmy," he said.

Andrea pressed her lips together and took another sip of her coffee.

"I shouldn't have?"

She played with the lid of her coffee. "I don't know. I'm okay. You guys are here."

"He knows about Aaron. He might be able to help us feed info to Tamarin."

"He's already in trouble. Won't it be worse if they think he's stepping on their toes?"

"Those guys would have stopped talking the second they saw you," Karie said. "If you go to Tamarin, what are you going to tell him? Why did you stop to listen?"

"I heard a name," Taka said, slowly, thinking it out. "Skinny. I heard a kid say it yesterday, too. When Fields had me looking for the van before he knew Andrea was involved."

"I wasn't involved," Andrea snapped. "He involved me with those photos."

He kept his tone even. "But now you are."

Andrea crossed her arms over her chest. "Jodie King's dad is named Skinny."

"How do you know that?"

"When I met Scott, at the smoke shop. Dewey and Glenn both called his dad Skinny. And Jodie's nickname"—she scrunched her eyes closed and pressed a fist against her nose, but the tears came anyway—"is Candy."

Taka frowned. They already knew that, so why was she so upset? "We're alone, you have to tell me what happened now."

"Hang on," Karie said. "Let me make notes." She dug in her purse and came up with a pen and a small pad. She flipped to a clean page and scribbled for a second. "Jodie 'Candy' King, dad Skinny."

"Let's talk about the garage first," Andrea croaked. She swiped at her eyes with the balled-up tissue in her hand.

"I heard the name Skinny. I stopped you."

"They were arguing over the first guy not knowing something and—"

"A woman making a call on someone named Eddie's phone."

"Do you remember the name one of the men called the other?"

Under her breath Karie said, "Eddie, killed by Lucy Garcia."

Taka stared at her. She lifted the pen and looked back.

"Derek," he said, answering Andrea's question. "The one who drove away first. White Chevy Equinox. Maryland tags."

Karie wrote it down.

"Those three guys at the party above the gallery? They said they were at Derek's. The apartment he said he wiped down must have been his. And the girls that are gone? That Skinny wants buried? Maybe they were talking about Anna Lansing and those two girls I saw."

"We can't assume that. Why does Karie think Lucy Garcia killed the Eddie guy?"

Andrea sniffed, her tears welling over again. "I know what happened, Taka. I saw it."

"Tell me," Taka said. "Start at the beginning."

23

Two o'clock and Jimmy was just getting to stick his head up for air. He slid the report he'd just collected from the printer into a folder and slapped it onto his "completed for now" pile. His stomach growled. "I'm going for a sandwich," he announced.

He opened his drawer, pulled out his cell, and turned it on. Shit. Taka and Scott's burner had blown it up.

"Before you leave, Boss," Nina said.

He held up his hand while he read the texts. All right. She was okay. "Yeah?"

"Remember last year when Andy Detweiler got all obsessed with Dewey Sanderson's mom looking nothing like him?"

And how he and Andy had blown up at each other about the swab and print Andy pulled off her drinking glass at a restaurant? "Hard to forget."

"Well, the DNA finally came back."

"He actually sent it?"

"It's not a match."

"Dewey's birth certificate is falsified?"

"We know he's him and the print shows she's her, but she is not his mom."

Falsifying paternity was pretty common, but falsifying the mother took more than one person to pull off. "What does that get us?"

"Nothing on Dewey and the senator's dead. Ten-thousand-dollar fine, possibility of five years in jail for mom?"

"Not what I'm looking for."

"We could use it to lean on her for info on Dewey's activities?"

He shook a finger at her. "There's a thought. We'll need to know exactly what we want from her first. We don't want to waste our shot." He held up his phone. "I gotta go take care of a couple of personal things over lunch. Call Andy and tell him he was right and I'm an asshole."

"There's more."

"There's more?"

"Yeah. Three of those casings came back as a possible match."

"To?"

"The senator's murder."

Jimmy's skin flushed cold, then hot. He forced himself to take a breath. Casings didn't mean much. It was always and would always be a Hail Mary play to have bothered collecting them in the first place. "Possible."

Nina nodded. "Possible."

No one on the federal task force had called him, yet, but they would once they saw the report. But it had only been two days since he collected them so... "You didn't send those through the federal lab."

She laughed. "No, that'd take months. Bill has the photos and federal and state reports on the casings for the four murder-arsons we've been looking at Dewey for, so we've been running the casings through the state ballistics team first for comparisons."

"And there's three possible matches."

"We need the gun."

"Text me which one. I'll see what Scott can do."

"Will do, Boss."

"Good job, Nina. Tell Bill thank you, too."

He hightailed it out, calling Andrea as he pulled out of BCI's parking lot.

She didn't pick up.

He called Taka.

He didn't pick up.

He called Karie.

She didn't pick up.

He hazarded a guess that they'd be at General, rather than Memorial, and headed that way. Five minutes into his drive, his cell binged an announcement and told him Karie sent him a message before relaying it out loud in computer monotone. *Andrea's being discharged. Don't know how long it'll take. I'm going back to work. They're going to talk to Detective Tamarin.*

"Reply 'what happened?'" The phone read it back and asked to send. "Send."

He pulled into the next parking lot. An air-conditioning company. He pulled around to face the road and ripped his phone from the holder as Karie's reply came through. The phone binged. He opened it before it could talk to him. *Having Taka there worked too well. Aaron gave her more than she expected. Treated for a panic attack.*

Thank you he texted back.

He tapped his fingers on the steering wheel. He had nothing to share except Cotton Candy's last name and that wasn't critical at this point. If Taka was going with her to talk to Tamarin, they must have info to relay and a plan to do so without yelling "ghost." He'd probably be more of a liability than a help if he showed up at CPD now. He had a court appearance to prep, and he needed to connect with Scott to talk about the gun and whatever Bulldog Bailey thought the senator still owed him that Dewey could get for him.

He typed Andrea with both thumbs. *Karie told me trouble with A. I'm sorry I wasn't there for you. Please call Sweet Joe if you're really going to talk to Tamarin. Take care. Call me when you can.* He hesitated and then added a heart emoji.

RAIN PATTERED ON THE WINDSHIELD. In the passenger seat of the Yukon, Andrea grimaced.

On hyper alert as he pulled into a reserved CPD spot in the City Hall parking garage, Taka said, "What?"

She held her phone up. "Jimmy says we should call Sweet Joe before we talk to Tamarin."

"I texted him. He's in court." He turned the truck off and asked for the umpteenth time, "You sure you're okay with this?"

Andrea couldn't see a way out of it. "They have to know what we heard."

"But I can tell them. You don't need to go in."

"I'm good, Taka." Andrea attributed her relative calm to the Valium still onboard and her resolve to convey what they had learned from the conversation in the garage. "I can remember not to tell them what Aaron showed me."

After hashing it out with Karie, they'd decided to withhold everything Andrea had gotten from Aaron. Mostly because neither Karie nor Taka thought they could trust the visions as truth. Karie had taken a theoretical approach of spirit and memory and no one knowing anything about how memory, especially other memories than the spirit's own, might be twisted by the spirit's beliefs or perspective.

Taka had simply wondered how going in and declaring that not only had Andrea overheard the nonexistent Derek talking about, presumably, the girls with Anna Lansing, but that she also knew that Lucy Garcia had killed the van driver, who, by the way, was named Eddie, and that the guy with a protection order against her was also involved, would keep her from being arrested on the spot.

Andrea had decided to choose her fight and for right now, this was what they could do without coming all the way clean. They had even taken the time to write out careful statements from Karie's notes to make sure they didn't cross over.

"Just the conversation in the garage."

She glared at him. "You're pissing me off."

"I'm sorry. You scared me."

"Aaron scared you."

"That, too."

"What if it's all real, Taka? What then?"

"That'll be then. We'll deal with it then. Ready?"

She downed the rest of the water bottle in her hands, took another deep breath, just checking that she could, and pulled the door handle.

They went straight up to Ronnie Horton's office. He excused the admin assistant he was speaking with, a woman Andrea had seen several times at various functions. "Detective Taka," she said as she passed by them.

"Jenny."

"You two look serious," Horton said, his gaze bouncing between them. "Didn't I assign you to your home, Taka?"

"I took a personal day, sir."

Horton leaned back in his swivel chair and tossed the pen in his hand to the desk. "I'm not going to like this, am I?"

"I wasn't investigating, sir. Andrea's car was impounded, and I drove her over to Louie's."

"I'd think you'd be staying away from there, Miss Andrea, considering."

"I was working, Lieutenant Horton—"

"Ronnie, please. Not like we haven't met before."

"I was working. Louie's great-aunt and sister invited me for coffee so we could discuss their genealogy and how the family came here to Charleston."

"Louie has that photo, right? In the bar? Of the plantation where his ancestors were slaves?"

Andrea glanced at Taka, but he was looking at the floor. Small talk it was then. "His family's included in that photo, yes."

"Really? The slaves in the photo are related to him?"

"Yes."

"That's really something. So, you were at Louie's and…"

"Afterward, in the parking garage," Taka said, coming to life. "We overheard a conversation that we think Pete Tamarin should know about in relation to Lucy Garcia and Anna Lansing."

"And you're here in my office because?"

Taka's voice hardened. "Because I want it crystal-clear that Andrea and I were bystanders and not seeking information on our own. That this was a coincidence."

"You know the investigative process inside and out, Taka." He very carefully did not look to Andrea. "We follow the leads, wherever they go."

Andrea's sinking feeling intensified. "This is information Pete needs if he doesn't already have it."

"Will you sit in?" Taka asked.

"Will you let us record?"

"Yes. But here, in a conference room."

"You want to wait for Sweet Joe and Carson?"

"Yes, but Sweet Joe's in court, Carson didn't pick up, and Tamarin needs this info now."

He was intrigued but trying hard not to show it. She shifted in the doorway. If he was already in suspicious mode and it wasn't even his case, what would Pete be like? "Have you located those girls who were with Anna Lansing? Any of the kids at her house? Or is Pete just focusing on the murders?"

"I've got extra hands on. We're looking."

"Then you need this info."

"Carson's downstairs with another client. I'll make sure he comes up. Wait in the conference room while I pull everybody in."

"Can we talk to him first?" The relief in Taka's voice was palpable.

"Of course," Horton said.

"WE COULD JUST SUBMIT YOUR STATEMENTS," Carson said twenty minutes later.

"And at this point," Taka said, "they'd just send someone to bring us in so they can ask their questions."

"And you just decline."

"Andrea's already been arrested once to compel her appearance."

Carson considered her for a long moment. "No offense, Andrea, but you're not my client. It's in Taka's best interest to submit his statement through me and keep his mouth closed. I'd recommend you do the same. Submit your statement. Keep your mouth closed."

She looked at the gathering of men outside the glass wall. "We just tell them never mind?"

"You're still giving them the info they need."

"Carson," Taka said. "If you tell me not to answer something, I won't. But let's get this over with now. Please?"

He sighed and raised a hand.

Pete, Fields, Horton, and a guy she'd never liked much, Karl, sat across from them. Sheryl, the lone female to have breached the male investigative ranks, sat at the end of the table. Two other guys stood by the back wall and another Andrea vaguely recognized sat down next to Carson and slid a digital recorder onto the table.

One of the gophers took the statements Carson handed him and went off to make copies. They went around the table introducing themselves. Karl and Sheryl were heading up the search to ID and locate the missing kids. They established Taka and Andrea were there of their own free will to provide information they thought would be relevant to the current case.

"Ground rules," Horton said. "This information will not be shared with anyone outside this room except on the okay of Detective Tamarin. You will not share this information with anyone"—he looked first at Taka and then Andrea—"including the state police and, specifically, Investigator James Hoyle." He slid two personalized NDAs, non-disclosure agreements, across the table to Carson.

The gopher returned with the copies, a little wide-eyed at the content.

"Hold onto those a second," Horton told him.

Carson read the NDAs and slipped them over in front Andrea and Taka. Jimmy was already in trouble with his boss. He was, for all intents and purposes, her boyfriend. He'd become part of the investigation on the wrong side. She got it. But he was a valuable asset they were throwing away. Next to her, Taka scribbled his signature at the bottom of the form and dated it. She blew out a frustrated breath and signed her own.

Horton nodded at the gopher.

The statements were brief but included descriptions of the men and their cars. Everyone read for a couple of minutes. "Oscar," Pete said. "Get these descriptions to the patrol officers who canvassed that building and get someone to see if the garage has cameras on the third floor that aren't broken. Run the tag and find out who owns that Equinox."

The copy gopher hurried out. Everyone else looked at Andrea and Taka.

Pete read the statements out loud for the recorder.

"No tag number on the Mercedes?" Pete asked.

"No, it wasn't visible from where I was," Andrea said.

"And this is a man you saw come out of the building after you saw Anna Lansing exit on Tuesday night?"

"Yes."

He turned his focus on Taka. "And this is the same man you saw on the third floor of the garage today, talking to a man he called Derek."

"I didn't see him get in the Mercedes, but Andrea described the same man I saw."

Pete read through the statement again. "This conversation—it seems unbelievably stupid that they'd have it in a public space."

"Only if you know what they're referring to," Carson said. "Business terms often sound literal."

Taka said, "They were angry, the rain was loud, and there didn't appear to be anyone around."

"The unknown walked right by you."

"We were a floor down by then. He wouldn't know we heard him."

"Someone besides Louie can verify when you left the pub?"

"Yes."

"And following this encounter, you, Andrea, suffered a panic attack for which nine-one-one was called."

Her face flushed hot. "Yes."

"Convenient." Pete leaned back in his chair, apparently to think.

A long silence fell.

Karl picked at a hangnail.

Horton stared down at the statement.

Pete cleared his throat and when Andrea looked at him asked, "You know what happened to those kids?"

"No."

"You have any prior contact with Anna Lansing before two nights ago?"

Andrea's anger stirred under the Valium calm. Really? Still?

"No," she said as emphatically as she could. "Despite the photos you showed me, I never saw her before then."

"You have any prior contact with Jodie King before two days ago?"

"No."

"You know any Eddies?"

"Yes. Eddie Alvarez is a music historian at Waltham-Young."

Pete and Horton both made a note of that.

"You have any prior contact with Lucy Garcia before finding her body?"

She shook her head.

"For the recording, please."

"No."

"Okay," he said. He stated the date and time and that the interview was concluded. The guy beside Carson turned off the recorder.

But no one moved.

Pete picked up the statement in front of him and made a show of placing it in his case file. "I know you're withholding information. Both of you. When it comes back to bite you, don't look at me to save you."

Andrea knew she'd be shaking normally. For this one thing, she could be grateful for being drugged. She stood up. Bracing her hands flat on the table, she leaned towards Pete. To make sure he heard her. "Pete, if those kids suffer further harm or lose their lives because you couldn't focus anywhere but on me? Don't look to any of the people in this room to save *you*." She shoved her chair in and walked out.

Pete yelled after her, "We'll need you to sign official statements later!"

Taka caught up to her at the elevator. He kept his mouth shut.

Outside City Hall, the rain had stopped, but the sky seemed lower, the day's gloom thicker. Andrea pulled her jacket closed and zipped it all the way up. An older gentleman stood nearby in a wool coat and scarf. "Is it colder?"

"Snow tonight," he said.

"Feels like it," Taka agreed.

"A little early for snow," she said.

Taka looked up into the grey. "Way early for snow."

"S'what the news said this morning," the old guy said. "But if they say it's going to snow—"

"It never does," Andrea finished.

"It never does what?" Taka asked.

"Snow when the news calls for it."

"Are they calling for snow?" Taka said, walking off.

"Snow tonight," the old guy said again and disappeared.

"Are you coming?" Taka called back.

24

"Foodland?"

She'd been silent since they left CPD.

"I have hamburger in the freezer."

"I think Jimmy and I only left you one slice of bread."

"I ate it."

"So we'll stop."

"No. I don't want to. There was a guy back there at City Hall. Talking about snow. And a couple at the hospital and three, including Aaron, this morning, and that weird family. By the side of the road. I don't want to see any more." She covered her face. "Not today."

The scent of baby shampoo filled his nose. He tried not to shudder, but that just made the chill that ran up his spine worse and the shudder larger than it would have been. "You still have eggs."

She lowered her hands and bent over to pluck Mrs. Dunbar's journals off the floorboard. The plastic bag was still wet. She hugged it to her. "I have my laptop and my files for Aaron and the new plantation job to work on until I'm allowed back."

He dug his phone out of his jacket pocket and handed it to her. "Call CPD Jenny."

She found the right number and hit dial. Jenny answered on

Bluetooth. "Hey, Jenny, can you change my duty station for tomorrow to my second address? Yeah. Andrea Kelley. 653 Double Branch Lane."

"Any scheduled court dates next week, Taka?"

"No, I'm clear for next week."

"I got it. Good night."

A moment of silence and then his dash lights switched back over to the radio display.

"You didn't have to do that," Andrea said, a quiver in her voice.

"I want to. I told Scott I'd be home tonight, but he won't be by until late. We'll make dinner and I'll be back by eight tomorrow morning."

"You don't have to stay. I just want to work."

She looked washed out. On the verge of crying again. "They're good people, Andrea. Pete's a good person. They're looking for those kids."

Wrong thing to say. Silent tears slid down her cheeks.

He watched the road instead. Passed the One Stop. Passed Foodland.

"It was me," Andrea said. "It was less than real life, but it was more than a dream. I can't remember everything now, like the surroundings. Or exactly who they were, except you and Aaron and Lucy Garcia. I don't know their names, but those details they gave me? The fear, the violation, the odors, the sounds, the high, the self-disgust, the shame. The wretchedness of those moments, the wretchedness and despair of their lives, those I got. I'm them," her breath caught. She fisted her hand in her jacket over her heart and hit her chest with each word. "They're me. We're all the same. We could all be each of them any given day depending on our choices. Depending on other people's choices that we can't even control."

In the wan late afternoon grey, the unlit Christmas decorations on her street looked surreal and out of place. He could tell her. That Karie was both right and wrong. That maybe the memories were skewed by Aaron's perspective, but that didn't invalidate the truth of them. All his important conversations seemed to be taking place in cars and over phones the last couple of days. He pulled down Andrea's drive into the empty carport and shut the Yukon off.

"It's hard to not be in control," he said carefully. "I didn't like it. Those days I was...held captive. I don't like it now. I'm more aware of my freedom. And my lack of it if I want to keep my job. If I want to keep my relationships. Every day is a compromise. What decision can I control today?" It dawned on him that he sounded like his therapist. As much as he had resisted the process, it had proved useful again and again the last few weeks. "What decision can you control right now?"

"I want a shower," Andrea said right away. She swiped at her wet cheeks. "But I'm afraid all I'll feel is the cold water."

The recognition shocked him. All these weeks he hadn't been able to put that fear into words. "I'll start it for you," he heard himself say. "I'll make it hot enough to steam so you can see it, so the bathroom's hot before you even come in." Scott had done that for him, until he could do it on his own.

"Okay," she said. "I don't want anyone else here tonight. Just you. I don't want dinner. I'm not hungry. I just want a hot shower. And I want to curl up under my covers and cry."

TAKA MADE hamburgers while she showered. Louie's cake had carried them a long way, but it was long gone now. Burning his mouth, he wolfed one down straight out of the pan, along with two eggs over easy, and put the rest away for her to re-heat tomorrow. When he heard her steal into her bedroom, he made a cheese omelet for her and tea for both of them. He arranged it on the wooden tray she kept on top of the refrigerator. Her laptop sat out on the kitchen table, but at the last minute he didn't pick it up. He'd come get it if she wanted it.

Upstairs, she was just crawling into bed, in worn T-shirt and loose shorts. It was cold in the room. The only light spilled from the open closet door and in bars through the plantation shutters. The muted dark blues and greens of the duvet and the just-visible patchwork of books filling the dark wall cabinets soothed his turbulent half-formed thoughts.

She didn't fuss at him for bringing the tray. He set it at the foot of the big bed and handed her the tea. He took his own and sat in the chair cocked between the bed and the bookcases. She didn't have a TV in the room. They sipped their tea and listened to the heater cut on and off and the wind pick up outside and the occasional pebble-shot of rain against the window.

Eventually, Andrea snagged the tray and he watched her eat, the slow tap of the fork against the plate ringing in the silence. He could still feel her lips on his. He wanted to kiss her again.

"You know," he said when his teacup was empty. "Karie's both right and wrong. Aaron's perspective may skew what he showed you, but that doesn't invalidate the truth."

"The cowboy boot on my chest?"

He nodded.

"You died. I know it. The same way I know I was in Aaron at the battle at the creek, that that girl was my sister, that Lucy took a pull on that guy's joint before she picked up the cash to give to Eddie. That she always gave it all to Eddie, never kept any. He needed it to pay for her room and buy her food and the drugs she needed. He needed all of it to take care of her. But she still wanted to come home to Charleston. She knew, just knew, that Candy loved her. She thought Candy must've been looking for her the whole time she'd been gone, that maybe she'd let the ladies at the VFW find her a rehab through the VA, that she'd be more grateful for her life and being back in Charleston was her chance to get away. So I know. You died."

He remembered coming to, how literally sweet the air tasted on his tongue as he breathed. How he choked on it because of the competing water in his lungs. Maybe he did. It wouldn't be the first time. "If I did, I don't remember. But I don't remember falling out of the buckeye tree when I was nine, either. My Uncle James thumped my chest and my heart re-started."

"You died when you were nine?"

He'd been lost in thought, staring at the bed but seeing the orange and yellow leaves of the buckeye tree far above his head as he lay on the cold ground. Her stricken voice slammed him back into the moment. "What?"

"You died. When you were nine."

He shrugged. "Technically? I fell on my back. It stopped my heart. My cousin Richie ran for Uncle James. He didn't have to do CPR, he just thumped me." He rubbed his sternum. Funny how it all came back although he didn't think he'd really remembered the details. "The bruise lasted all summer."

"Taka."

"What?"

"You keep asking why you're my conduit, 'how can that be?'" she said, mimicking his voice. "Should we do a survey of anyone else I'm around a lot and see if they've, oh, I don't know, ever died before?"

He lifted his cup to his lips, but it was empty. He lowered it again.

"And how come you never told me that?"

"It never came up."

"And it never occurred to you that it might be related to this ghost thing?"

He got up and collected the tray. "I don't really remember it, so it's not, like, something I ever think about."

Andrea cocked her head and really looked at him, maybe for the first time that day. "There's too many other moments you do remember."

She meant his moments that she now remembered, too, but there were way more than those that he would never forget. Like the gas station that haunted his sleep. He could feel the heat on his skin right now, smell the unmistakable scent of roasting human flesh. "You can say that twice. Are you still hungry?"

She shook her head. "I didn't realize I was. Thank you."

"Want the light off?"

"Will you come back up for a few minutes, while I fall asleep?"

God, he hated that she now knew, really knew, even a tenth of what had happened to him. That it would hurt her the same way it hurt him. "I'll be right back," he said.

Jimmy wasn't sure what to think about the text he got from Taka. It wasn't like he saw Andrea every night, but he had expected to tonight. On impulse he texted her anyway *I'm here if you need me. Don't hesitate.*

Bubbles a few seconds later, then *Breakfast?* with a heart emoji.

He sent back a thumbs-up.

A soccer ball rolled into his feet. He looked over at the closest game.

The wet air shimmered under the park's light. Parents stood or sat in sling-backed cloth chairs up and down the sidelines, both teams at the far end driving for the goal.

"A little help?" Scotty said from the other direction.

Still sitting backwards on the picnic table's bench, Jimmy booted the ball over. "You play soccer?"

"I used to. Now it just adds a little challenge to my run." He sat down on the top of the same table. "I'll tell Dewey I met up with you. Maybe you and Andrea can make a random appearance at the Coliseum next week."

Dragging Andrea along into an undercover ruse where the subject knows he's being investigated? No. "Noted. The Beretta 92 nine-millimeter casings with Chet's name on them came back as a possible match."

"To?"

"The unknown casings at the senator's scene."

"Nine-millimeter rounds killed him, right?"

"Correct."

"I'll see if I can get the gun for you. I don't think Chet owned it. And Dewey doesn't sell the 92, only the newer variations. If I remember right, it might be from Dewey's personal collection."

Jimmy tamped down his hope. "If you can get it, Nina'll drive it to the lab and wait on it so it's not missing too long. You ran into Andrea?"

"At a smoke shop in South Charleston. We were collecting rent. She was asking about Lucy Garcia. I saw it on the news, that's the victim she found in the alley?"

"Yeah."

"Crazy that she just happened to see her photo."

"Bulldog Bailey?"

"We already knew he had single moms and college kids selling drugs for him, but Chet says he also uses them as a bit of a local stable. He doesn't go out of his way to pimp them, but he will if the opportunity comes up."

"Sellers are willing participants?"

"Sounded like it from Chet, but you know how that goes."

He did. Half would need drugs and the other half money when they started, but even when their circumstances changed, they'd find it difficult to extract themselves with the threat of exposure hanging over their heads. A different type of trafficking than he'd been talking about with Taka and Andrea, but still trafficking once consent was withdrawn.

Suddenly he felt bad for all the thoughtless comments he'd tossed at drug mules and prostitutes over the years. How many of them were trapped in their tough-bitch armor due to threats and coercion and not by real choice anymore?

"We're still working on the audio. What did he want?"

Scotty hopped off the table. "I was on a rooftop across the street, Jimmy. That's why we have the audio, no?" He batted the ball sideways and lazily followed it to bat it back. "Chet said he was asking for hush money for a woman he claims the senator knocked up. No names, no time frames. That's all I got. I'm still working on building trust."

"Fair enough. Why was Taka on the roof?"

"Dewey wanted him as backup. He passed, but I guess he thought he'd check up on the situation anyway. He made me with one look." He bounced the ball up on the edge of his foot, caught it on his toe.

"Good call on version two then. But he tripped every alarm on your background. He got an officer in Idaho to pull your military discharge."

He'd let the ball fall while Jimmy was talking. He made the same move to his toe again, but then kicked it up to catch it in both hands. "Everything hold up?"

"So far. What can you tell me about Skinny?"

"Nothing. Never seen him. He leases shop space from Dewey."

"No other dealings?"

Scotty tucked the ball under his arm and leaned against one of the pavilion's supports. "Not that I've heard. He wasn't there. His stepson called him. We collected the rent and a few free cigars and that was that. I've told you before, Dewey's tight. Crew's tight. Keeps his office locked."

Stepson. Were Candy King and Alexander Conlon related through a marriage somewhere? "Skinny's name?"

"I don't know. Dewey knows him pretty well, though. He was brutal to the old guy over the phone."

"Candy King ever come around?"

"I've seen him at the club."

"Put him on your radar. Log any contact."

"Done," Scott said. He dropped the ball between his feet and slid his hands in his hoodie's pockets. "Can you tell me who we visited Tuesday night?"

"You've lost me."

"We went to a house across the Corridor from here, after the meeting with Bulldog. About midnight. On Beaumont." He threw a hand up in the air at Jimmy's silence. "Tell me we lost Detweiler again."

"I don't know." Wasn't Beaumont the street Anna Lansing lived on? "I'll check the report. We were dealing with the alarms on your cover."

"I told Taka you knew about my addiction and discharge."

"I told him I didn't."

"Let's just play it that you were keeping my secret."

Jimmy palmed the tiny bag with the bugs in it from his jacket pocket as he stood up and then stretched. "Got it." He held his right hand out to shake and Scotty took the bag from him. "On the deck. Out of the wind if you can."

Scott lifted his chin in the briefest of nods. "See ya." He kicked the ball away and went chasing after it.

Jimmy called Andy Detweiler.

No answer.

He searched local homicides. Anna hadn't been named, but Wednesday's big news was the murder on Beaumont Road.

25

On the drive home from Andrea's, Taka called Dewey. Music and the muted murmur of a big crowd when he picked up. Dewey was at the club, probably sequestered in his VIP booth since he could talk. "Heard Andrea had some trouble," he said right away.

Taka would love to know his sources. "Of course you did."

"I can have my guys step on Candy a little. Persuade him to withdraw his complaint."

"What do you know about him?"

"Buys off Bulldog. Spreads quite a bit of it around for free."

"That's why they call him Candy?"

"Cotton Candy. Panties melt around him like spun sugar."

Taka groaned at that.

"He never goes home alone," Dewey continued.

"His dad?"

"Skinny?"

"What's he do?"

"He owns a smoke shop," Dewey said, his words more pointed. "If you're going to 'cop' me, I'm hanging up now."

"I'm pretty sure that after today 'cop' is no longer my career path."

"So you'll come work for me."

Taka laughed. "That doesn't mean I'm going to the dark side, no."

"I'm hurt, William. I'm an honest businessman."

"And I'm one-hundred-percent white."

"Okay, as honest as a businessman can be these days and stay in business."

"Well, then, I'll admit to being just as much color as it takes to be not white."

"You know you're beautiful, right?"

Taka rolled his eyes.

"Speaking of color, that Black detective was in tonight. What's his name?"

"Fields?"

"That's the one. He also asked about Candy and Skinny. Showed me a photo of Anna, too."

Anna. Andrea's blonde? "Lansing?"

"You know her."

He could say he did. See where that'd get him. But Dewey usually knew the answers before he asked. "No, I don't. I know of her. She's the cause of Andrea's cop troubles."

Taka listened to a good bit of "Lady Marmalade" in the background before Dewey decided on his next move. "Bulldog Bailey says my dad was Anna Lansing's exclusive client. He contracted through Bulldog to keep his hands clean. The money to maintain her ended when my dad died. Then she told Bulldog she was pregnant."

Bulldog was Anna Lansing's pimp. Was she in the same hole as Lucy Garcia had been?

"He wanted hush money and child support," Dewey continued. "Because she wanted to keep it. I told him no."

Dewey had hated his father for a very long time. Add the events of six weeks ago and his answer didn't surprise Taka at all. It was why he suspected Dewey of the senator's murder. He would absolutely delight in Senator Sanderson's name being dragged through the mud. "What about your mom?"

Dewey clucked his tongue in the way he did when exasperated. "My mom's a survivor. And I couldn't have cared less if it went public."

"But now Anna's dead. And if the ME finds her pregnant and Fields hears about the link between her and the senator, he'll think you have a pretty good motive for murder. But so does Bulldog. Maybe he didn't want to spend any more money on her if you wouldn't cough up."

And she knew Lucy. Maybe Anna didn't care for Bulldog's contracting on her behalf. Maybe Lucy's bid for freedom was catching.

"… to talk to her that night."

"What?"

"After Bulldog left. I went to Anna's. State babysitters followed me right over there."

"The state cops are following you?"

"You're going to pretend you don't know Jimmy Hoyle?"

"Depends."

"On whether or not I know you're sleeping with Scott?"

"Jesus Christ, Dewey, seriously?"

"Have you seen the way you don't look at him and then you do?"

"Christ," Taka muttered.

"It's how you used to look at me. It's how you still look at that girl of yours."

"I've never slept with Andrea."

Dewey was drinking. The ice in his glass rattled. "Well, that's a damn shame, William."

"Why tell me about Anna?"

"It might help if you stay a cop a bit longer is all I'm saying," Dewey said. He didn't say, *And I know a secret you don't want your cop buddies knowing,* but he didn't have to. "Before you come work for me."

"Did you kill her?"

"Of course not. I hope you just felt obligated to ask, or you don't know me as well as I thought you did."

"I don't think anybody knows you as well as they think they do, Dewey."

He laughed out loud, that big genuine laugh that could still turn Taka's head and hung up before Taka could ask about Skinny again. Taka didn't know what Dewey thought Taka could, or would, do if CPD's suspicion fell on him. Threatening to out him wouldn't do the trick, though. Reminding Taka that he owed Dewey his life would get him farther. He suspected Dewey already knew that.

God, he hoped Pete Tamarin was just dangling Andrea out in front of Candy King, that he had something that linked him to Anna's murder. If he was actually considering Andrea a real suspect, but she didn't do it, and Dewey didn't do it, that left Candy, who at least admitted to knowing her.

The better bet was Bulldog. But since Taka had failed to mention Dewey's meet with Bulldog to Ronnie Horton before it happened, it would be really, really awkward to bring it up now to get Bulldog posted on Tamarin's white board as a suspect. And bringing up the fact that he was talking regularly enough with Dewey Sanderson for Dewey to confide in him was its own quicksand.

He drove the rest of the way home on autopilot.

Miss Betty, in slippers and a jacket pulled on over her housecoat, stood on the bit of grass in front of the condos with her old Schnauzer. "And how are you tonight, Taka? Staying out of trouble?"

"Always, Miss Betty." He stooped to take the old dog's head in both hands and rub his ears, which made him groan and lift a hind leg to scratch at the air.

"It's good to see you out and about again. You tell that nice young man of yours I'm making more chocolate chip cookies this week."

Taka bit his cheek. Did everybody know? "Yes, ma'am," he said and beat a hasty retreat without looking up at her again.

Inside, he found Scott had left the condo spotless. He needed something mindless to do before he could sleep. He changed and worked up a sweat in the guest room, concentrating only on the texture of the weight bar's grip against his palms, the padded bench under his back, the tension of his muscles when he moved to bicep curls and triceps dips, the angle of his squats. It took every tool the therapist had given him to talk himself into the shower afterwards, but he did it.

He woke up from bad dreams at the key in the door. Scott turned off the kitchen light, disappeared into the bathroom, and started up the shower. Taka had almost dozed back off when Scotty pulled the covers back and settled in beside him.

Everything Taka wanted to ask him flew out of his head.

He held his hand out across the space between them and Scotty took it.

"I'm sorry," Scott whispered. "About all of it."

"It's okay," Taka murmured. "Let's just sleep."

But then he couldn't.

Who killed Anna Lansing was one impossible question, but who killed Lucy Garcia was the other. Andrea said she killed Eddie before he knew she was a danger to him. So, who killed her? Mystery Derek seemed the probable answer. Had Candy called him?

After Scott rolled away from him, taking his heat with him, Taka got up, padded into the living room, and pulled on the sweatshirt he'd left on the couch. He checked to see if his access was blocked on the department's servers. It wasn't. But any searches he made would be tracked.

He backed out. As long as he had access, he had a last resort.

He made a list of names and went surfing on the public domains. The only bit of this case elephant he had a hold of was a toenail. He'd not been officially privy to any details after meeting the commander, talking to the Summersville Conlons, and being mean to the rotten little boy at Alexander "Xander" Conlon's who had threatened to tell Skinny in reference to an uncle. Skinny wasn't a nickname Taka heard a lot, but it wasn't uncommon. Uncle could mean close family friend.

Still, through Skinny, Jodie 'Candy' King could, possibly, be related to Xander Conlon. By marriage at the least. What were the chances that Xander, Henry, and Linda Conlon, the Conlons living closest to Clay, weren't related? He hadn't asked, and he should have. It had felt like a wild goose chase by then.

Without a first name, there were probably lots more Conlons in Charleston and Kanawha County who could have thrown a dart at Clay for that random address on the rental agreement. He tapped in a White pages search. Okay, only six more Conlons in Charleston, so not as big a job as he had thought to question them.

The name of Conlon was probably real enough. And a mistake made by the crooked rental agent that the renter probably wouldn't know about until one of Tamarin's team went sniffing around. Unless

Taka had already tipped them off when he talked to the Conlons in Summersville and Tina at Alexander's in Hico.

He ran a search for Skinny Conlon. Various combinations of skinny meals by chefs named Conlon and skinny jeans articles by writer Conlons. He searched Henry Conlon and found about a billion of them. With the name Alexander Conlon, he found a LinkedIn profile listing him as an owner for an LLC in Charleston with a vague mission statement as an entertainment company. His Facebook page was entrepreneurship-motivational shares and check-ins to restaurants and an independent gym near Hico. His friends were nationwide, no apparent family. No Henry or Skinny Conlon. No Candy King.

He searched for both the LLC and the smoke shop at the WV Secretary of State's website and only got addresses and law firms for the Registered Agents. Through CPD's servers, he'd have had access to the owners' names.

Skinny King, the name he'd given CPD because he'd been thinking King's dad, not stepdad, got him nowhere on three different searches. The man could be named anything. It occurred to him that he didn't even know what Jodie Candyass King looked like. From Andrea, he knew Lucy Garcia had an Instagram, though.

The last post was from Philly, last February. She'd posted more and more infrequently over the previous year. There were two photos of Jodie King, whom she only labeled Candy. One of those was taken at the VFW. She had one arm around Candy and the other over the shoulders of a veteran, Tripp.

King had the big three. Nearly all the posts were selfies or featured the smoke shop. He was fond of the peace sign and the shaka. Some of his photos included a big guy with a full crucifixion tattoo on his throat, trailing onto his collarbone. No Lucy or Eddies in his feed or friends list, no dad or stepdad, no Skinnies. No Anna. No Alexander or Henry.

There were relatively few Anna Lansings to be found, and none connected to Charleston. CPD hadn't released her name yet to the press, so there were no photos connected to her death. The disappearance of Lucy Garcia from social media after she went to Philly and the lack of any social media connected to Anna Lansing bolstered the thought that they weren't free to act on their own. He closed his eyes. Trafficked. How many prostitutes and gigolos had he talked to over the years and simply thought they'd made different choices on purpose? How often had he overlooked someone in need of rescue?

He set the laptop down and went into the kitchen to pour a glass of water. Lucy was connected to King and, by association, Skinny. She was also, according to the photos Andrea was shown, connected to Anna Lansing. The conversation in the parking garage referenced the phone call Lucy made from Eddie's phone and Eddie's death, and almost certainly, by association, Anna Lansing. And, once again, Skinny.

The possibility that there was more than one Skinny in the mix? Skinny. Toothpick skinny. Dewey absolutely knew Skinny's real name. But if he'd been willing to tell Taka, he'd have offered to earlier. Dewey was calculating with both his words and his knowledge.

Maybe Scott could find out for him. But since Dewey knew about them, he'd know the request was coming from Taka. He could go back to the Conlons in Summersville and ask if they knew Xander and Skinny.

Or he could ask someone who probably already knew. He could have done that hours ago.

Re: Jodie King. What's Skinny's real name?

"Hey," Scott said from behind him.

Taka set his phone down and turned. "You know Skinny's real name?"

Scott blinked at him. There were lines on his face from the pillowcase. "Like, from the smoke shop?"

"Yeah."

"No. I'm cold," he complained, eyes half-closed and hair tousled. "Come back to bed."

"You could put some clothes on," Taka observed, but his blood was already stirring, his focus shifting.

"Or you could come back to bed."

LYING ON HIS BED, Jimmy tossed a handball at the wall and caught it on the rebound.

The doublewide simply absorbed the sound.

Usually he liked his isolation, but tonight the silence pressed too hard on his ears.

He could walk up through the fog past the family cemetery to his parents' house.

There'd be the TV on all night, the click of the baseboard heaters, the tick of the grandfather clock, his dad and the dog snoring, his mom re-heating her coffee in the microwave.

He threw the handball at the wall. Caught it.

SHE COULDN'T SLEEP.

Andrea sat up and turned the bedside lamp on.

Both Mrs. Dunbar's journals and her laptop were sitting on her nightstand, on top of the notepad that lived there. She waffled, then skimmed through four of the eleven small journals for dates. The entries varied in length and sometimes weeks or months were skipped between daily entries. The handwriting was conservative and very small.

At a guess, Andrea would say Mrs. Dunbar was making her pages last as long as possible before starting a new journal. Several times she had to tell herself to quit reading about the spat between the cook and the housemaids or the broody chicken with the largest eggs and the bad eye or the recipe for a brown sugar custard pie that Andrea thought was probably a pre-Civil War version of Jefferson Davis pie.

The fourth journal she tried covered the dates during which Aaron would've been sold. Mrs. Dunbar used her slaves' names, not just calling them by the name of the role they occupied in her household, so Andrea was hopeful, but a quick skim didn't pick up an Aaron or various spellings of that name.

There was a toddler underfoot in the kitchens that Mrs. Dunbar called Tom. Andrea scrolled through her photos to Louie's family tree and looked through until she found Aunt Sally's grandfather, Thomas Jaffee Orengo. His birthdate was approximated as 1849, so 1851 could definitely put him in the kitchens if his mother was the house cook.

But the wisp of white in the alley kept rising over and over again in her mind.

Lucy's ashy face and glazed-over eyes.

The drive of the knife.

Downwards and back.

Into Eddie's chest.

The overseer's sweat hitting her skin as he thrust into her.

Shhhh. This ain't forever.

Stomach roiling with nerves, Andrea stacked the journals back up, made herself more comfortable, and opened her laptop. She'd started putting the word out yesterday morning before the sheriff showed up with the summons from Candy King. She wanted anything her contacts could dig up on human trafficking in Charleston. She wanted anything on Candy from the smoke shop.

She wasn't very used to hunting current people down except as related to property records or specialties. But she'd made friends of her friends' friends while searching for info in October and learned a couple of new tricks. After she had Candy's full name to work with, she'd deployed those, too.

But with the feel of the knife in her hand and the overseer's stink in her nose, she couldn't quite make herself pull on those ugly strands that would expose the darkest shadows of Charleston's underbelly in real time. Not yet.

Instead, she surfed through her network for any new and useful responses related to her vague inquiries over the past month for possible ways she could pin Aaron down in the historical record of either Charleston or South Carolina. She'd also requested any official records or personal journals researchers came across related to Live Oak and Black males named Aaron, or any variation of same, in the slave markets in the 1840s and '50s, especially in Charleston, New Orleans, Atlanta, Louisville, Lexington, or Norfolk. And she'd asked everywhere about any plantation names, known slave owners, or buyers with the initials SH.

Nothing new.

She still had lots to go through based on Talisha's thoughts, though.

While she was thinking about her, she emailed to ask her to show intern Megan how to fill out the archival document forms.

Then she posted a few new questions looking for someone who could educate her about slave stockmen. She asked Antebellum and Civil War researchers to tag her on any notations they came across regarding stockmen or slaves of any age in Confederate service named Aaron or the like, or any owners with the initials SH in military journals, impressment or reimbursement records, or, on the off chance, in service to the Union.

Now that she could talk to him, she needed to find out if Aaron was related to Louie and whether his name remained the same throughout his slave life. Had he survived slavery? And if so, what last name did he adopt? But most of all, she needed to know what, exactly, he needed from her, who the Ned he wanted found was, and if he could tell her who killed Lucy Garcia.

Even as she wrote down one question after another, she remembered Billie Mae and Bruten Wilder's limited communication, thought again about the ghost outside City Hall, *snow tonight*.

But she could try.

A little more primed, she swapped browsers again and checked the private forums where she had posted her trafficking questions, both slightly sickened and unsurprised at the answers. Then she fired up her Tor browser and went hunting for her answers regarding Candy on the dark web.

26

At six, Andrea debated going for a run. She'd missed a couple of days already. It would clear her head and might make her feel better. On the other hand, the dawning day was just more grey and wet and if Candy King or another cop were waiting for her to step outside, she didn't want to know about it yet.

Instead, she texted Karie to see if she was awake. *I'm going to Louie's this morning about 8:30. Bringing Taka. Could you meet us there?*

Karie sent back a thumbs up. *Can I try and capture activity?*

Although they'd bonded over ghosts, she and Karie just clicked.

They had a lot of common interests. They were closer now than any other women friends Andrea had in Charleston since her girlfriend Lauren moved away. Andrea could say no and Karie would still come and support her. Taka would probably prefer no equipment.

But she had let Karie in at the start knowing Karie's goal as an investigator was indisputable proof of life after death. And Karie had helped save Taka's life by capturing an electronic voice phenomenon, or EVP, from a ghost Andrea couldn't hear. And who knew what they were walking into after yesterday?

Yes. IDK what to expect. If Aaron even shows.

Are you okay? Karie texted.

No, she really wasn't. She was having half-baked ideas of trying to find out who the women in the visions were even after discovering how hard it was to find any evidence of any one slave that could be verified as a certain individual.

I can't stop thinking about them, Andrea texted. *All of them are dead now so there's nothing I can do to help them.*

I can't get over the fact that people are still buying and selling people, Karie texted back. *I mean, I knew that, intellectually, but here? In Charleston? That sounds so naïve, doesn't it?*

No. Or maybe yes. It's just not visible unless you're looking for it. I actually told Taka and Jimmy yesterday that I thought it just happened to Asian maids in Abu Dhabi or Thai girls in Bangkok. What a privileged life I've led.

I've been up half the night, Karie replied, *reading about Bangladeshi girls taken across the border into India and sold into brothels.*

I've been up half the night asking for info on sex slavery here and who the players are—it's definitely a thing here in WV. Nothing definite yet on names of sellers, but that guy Candy, his selfies on social are all code for new shipments of drugs and where he'll be.

Seriously? Can you report it? Can Taka? Or Jimmy?

Andrea had been wondering herself what she could do about any of it. *After this week IDK. We'll have to figure it out. Maybe I can get someone else to—at least I can give the info to Sweet Joe? And the info on trafficking, too. There's groups that help women recover after being rescued —gotta go, breakfast with J—8:30?*

I'll be there.

AT SEVEN, she let Jimmy in the kitchen door.

He hugged her hard. She looked worn and a little shell-shocked.

They made coffee and cheesy toast.

"So," Jimmy said once they were seated at the kitchen table. "Why'd you go to Tamarin yesterday?"

"We were warned off telling you. We signed NDAs."

He'd really fucked up not coming clean with Tamarin and letting

Taka take his lumps for calling to tell him about the nine-one-one dispatch to Louie's.

"Okay. Tell me about the panic attack, then. What did that have to do with Aaron?"

She thought for a second. "Did I tell you about the stripe I've been seeing on his trousers?"

"No?"

"The first time I saw it was in the alley. But I've seen it a couple of times since. His clothes were already Civil War era. I found out that a fifteen-year-old slave named Aaron was sold by Live Oak in 1851. During the war, that'd make him about the same age as our Aaron appears to be. That stripe made me wonder if he served the Confederate Army in some way."

"That's why you met that guy at the VFW."

"He definitely saw a battlefield, at the very least."

Then she gave him what was almost certainly an abbreviated version of her encounter with the ghost and the visions he gave her.

"Candy sold her," she said about Lucy Garcia when she was done. "Just flat-out sold her and walked off."

"But he didn't kill her."

"I don't think so unless he was close by. I need to talk to Aaron."

"You held Billie Mae." He automatically looked past Andrea to where it had happened. Movement outside the window caught his eye. For just a minute he wondered, but no, it was a handful of leaves drifting to the ground. "How come you didn't get anything off her?"

"She was solid, a real girl, for a couple of minutes. Like the stories of hitchhiking ghosts, Karie says. But this was different. I was—I don't know what I was. I've never *felt* so much as in the last two days. This looked like a shadow. I was standing in front of Taka and then I wasn't me anymore."

The back of his neck went cold. He ran a hand across it and resisted the urge to look over his shoulder at whatever he was certain was standing behind him. "Possession?"

"That sounds creepy, doesn't it?"

Jimmy took a bite of his toast, trying to shake off the chill.

"You know what was weird?"

He laughed and choked. She pounded him on the back while he wheezed, still laughing, his eyes watering, until she was laughing along without knowing why. When he finally caught his breath, between helpless silent bouts of laughter, he said, "No, what was weirder than this whole 'ghost sharing memories' thing?"

"That he was loud," she said and then dissolved again, which set him off all over again.

"Okay," he said, after a couple of minutes. "Okay, okay." He took a couple of deep breaths and settled himself. "Explain?"

"I was just thinking about the boy on Louie's bar, playing jacks and how loud he was. At one point I could hear his hand slide across the wood like—" she searched for the right sound. "Like wind through trees. The ball was thundering down. And the jacks were clanging like horseshoes."

"Horseshoes?"

"Have you never played horseshoes?"

"The ones we had were rubberized. And what boy on the bar?"

"Did I not fill you in on Savannah and Great-Aunt Sally?"

He shook his head.

"It was a long day."

"No kidding."

She gave him what he was sure were only the highlights and then told him about the other ghosts, including the boy. He wanted to be fascinated by it. And supportive. But he found himself trying to form a response with a mouth and throat and brain gone stiff, like he'd been out in a frigid wind for far too long.

"I've said too much," she said.

"It's just," he managed, "the thought of not an occasional ghost. Or two. But multiple ghosts. Anywhere. Anytime. It's an obvious thought, isn't it?"

She nodded.

"I just hadn't had it yet. I mean, probably, I had. Just not about *you* seeing them. Somehow that hadn't occurred to me." Everything was loosening up now. He stood up to walk it off, pacing to the stove and back, aware of her gaze on him. "I don't know why it's surprising to me.

Of course, you'd see more than just the ones directly in front of you. What if they all start trying to talk to you?"

Immediately, he wished he could take the question back. How would she know? This was all new to her, too.

"I've been worried about that," she said. "Karie says she thinks there'll be rules of a sort to my—"

Curse. He clamped his mouth closed on that one quick enough to stop it leaping from him.

"Ability. And I've already noticed that some ghosts notice me and don't care. Some notice me, but don't try and talk to me. Some seem to be echoes or don't notice me at all."

"And the boy playing jacks was loud?"

"It was weird," she said smiling.

Jimmy made himself smile back. That helped. "It's all weird."

Someone was pulling into the carport next to his RAV4.

"Taka," Andrea said.

Jimmy grabbed their plates off the table, dumped them in the sink, and was pouring coffee into a third mug when Taka came into the mudroom from the carport on a gust of cold air.

"Who's Jodie King's dad?"

Jimmy brought the hot coffee to the table. "He's dead."

"His stepdad, Skinny?"

Andrea caught her breath. "Taka."

They exchanged a complicated look.

"I don't think I have much to lose, Andrea," Taka said.

"This is related to the NDAs?" Jimmy asked.

"And two open homicide investigations."

Andrea said, "Do you know, Jimmy?"

"I don't. And I have no legal reason to go ask King. CPD would probably have my head if I tried. I do have somebody working on it, though. We can't use official channels right now for various reasons."

Still standing in the doorway between the mudroom and the kitchen, Taka shoved his hands in his jeans pockets. He stared at the floor while he thought. "Tamarin and the rest of them. They don't know what King did to Lucy Garcia." He looked up. "Fields was at the

Coliseum last night, asking Dewey about King and his stepdad, Skinny. Obviously, they're thinking the same thing we are."

"That smoke-shop Skinny and parking-garage Skinny are the same guy," Andrea said.

"I texted and asked him to tell me smoke-shop Skinny's name. They must know it by now. But then he called this morning from a burner. They're nowhere on the IDs for the men in the garage. The Maryland plate was stolen. The cameras were nonfunctional. No one in the gallery building knows their names. The leasing company took cash. The name they have is false. The only thing we gave them that could be verified was the guy that died in the van was named Eddie."

"Which just puts suspicion back on me," Andrea said.

Taka's constipated expression said it all. "The van was also paid for in cash, by a woman. Fake address, but the leasing agent also wrote down a last name, Conlon. I gave that to Fields yesterday from the hospital, but the agent's gone. His parents reported him missing yesterday morning."

"An Alexander Conlon is part-owner of the smoke shop," Jimmy said. "With Jodie King. There aren't any other owners."

"I heard Skinny on the phone," Andrea said. "He's a real person. And he was giving the orders. He's an older man."

Jimmy couldn't say that Scott had said the same.

"You could ask Scott," Andrea said to Taka.

"I did. He doesn't know. I went to Alexander Conlon's farm to ask about the van," Taka continued. "A woman there mentioned an uncle named Skinny. Can you find out if he and King are related, Jimmy? Maybe by marriage?"

"I can try."

Andrea slid her coffee mug away from herself, drawing Jimmy's attention.

"I'm trying to get some firmer details," she said. "But I think Alexander Conlon provides sexual entertainment at parties his clients hire him to manage."

Taka recovered faster than Jimmy. "Trafficking?"

"I don't think so, or at least not all of them. He pays two-hundred-and-fifty dollars for four hours, plus drinks. And a drug of choice.

There's whispers that some students have left school to work for him full-time. I'm trawling for any who are willing to talk to me."

Jimmy's brain wouldn't settle on a single thought. He knew she'd found more than he'd expected on their last go around, but this? How deep did Waltham-Young's information network go? Should he mention the dead girl and that Conlon's dad and the senator were buds?

"What about King?" Taka asked, like he expected Andrea to know.

"Wait," Jimmy said. "Conlon's dad, Harrison, and Senator Sanderson were good friends. They both attended a series of exclusive parties until a young woman died at one of them and the senator bowed out."

"Xander's been running them awhile now," Andrea said.

Taka's gaze shifted to the window. Jimmy could practically hear his hamster wheel turning. "Where does Harrison Conlon live?"

"His address is an attorney's office in New York." Jimmy said. "After a DUI, he let his driver's license expire and apparently he doesn't own any property. At least not in his own name."

"No wonder I didn't come across him."

"I'd request IRS files, but I can only justify so much digging on Candy King and the Conlons. Dewey's just their landlord so far. There doesn't appear to be any other ties between them, certainly nothing criminal."

Biting his lower lip, Taka looked away again.

Letting his tone sharpen, Jimmy said, "You know something I don't?"

"No," Taka said, decisively. "Just trying to connect the dots."

Jimmy could see the effort it took him to shake off whatever his gut was giving him and focus on Andrea, who was still ping-ponging her worried attention between them.

"Did you find anything on Candy King, Andrea?"

If Taka had a hamster wheel in his head, Andrea had an old-fashioned filing system. Her brain was a hand-carved mahogany chest holding a thousand manila folders. She sorted for a millisecond, filing info away, and pulling out what she needed. "On his social media, a peace sign means a fresh load of imported marijuana's come in and he's selling. He always has domestic on hand. A shaka is extra quantities of pills available to his regulars beyond their standard amounts. Tongue out means he's got something he doesn't normally handle, like special K or mushrooms."

"And he sells women into sexual slavery," Taka says.

"He does. But I have no proof yet except from Aaron. I've got feelers out."

What? "Whoa, whoa," Jimmy blurted. "Where are you getting this info?"

27

"All the archivists I know are research geeks and I've developed a lot of connections. Most of the projects I work on involve property developers, community politics, historical preservationists, and environmentalists, so I've learned how to verify anonymous sources and find buried documents. Sometimes it's just enough to get a demolition hold for a few months until a property can be documented before it's destroyed."

Property records and water sheds were a long, long way from sex trafficking. "How does that translate?"

She narrowed her eyes at him. It reminded Jimmy of how distrustful she'd been of him when they first met. And how he'd deceived her. How he was still deceiving her in some respects.

"An honest question. I don't know how you get from property research to sex trafficking."

"The deep web and a trustworthy reputation for protecting your sources."

"It's just research," Taka said. "But she's an expert in it."

Andrea nodded.

Jimmy held his hands up. "I didn't realize when we've joked about hackers before, you meant literally."

"It's research hacking, Jimmy, like biohacking, not illegal-breaking-into-secure-computer-caches hacking," she clarified. "Mostly it's asking one person to go ask another to find someone who has the info you need and getting them to feel safe enough to give it to you. Then you verify its authenticity through multiple sources while trying to find or make more public sources as you go."

"I get it. I do. I just didn't realize how good you are at it." He suspected Nina and Bill would want to adopt her if they ever found out.

"Given enough time, she can get Skinny's name," Taka said, still standing in the doorway. "But I don't think we have the time."

Jimmy gave him a sideways glance.

"They're going to rule Lucy's and Eddie's deaths a double homicide and pin each death on the other. They don't have the knife, but the theory is that they fought and stabbed each other with the same knife."

"So, where's the knife?"

"Carried off by a vagrant in the alley. He's the one who covered the body with the pallets. It's on the bakery's CCTV. They can't find him."

Jimmy frowned. "They saw him take the knife?"

"No."

"Because Eddie didn't stab her," Andrea said, voice rising. "She was bloody, but she wasn't hurt."

"King has a solid alibi for Anna Lansing's murders." Taka ground to a halt. He wiped a hand across his mouth.

Andrea stood. "What?"

"You don't."

"But you were here the night of Anna's murder," Jimmy said.

"They're considering me unreliable. You, too. Just"—he held up his hand—"wait. There's more."

The blood had run out of Andrea's face, leaving her stark white. Jimmy was afraid she might faint. "Like what?"

"They're saying there's suspicious activity on your computer, that they have the Tor nodes you used, and they can demonstrate stalking behavior."

Jimmy was happy that a little color flushed back into Andrea's face with her anger.

Taka turned his head away again. Jimmy's gut said embarrassment this time. "I can give them two better suspects. For Anna at least. But I'll be done when I do."

Andrea seemed speechless. Jimmy said, "Why?"

"I have knowledge of a meet between Bulldog Bailey and Dewey Sanderson and didn't report it ahead of time so that my superiors could decide if CPD wanted to monitor it."

Jimmy's relief that they didn't have to work around CPD getting involved on that one almost opened his mouth. He could tell Taka not to worry about that, that he could say he asked Taka to keep it quiet. He'd probably earn another reprimand. He bit his tongue.

"Two guys can't meet to talk?" Andrea said.

"Two guys under constant suspicion of illegal activity and the subjects of several fruitless investigations that have taken hefty chunks out of the budget? Maybe. If no sworn officers are aware it's taking place or if a sworn officer in a position to be aware of those investigations who does find out takes it up the ladder when he becomes aware of it and the chain of command says let it go? Yes. Me? After that suspension? No."

Andrea frowned at him. "What does that have to do with Anna?"

Jimmy wanted to know, too. Was she the one the senator knocked up?

Taka eyed him, wary. "You should go. Plausible deniability."

He would, if he knew the techs could clean the audio from the meet up enough to hear. Otherwise, this might be his only chance to find out more. "Do you have knowledge that a crime was committed?"

"No."

"You've already broken your NDA and I've already heard that Fields broke investigative procedure by talking to you."

"I'll deny Fields said anything to me." Taka cut a hard sideways glance at Andrea. "If I have to, I'll say I channel ghosts."

Jimmy ran both hands through his hair and then plopped down on the kitchen chair at the end of the table. "I'll deny you said anything to me. I'll say I witnessed you channeling ghosts."

Taka stared at him. Jimmy stared back.

"That coffee still hot?" Taka finally said.

Jimmy stuck his pinky in it. "No."

Taka stalked over and snatched it up.

Stomping to the counter, he shoved it in the microwave and hit buttons.

Still trying to be pissed, Andrea sat down and sipped from her own cold coffee.

Taka jerked the zipper of his jacket down and then prepped his coffee before he turned back around.

He leaned against the counter and took a long swallow.

"Anna," Andrea prompted.

Jimmy didn't know where to look.

"Bulldog Bailey pimped her on an exclusive contract to Senator Sanderson. She came up pregnant after he died and wanted to keep the baby. Bulldog pressed Dewey for maintenance, child support, and hush money for both of them to keep her from going public."

"Dewey hated his dad," Andrea said.

Jimmy leaned back. And his mom's not his mom. And he was on Beaumont around midnight. "So Dewey killed her?"

"No," Taka said like Jimmy had disappointed him. "He told Bulldog no."

"My network says Candy King and half the city buys from Bulldog," Andrea said. "He could probably skywrite it over Charleston, add that the senator bought meth from him every day, and Dewey still wouldn't care."

"Still, it's more motive than you have."

Jimmy saw Taka's other suspect then. "And Dewey's answer gives Bulldog more motive than anyone."

Taka nodded. "Why keep feeding her with her meal ticket gone? A pregnancy and birth would take her out of profitability for months. An abortion would risk her needing medical care."

"And," Jimmy said. "If she was being trafficked, give her too much opportunity to talk."

Andrea crossed her arms like she was hugging herself. "Anna Lansing has no footprint at all online. She was a living ghost. I doubt that's even her name. What would he have done with the kids? Sold them on?"

Scott had said Bulldog was only an opportunistic pimp, but if he'd handled the logistics for Anna and the senator, he'd probably know who to approach about the kids. "That'd be a problem for CPD with Andrea as well. What did she do with the kids?"

Taka swirled the coffee in his cup. "Dewey went to see her. Tuesday night. After meeting Bulldog." He drained his mug and place it in the sink.

"Well," Jimmy said into the long silence. This could be it. What they finally nailed Dewey on. And now he had a second witness. He was going to chew Detweiler up one side and down the other for not answering his phone, even if he was off duty.

"What would he have done with the kids?" Andrea asked, her hand tightening on his.

"Nothing," Taka said. "He didn't kill Anna and he never saw any kids. She was fine when he left her. He'd have cut Bulldog out, but still made a deal with her."

Scott didn't go inside, and Taka was definitely not there. "You sure about that?"

"Certain. I think garage Skinny killed her, one way or another."

"But if you can't identify him, you're after turning this on Bulldog," Jimmy said. "And you'll throw Dewey under the bus as well if you have to, along with your career."

Taka had been avoiding looking at Andrea but now he did. The determination in the hardness of his face made his always large presence seem to fill the room. Jimmy couldn't look away. When he was thirteen, he saw his grandfather sitting at his bedridden wife's side after she'd had a stroke. At the time, the only word in his head was *devotion*. That's what he was seeing again right now. A spike of jealousy pierced Jimmy's heart.

Taka shrugged and addressed Andrea directly. "You didn't have a secret side hustle flipping women down the street from Louie's until things went sideways, did you?"

"No."

"Sell any kids this week?"

She rolled her eyes. "No."

Taka turned his disconcerting largeness to Jimmy. "I'm good."

It wasn't jealousy of Taka, Jimmy discovered in that moment. It was for that level of devotion. He wanted that one day. He wanted to give it, too.

Jimmy sighed. "You can't go to CPD until after they approach Andrea." Focused on Taka, he reached out blindly towards Andrea and was grateful when she took his hand. "*If* they approach Andrea. It'd all be so circumstantial, who knows if the DA will even let them try for her. You don't want to give away that you were tipped off whether anything comes of it or not."

Taka stuffed his hands back in his pockets and huffed his breath out. "Fields is Black, and I'm brown, so he'll be at the top of the list." His lips twisted and his gaze wandered to the window.

"If there's nothing to be done about that right now then," Andrea said, "I want to go ask Aaron who killed Lucy."

"Ten to one, it's Derek."

28

The deadbolt clunked over and Karie pulled Louie's door open to let them in. Her eyes were lit up with excitement. She pointed at one of the EMF meters sitting on a table by the bar laden down with her ghost-hunting devices. "Look!"

Jesus and the crew could probably hear her stage whisper in the kitchen.

The boy with the jacks stood entranced by the meter's red lights. He trailed his open hand through the air above it. The lights extinguished, one by one, the meter's distinctive squeal rising and falling with a sharp crackle. He reversed his motion and the lights lit up, until the meter pegged out at top volume.

"What is that?" Jimmy asked and Andrea realized that for how familiar she was becoming to Karie's investigations, Jimmy hadn't witnessed one.

"It's a ghost," Taka told him at the same time Karie said, "It's an electromagnetic field meter."

"It's both," Andrea said. "The boy with the jacks is doing it. He's standing and moving his hand over it."

Jimmy frowned at the meter on the table. "So he's putting out the same radiation as a leaky appliance or a power line?"

"Nobody knows, exactly," Karie said, keeping her voice low. "Probably not? A cell phone can set it off, but Andrea's proven a ghost can literally be on top of it and not set it off. They do it purposefully, so it's more that they can either produce electro-radiation at will, or they can manipulate the mechanics of the meter. Based on anecdotal evidence, I'd say the former. Some ghosts that are extremely active or emotional seem to stream an electromagnetic field. And people sensitive to EMF sometimes think their house is haunted because they feel off-kilter from stray EMF."

Jimmy's eyes got wider the whole time Karie was speaking. Andrea couldn't help but laugh. "Meet the real investigator, former skeptic, and science geek, Karie Wilson."

Karie gave a little bow.

The boy had noticed her laugh and stopped what he was doing. He was looking right at her. But then his attention drifted away. And then so did he.

"What's happening?" Taka said.

"He's gone."

"Is Aaron here?"

"No. This isn't a morning I'm usually here."

Karie trotted over to the table. "We got good activity in the dining room the other night on the spirit box. I think we should move in there. We'll be further from the window and the kitchen, too." She picked up the meter and hit a button. "Oh, look, he recorded a temperature drop, too. Nice."

Between them, there were enough hands to move everything in one go, with Karie chattering away about what each gadget did or measured. As she continued to answer Jimmy's questions, Taka muttered, "I'm getting more coffee," and left.

Andrea watched him go. There had to be a way that he could keep being a cop. She didn't want to be the cause of him losing his purpose in life. She already felt guilty for forcing him to help her. Although it's not like she'd courted this ability. At first, she hadn't minded. But now she shivered despite still wearing her jacket.

Karie fell silent. "Did it just get colder in here?"

Jimmy got that alert, bloodhound-on-the-trail expression that meant he was super interested.

When Karie turned it on, the spirit box crackled rapid-fire across the radio frequencies, making them all jump. A single word blasted out of it that Andrea couldn't understand. Then the air warmed back up and the odd tension in the room she hadn't noticed until it was gone lifted.

"That was interesting," Karie said. "See anything?"

"No."

Jimmy was staring at the speaker.

"I didn't catch it," Karie lamented. "It sounded like—"

"'Here,'" Jimmy said.

"That's what I thought, too," Karie said. "Good!"

She busied herself with making sure the recorder was on and then setting up one of the two video cameras she'd brought. Andrea sidled over to Jimmy. He considered her for a long moment, then leaned over and kissed her. "It's gonna be okay," he said quietly. "We'll sort it."

He looked at his watch and raised his voice so Karie could hear. "I've got meetings. And court this afternoon."

"Taka's officially at mine, today, so we'll be at the house after we get done here."

"I called this morning and took another personal day," Taka corrected, coming in with a laden tray and Aaron in his wake. "Seemed the least I could do for the department, considering."

Taka set the tray on an empty table. Aaron, looking whole in his drabs and knee boots, chambray shirt, and waist apron, stopped next to Andrea.

Jimmy thumped Taka on the shoulder and left.

"No trouble in the fields today," Aaron commented.

Andrea translated that to neither fake Derck nor the man in the Mercedes was around. "Good," she said.

"What?" Taka said over his shoulder.

"Could you pour me one, please?"

"Me, too!" Karie said, her head under the camera as she adjusted the tripod.

He turned his head, noting the camera placements. "This video stays with you, right?"

"Of course. That's stipulated in the release you signed."

"Good," he said, pouring milk in all three mugs.

"Aaron needs to clear a few things up," Aaron said.

The repeated phrase didn't bode well for answers to all the questions Andrea had for him.

She wanted to wait until Taka was settled and Karie was set up before trying to talk with Aaron. But she was also a little worried that Aaron would dissolve into shadow and take matters into his own hands before they were ready. "I've got Aaron here."

Taka froze midpour. After a second, he set the small pitcher down and turned around to look in her direction. Aaron wandered over to inspect the equipment. One of the EMF meters bleeped and then all three lit up, emitting their wavering squeal. Taka's head whipped around as he dropped into a defensive crouch.

The lights and noise died.

"It's okay, Taka," Andrea said.

Karie adjusted the camera she stood next to, making sure the table was in full view.

Taka relaxed a little but remained ready to move. Smiling, Aaron watched Taka flinch as he set just one of the meters off. He set off the second. On the third, Taka straightened all the way up, scowling. "Is it my imagination or is he really giving me a hard time?"

The steady crackle of static from the spirit box sped up then it spit out, "Hell-O."

Karie threw her a wild, gleeful grin.

"Kin-DREAD."

Karie chortled. "Was that 'kindred'? Did he say, 'kindred'?"

"He's looking at Taka."

"Soldier," Aaron said, the word absolutely exploding in Andrea's ears. Her hands flew up to cover them. "Brother."

"Too loud," Andrea yelled.

In two huge strides, Taka stood in front of her, his hands landing on hers. "What's wrong?"

"Aaron's voice. It's too loud."

Aaron peered around Taka's shoulder at her.

She lifted her hands a couple of inches from her ears, Taka moving his hands with hers.

"Say 'soldier' again."

"Soldier," Aaron said at a normal volume.

She lowered her hands. Taka stepped back a little. "Say 'brother.'"

Aaron placed his arm around Taka's shoulders. "Brother," he said at the same time Taka hesitantly did the same.

"Not you," Andrea said to Taka. "It's okay now. He was talking about you. Soldier. Brother."

Still looking worried, Taka said, "Okay."

"He's standing right next to you, to your right."

Eyebrows peaking together, Taka turned his head. Andrea wished she could take a picture of them almost nose to nose, Taka scared witless and Aaron grinning like he'd just won the lottery.

"Brother," Aaron boomed. Andrea slammed her hands back to her ears, hunching over and spinning away. "Jobah."

"Stop!" Andrea yelled.

Taka grabbed her, bundling her against his chest.

Karie's hand landed on her back. "What's happening?"

"His voice. It's like standing in front of a stage speaker at a heavy-metal concert."

"Oddly specific, but okay."

"I thought you said it was okay now," Taka said.

"It was, for a second."

"So it comes and goes?" Karie said.

The dining room door cracked open. Through the opening, Jesus said, "You need help?"

"We're okay, Jesus," Karie reassured him. "Just a technical issue."

The door shut with a firm click. Andrea patted Taka's chest and he let her go. Aaron stood behind him, looking mystified. "Is Jobah a name, Aaron?"

"Brother."

"It's fine now," Andrea said. "I don't get it."

Taka turned to look where she was looking.

"Aaron nee—"

Damn it. "Stop! Too loud!"

"Let's try something," Karie said. "Hey, Aaron, could you stay, but move somewhere else in the room? Don't look at him, Andrea."

Aaron's first couple of footfalls sounded like mortar rounds, and she could hear the rustle of his clothes underneath, but then they grew softer until they were just the normal fall of boot heels on hardwood. Andrea lowered her hands again.

"Don't look," Karie reminded her. "Taka, close your eyes."

Andrea could see he didn't want to. She took his hand, and he immediately threaded his fingers through hers. He closed his eyes.

"Okay, Andrea. Can you see Aaron?"

He'd not gone far. Just back to the equipment. "Yes."

"Ask Aaron something."

She blanked.

"Anything," Karie said.

"What do you need from me?"

"Find Ned. We're in the wrong place. Talk to Sally."

"We talked to Great-Aunt Sally."

"My Sally."

"How can I find her?"

"You already have."

"Great-Aunt Sally?"

Aaron shook his head. No. "My Sally."

"And I've already found her."

He nodded. Yes.

"Are you related to Louie?"

He glanced at the dining room doors but didn't answer.

She thought about answers and what he'd said to her in repeated phrases. They were all related to his past, weren't they? Maybe she needed to find a different way to ask. "Who was Whay to you?"

He smiled. "They said he could track boar in the pouring rain without a single hound."

"Who were Whay's children?"

"They are many."

Right. And he'd have had many sons, too. She squeezed Taka's hand. "What was Whay's wife's name?"

"Athena," Taka said.

But then she thought of a better way to phrase the question. "Who were the sons Whay gave rings to?"

That got Aaron's approval. "Boway, Kitch, Tooar, Jeer, Tendy, Tattio, Gowar."

"There were seven rings, not four!" She repeated all seven names out loud, so they'd be recorded. They'd spell them as they sounded and consult an expert later. Though, without knowing where Whay came from, authentic spelling might not be possible. On the other hand, maybe the names would give them a clue. She needed clues for the records search, too. "What were their slave names?"

He smiled. "Michael, Tom, Sam, George, Ben, Homer, Jacob."

Again, she repeated them out loud.

"Where are you buried?"

He just looked back at her. After a moment he put his hand on the spirit box. "Bo-BON-ez."

"I don't understand. Bones?"

He disappeared.

"He's—"

He stood directly in front of her. If she reached out, he might be able to give her more, but she shrank back instead, pressing herself against Taka's arm.

"You okay?" he murmured.

She nodded but then remembered his eyes were closed. "Yes."

"Find Ned." Aaron's tone had a note of urgency. "We're in the wrong place. Talk to Sally."

He flickered.

"Wait," she said. "Did the men in the garage kill Lucy?"

"I was a stockman, too," he said, much louder as he lost most of his form.

"Wait," she cried out. She couldn't think of a way to rephrase. Descriptions? "Who killed her?"

"Soldier."

Too loud. Too loud.

He was almost gone. She tried to grab him.

"Brother," he sighed somewhere inside her.

Boot on her chest.

Drowning.

She strikes out, arm and head above the river.

The riderless horse.

And then she's cold, walking down the back alley in the opposite direction of the van. The rough asphalt makes her wobbly in her heels. Her legs are bare and the hoodie not near warm enough. "Did you leave?" she asks Eddie.

"Yeah. One of the girls got a little roughed up. She's okay."

Tucked into the hoodie sleeve, the cold blade of the knife jiggles on her forearm as she walks. If she'd known, she could've walked out. Kept the cash and found a ride out to Candy's. But this is better. She can still do that but this time she won't have to try and convince the cops she's been kidnapped and forced into sex work.

Eddie will be dead.

She can find Derek one dark night and kill him, too.

The van. The knife. The blood. The call. Call your handler before I do, or you'll be flipping dime buys thirty a night.

The wail that comes out of Andrea hurts her throat, her ears. She didn't know crying could cause so much pain. She writhes on the floor, trying to get any breath at all through the storm of wailing sobs until she's exhausted. She can barely move. The burning pain of her shattered heart drives her to her feet.

She slides the van door back.

Sees the strap to her sling bag poking out from under the seat and jerks it out.

Jumps down, knife still in her hand.

An arm slides around her neck and pulls up. Her heels fall off.

She scrabbles at the hard muscles cutting off her breath, bag swinging.

She knows that scent.

He plucks the knife from her hand, then drives his fist into her stomach twice from behind. Traps her between his blows and his body. Three times. Four. Five. Six. Drops her to the ground. Stomps on her. Grunts when he kicks her in the face, the back. When she arches away, he stomps on her belly again.

He pants for breath.

Steps over her.

That scent. She knows that scent.
She pushes herself up.
So tired.
Gets her feet under her.
Stumbles down the alley.
Hits a dumpster. Falls.
Wall.
Hide.
Crawls.
Plunges down into the cold river.
Boot on her chest.
Andrea gasps.
Louie's. Taka's hand in hers.

29

S he didn't fall this time.

Taka didn't have time to do anything but swing around to face her, his hands on her upper arms, getting ready to support her. "Are you okay?"

"Lucy was beaten and kicked. Her stomach hurt really bad." She put her hands on her upper left abdomen. "And then it didn't."

With his bit of military medical and first-responder training, Taka didn't hesitate before he said, "Probably her spleen. You can bleed out fast. Did you see who did it?"

One thing she'd always admired about Taka was his ability to adjust with lightning speed to changing circumstances and not question the how of them. Like his acceptance of a power larger than himself, now that he'd decided to help her, the strange impossibility of it all wasn't something he had to wrap his head around.

"Yes, I think so." Andrea closed her eyes and concentrated on the memory. "She knew his scent, the cologne he was wearing. It's distinctive. It seems like I know it, too. That I almost know who wears it. She knew. She just couldn't—" She shook her head.

"She couldn't what?"

"She couldn't believe it."

"Was it Jodie King?"

"No."

"Is Aaron still here?"

"No." Andrea leaned into his hands. He let go and folded her in a huge hug instead.

"That was incredible," Karie said, and threw her arms around both of them. "And terrible. I was way scareder than I thought I'd be."

"It's scary," Andrea said under Taka's armpit.

"Way," Karie said.

"I need alcohol," Taka said.

The door creaked. "Whiskey?" Jesus asked.

"That'll do," Taka said as their cuddle puddle broke up.

A few minutes later they had a bottle and shot glasses in front of them and Karie was hooking the first of the two cameras to her laptop. Taka poured. He tipped his back, but Andrea dumped hers in her lukewarm coffee.

They watched the playback in real time.

"See," Karie said, pointing at Taka on the screen.

'No," Andrea said. "What?"

"When he knows where Aaron is, you say Aaron's too loud." She ran the video back and played the first part again. "We're all watching the meters and the spirit box. Did Aaron say anything before he used the spirit box?"

"No."

"The first time he speaks just to you, he's too loud, right?" She hit the fast-forward. "And here's where Taka closes his eyes." She zipped the video forward again. Missed the spot, ran it back. "And here, when you yell 'wait,' Taka opens his eyes. And here, see his head move to look where you're looking?"

"I'm not going into any more encounters with my eyes closed," Taka declared. "It was too hard not seeing what was happening."

Andrea thought about the boy on the bar playing jacks. Taka had looked over, hadn't he? Given her the side eye, shot a glance back at the bar. He'd known she was seeing something else. "I think you're right, Karie."

"I am, look." She ran it back again and they watched through it once more.

It was more obvious when Andrea knew what she was looking at and then— "Stop!"

Karie paused the video.

"Right after I say, 'who killed her.'" There'd been a shifting in the frame.

Karie played it again. "Oh my God."

She ran it back.

"There," Taka said.

Karie fiddled and managed after several tries to freeze the frame on the dark blur slipping between Andrea and Taka. "It's really there."

"It could just be the light," Taka said.

"I have people," Karie said. "If we ever wanted, they'd be able to isolate it and determine if that's a possibility."

"If we ever wanted," Andrea said.

Karie took a screenshot. "*Only* if we ever wanted."

"Which we don't want," Taka said.

"Correct," Karie said.

"That's Aaron," Andrea said. "That's him."

Taka poured himself another shot.

JIMMY FLIPPED through the night team's reports. Tuesday night. No report of a visit to a house on Beaumont Road. On the attached timeline, Detweiler was held up at a traffic light crossing Corridor G. Lost subject vehicle. Lost signal on undercover's tracking chip. Returned to surveillance at subject's home. Subject arrived home at 1:24 a.m. Wednesday.

Detweiler or his team had lost visual a handful of times throughout their surveillance. Scott's tracking chip, hidden in his shoe, glitched with the available reception across the dips and peaks of Charleston's terrain. But to lose both along with Scott being shut out of learning who Dewey had visited was a triple strike.

He walked down to his chief's office. Maddox was head down over a thick stack of folders. "Speak," he said when Jimmy hesitated in his doorway.

"A woman named Anna Lansing was found murdered at her home on Beaumont Road Wednesday morning. Scott reported that Dewey Sanderson went to a house on Beaumont Road Tuesday night around midnight, but the team can't confirm."

"Street number?"

"Scott didn't mention one. I didn't ask. I can ask for a description of the house in his written report."

"Do that."

"Should I inform CPD for their murder investigation?"

Maddox looked up. "Your UI witness a crime being committed?"

"No, sir."

"Did he hear the subject talking about having committed a crime?"

"No, sir."

"Let CPD run their investigation. If they start looking in Dewey's direction and it won't jeopardize our investigation, we can throw them some anonymous info."

"Yes, sir."

Maddox narrowed his eyes at Jimmy. "On your best behavior now?"

Jimmy smiled and shook the folder at him. "Just keeping you in the loop, sir."

"Fuck off, Jimmy. This paperwork ain't going to sign itself."

Jimmy headed for the team room. Andy came back on call at noon. Jimmy's gut said they had a come-to-Jesus meeting on today's agenda.

OUT ON THE street outside Louie's, Taka spotted a CPD cruiser down the way, tucked between a Lexus and a Honda Accord. Maybe Tamarin actually gave two hoots about finding the guy that drove the Mercedes. Or maybe he was serious about suspecting Andrea. He couldn't tell anymore which was more likely.

As they crossed to the garage, though, he also noticed a small, white pickup truck with a Clay County Public Works logo on the door and tailgate. That was interesting. A small part of him wanted to be paranoid. He shook it off.

"Here," he said, palming his keys off on Andrea. "I had three shots. I can't feel 'em, but you should drive."

He watched as they left the garage and Andrea drove them to the highway, blocking the side mirror enough for Andrea to snap at him once. No one followed them.

Not far from her turn-off to Greenbrier, Andrea said, "There's nothing we can do with the info we have on Lucy, is there?"

"Not right now."

"And we're going to wait to see if Tamarin's coming after me for Anna before you do anything rash."

"Yes," Taka said, his tone turning wary.

"And you cashed in a personal day."

"Yes."

She turned left at the bottom of the ramp instead of right, went under the overpass and got back on the highway towards town. "Then I need to go look at the stuff a client brought me at Waltham-Young."

"Are there going to be ghosts?"

"Never seen one there before," Andrea said.

"Now you've done it."

"If there is, I won't call your attention to it, that's for sure."

Taka leaned his head against the passenger window and closed his eyes. He wasn't buzzed, but the whiskey had relaxed him. He should've tried to sleep more.

A few minutes later they were jostling back over Charleston's surface streets, and he had to sit up. There was a small wedding party gathering on the steps of City Hall. Three or four cruisers sat out in the small lot around HQ's side of the building. The Kanawha River was running high and fast after the rain, the water dark and turbulent. A line of loaded coal barges ran the middle current. Andrea turned right, past the riverfront park, the double sails soaring over the steps of the amphitheater down to the river and the huge, sculptured paddlewheel arch blinding white against the grey day.

At Waltham-Young, Andrea drove through the front lot where she usually parked and around the left side of the building. He recognized the shape of the gardens visible on the opposite side of the building from Andrea's office. She drove down a wide ramp to reveal a below-ground series of large garage doors in the side of the building to their right and underground parking and detached storage to the left. There were four drive-in spaces and another four dock-high doors for semi-trailers. Taka had never known this area existed.

With Waltham-Young occupying a narrow spit of land between the river and Kanawha Boulevard near the Patrick Street Bridge, this was a bona fide engineering marvel. "Wow. How is this even possible here?"

"Rock,' Andrea said. "A huge amount of it between here and the river. They blasted this area out."

Taka snorted. "Very carefully."

"Very carefully," Andrea agreed.

She parked, led him to the pedestrian door next to the third drive-in garage on ground level, and swiped her card. The door clicked and she tugged it open. He caught the edge and held it for her. To his surprise, the interior was well-lit and undivided along the entire side, the other doors opening into the same massive space. A series of huge chain-link pens held pallets of material and equipment throughout the interior.

An unmanned security desk sat over to the left, midway down the wall. Andrea held her key card up in that direction for whatever camera they had running.

Andrea walked him deeper into the building past three of the larger pens before she stopped at one marked 14-17 R and again swiped her card. Pallets of boxes and assorted stuff—chairs, old desktop computers, ten or fifteen large plastic-wrapped neon signs—formed short rows. A couple of rows down, a college-aged girl—woman—he corrected himself, sat on two stacked pallets. The contents of an empty box lay all around her as she scribbled on a clipboard balanced on her knees, an open book in her lap.

"Hey, Megan," Andrea said.

The girl, Megan, jumped hard with a bit-off scream, dropping the clipboard. Her blue-gloved hands flew to her chest.

Andrea stopped hard. Her own hands going up to cover her mouth. "I'm so sorry, I didn't mean to scare you!"

Megan laughed. She pulled one wireless earbud out from under her hair and then the other. "I seriously didn't hear you. I'm so sorry."

"You're fine." She waved her hand between Taka and Megan. "Taka, Intern Megan. Megan, my friend Taka. Did Talisha show you what you needed?"

"She did," Megan said with cheerleader enthusiasm. "And she carried off a stack of records and a logbook from the first box I went through, too. Mr. Pederson held it out for last when we unloaded. He said it held the oldest documents related to the plantation. She was so excited."

Taka didn't know who Talisha was or why she'd be excited except that it's the kind of thing that would have Andrea beside herself, too. "This is your latest project?" he asked Andrea. "The one in Falling Waters?"

"Yes, Ivystone Farm. How far have you got?"

"This is the thirteenth box," Megan said. "It's so hard not to stop and read."

"And what have you found?"

"There's so much! Account books and crop rotations, lists of livestock. Seed catalogs. One box was all cookbooks, with a few notes tacked into them, like grocery lists and stray handwritten recipes. There were two really old ones, from 1809 and 1821. I already took them and the seed catalogs to Ms. Michaelsen. I hope that was okay."

"Perfect! Where's the stuff you've been bagging?"

"On the shelves?"

Taka smiled at the statement in a questioning tone, which reminded of all the girls in school growing up.

Taka followed Andrea to the last row in the section, where metal racking with plyboard shelves ran the length of the fence. She stopped at the three wide shelves with paper signs labeled "Pederson/Randy." They were chock full of bagged items from the boxes. "This is incredible," Andrea breathed. "I can't believe I'm missing this. It's a once-in-a-lifetime cache. Even if three-quarters of it is pure junk, it still tells the history of who lived there all these years. Just the cookbooks and seed catalogs will make this project worth the time, let alone what Talisha ran off with."

"You'd have had interns doing a lot of this anyway, right?"

Andrea nodded. "I guess."

"It's all being documented. You're the analyst of that stuff, right? The one who will write up a big picture from the details?"

"Yes."

Taka could see he wasn't swaying her much. "You still get to touch the stuff? Or is it off-limits now that it's been bagged?"

That got a smile.

"It's not evidence," she said. "It needs preserving if it's worth it, but yes, I can touch it."

He walked down to the middle of the racking and reached back into the center shelf. He ran his hand over the tops of the bags.

"Stop," she said.

He pulled up the bag, a paper lunch sack, and took it to her.

She held it a second before opening it, then leaped back, shaking her hand. Taka caught the bag midfall. "Mouse," she squeaked.

"Mouse? There was nothing there."

Her gaze darted and landed at the bottom of the racking. He turned to look. "Nothing there, Andrea."

She watched the nothing climb the racking.

He watched her.

Apparently, it disappeared back into the bags.

"Are you telling me mice have ghosts?" he asked.

She shook her head. "I don't know. Yes?" Her gaze darted from the shelf to the bag in his hand and back to the shelf. "What's in the bag?"

He opened it and pulled out a folded paper that he handed to Andrea.

"Megan's form," she said, finally focusing again.

Taka tipped the remaining item out into his hand. A small, sealed paper packet labeled Corn, F3West/1868/SH in faded ink.

"What is it?"

He held the packet up for her to see. "Feels like corn kernels."

"Megan," Andrea called out. She turned and hurried back down the row. "Megan! Have you run across anyone with the initials SH?"

"That's what Talisha was excited about," Megan said. "About 1830, the farm became known as Sutter's Hill."

"It was still Virginia then," Andrea said to herself. "That'd be too big a coincidence, though, just running across it."

"What are you muttering about?"

"Aaron or another slave named Aaron was purchased in 1851 from Live Oak by a person or a plantation with the initials SH. I've been looking since I found the sale and couldn't find one that fit. But the luck of Pederson just handing it to me, that it'd be this project—"

"When did you land it, before or after Aaron showed up"—he looked down at Megan, who was staring up at them from her pallet perch, wide eyed—"in Louie's family tree?"

"After."

There went his theory. She was still thinking though, staring vacantly at the pallet of neon signs. At least he could tell she wasn't looking at something not there.

"But the curtains for Berrylane," she said.

"The ones we were talking about that, uh, one night before Louie mentioned Aaron?"

She nodded. "Yes. They were from Ivystone. They were used as burial shrouds about the time of the Civil War, so Pederson had samples cut for Berrylane."

"Burial shrouds?"

Megan stood up. "I called about the burial! You were right about the forensic anthropologist in Charlotte. One of the soldiers was Union and one was Confederate. The third one was just a guy. They're sending hard copies of everything they have so far."

Andrea shook off her fog and looked up at him. "The *photo* of Aaron indicates Confederate affiliation, but slaves weren't soldiers for the Confederacy."

"Got it," he said.

"But still." She thrust her chin out at Megan. "Have you seen any mention of a Sally yet while trying not to read everything right away?"

Megan blushed. "A Sally Thorpe from a neighboring farm who raises sheep."

"Thank you, Megan. And you're doing a fantastic job. Could you let me know when the report from Charlotte arrives?"

"I will. Are you back?"

"No, not yet. I just wanted to see this for myself."

"If I come across another Sally, should I text you?"

"Please."

Back in the Yukon, again with Andrea at the wheel, Taka said, "I think it still fits. Aaron's here because of this Falling Waters project. The burial shrouds you handled."

"I can believe he's here because he's related to Louie, or I can believe he's here because of the fabric samples from Ivystone but I'm having a hard time believing both. And what the frig with the mouse?"

"But you didn't see any human ghosts."

"Not unless the security guy whistling 'Dixie Chicken' was one."

He opened his mouth and shut it again. No need to tell her he never saw a security guy or heard anyone else in the warehouse.

After a minute, Andrea began to hum 'Dixie Chicken' under her breath.

Taka reached over and turned the radio on.

30

They'd just made the turn from Patrick Street onto Washington when Andrea straightened. "Hey," she said. "Why don't we just call the smoke shop?"

"For what?"

"We'll just ask for Skinny's real name. Then you'll have a place to start trying to differentiate him from parking-garage Skinny."

"Just call and ask?"

"Yes. I doubt Candy answers the phone and I got the feeling Skinny's more of an absentee owner."

And the smoke shop a front for money laundering, now that he thought about it. "Jimmy said he's not an owner at all."

"Believe me," Andrea said. "He's in charge. Tattoo guy or another employee'll answer the phone."

"The guy with the Jesus hanging from his ears?"

"That tattoo is kind of amazing, isn't it? I'm pretty sure Christophe Arnold over at Tattoo Knight did it."

Taka laughed. While not having any tattoos herself, Andrea had become slightly obsessed with tattoo art in high school. She'd chosen the artist for his own work. "Just think, if you'd never gotten hooked by Angel's tattoo, you wouldn't be a tattoo connoisseur today."

"I probably wouldn't be an archivist today. Buffy fanfic sparked *all* the questions."

"So what questions do I ask to get Skinny's name?"

She slowed down while she thought, drafting the semi in front of them rather than going around it. "Let me give it first crack. If I can't get it, you can call again later and try."

He Googled the number on his own phone and hit call. It rang twice before a very mellow male voice answered. "Hi, my name is Andrea. I work with a Virginia Beach cigar distributer, Longfellow Smokes. Do you know of us?"

"No, I don't."

"A customer I have in West Virginia gave me the name of your store and said I should talk to a Skinny about buying product."

"I actually do a lot of the purchasing myself. Can you send me your product catalog?"

"I can. You can authorize purchase orders?"

"Yes, up to a certain amount."

"And your name?"

"Daniel Long."

"And Skinny's name?"

"Henry Conlon."

Taka clamped his mouth shut. Henry Conlon. The one he'd spoken to?

"I can use the address in South Charleston?"

"On D Street, yes. But could you send a second catalog to a different address?"

"Sure."

Daniel rattled off a PO box number in Clay, West Virginia, and the zip code.

Taka pumped his fists in the air. This is why he loved her. Why hadn't he thought of that? Just call and ask.

They disconnected and Taka whooped. "I can't believe you just did that."

She shrugged. "I can't believe we didn't think of it before."

"Okay," Taka said. "So, Candy King's stepdad Skinny is Henry Conlon. His business partner is Alexander Conlon. Skinny is

Alexander's uncle, so Harrison Conlon, Senator Sanderson's old friend —Alexander's dad—is Henry's brother?"

"Henry is a diminutive of Harrison."

"A what?" Taka said.

"A nickname of Harrison is Henry."

"Henry. Why not Harry?"

"That, too."

"You're saying Harrison and Henry could be the same person? That Alexander's dad is Candy King's stepdad?"

"Makes sense, right?"

"I was told Skinny was Xander Conlon's uncle, not his dad."

Andrea turned the radio off. "Maybe you were told wrong. Or lied to. Not like there'd be two brothers with basically the same name."

"George Foreman named all his sons George Edward."

"True. Cousins?"

"Jimmy said Harrison didn't own any property in his own name, right?"

At Andrea's nod, Taka continued feeling his way through the idea. "The house I visited was owned solely by his wife. But the Henry I met was cancer-eaten and appeared bedridden." He thought about Tina, at the Conlon farm, and the missing kids and the guys in the parking garage talking about wanting Eddie and "the girls" buried deep. "It doesn't seem likely he could be in charge of a multistate human trafficking ring."

Andrea made the next turn. "I don't know. Strength of will. Training Alexander and Candy up to obey him. Haven't some gangs— oh! Hasn't the mob been controlled by old guys from prison cells?" She took the ramp onto the highway.

"Let's go see him."

"You can't, Taka. You're off the case."

"He doesn't know that. And from what Fields said, they have nothing to go on. They have to know by now his nickname is Skinny, but they have my report dismissing him and the fact that the renter of the van was an older woman. Since they couldn't corroborate our story, they have nothing to ask him."

"Maybe they're trying to link him to the dead guy, Eddie."

At this point, what did it matter? He texted Fields on the burner number.

Found the gold Mercedes?

Fields must have been at lunch because the reply came immediately. *No.*

Have you linked Henry Conlon to van driver Eddie?

1) Stay out of it, Fields returned. *2) No.*

Taka decided to push it. *To Anna Lansing?*

1) Seriously. Stay out of it. 2) No. 3) She went to Marshall at the same time as Andrea. They had two classes together. She went by a different name.

Damn.

JIMMY HIT print on his report and sat back. Just after noon. Nina spun her chair away from her computer screen. "You done?"

"Yeah, on that one. Court at one."

"Remember asking what I could dig up on a Skinny related to the Candy King?"

"Yeah?"

"Remember that Harrison Conlon went down for distribution, but a pimping charge was dropped?"

"Yeah?" Jimmy got up and collected his report.

"His older brother, Laurent, took the hit on that one, in '74. And pedophilia after his fifteen-year-old wife took issue with him sleeping with her thirteen-year-old sister."

Good for her. "And where is Laurent now?"

"Went off a bridge in Jersey in '80."

He pounded a staple into the corner of the report and slid it into a folder. "Suicide?"

"Winter car wreck. Body never recovered."

"And I want to know this why?"

"His nickname was Skinny."

"HEAR ME OUT," Taka said. "I need you to go east on 64. It's stupid, but you really are it for them on Anna Lansing. Candy's managed to wiggle his way out. Unless we come clean on the ghosts, there's no way to pull him back in on Lucy Garcia to help figure out who killed her. If you tell them what you know, they'll assume you lied from the start, and they'll use that against you."

"What can we do at Skinny's?"

"See what we can see. He's the only lead we have. If we can, we ask some questions of the neighbors. I won't use my badge."

"But why, Taka? What good will it do?"

"If we see the Mercedes, we'll document it. Maybe somebody will recognize that guy's description or will have seen the van. Christ, Andrea, I think I got that kid at Enterprise killed by tipping them to the fact the name Conlon was on the paperwork. If we see Skinny's wife, maybe we can convince her to talk to us."

Obviously, he was going to blow a gasket if she took him home. Once he knew she was giving in, she could convince him to stay in the car. Otherwise, he really would be throwing his career away. "Okay. But we're just taking a look. Nothing else."

"It's in Summersville. Off 19, just over the lake."

He got busy on his phone. She drove. They had spent many hours in and around Summersville, on the lake, which was a wider portion of the Gauley River, and hiking and climbing in the woods. Dewey owned a home out here now, according to Jimmy.

Once they crossed the river, Taka directed her to an informal subdivision on wooded, terraced lots. A battered wooden sign announced it as Longleaf Acres. A couple of winding streets in, Taka pointed out the house as she cruised by it. Short drive. One-story wood frame with a brick addition on a double lot. Detached garage.

They doubled back on an adjacent street uphill from Henry Conlon.

"That house for sale," Taka said.

She pulled into the drive and stopped. He got out, looked around, and then sauntered to a window and peeked in. Exaggerated checking his watch by holding his arm up, elbow high, as if they were waiting on a tardy Realtor. Walked back to the car and down to the garage, peering into the back yard. Came back to the truck.

"Good view of the drive and front. If you pull down like you're pulling into the garage, we'll be able to watch the house and still see if someone's coming to check on us."

Glad he wasn't leaping into action to talk to people or knocking on Skinny's door, Andrea pulled around and parked. Her experience as a native had been that as long as you weren't parked on their curb or blatantly carrying furniture and TVs out the door, neighbors might be watching, like Dr. Huntley, but they wouldn't come asking why you were there.

Taka pulled his back door open and rummaged around. "Lunch?"

"Sure."

He closed the door and got back in up front with bottles of water and granola bars. Andrea cracked the windows open. They watched Skinny's house while they ate. An hour later, Andrea was bored and wishing she hadn't left her laptop at home. She cranked the Yukon up and ran the heat for a few minutes. It was another hour before a white Lexus arrived at Skinny's place. And, of course, the neighbor across from where they'd parked also pulled in. She gave them a long, hard look.

"It's Tina, the woman I saw at Alexander Conlon's," Taka said.

Andrea lifted a hand at the woman across the street. She lifted a hand in return and went inside. "Neighbor just clocked us so we only have as long as a reasonable couple would wait for a realtor."

"I'm working on what I could say if I go knock on Skinny's door. Maybe he's not parking-garage Skinny."

"But if he is, you don't want to tip him off that you know he is."

"Maybe I do. Maybe I just up and ask about Derek and Mercedes boy."

"And then maybe he shoots you and I drive home alone."

He didn't look at her.

A few minutes later, he said, "I was thinking I'd ask about Anna Lansing. In reference to Candy. Maybe I ask if he knows an Eddie."

"Maybe Tamarin already followed up."

"We go back to ask people the same or different questions all the time. At least he knows me already."

"Maybe we sit here another half-hour or so and then decide."

Evidently someone lit a fire. Smoke drifted from the chimney.

At fifteen minutes in, Sweet Joe texted: *Tamarin wanted you to come answer more questions tonight, I told him we'd be there Monday at ten am. That okay?*

She turned her phone so Taka could read it.

She couldn't read him and didn't even know what to call the dread anxiety that curled up her gut. She wanted to call her mom. The ripple of grief that thought brought with it was at least familiar. She imagined for a second the earful her momma would have given Pete Tamarin by now.

Yes, she texted back.

At thirty-five minutes, Andrea started the Yukon.

"I think we can park down the street from them," Taka said. "Somewhere we can still see the drive."

Andrea pulled out of the driveway nose first. "Should I go back the way we came or does this road loop around?"

"It loops."

She decided to loop, check out the rest of the street.

Taka sat tense and uneasy in the passenger seat. "I'm gonna go talk to him. We could sit here for days otherwise."

"Maybe we should do that. We could park across the road and just watch for who goes in and out of the subdivision. See if we get lucky. Wait until we find out if they're going to really name me as a suspect. If they don't, you go back to work, you keep collecting info, I help under the radar, eventually you stop these guys."

"And if they do take you in?"

"You can come back out here, go crazy with all the questions."

She pulled up to the stop sign. Right, they were back out on 19. Left, back to Skinny's. A light-blue Ram dually with window tinting passed by, four men inside. Taka scowled. He leaned forward to watch it go down the street. "I think that was Bulldog Bailey. Give it a minute."

Andrea checked her rearview. No one.

"Let's try and park down from the house somewhere."

As Andrea pulled out, the white Lexus exited Skinny's driveway and came right at them. There was nowhere to go. Tina spotted Taka, her head turning as they passed each other. There was nothing to do about it.

"It's okay," Taka said. "I'd say given Bulldog Bailey's presence, the likelihood of smoke-shop Skinny and parking-garage Skinny being the same Skinny have just skyrocketed, but as far as he knows, I'm just trying to figure out who rented the van and maybe who killed Eddie."

"Okay."

"So pull into the drive."

She hit the brake instead. A car coming up behind them honked. She pulled to the side of the road, and it whooshed by, the driver glaring over at her. "What are you going to do?"

"Go follow-up about the van and Eddie. I'll record the old man. You can tell me if he sounds like the man you heard."

"Taka."

"Better that than Tina telling them I was lurking. I can control their perception of me. And I can see if that was really Bailey."

"This is really dangerous."

"Andrea. Pete Tamarin is trying to make a circumstantial case that you were involved with Lucy Garcia and Anna Lansing and killed Anna. We have to hand him another possibility. Something they can follow-up on. Since they don't have a leg to stand on with any further investigation in this direction, we're on our own. I've got this."

Her head hurt trying to think around corners the last few days. Andrea pressed the heels of her hands to her eyes. She could drive them home and sit in her house playing cat-and-mouse information games with anonymous information brokers and hope for the best by Monday. Or she could let Taka poke the bear. Either choice seemed likely to land them both in jail. She either trusted him or she didn't. And hadn't she told him just days ago she trusted him?

She pulled back into the street, past the next four houses, and into Skinny's driveway.

31

S kinny's wife opened the door. Possibly Candy King's mom if they'd gotten the relationships correct.

"Hi, ma'am, I'm Detective William Taka, with Charleston Police Department?"

"I remember. You came about the van," she said. "We had another fellow down here yesterday morning. Oscar, I think his name was."

The rookie in investigations. Tamarin was good at his job. It was smart to re-document the contact after Taka became part of the investigation. "Yes, ma'am. I'm sorry to bother you again. It helps sometimes when we have a rapidly changing situation to revisit people."

"You mean like my son knowing those women."

"Yes, ma'am."

"The young man said Jodie wasn't in any trouble."

"No, ma'am. May I come in?"

"My husband has visitors right now."

"Yes, ma'am."

She gestured him back and stepped outside with him. "My husband had nothing to do with the van. And we never met those women. What more could you possibly have to ask him?"

Is he running a sex trafficking ring? Taka took out his phone and tapped to his photo roll. "I just wanted to show you both a photo. It's come to our attention that the women in question may have been using different names. Maybe you had a conversation with one of them if you saw them with Candy?"

"Candy," she said with disgust. "Jodie picked that name up in high school and I've never cared for it."

He held up Lucy Garcia's photo.

She didn't look at it.

"Candy hasn't brought a girl around since senior prom. I'm sorry I can't help you."

"We ID'ed the driver of the van. His name was Eddie."

Her lips tightened. She shook her head. "We can't help."

"You can't or you won't?"

"I don't like your tone, Officer. My husband had nothing to do with any of it."

"What about you? Do you know anything about the van or Eddie?"

She sighed like she was disappointed in him and crossed her arms.

"Okay, you don't know anything about that."

"We don't."

"Your husband's name is Henry, correct?"

"Yes."

"Could you confirm his legal name is Harrison?"

That threw her, but he couldn't tell if it was surprise or fear. "Of course, he's Harrison. Who else would he be?"

And that was not the answer he was expecting.

"I'm going to have to ask you to leave. I'll be calling your supervisor to complain about harassment."

Ten to one she wouldn't expose herself by calling. "That's fine, ma'am." He pocketed his phone and fished a business card out of his money clip.

She watched him climb back in the Yukon.

Andrea backed down the driveway and headed back to Highway 19.

"She's the weak link," he said. "I can give Fields that much. If he can crack her on Eddie, the rest of what we heard might surface."

"I filmed you speaking with her. And took another video of the blue truck with the house visible."

"Thank you. Maybe they can get a back door in through Bulldog. If we park in the Pirate's Cove lot, we should be able to see when he leaves. Confirm it's him."

"We should go. You can text Fields the video and he can check the plate."

"Just pull over. Let me make my notes on my conversation with Linda Conlon and watch the videos. Bulldog's who I'm giving them if they come after you, I want to make sure it's him before I send anything. If he comes by while we're still here, I can note how long they met for, which will help later. If they don't, we'll go home, okay?"

"I thought about sending the plate to Jimmy."

"But you don't want him getting into any more trouble. I get it."

"I never wanted you in trouble either."

"I know." And he did. It wasn't her fault. Even if he'd never shot Zach Taylor, he'd have had to deal with her ghost problem. It was always going to be complicated. And with a higher current shoot rate at CPD than anyone besides Ronnie Horton, his career was blazing out anyway. Might as well go out with a bang, as long as it freed Andrea up as well.

Andrea crossed the highway and turned right into the dirt lot. Two cars, both empty.

"You ever think about Sarah Mack?" she said.

Sarah Mack was the girl Bulldog helped. In eighth grade, she was diagnosed with some rare cancer. All of them figured "rare" was meant as an adult reassurance that they didn't need to lay awake at night wondering if they had cancer, too, even though they all knew someone with lung cancer from the mines.

"Yeah."

What Andrea was really asking was, do you remember how Bulldog supplied Sarah Mack so she could make it through the day. He remembered. He also remembered the back of Scott's head as he sighted down the rifle scope aimed at Bulldog's head on Dewey's warehouse deck because Dewey thought Bulldog was capable of murder. And that Bulldog had added pimping to his drug dealing at some point and now Anna Lansing was dead.

On his phone, he wrote down everything as closely as he could recall while Andrea watched for the blue truck. When he finished, he told her how Linda didn't give him a yes or a no when he asked her to confirm Skinny's legal name as Harrison. "She asked who else he'd be. Which, I get it, we live in West Virginia where no one can say anything straight up, but still. It was odd."

"And then she asked you to leave."

"Yeah."

He watched the videos. He should've thought of making them himself, but between the swirl of discovering Aaron and Lucy Garcia's backgrounds, figuring out where Anna Lansing fit in, the confusing crossover of Scotty and Dewey and frigging Bulldog into all of it, and plain trying to just figure out who was who, his head was done in.

"I've been trying to figure out Aaron's background since October," Andrea suddenly said. "But nothing came together until he found Lucy Garcia in the alley. And we only found out who she was because I went to see Glenn at the VFW about the pants Aaron wears. Oh!" She threw her hands in the air. "Miss Ava said Lucy's name started with a 'K' sound. But Lucy meant Candy, didn't she? Candy King."

"I saw another guy in a photo with them at the VFW," Taka said. "Tripp."

"Tripp went to the smoke shop with us. I gave his name to Pete. He seemed really sad when Glenn told him she'd had drug issues. I think he was sweet on her."

Stalling for time, Taka hit his Instagram app and punched Candy back in. "Remember Tripp's last name?"

"No. I told Tamarin all about going to the VFW and the smoke shop, though."

"I know he talked to the reenactor," Taka said and then wished he hadn't. But Andrea let it go.

He scrolled down through Candy's thousands of followers. No Tripp outright. He started tapping on the military-sounding usernames.

"Almost done?" Andrea said.

"Yeah, couple more minutes."

Rifleman56, bullit1998, camo_stan. Click. Scroll. Click. Scroll. All these people needed help organizing their posts. They were so random. Not that he could say much. He hadn't posted to his Instagram in six months at least. The pics he posted were at least consistent though. Fish and climbing ropes and trees. On the seventeenth try: ghillie360.

Trucks and muddy ATV trails and lots of different dark-haired women. In bars. In trucks. Mud-spattered and laughing with bottles of beer in their hands. No last names, no tags, no usernames, no repeats. A year ago, Lucy Garcia. A dozen photos.

Andrea tapped his arm with the back of her hand and then pointed at the road. "There's the truck."

Taka glanced up at the blue dually and went back to his notes. He entered the time. A thirty-six-minute meeting between a known drug dealer and sometime pimp and a smoke shop owner with a sex trafficking son and drug-dealing stepson. One guess as to what the meeting had entailed.

Andrea shot an exasperated look at him, started the Yukon, and pulled back out across the four-lane highway. Mirroring his line of thought, she said, "Bulldog pimped Anna Lansing to Senator Sanderson. He's Candy's supplier, so Anna didn't need Candy to provide drugs. Why was Candy familiar enough with her to go to her house?"

"It's a small world. Maybe they knew each other growing up. Or met at the Coliseum. Maybe Candy was horning in, pushing his boundaries. Maybe Bulldog and Skinny have a working relationship. No way to know unless we ask."

"Do you think Pete asked?"

"It doesn't matter if he did or not. Candy's out of the fire."

"Or he thinks he is. You said going after me could be a ploy."

"If it started that way, it's gone too far. Pete's going to have to play you out before he can reverse tracks unless we can stop him cold."

She went back to thinking.

He tried not to urge her to speed up.

Bulldog would definitely be keeping an eye out for the Yukon. How he reacted would affect every decision Taka and Andrea made from here on. He watched the truck's tail lights in the right lane for a couple of miles.

Then the couple of cars between them pulled into the left lane. The truck was slowing. Andrea slowed down, too.

"It's okay," Taka said. "Drive on up behind them."

She set her jaw but did as he said.

Before Mount Nebo, the guardrails gave way to a wider paved shoulder with terraced rock ledges beyond. Taka thought Bulldog would use the shoulder, but a nearly hidden road appeared, and Bulldog turned right.

A small white utility truck and a red sedan passed by them in the left lane.

Taka thought Andrea would drive by, but she sighed hard, hit the brakes, and turned in, too. It was just a short wide drive to a locked pipe gate. But they were off the road. Bulldog had let them block him in.

The blue truck idled.

Taka couldn't see anything much through the tinted rear window.

Then the engine shut off.

"Shut it off," Taka said.

Andrea turned the truck off. She reached back and pulled her FN nine-millimeter from the holster at her lower back and placed it on the seat beside her.

He pulled his own gun and set it down then got out and closed the door. He walked to the front of the Yukon with his jacket in his hand and turned a little circle to show he wasn't armed. He pulled the jacket on and then leaned back against the warm hood. The driver and passenger doors of the truck opened, but only the driver got out.

Bulldog came and leaned on the hood beside Taka.

The day was fading, and the air felt wet. It was colder already than when he'd been standing outside at Skinny's. It'd be full dark within the hour. His phone vibrated in his jacket pocket. It rang inside the Yukon. He thumbed the home button to mute it.

"Give me your phone," Bulldog said.

Taka pulled it out and handed it to him.

He turned it off. Set it on the hood. Took his own out and did the same. "Nothing I say goes anywhere with my name on it."

"Agreed," Taka said.

"Skinny's all up in my grill over that girl," Bulldog said.

"Heard she was your contract to the senator."

"You still in with Dewey then?"

Taka shrugged.

"She's a local girl. She and I known each other a long time. She should've been in my stable all along."

"Skinny owned her?"

"Technically."

"He owned the senator's contract?"

"Technically. But she didn't want to get shuttled out of town on Skinny's party circuit. She got spoiled on exclusive. She still got appeal. I said I'd buy Skinny out, she got to work the deal, though."

The click of the pieces falling together felt good. Smoke-shop Skinny was parking-garage Skinny. If Bulldog was buying Skinny out, what went wrong? "Then she told you she was pregnant."

"Right there. You still Dewey's. I knew it."

Taka wanted to walk away. He made himself stay still. Didn't shift his slouch against the hood. Kept his mouth shut.

"She wanted to keep it," Bulldog said. "Fine. But that complicates things. Her earnings go down. I gotta use a girl to watch the kid. I wasn't gonna pay the man what he wanted when I wasn't going to get full use of her for the next few years and then she be older."

Taka tamped down the churn of outrage trying to rise inside him. "So you went to Dewey to see if you could shake the difference out of him."

"Figured it couldn't hurt."

"But what—Skinny found out?"

"I got a rat somewhere. I'm putting poison down now."

"Why tell me?"

"Everybody know you on thin ice. I'm pretty damn certain you not allowed to be talking to nobody. Especially Skinny. Everybody know your girl there's in Candy's sights 'cause Dewey embarrassed him in front of her. And Skinny made sure he clear of that mess. You want her off the hook, you can"—he held up one finger—"throw me under the bus 'cause I went to Dewey, and he said no." He held up a second finger. "Or you can throw Dewey under the bus 'cause he don't want no baby brother messing up his life. We both know you ain't throwing Dewey under the bus."

"So why shouldn't I toss you under?"

"I didn't kill her."

"What happened to the kids?"

"They gone."

"Skinny off them or move them?"

"Those kids thousands of dollars in his pocket. He moved them. They on the circuit now. I can't tell you nothing about them."

"Anna Lansing?"

"I did not kill her," he said again, enunciating every syllable. "I wasn't gonna buy her, though. She knew that. Skinny knew that. Skinny has this thing about loyalty. Guess we all do, really, but he's...over the top."

Taka heard the boy at Conlon's farm in his ear, *I'm unknockable.* Street slang for loyal. "Skinny didn't kill her."

"Naw. He put his old bottom bitch on it though. Now, *she's* unknockable."

"He tell you that?"

Bulldog tsked better than a teenage girl and rolled his eyes. "I'm not answering that."

"His old bottom bitch?"

"You were talking to her. She don't allow other wifeys in the house no more, and she don't recruit them, but she was a legend. Brought Anna in. Took her out."

Linda Conlon.

Unknockable enough for Skinny to put property in her name. Andrea had been right about Skinny training his sons up to obey him. He'd had lots of practice. The few details Taka knew made sense. Anna opened the door to her murderer. She was shot point-blank in the foyer. There was no attempt to move her. No cleanup. The door handle was wiped clean. He didn't know the setup of the house, but the kids would be more trusting with a woman, even if she was a stranger to them.

And she might not have been.

An older woman, acting like a grandma.

Plaques in the front hall.

Christmas Charity Drive. Food Bank Volunteer. Big Brother, Big Sister.

Taka suppressed a shudder. "She still recruits vulnerable kids."

Bulldog side-eyed him. "Bro."

"You know an Eddie who works for Skinny or a heavyset guy who drives a gold Mercedes?"

"Naw. Most of his crew on auto these days. They blow through town a few weeks at a time."

But there was still one thing he didn't get. "What was with Candy and Anna?"

"Trouble, that's what. Candy like sampling, but he kept going back to that well. Maybe that baby his. Just another reason for his mama to put that particular wifey down."

A tiny drop of wet hit Taka's cheek. And then his hand. Bulldog jerked his hoodie up over his ball cap.

"You're hoping we take Skinny and his sons down."

"Xander's okay. He cuts me in. His parties are a bit above my network grade if you know what I mean. But yeah, Candy cramping my territory. And Skinny has him sending girls out on the street when they in town. Drawing a bit too much attention. Hurting the locals."

"You afraid of him?"

"I deserved a beat down for Anna."

That didn't answer his question, but Taka could read between the lines. Bulldog couldn't touch Skinny. And at any time, Skinny could let Candy off his leash, push Bulldog out altogether.

"I'll see what I can do."

"Tell Andrea we even." Bulldog turned, scooped his rain-dotted phone up, and walked off.

32

O ut on the highway, wipers struggling against the misty fall that screamed snow on the way, Taka said, "What'd you ever do for Bulldog?"

"I did some economics research for him back in high school."

"You taught him business principles. You're the reason he stays too low-key to catch out."

"I didn't know at the time that he was a drug lord in the making," she said, her voice tight, like it got before she started crying. It cracked as she said, "I didn't know he'd hurt people."

"If you ask him, he'd say he's helping more people than he's hurting."

"Every villain thinks he's a hero."

"Librarian wisdom?"

"I heard it at a conference years ago. I think about it a lot."

The wipers squeaked across the windshield.

"So, what'd he say?"

"A lot more than I expected."

His phone rang across the Bluetooth. "Hang on."

West Virginia number. The same he'd missed before.

He thumbed it open. "Detective William Taka."

Silence.

"Hello?"

"It's Tina," a woman whispered into the phone. "You gave me your card a couple of days ago."

"I remember."

Andrea met his gaze.

"I saw you today and I just thought—you said I could call you, if—" She caught her breath and held it.

"Are you in immediate danger?"

"No. He's with the boy. He'll be awhile."

"I can have someone to you in a few minutes. Are you at the house?"

"No, no. I don't want anyone else. Can you come get me?" She started to cry. "Please?"

"It'd be safer for all of us if I call and have a sheriff's deputy come get you."

"I don't want him to know, please, he might hurt him. He has a gun," she whispered, her words so soft and jagged, he could barely understand her. "Don't send anyone, please. Please. I can sneak out. I'll be in the barn. You can take me anywhere. You can take me to the sheriff's, I'll tell you anything, and you can come back later, please. But you just come now. I'll be in the barn. Don't let him find me there, please."

She hung up.

He didn't dare call her back. And now that it registered, what did she mean by *he's with the boy*?

"Where is she?"

"Alexander Conlon's place in Hico has a boy and a barn. That's where I talked to her."

"You can't go. That's not Kanawha County, is it?"

"It's Fayette," he said. "I don't think it matters, though. She's asking me to personally come get her."

"But if Conlon interferes?"

"I can do a citizen's arrest, sort the details later."

"We should call nine-one-one."

They were coming up on Mount Lookout already, but Conlon's

house was on a long rural route outside Hico. Emergency vehicles would still get to her faster than he could. On the other hand, she wasn't in immediate danger and thought the boy would be if the sheriff's office showed up with sirens blasting in marked cars.

Could he get Tamarin on board to talk to Fayette County and make a plan to go in quiet? How long would that take? Shit, what was the address? Something Ridge Road. He'd made his notes on paper, not his phone. He Googled Alexander Conlon, found the entertainment company. No home address. Tried Spokeo, no home address. Call Tamarin? Fields?

"Taka?"

"I'm trying to find the address to call it in."

He tried a couple of other websites and then dialed CPD. "It's Detective Taka, I need an address. Alexander Conlon of Hico."

"Checking. I'm sorry, Detective. I'm not authorized to give you that address."

"Could I speak to Detective Tamarin?"

Voicemail.

He hung up and tried again. "This is Detective Taka. I need to speak to Detective Tamarin now. It's urgent."

"He's unavailable, Detective. Is there someone else I can connect you to?"

"Detective Fields. Not his voicemail."

"He's still in court. I can take a message."

"Lieutenant Horton?"

"He's in a county meeting and can't be disturbed."

Taka hung up.

"Map?" Andrea said.

"I can get us there, but I don't remember the street address. We'll get her and then take her to the Sheriff's Office. They can sort what needs doing and get her to a shelter."

"And you can ask her about Skinny," Andrea said, a hint of accusation in her voice

"You just heard me try to get help from CPD. Bulldog confirmed the Conlons are trafficking. You wanted one of his people to talk to you. Now's your chance."

"Maybe once the deputies get her out of there, we can talk to her."

"There's nothing to tell them. She's not in immediate danger. I talked to her before. If they get there first, I'm pretty sure she'll deny anything's wrong, and the nine-one-one call will come back on me in a bad way."

"Look at a map."

He pulled up a map of Hico. He narrowed the possibilities down to two roads off the loop of Arrowwood Creek, both named something Ridge Road. He couldn't tell on his phone. It started with a D. He zoomed in as far as he could. Dotson Ridge sounded right. He racked his brain for the road name off that—it started with an M—but there were no names on the smaller roads on the map. "Dotson Ridge runs for two or three miles. I don't know the name off that or the number." He wished he were driving.

Andrea's hands were clenched so hard on the wheel, her tendons were standing out in her wrists. The wipers squeaked.

"We can't just leave her there after she's asked for help." He whipped his head around, squinting back at the road they just passed. "Turn around."

Andrea still didn't look at him, but she checked her mirrors, stepped on the brake, and U-turned across the grass median.

As dusk fell, it took three tries to get the right road off Dotson Ridge, the barbed-wire fence, the two small houses backed to the steep hillside before reaching Conlon's farm. The porch lights were on, emitting a warm glow.

"Turn off the headlights."

They drove past. Taka had been half-expecting to see the gold Mercedes, but there was only the new Chevy, the old Kia, and the Eldorado.

Tina had implied Conlon was home, but maybe he'd taken the boy elsewhere. Except there'd be no need for her to escape to the barn then. Maybe Xander Conlon had been home the day Taka had come knocking?

One of the hounds leapt up and chased them down the length of the yard. Taka hoped the road led to other houses, but it ended around the next curve, about a hundred yards on, at a chained gate over another cattle guard. A shallow stand of mixed hardwood trees on either side gave way to a fog-shrouded rolling field of tall grass. The tight rain fell in a near-invisible curtain through the dusk. A couple of cows flicked their tails, grazing on the side of the closest hill.

Andrea swung around to face back the way they came and shut the engine off.

Behind them, the dog bayed twice more, deep and mournful, and then fell silent.

He opened the Yukon's door, the cold a slap after the warmth of the ride. He jerked his jacket back on. "If anyone drives up out of that field or comes down the road here before I get back, just wave your phone at them and go. I'll call you and we'll figure out meeting up."

Her lips a thin straight line, she nodded.

She was rarely outright mad at him. Her curt nod hurt.

He closed the door as quietly as he could.

ANDREA WATCHED Taka skirt the dark tree line leading to the house, heart in her throat.

He disappeared around the uphill curve in the crumbling asphalt road. It would take a few minutes for him to get by the dogs. He'd been there before, so they must've been okay, or he'd have said something.

Maybe.

She turned the Yukon's key just far enough for the battery and rolled the front windows down.

Nothing.

She relaxed her fingers. They were stiff from gripping the wheel so hard for so long. The woods were silent. She checked the side mirror. She could see one cow's back, the bony rise of its hips between ribbons of mist.

She'd only just started pulling in her information. And yes, it would take time they didn't have, but if this went wrong, Taka wouldn't have choices when it came to ending his career. If they'd only gone home instead of to Waltham-Young, maybe she'd have more answers by now.

No movement on the road.

Then again, what would more answers matter?

Taka would never ignore someone in need.

And the one sure answer she already had was that Xander Conlon took advantage of vulnerable people in the worst way possible, encouraging them to sacrifice their health and mental well-being as drugged-up toys to be tossed away when they were no longer wanted.

Maybe this Tina was their silver lining.

Taka could help her even if he couldn't help himself.

And maybe clear Andrea of any suspicion if Skinny was the one who ordered Anna Lansing's death and moved the kids.

He'd be exploding his career on his own terms.

Side-view mirror. A flock of small dark birds, darker than the falling night, exploded from the grass.

"Stay still," a hard male voice commanded from the passenger window.

Her heart thumped, forcing the breath from her lungs.

"Look at me."

She turned her head, very slowly. The hole at the barrel end of the handgun pointed at her was very big. Her gut filled with liquid ice. She had to consciously tighten her muscles to make sure everything stayed inside.

The hand holding it was large and white and steady.

Taupe wool covered the arm attached to the hand.

It became a dress coat over a torso in a grey suit and striped tie.

The gold Mercedes guy stared back at her when she reached his face.

Someone opened her door. She flinched but didn't look away.

She saw his mouth moving, but the words came from far away.

"Leave the keys. Get out."

Get out?

"Get out," he repeated. "Now."

She didn't fall out only because her muscles were bricks, stiff and heavy. Her jaw hurt, but she couldn't unclench it.

The second man was a boy.

Maybe twelve or thirteen.

He seemed sure of his grip on his gun. Casual, even.

Mercedes came around the front of the Yukon. "Pat her down."

The boy found her gun right away. He pulled it from the SuperSlide and put it on the front seat of the Yukon. Took the pocketknife and cash from her front pocket and stuffed them in his own.

"Where's your phone?" Mercedes barked.

"In the truck," she rasped through her closed throat, her frozen lips.

"Step out of the way."

She moved closer to the grassy shoulder.

The boy scrambled into the Yukon and found her phone.

"Passcode."

She gave it to him.

"Works," the boy said.

"Go ahead, now. Don't wreck it."

The boy whooped and slammed the door shut.

"Move," Mercedes said, tilting his head in the direction of the house.

Andrea was loosening, bit by bit. Her back crawled with the knowledge of the gun, what a bullet does to flesh as it travels through it, blowing the tissues wide apart before they fall back in on themselves, catastrophically damaged.

Twenty yards down the road, the Yukon roared to life behind them. The headlights hit them, threw their shadows up the road into the night. It rolled past, the boy bolt upright behind the wheel, focusing hard through the windshield, his tongue tucked in the corner of his open mouth. He was probably sitting on her jacket.

With her initial fear thawed, her hands were freezing. The damp cold seeped through her clothes. The thin wool sweatshirt she'd pulled on over her long-sleeve Henley was neither warm nor water-resistant enough to be outside for long.

The hounds barked and barked, sounding like a pack instead of just two dogs. When she rounded the curve of the road, she could see them rush the Yukon as the boy crossed the cattle guard. He kept going, driving straight into the dimly lit barn.

Taka wasn't outside. Maybe they hadn't found him.

Andrea kept her mouth shut.

There was a worn-in dirt path between the road and the gate in the fence.

She lifted the latch and passed through it.

"The barn," Mercedes said.

The hounds came bounding over and crowded her legs.

The boy turned the Yukon off and came out to stand in silhouette in the middle of the open double doors, her shoulder bag in his hands. As they got close, he said, "They're inside."

The barn was less ramshackle inside than out.

The light rain sounded twice as hard on the metal roof.

There were a couple of stalls along with big concrete pads on either side. A tractor sat on one, pallets of stacked feed and bales of rolled hay on the other. In the central aisle at the end of the barn, Taka knelt with his back to her, feet crossed, and hands laced on the back of his head.

A bald man stood in front of him with a gun to his forehead.

Behind the bald guy, a ghost sat in a barely-there ladderback chair, his head at an awful angle. The hangman's noose still hung around his neck. His hands rested on the coil of rope in his lap, but his fingers moved restlessly over the rosary he held, and the whisper of his prayer tickled her ear.

"Go on, get down there beside him."

She laced her hands the way Taka had and knelt so that their shoulders brushed.

Mercedes came around to stand beside Taka as he dug through her bag. He held up her Waltham-Young ID. "Andrea Kelley. You are in the wrong place at the wrong time, girlfriend. Again. This one"—he kicked Taka's feet—"came round here asking about a van we don't know nothing about and handing off his card to Xander's maid. In case she needs help. Like she'd ever want to leave the cushy situation she's landed in. Only he's internet famous after shooting that boy."

While Taka's name had been officially withheld, he wasn't indicted by the grand jury, and hadn't made national news, video footage had gotten out and he wasn't hard to recognize. Zach Taylor's relatives had made sure Taka's name was attached to it, at least in certain circles. More widely, it wasn't hard to find both detractors of "dirty WV cop" and admirers of "sexy WV cop."

"When I saw you kissing him yesterday," Mercedes continued, "I knew exactly who he was. And I didn't like it. I don't like being followed."

"I work on Hale Street, part-time," Andrea blurted. "He wasn't following you."

"Nuh-uh. I called that dress shop and described you. You've never worked for them. Now you both sneaking back 'round to Skinny's?"

"Where's Tina?"

He laughed. "Doing our laundry. 'Bout got supper on the table, I'm sure."

"She fooled you," the boy shouted.

"At-at, boy," Mercedes barked. "What'd I tell you?"

"To keep my fucking mouth shut."

"Now come here and point your gun at her back. Not too close. Like I taught you. Good."

"If you have nothing to do with the stolen van," Taka said, "why risk bringing us here? The department will be re-tracing every step I took the last few days if I go missing."

"Nah. Xander and Tina talked to a fellow came 'round yesterday to follow-up. Wanted to see Tina for himself. Don't you know it? She doesn't match the description of the lady who rented that van. Cop said that only left him with a hundred more Conlons to check on. Xander gave him a couple of suggestions."

"So Xander's both in the clear and innocent as well. Why are we here then, Mister..."

"Like I'm gonna give you my name. You're here because a lot of people would like to get their hands on you." He chuckled like he was making a joke. "She's here because she's unlucky. Get up. Slow. Any attempt to attack or escape and she's dead."

The bald guy followed Taka's head up with his gun. Taka's gaze never left his face.

"Remove your jacket." Mercedes circled. The light on his phone flashed again and again. "Take off your sweater and shirt."

Andrea's brain finally caught up to the joke.

When Taka hesitated, he said, "Finger on the trigger, boy."

Andrea didn't think it possible, but her mouth dried out even further. Her throat tickled. She held her breath, afraid if she coughed, the boy would shoot her.

Taka reached back with both hands and jerked his sweater and polo off together.

"Drop them."

When Mercedes was done taking pictures, he said, "Down."

Taka knelt.

He repeated the same moves with Andrea, then, "The bra."

Taka continued to stare at the bald guy.

"Bra."

It took her two tries to get the clasp undone with her trembling fingers. Her skin was goose-pimpled from the cold. The bra fell away. Her taut nipples ached. Mercedes stepped in to get a closer shot. Hands already fisted, she closed them tighter, shifted her weight.

Mercedes clucked at her. "No." He tilted his head at bald guy.

Bald guy deliberately moved his finger onto the trigger of his gun.

"Dress."

As they gathered their clothes, Taka's warm hand found her cold one. He gave it a quick squeeze.

Mercedes's thumbs worked his phone. "Prime buck. Cop. Soldier. What are you, Detective Taka? Six foot? Muscular. Premium pricing in effect. Sale by private bid. Delivery not included. Mature, experienced white female, five foot ten, fit, suitable for rough play. Highest bidder. Delivery not included. Companion bids welcome but must meet or exceed individual offers. Standard terms and conditions apply. Sold as-is, no warranties or guarantees. Bid window ends six a.m. EST. Must be removed by ten a.m."

33

Andrea's teeth wouldn't stop chattering. She couldn't stop shaking. Her knees and shins seemed to be sucking the cold from the ground beneath them. The rain had changed to sleet, playing its unique tune across the tin roof, accompanied by the wood siding, the old car up on blocks.

She'd grown up under an uninsulated tin roof. The sound had always meant curling up in a deliciously warm bed with Christmas on the way. She already knew that from now on, it would mean unrelenting cold and the hollow dread of what would happen next.

The boy seemed an easy target while Bald Guy and Mercedes had a whispered conversation, Bald Guy keeping his aim true on her while Mercedes studied the rattling dark outside the barn. But Andrea couldn't see him. Obviously thinking the same, Taka turned his head and got a sharp command to look forward from Bald Guy.

Making a decision, Mercedes found two discarded feed sacks. He rolled the edges down with lithe twists of his hard hands and dropped them to the dirt floor in front of them. He pulled several thick strips of black plastic from a tool chest near the tractor. Andrea didn't recognize them as industrial zip ties until he pulled Taka's arms behind him, and she heard the first rip of plastic sliding through the lock.

He shifted to her, Bald Guy's gun smoothly tracking onto Taka instead.

He grabbed her wrist. "Wow, you're really cold already." Looping a zip tie around each wrist like handcuff bracelets, he pulled them tight, closing the gap between her wrists. She suddenly knew. This was how Lucy Garcia got her scars. She couldn't remember from the YouTube self-defense video she'd once seen if she was supposed to bring her wrists together for zip ties or keep them as wide apart as she could. "Boy, grab her jacket. Can't have her losing me a sale by freezing to death before transport comes."

"They might do that anyway," Bald Guy said.

"At least we can tell Skinny we tried."

"I don't really think he cares. There'll be buyers for the cop dead or alive."

"Skinny might not care," Mercedes shot back. "But I always like more in my pocket. Boy. Now." He yanked one of the feed sacks down over Taka's head.

Even though she knew it was coming, the slide of the bag over her face nearly undid her. She sank, her butt hitting her heels. Mercedes jerked her up by her elbow. Pain corkscrewed through her shoulder blade. She yelped and felt Taka surge to his feet, both Bald Guy and Mercedes yelling she couldn't tell what with the sweet-smelling sack over her ears and the relentless rattle-crack-hiss of the falling sleet.

Mercedes propelled her forward. She concentrated on picking her feet up and putting them down. She thought the barn was cold until she stepped out into the stiff breeze. The sleet stung her hands and pelted the bag. She tripped and stumbled over the hillocks of grass under her boots. The overgrown stems brushed across her hands and whipped over her thighs, soaking her jeans.

They were walking the wrong direction and over the wrong surface to be going to the house. Was there another barn out in the pasture? A shed? Did they think if they dropped them in the woods that they'd stay put? Mercedes swung her around to a stop. Was that her panting? There was no air in the bag. She tried to stop and couldn't.

The sleet had stopped, replaced by a resounding silence.

"Snow!" the boy crowed and then whooped. He took off on a loud, joyous, galloping lap around them, his yells seeming to come from everywhere, even above her.

One of the men grunted.

Something scraped across the ground in front of her. Door. She could sense the open space yawning before her, smell the basement mustiness of the earthy, stale air that wafted out.

Mercedes planted his hand on her back and shoved her forward.

She ran her aching shoulder against the door, hard and immovable, stubbed her toe on something blocking her path forward, and then fell face first onto a hard downward slope. One of the men cursed, stepped over her, and dragged her further downhill by the back of her sweater, making it cut into her armpits and scraping her bared belly along the rocky ground.

He dropped her.

The last of her gasping breath whooshed out of her lungs. Taka fell somewhere near her in a rush of curses and meaty, flesh-on-flesh hits. Something fairly light landed on her calves. Her jacket? Please let it be her jacket.

A solid thunk beyond her feet.

"Damn thing's stuck," Mercedes muttered.

"Just give it a whack," Bald Guy said.

One of them gave it more than one whack and then made a satisfied sound.

"Lock?"

A distinct snick from that side of the door.

She couldn't hear them leaving.

Then she heard the boy whoop again in the far distance.

She was freezing.

But maybe not quite so much as in the open barn.

The floor was loose, pebbly dirt. A thin layer. Parts of her were touching colder, harder ground.

Taka thrashed around. He must've gotten the bag off his head. His voice rang out, "You okay? Andrea? You okay?"

"Right here," she mumbled into the dirt and the bag against her face. Past the dry grassy sweet of the bag was the reek of wet clay and rotting wood. "I know where we are."

JIMMY PUSHED through the courthouse doors at a quarter til six into spitting sleet. He pulled his coat closed and buttoned it up. He'd arranged to meet Detweiler at BCI to discuss Dewey's Beaumont Road visit. He texted Andrea.

Glad Aaron showed. Meeting at six and paperwork. Late takeout at yours?

By the time he was warming up in his car, she texted back. *Planning to turn in early.*

That was fair.

CU tomorrow he sent back.

Thumbs up and heart emojis in reply.

Someone tapped on his passenger window.

He jerked his head up.

Fields.

He hit the door locks and Fields slid in with a blast of cold air and a hint of expensive-smelling cologne.

"Detective Fields," he said, by way of introduction.

"You're one of only two Black detectives in Charleston, Fields. I know who you are."

"You know Taka doesn't consider himself Black, right? Black's more than just a skin tone and a couple of common features. It's a dynamic culture. One he's largely unfamiliar with except for the discrimination and the slurs."

Jimmy couldn't control his blush, but he could accept the mild admonishment. "Point taken. Thank you."

"He's up to no good. Sent me a video of Bulldog Bailey's truck outside Skinny Conlon's house in Summersville. A little while later, he suggested I look at Linda Conlon for Anna Lansing's murder. I assume due to your relationship to Andrea, you're familiar with the details of her death?"

"I have my sources. By Linda Conlon, do you mean Linda King, formerly Linda Rogers?"

"Yes. I tried calling, but he didn't pick up. No response to my texts. Do you know where he is?"

"Candy King's mom. She married Skinny?"

"On my to-do list. Please don't help."

"Andrea just texted me from her house."

Fields raised his brows. "And that's relevant how?"

"They're attached at the hip again."

Fields nodded. "You indicated in your interview that you have a romantic relationship with Andrea."

Jimmy didn't like the turn of Fields's tone from I've-got-a-question to probing. "We do. Taka's her best friend. I'm okay with that."

"You're assuming Taka's at her house."

"I'm assuming I can ask, and she'll answer."

Fields's gaze slid to the phone in Jimmy's hand.

Jimmy typed. Sent.

Fields sat perfectly still. The heater fan blew stale air on them. Sleet collected at the bottom of the windshield in tiny drifts. Jimmy wrinkled his nose. He really needed to throw out the takeout bag he'd tossed into the rear footwell. And maybe wash his gym shoes.

In the shower. His phone is dead.

Jimmy held it up for Fields to read. "There you go. Whatever skulking they were up to, they're in for the night."

Fields looked no less worried than when he pulled the door open. "If you talk to him before I do, please tell him I'll do my due diligence on Linda Conlon, but to cease and desist any investigative actions. Tell him I'll make sure Tamarin dots every i and crosses every t before we make a move on Andrea."

"See that you do" were the words that tried to unfurl off Jimmy's tongue. He caught and swallowed them. "I will. Thanks for helping them."

SHE KICKED, hitting Taka twice, and wiggled and grunted and finally got herself turned over.

"It's so dark I can't see my hand in front of my face."

Having her full weight on her bound hands hurt. Andrea rolled to her side.

Taka shifted and shifted, bumping and hitting her. Then there was a different feeling when he got onto his feet.

A thud.

"Damn it. Ceiling's low. And hard."

Definitely an old root cellar.

Rustles and his zip ties zinging. Meaty thumps. "These ties are too thick. Andrea?"

Here.

"Andrea? Ands. Andrea!"

Could he not hear her? "Here," she said. It came out softer than she thought it would. She cleared her throat. "Here."

He sat down again. Listening felt like watching. She could see him clearly in her mind's eye. But then his hands were scrabbling at the bag over her head, and she was blind and short of breath. His cold fingers dragged across her cheek. She tried to lift her head to help him. It was hard. Her head was heavy.

When the bag came off, the cold wet air rushed into her. She opened her mouth and breathed it in. Her face was cold now, too. But oxygen was way better than no oxygen.

"Andrea?"

"Better. Thank you."

He'd said it was dark, but she could make out the outlines of his body, the boundaries of the small space beyond him.

"Was that bald guy Derek?"

"No. You need to sit up. Less body against the ground."

She couldn't get upright until she'd squirmed around so much that she ended up curled around the solid bulk of his body. Knee hooked against his thigh, she kicked her other leg out and levered herself up.

"Good. Can you stand up?"

She pressed against him, worked her feet under her and then shoved up. She tilted forward, stumbling up two steps and hit the wall. Uneven. Jagged. Some sort of shelves. She put her back to it and gasped at the sight of another person in there with them.

The girl sat huddled against the back wall to Andrea's right. She gave off the same sort of faint glow Billie Mae had. She frowned at Andrea. "Is it still locked?"

"Andrea?" Taka said, uncertain again.

"I'm good. Just breathing for a second."

He scrambled to his knees again and stood, slouching to keep from hitting his head. "Move around a little, work up some warmth." He swayed and then hopped from foot to foot. "Are you moving?"

She had an extra inch of clearance from the roof, made of unstripped logs laid side by side. She stepped sideways and back. The movement made her aware again of the cold. Step and back, step and back. She shivered, which set her off shaking again. She clenched her jaw shut.

"Keep moving."

"I am," she gritted out.

The girl rose easily. She was maybe twelve or thirteen. She wore jeans with holes at the knees and a Nirvana T-shirt. She mimicked Andrea's step. "No one came," she said.

Over and back. Over and back. Then hopping, following Taka's motion. Although she really just wanted to lay down again, within a few minutes she was warmer. Her shakes eased. "You couldn't break the ties?"

"I couldn't get out," the girl said.

Taka fiddled with his wrists, adjusting the zip ties where he wanted them. He put his legs together, bent over slightly, and brought his hands down hard against his lower back at the top of his butt. Nothing.

"I couldn't get out," the girl said again and sprang forward. Andrea cringed away so she wouldn't touch her. The girl slammed into the door, beat on it with both hands. "Brendan, you little monster, let me out right now!" She screamed bloody murder. Andrea couldn't watch. She crouched down and covered her head with her arms.

Taka tried again, jerking his hands apart hard when his hands hit. Nothing. "Are you warm enough to sit down for a couple of minutes?"

"You're going to be in so much fucking trouble," the girl screeched. "Let me out! Let me out!"

She scrabbled at the edges of the door.

"Andrea?"

"I'm good."

"My shoelaces are paracord," he said, dropping hard onto one knee.

Of course, he'd actually done that. They'd joked about it two Christmases ago when she put the cord in his stocking, but she never noticed he'd done it.

He plopped himself down. "I'm sitting down with my boots facing you. If you can undo one lace, we can use it to break the ties."

It helped that she could see a little. The panicking ghost was still scrabbling, with small sobby breaths. Andrea glanced over as she turned around to sit with her back to Taka. Dark bloody streaks under the girl's hands. She'd torn her nails trying to get out.

Andrea was grateful for all of two seconds when the ghost blipped away, taking her light with her. She patted around, found Taka's feet. It took forever to fumble the lace free. She was cold again. They got up and hopped.

The dark had her straining to hear the scrabbling that wasn't Taka and wasn't at the door. Was it the girl? Angry squeak. The patter of tiny running feet. "Are there rats in here?"

"Don't think about it," Taka said. "Give me the cord."

They stood back-to-back. His hands were cold against hers as he passed the cord through her zip tie.

"Pull back against the cord."

He sawed through her ties in seconds. Within a minute they were both free.

She grabbed hold of him, and he held her tight.

34

"Jimmy, it happened. And the backups failed, but that happens, too. Let it go." Sitting at his desk where he'd been ass-deep in paperwork when Jimmy walked in, Andy Detweiler stuffed the last of his sandwich in his mouth.

"If we'd managed to document it, we could report Dewey's presence at the house, buy a little goodwill with CPD, give them someone else to look at besides Andrea."

"But we didn't," Andy said around his mouthful.

"And why is that?"

He rolled his eyes. "You want me to say it was all my fault? Fine, it was all my fault. It's noted in the record. Can we move on?"

"I need you to answer your phone."

"I was sleeping, Jimmy. It's been five months. I had two days off in a row. I wasn't on call. I was sleeping. And fishing. I was sleeping and fishing." He kicked his feet up on the desk. "I may have been sleeping while fishing."

"You have to stay with him, Andy. You've lost him a couple of times."

"You're getting in tight with this girl. Scotty's parking overnight at

Taka's place. You sure you want to call me out on a bona fide unavoidable mishap?"

It was a subtle threat. "Yeah, fine. Just do better."

Andy waved his arm across his desk. "Okay if I get on with my night of paperwork?"

"Nina tell you your hunch paid off?"

"I told you Dewey wasn't related to his mom!"

"You did. I apologize for brushing you off. If Maddox gives you any shit about the expense of the DNA, I'll back you up. Even if it doesn't prove useful in the end."

"It will," Andy said with confidence. "And your chasing after those casings will, too."

Tit for tat. He deserved that.

"MOM HAS A ROOT CELLAR," Taka said into her hair. "I guess you'd call it that. But it's built partially under the house. I don't hear anything that might be a house near us."

"Root cellars can be built a bunch of different ways."

"You've seen one before?"

"Most of my restorations have them, sometimes several."

"You warm enough to explore a little? See if we can break out?"

The ghost girl's scream echoed in her ear. She shivered. He'd been letting go of her, but now pulled her in closer again. "I saw a ghost in the barn," she said. "A hanged man."

"As long as there aren't any in here with us."

"Not right now," she said.

"I don't want to know if one shows up."

She leaned back but kept her arms around him. "I don't think you have a choice anymore, Taka. I can't help them without you."

"You don't actually know that you can help them. We got lucky last time. The circumstances aligned."

"I think that's how it works. Call it crossover circumstances. I'll bet you a steak dinner that Ivystone is where Aaron lived after he was sold from Live Oak. And that he either wasn't aware of me until I got attached to the project or couldn't make me aware of him."

"To claim that bet, we need a way out."

"It's a root cellar, Taka. If we can't get through the door, we dig our way out."

"Seriously?"

"From what I saw it's old, there's no concrete. The mortared rock is only at the front to secure the door."

"From what you saw?"

"You said you didn't want to know."

He ran his arm up and found her head, pressed her back into his chest.

"I didn't get raped," she whispered.

"I'd have killed them before I let that happen," he whispered back. "If we have to dig through a mile of dirt, we're getting out of here."

She clung to him a moment longer. "It's maybe eight feet by nine. You take the door; I'll check the walls. The roof's a series of logs. We can see how soft they are. They only last thirty or forty years."

He shuffled sideways, feeling for the upward slope to the door. She turned herself around, feeling for the wall. Moldering and rotten wood crumbled beneath her hands before she hit the solid wall. Saplings stacked lengthwise by the feel of it. At a guess, milled rough-sawn planks had been wedged between them to act as shelves, but over the years, the high humidity and wood mold had destroyed them. Her feet hit something against the base of the wall.

She dropped to her knees, feeling. A hard bowl, crusted something still inside it. Two more like it. The remnants of a basket or several of them. She stood again and walked her hands along the wall, fingers feeling for the soft spots. Not many, mostly around the metal stakes driven into each log to pin it to the one below.

Thinking weapon, she tried to wiggle one free but that wasn't going to be an easy task. It could wait unless there was no way out. "Sapling wall," she said. "In decent shape. Maybe there's an axe or hoe in here."

"Door feels impenetrable. It's like one of those thick dungeon doors in old movies. It pulled open, right? Is that what you heard? So it should push from this side?"

"And the hinges would be outside. There's more room to work outside. Hard to hang the door from the tunnel side."

"I don't think it's an option."

"Check the roof above the door."

"Rock. Past that the logs. They seem pretty sturdy."

"Ventilation pipe," Andrea said. "It's rusted, but not falling apart yet."

"That how the rats are getting in?"

Andrea had been hoping the back wall would be dirt. They could dig up around the edge of the roof. But it was saplings as well. She broke away the rotting shelves and ran her fingers across the logs. She could hear Taka doing the same on the last wall. A light rose so slowly she was hardly aware of it until she could see the shadows of her hands.

It was the girl. She stood back in the doorway, watching Taka sweep his large hands across the side wall. She crossed the small space, her light brightening the back wall. Another pipe in the corner where Andrea and Taka would meet. Water had hollowed out a wide space in the ground where water now pooled. This pipe was rustier than the other. Water seeped down from above. Andrea couldn't reach, but she thought the space around the pipe had been dug out. Mud caked the sapling logs below it.

"I found where the rats have been getting in."

"Rats," the girl said, squeezing a whole scenario of terror and helplessness into one word.

Andrea expected her to disappear but as Taka crowded her, his arm sweeping right through hers, the girl crouched instead and slammed her fist into the saplings directly above the water. The soft wood exploded silently outward. The wet scent of decay rose.

"What's that," Taka said, eyes blind.

It was disturbing. Andrea leaned in and dug at the wood, scooping it away. "Soft spot. There's water collecting here from another old vent pipe."

He sidled over, and she placed his hands where she was working. But a few minutes later, the rot was dug out, giving them only a two-handsbreadth width of hard-packed earth behind it. Taka grabbed the pipe and rocked it. A shower of sharp rusty pieces fell around him, but he freed it. Feeling carefully to place the pipe where he needed it, he jammed the end under a rotted sapling to try and pry it from the wall.

Andrea went for the hard bowl, which turned out to be ceramic. "Here, I found a bowl, let me try." But it was too wide to get down to the dirt.

"He came back," the girl said.

So why was she haunting the place?

"Pipe's usable," Taka said. "Maybe we can get some dirt dug out to give us more room to lever the wood off the wall."

The girl pointed to where the bowl had been. Moved her hands in a digging motion.

One hand marking the opening, Taka was using the pipe as a spear, chunking it in over and over to loosen the compacted soil. Andrea shoved the basket remnants and other bowls aside. Age broke one into several pieces. She scraped the bowl across the ground, but the edge was too rounded to dig in.

Using one of the bowl shards instead gave her a digging edge. She dug a small patch of hard earth and then a couple of inches over on her next pass, hit turned earth. Andrea's stomach dropped.

She sat back on her heels.

When she looked up at the girl, the girl was staring at the patch of looser dirt.

Andrea explored the patch. Large but not grave large. She could try asking, but then Taka would know they weren't alone. She scooped a couple of bowlfuls out and then went to work with her hands.

Hard ridges under her fingers.

Lying less than six inches deep, the left side of a human skull reflected the girl's spectral glow.

KARIE W: *Andrea's not answering - she's not stuck at CPD again is she?*

jhoyle: *She's home. Shes plnng to turn in early, but that prbly means 'read all the things" that Louie's gr aunt gave her.*

Karie W: *Did she tell you about our session w/Aaron today? Amzballs!*

Jhoyle: *In mtings and court all day. Can't wait to hr abt it at brkfst tmmrow*

Karie W: *When's breakfast?*

Jhoyle: *7am @Andrea's*

Karie W: *:thumbsup:*

"ARE THESE YOURS?"

"What?" Taka said as the girl said, "Yes."

"When did you die?"

Taka stopped digging.

"I was bones when he came back."

"Did you live here?"

"Yes." The word rebounded off the walls in the small space.

"Taka! Close your eyes!"

"I can't see anything. I don't know where you're looking."

"Just—"

"Okay, okay. They're closed."

"He was afraid to tell them after they called the police." Her voice boomed like thunderclaps.

"Turn it down," Andrea shouted.

"They're still looking for me," the girl said, her volume dropping as she spoke.

"What'd you do?"

"I waited," the girl said.

"Taka?" Andrea said. "What'd you do?"

"I don't know. Nothing. Is it better?"

"I found her bones."

"This pipe is disintegrating."

"We can try to break the other one free. It's on the same wall, in the other corner."

"How strong are bones?"

"You can't be serious."

"They're still looking for me," the girl said again. Her tone was different. Decisive.

"I need a lever. The other pipe's not going to hold up any better than this one."

She dug around until she found a longer bone.

"I'm going to see if I can wedge the pipe in behind the edge of the rotted logs," he said. "Is it still here? Can you see?"

"She's a tween and yes."

He wedged the pipe and then crouched, holding it at the bottom. "Hit it, hard as you can. Try not to hit my wrist, okay?"

The girl's ghost light flickered with every swing of her leg bone.

Once the pipe was wedged, Taka pulled down on it, twisting as he laid his weight on it. The log shifted. They moved the pipe across the log and Andrea swung the bone again. On the third wedge and lever, the end of the sapling popped free of the stakes connecting it to the logs above and below. Taka rocked the log until it was loose enough to push that end to the floor.

He waited while Andrea positioned the pipe above the next log. She whacked it in as hard as she could. On the last strike, the leg bone splintered, the ghost light winked out, and the log dropped off the stake above.

"Did you get it?" Taka asked.

"Yes. Lost my light, though. And the leg bone's done."

"I'm getting used to the dark." The log pressed against Andrea's legs, and she stepped back while he worked it loose and pulled the end down. "Now we dig."

There wasn't quite enough room for both of them to dig, so they took turns using the bowls, bowl shards, and pipe remnant to dig out an area beyond the log wall to sit in. Then they dug up, hoping it'd be no more than six to eight feet to the surface. At the point where she could no longer sit, but couldn't stand up straight, Andrea was sure her arms were going to fall off.

Breathing hard, she stopped, and sat down.

Taka didn't tap her out.

"You okay?" she said.

"I wish we had water."

She wished he hadn't said that as suddenly she was aware of her desperate thirst. "It's so humid in here it's practically raining."

"If I could lick water from the air I would."

Andrea leaned her head back against the dirt and closed her eyes. "There's lots of rock on the ground if you want to give the pebble in the mouth trick a go."

"If they weren't waterless pebbles, I would."

"Uh-huh."

"Don't go to sleep."

"I just need a couple of minutes."

He poked her side. "We're warm right now, but we're also wet from sweat, and it's still cold in here. Get up. I'll dig, you clear."

With great effort, she swung her legs out of the space and put her feet back on the cellar floor. Taka took the bowl shard she'd been using and helped her stand. She leaned against him. He let her for a moment. "Come on. I'm ready to be out of the dark."

He clambered in. He started digging again, the bitter, rooty soil falling down around him, Andrea swept it away onto the floor and when it got too high, scooped it to one side with one of the bowls. Eventually they switched again. And again. At some point they both made their way to the front corner and peed.

"Hey," Taka said. "I never told you what Bulldog said, did I." And he launched into a detailed recreation of their full conversation, going back a couple of times to amend himself. Andrea gleaned the random bits of knowledge he had about how pimps worked. And then they covered entry into trafficking again and what counted as trafficking and a debate about whether women, or men, could ever choose that life, or if they were only bulldozed and exploited into the life by manipulative profit-seekers and taught to say, 'Thank you for taking care of me.'

Andrea was pretty sure she fell asleep standing in the hole during a rest from using the pipe to scrape at the dry, stony clay, her arms folded over her head. Taka's hand on her ankle woke her. She told him all about Mrs. Dunbar and all the places in the historical record she'd looked for Aaron.

She told him how some slaves had both a slave name and a family name. Since Whay was African, he'd probably given the seven sons Aaron had named their family names. Using their slave names, they'd be easier to find in journals or letters or sales, but only if they'd actually been recorded anywhere. She might be able to find at least a couple of them in Mrs. Dunbar's diaries now.

And she explained how she was going to go through every artifact Mr. Pederson had boxed and then going to Falling Waters and Ivystone Farm when this was all over to find Sally.

On and on they dug.

Until Taka shouted something garbled, and the dirt started falling faster. It felt different in her hands, slightly moister, still filled with dry chunks of shale, but easier to pack. It smelled different, too. It was easier to dig. When her turn came again, she could stand with her arms partially extended. When she gave out again, she was braced between the first sapling above their entrance and the shaft wall, her arms fully extended. She was starting to wonder how high the slope above the root cellar rose. She'd lost all sense of time, but they had to be running out of it.

35

Jimmy scraped the snow from the windshield while the RAV4's engine warmed up. His phone vibrated in his coat pocket. He ignored it until he got back in and slammed the door shut on the arctic air.

Scott. *Call me*

That couldn't be good. He dialed Scott's burner.

"Dewey got a text on his phone about midnight. From Bulldog Bailey, I think. Been behind closed doors ever since. Kept me til Chet came back on at six. Something big's going down."

"He sent you home?"

"Yeah. Said he needed me on call. To be ready with an hour's notice."

"No way for you to stick around?"

"I told him I'd just stay, but he said no."

"Then you should get some sleep."

"This might sound crazy, but I swear after he got that text, he said, 'Goddamnit, William.' Then he called Bulldog while we rushed out to the car. Made us stand outside in the snow until he was done. Taka's the only person I've ever heard him call William. I've been calling him since I left, and it goes straight to voicemail."

"He's at Andrea's. His phone was dead." Though it'd be charged by now and Taka wasn't the type to leave it off.

"Guess I'm meeting Andrea then. What's her address?"

That seemed like a bad idea. "I'll go. They might have gone for a run. Blow off some of the stress CPD's putting on them. I'll text you."

"I don't like it," Scott said.

"Go home. That's an order."

"Roots," Taka yelled.

And a minute later, "Snow!"

Cold air and wet snow plunged down the shaft. Taka dropped down and faint light followed him.

"It's light out?"

"Past dawn. Snow on the ground. There's no cover, so it's up and run for the woods or the barn." His face was smeared in dirt. It was clumped in his hair and covering his clothes.

"You're a mudpuppy."

"I know you are, but what am I?"

"Do you think we can take the Yukon?"

"I can hotwire it if they took the keys."

"Barn, then."

"Jackets."

She handed him his and slid hers on. "What about the bones?"

The light didn't reach far enough to see them.

"Let's cover them. Fast."

Andrea placed the splintered thigh back in the hole and they shoved the dirt back over it. Taka smoothed it down while she pulled the basket remnants and pieces of broken bowl back over it. When Mercedes found them gone, hopefully he wouldn't notice the disturbed earth and the bones would still be there when they reported them.

Taka went up first. When Andrea reached for the lip, her feet braced against wall and logs, Taka grabbed her wrists. When she looked up, he said, "Shhh, they're coming."

He helped her snake out on her belly into three inches of snow. The men were just outside the barn, only movement and flashes of color through the trees and patchy fog. She and Taka were at the top of a small hill, the door to the root cellar invisible at its base. Taka scooped up a handful of snow and took a bite. "Just wet your mouth and throat," he whispered.

She copied him. Initial burn of cold and then the most sensuous sensation of water running off her tongue and filling her mouth she'd ever experienced. It was the best mouthful of anything she'd ever eaten in her life. She'd grown up here. In the winter, you carried water and blankets in the car in case you got stuck on the road. She knew to eat more would just make her colder, but she still wanted to gobble more down.

They wriggled further over the back of the slope on their bellies, then jumped up and ran down the backside, sliding on the snow, and into a fringe of trees. Taka nearly hit a cow before they saw each other. The cow snorted and shied away, scaring three others who trotted off a few yards between the trees and then turned as one to assess the threat against them. Taka crouched at the base of a tree. Andrea kneeled down beside him.

One of the cows mooed and then they all strolled away. Taka and Andrea's tracks led straight down the hill into the trees. "They won't see the shaft until they've opened the root cellar," Taka said, his voice low. "And they won't see the trail until they've walked up the hill to check the top of the shaft. That gives us at least a few minutes to work our way out to the road and try to circle 'round to the barn."

"In your footsteps," Andrea said.

No one was there when Jimmy pulled in at Andrea's. Taka's Yukon wasn't in the carport. No lights were on. The house had a distinct air of emptiness.

He looked back down the dark street. Five of the houses' Christmas lights were on. There were lights on inside in all but one. And Susan Pepper's, of course, was dark as well, feeling more desolate than

Andrea's. He could see Huntley, across the street, drinking coffee or tea while he read in his kitchen.

At the top of the street, someone came out and started a car up, the exhaust pluming, and went back inside.

He texted Scott: *653 Double Branch Lane*

His reply bubbled up instantly. *On my way*

Jimmy was pretty sure he'd never gone home.

TAKA MOVED FASTER than she expected. There was little snow under the trees. He ran, choosing the straightest line possible. He didn't look back, knowing she could keep up. The cold air burned her lungs. The digging had wrung everything out of her, but her body knew how to run, and she let her muscle memory carry her into a steady pace. Two full minutes, maybe three, and Taka dropped in front of her from run to crouch. She fell in behind him.

He pointed to the tree line but then motioned her to stay. He crept to the edge of the field. Watched for a moment and then crept back. "They're almost to the cellar. We shouldn't be visible. Ready?"

She'd caught her breath. But her throat was so dry, she didn't think she could produce the spit to talk without coughing. She nodded.

They ran. Within another two minutes, they ran out of woods. They trotted along the tree line back toward the road. Over the next hill, they spotted the pipe gate, a dull red against the white snow-covered field and stretch of road beyond. The sun was burning off the remnants of fog and it looked like the sky would be a brilliant blue before long.

"Do you think they'll follow us or go back to the barn?"

"Instinct would say follow, at least for a few minutes, right? They'll be pissed and want to know how we got out."

He held the barbed wire of the fence for her to slip through. She turned and stepped on the lower strand, pulling up the middle for him. They bolted down the grass verge along the road, hoping for better traction. It was like running in sand. Taka slowed to a trot when they got near the gate beside the driveway, then stopped dead, holding his arm out to catch her. He backed up into the trees, hauling her with him. "Dogs," he whispered.

They were between the road and the gate, busy sniffing along the road and digging through the snow for something they gobbled up as soon as they found each piece.

Taka let her go and turned into the fringe of trees between them and the barn. Creeping forward one careful step at a time, they got to the fence. Again, barbed wire. They eased through. The doors on the barn were closed. A figure rose out of the brush to their left, gun in both hands at the low ready. Taka shoved Andrea behind him.

"Dewey said you'd come for the truck," the gaunt man said.

Taka's breath rushed out. He leaned forward, hands on his knees.

"What's happening?" Andrea whispered.

The gaunt man patted the air, lowering himself again. Taka dropped to a knee. Andrea did the same. The man touched something on the headset he wore and said, "Got 'em. Go one and go two."

"How'd you know?" Taka said.

The corner of the man's lips lifted, but it could hardly be called a smile, maybe just an acknowledgement. "Long story."

Engines, coming down the road. The hounds lifted their heads and bayed.

"Meat's gone," the man said. "Let's move."

"The gate?" Taka said.

"Visible from the house."

They went back the way they came, though the man snipped the top two fence wires at the posts rather than climb through them. A black four-door BMW drove past them, braked hard, and made a sliding one-hundred-and-eighty degree turn. The hounds lost it, barking wildly.

The man pulled the rear door open and Taka dove in, so Andrea did, too.

A scent she'd never forget teased her nose.

The man squeezed in beside her and shut the door.

She bends over and shakes her hair out and then flips her head back up, so it settles in soft curls around her face and over her shoulders.

He shakes the Tupperware at her. She used to put meatloaf in one just like that. She's just drunk enough that she can let herself say her daughter's name. Elsa. Like in Frozen.

The driver floored the gas, the tires spinning on the packed snow, before they caught, and the car leaped forward.

They just missed hitting a black SUV with dark tinted windows turning into the drive. As they passed by, it trundled over the cattle guard. The hounds raced under the bit of three-board fence by the gate and chased the SUV down as it headed for the barn.

"Is that Dewey?" Taka said.

The man slid his gun into his chest holster, and pressed his shoulder to the door, shifting to give her more room. "Yes. He saw the sales page."

"Hi, Andrea," the driver said.

It took her a second. "Glenn?"

He hooked a thumb back at her. "That's Commander Luke Bowman." He swiveled his thumb at the man riding shotgun. "You remember Tripp."

"Yes," she said, and shrank back against the seat.

Bowman shot her a concerned look.

Taka picked up her hand. "You okay?"

She nodded and held on tight.

SCOTT PARKED behind him and joined him in his car.

"If we report them missing," Jimmy said as they studied the dark house, "CPD's going to think they ran."

Karie pulled in next to him in the snowy drive, took stock when she got out, and pulled his back door open.

Jimmy made the introductions.

None of them had a key. Would getting inside matter? "Andrea texted me around ten-thirty," Jimmy said. "Said she'd had a good session at Louie's."

Scott scrolled on his phone. "The last text I got from Taka was about three-thirty. Just a thumbs up when I asked if I should go to his after work."

"Andrea texted me at"—Karie squinted at her phone—"two, that they'd been at Waltham-Young to check on some stuff in the warehouse and she's certain her latest project is connected to Aaron."

"Well, that's something," Jimmy said. "She's been trying so hard to find a foothold with him."

A CPD cruiser came down the street. The uniform driving looped it around the cul-de-sac, drove back by Andrea's, and pulled in at the curb four houses down. He shut the engine off. Through the back window, Jimmy watched him reach up and adjust the rearview mirror.

Breaking the silence, Scott said, "Who's Aaron?"

"Someone at Louie's," Jimmy said at the same time Karie said, "One of Louie's ancestors."

Scott's gaze shifted between them.

"He's one of Louie's nephews," Karie said at the same time Jimmy said, "I meant someone on Louie's wall."

"I've heard Taka say his name on the phone with Andrea."

"I know Andrea's security code," Karie said. "Sooner or later, that officer's going to wonder why we're just sitting here."

Jimmy glanced back at her. "Let's break in then."

THEY RODE in silence for a while. The only way back to Charleston was two-lane highway 60. Plows from the small towns along the way were out, but large sections remained covered in snow that was packing into ice with the weight of every car before them.

After downing half a bottle of water and sharing a thermos of steaming black coffee with Taka, Andrea's shakes eased off enough for her to think. She knew the warmth and exhaustion would catch up to her, but the coffee and that distinctive, light grapefruit-and-old-leather scent kept her on edge.

She stole glances at the men.

Soldier, Aaron had said. *Brother*.

One of them killed Lucy Garcia.

Beside her, Bowman had gradually relaxed. Besides being unnaturally thin, he was pale. He'd let his head fall back a little, but under his half-closed eyes, he was watching Tripp fidget with his phone.

She suspected Tripp felt the weight of his gaze and that was why he was so engrossed. Glenn seemed content to focus on the shifting conditions. He was humming under his breath to the song playing low on the radio. Something country. She could barely hear it. Taka shifted restlessly beside her.

"About that long story," she said in Bowman's direction.

He shifted his lidded gaze to her but didn't lift his head.

He pulled his sweater and shirt down so she could see his port. "Had some time off, so I'm here for the Conlons," Bowman said. "Found Dewey a couple months ago and paid him for some information. He called me. I spent half the night checking all their hides. Found the Yukon here. That wouldn't normally mean much, but"—he waved a hand in the air—"snow. And you weren't anywhere else. He wanted me to head Taka off if you managed to escape before he sealed the deal so you wouldn't go getting yourself killed."

Andrea cleared her throat, almost sure what he meant, but... "Seal the deal?"

"He bought you." His face hardened and he sat up.

Glenn turned the radio down.

"How kind of him," Taka drawled.

"The Conlons know you're after them?"

"Yes."

"They were trying to frame you by using your address," Taka said. Andrea didn't know what he was talking about and didn't know if she should ask. But then Taka went on. "Except that kid screwed up, put their name on it."

They were talking about the rental van under the name Conlon. Bowman's address was on the rental agreement.

To try and frame him.

But that made no sense. "But when they rented the van," she said, "they didn't know what was going to happen."

"They don't usually rent vans at all," Bowman said. "I don't know what they were planning to frame me for, but everything went sideways before they could execute."

"That's a good thing," Glenn said. "How'd y'all end up on the wrong end of town, anyway? Were you helping that Detective Tamarin with Lucy Garcia's case?

"Yes," Taka said. "Thank you for the assist."

"Happy to help," Tripp said. "We know Candy had something to do with Lucy ending up in that alley. Have to say, it's an awful surprise finding out Skinny and Candy's brother are involved in something like this. Up until he got sick, I used to see Skinny every week at the smoke shop. What does a van they rented have to do with Lucy? Candy said he talked to the detective same as us and they said he was free to go. Skinny's too sick these days to hurt anyone. Do they think she got mixed up with Xander? Did he kill her?"

"I can't discuss an open case," Taka said with finality.

"How'd you get here, Miss Andrea?" Glenn asked, his eyes finding hers in the mirror. "If you don't mind."

"We're friends," Taka answered for her. "Total fluke."

"Wrong place, wrong time," Tripp said.

Mercedes had said the same last night. "How did the three of you meet?"

"The VFW," Bowman said before Tripp could answer. "Needed backup I could trust."

Andrea glanced away, not wanting him to see her doubt. "If you can't trust veterans, who can you trust?"

36

When they finally reached the interstate, they joined the slow crawl to Charleston.

Taka leaned forward to see Bowman. "Can I borrow your phone?"

Bowman, who'd been staring into space, startled a bit and then patted his jacket and pants pockets, before finding his phone. He held it out, but when Taka took it, he held on. "I suggest a planned approach to involving CPD, Detective Taka. And keeping any mention of our intervention, and Mr. Sanderson's, out of the mix."

"Agreed," he said, and to Andrea, "You know Jimmy's number?"

She shook her head. "I don't know Karie's either."

He thumbed a number and texted someone. Scott, probably. Then looked up a number. "Hey. Detective Taka, CPD, could you please notify Jimmy Hoyle that Andrea Kelley is safe and not available by phone, but she'll call him as soon as possible? Yes. Kelley. Thank you."

"You should call whoever you texted," Bowman said. "They won't know if it's you or not otherwise."

Taka took a deep breath. "Yeah, okay."

He called. Scott picked up immediately. Taka's end wasn't illuminating, and he kept it short, making it sound like winter travel misadventure. "Yeah, Andrea found a connection out in Summersville with Aaron. We just didn't anticipate the snow." After he ended the call, he pressed the corner of the phone to his forehead, eyes closed.

"It's okay," she said. "He'll understand. Where'd he hear Aaron's name?"

"You texted Karie about thinking your Waltham-Young project's related to him. And Mercedes must've answered the texts they sent us later. They didn't know we were gone until this morning. Jimmy was smart enough to know Tamarin might see us being gone as you making a run for it."

She pressed a hand against the pang in her chest. "Pete wouldn't have thought that."

"There's a cruiser parked on your street right now."

Glenn cleared his throat. "If I can ask? Tamarin's that detective that I spoke with about Lucy. Why would he think you'd be making a run for it?"

"Maybe we should," Taka muttered.

"Mercedes is Diego Collins," Bowman offered, saving them from having to answer Glenn.

"And the bald guy?" Taka asked.

"John. Don't have a last name, yet. Who's Aaron?"

"Just someone..."

Andrea stopped Taka with a hand on his arm, a stupid and only half-formed plan not quite coming to her. She kept thinking about Miss Ava, and how she'd approached that family at Louie's. If she could only get one of the men to reveal himself, she could make a better plan. But if she got out of this car without knowing which of them killed Lucy, she might not ever have another chance. On the other hand, pissing off a killer in a car in a traffic jam and snow all around after the night they'd had didn't seem smart either.

"Not many people know, but I'm a bit of a psychic," she said.

Taka widened his eyes in alarm.

She squeezed his arm again. "Spirit keeps bugging me until I pass on their messages. It's inconvenient sometimes."

Bowman gave her the same flat stare he'd been practicing since they'd got in the car.

Glenn spared a glance at her in the rearview.

Tripp visibly froze and then cranked himself around to see her face. "Like, what, ghosts?"

He was a big guy. He couldn't hold himself there without hurting his neck.

He faced forward again with a huff. "My aunt lived in a haunted house. The lights used to flicker all the time. My mom said it was just a short and the house did burn down, but they didn't find a short. What they found was twelve dogs and a baby buried in her crawlspace. Not that she did that. It was a previous owner. Still, that's a lot of bodies. And then my sister—"

"Who's Aaron?" Bowman said again.

Glenn was looking at Tripp like he didn't know who he was anymore.

"Tripp's not wrong. Aaron's a spirit."

"I don't believe in ghosts," Bowman said. "Or psychics."

"Elsa," Andrea said. "How old is she now?"

She'd thought him expressionless before, but she'd been wrong.

Her recovering body temperature dipped several degrees.

He could reach out and kill her right now.

Taka turned his arm over and her hand slid down into his once more.

"Her mom is here. She wants you to know she never meant to leave her. She thought she was a great mom. And great moms deserve a girls' weekend in Atlantic City every now and then."

Andrea had truly been mistaken. He might be the most expressive man she'd met. With no obvious change of expression, the pain that rose in his eyes made her hurt, too. Now that she was thinking about that part of the vision, it flooded her, like something that had happened to her. "She doesn't even know what happened. They went to dinner, a nice one. They all dressed for it. Dressed for each other and themselves, not husbands or boyfriends. No demands, no accommodating, except for Julie who has a peanut allergy.

"They ate, they flirted with the waitstaff, they laughed a lot at the expense of said hubbies and boyfriends. Then they went for drinks. They sat outside, where they could see the beach from a rooftop bar."

Bowman's forehead drew down into a fierce frown. His eyes blazed. He blinked against the tears filling them.

She was hurting him.

It was too much, too fast.

Miss Ava had strung the family out, asking if they understood certain references. "She's showing me a volcano, like the kind kids make for a school project? Does that make sense?"

Bowman swallowed hard. She looked away, keeping him just in the corner of her eye and allowed the memory to come again.

She had two drinks. She texted Elsa a good night and sent a selfie with the girls. She texted her hubby a heart and then followed it up with a photo of one of three male strippers who had just come out after their show to pass out discount cards and smiles. She said she was running away with him.

"She told Elsa good night. Did she send her a selfie? With her friends. Elsa still looks at it. And she's showing me a stripper, a man. She's laughing? She's married and she's making a joke that she's running away with the stripper. But then she's showing me a pair of wedding rings. And a heart."

"How do you know all this?" Bowman demanded.

"Holy shit," Tripp said.

She enjoyed the slight buzz until she didn't. It got worse, like she'd had a lot more to drink than she had and excused herself for the ladies' room. Somehow, she ended up on the boardwalk. She woke up to a strange room with three men gang-raping her. And now she's in the back seat of a car, but her tongue's too thick to work and the flash of the streetlights are hurting her eyes, so she closes them.

"She only had two drinks, but she felt sick. She's showing me a restroom. And another woman. A blonde with an A name. Annette? Amy? Amanda—that's it. They left at the same time and ran into two men Amanda knew. She woke up to a gang rape in a strange room. She suffered beatings and threats to Elsa and her husband whenever she stepped out of line. So, she learned to play the game."

"She's dead?"

Andrea closed her eyes on the tears she couldn't stop from welling up. She thought of Miss Ava, of how she'd soothed. "She's showing me my symbols for drugs. For oxy and X. It's being offered to her. She's taking it. She didn't mean to die. It was just her time. And she knows now that none of it was her fault. Yeah, she was looking forward to that weekend. Couldn't wait for it. And yes, she threw her hubby under the bus at dinner. And she teased him with the stripper, but she loved him. He was the love of her life. And she was a great mom."

"Is she for real, dude?" Tripp blurted. "Is that all true?"

Bowman hid his face by turning to his window. Glenn was doing maybe twenty in a line of cars fifteen deep behind a plow. "I don't know," he finally said. "Some of those details were reported."

"It's true, man," Taka said. "She says it's true, it's true." Without letting go of her hand, he dried his palms on his filthy jeans. Glanced over at her and away again. "We wouldn't have got out of the root cellar without some help."

Again, Glenn found Andrea in the rearview. "You were locked in a root cellar?"

"Yes," Andrea said.

"All that dirt on you. You dug out?"

"Yes."

"I'll bite," he said.

"A girl, twelve or thirteen, was trapped inside and died. She lived there but her parents still don't know what happened to her. I think she had a younger brother. She led us to her bones, and we used one to help lever the log wall apart to get to the dirt behind it so we could dig out. Are there any reports of a girl missing from Conlon's address in the eighties?"

Taka let go of her hand and used Bowman's phone to Google the road name and missing child and 1980s. It took him a couple of tries before he stopped, reading. He said, "Lisa Elizabeth Townsend. They'd only lived there three weeks when she went missing. It was assumed she ran away because of the move. One brother, Brendan, seven at the time."

Bowman held his hand out and Taka gave him the phone.

Tripp was holding his own phone up for Glenn to glance at, his hand shaking.

"Stop the car," Bowman said. Before Glenn really had a chance, he hit the back of Glenn's seat and yelled, "Now! Stop the car now!"

Glenn swerved hard through the plow's leavings. The driver behind them laid on his horn as he flew by. Glenn's BMW lurched to a sliding stop. Bowman jerked the door open and leaned out, gagging. He got his seatbelt undone and practically fell out. Caught himself on his hands and staggered to the back of the car before he emptied his stomach.

Tripp opened his door as well. He got out, but just stood there, facing away from Bowman. Maybe he was a sympathy puker. Or maybe he was worried she'd start talking about Lucy Garcia soon.

Glenn sighed and turned the car off. He turned in the seat to look back at them. "There is no photo, is there? The slave you were asking me about, dressed in cast off bits of Confederate uniforms? Tamarin thought you wanted an excuse to be the one to ID Lucy, but you were really trying to ID a spirit."

"Aaron."

"Are there really ghosts? Or do you just know things?"

Andrea wasn't sure what to say. What would shake him more if he was the one? "I don't know anymore."

"What about Lucy? You see her ghost?"

"I have."

Tripp dropped back inside the car. He nearly knocked heads with Glenn to speak directly to her. "What does this have to do with us?"

"You guys knew her best. She didn't have family. Sometimes spirit shows us symbols or tell us things we can't understand, but someone who knew the person does." Taka was about to break her hand in two. She dug her nails into his hand as hard as she could. "Lucy keeps showing me a silver lighter. She was in the alley there off Quarrier, between Hale and Capitol, so CPD picked up a lot of junk, but they didn't find a lighter."

Bowman was retching again. Tripp blanched and wiped sweat from his temple. "She used those plastic Bic lighters, y'know, the disposable ones."

"I don't remember ever having seen her light up," Glenn said.

"She only smoked pot." Tripp put the back of his hand to his mouth, decidedly green.

Taka twisted his hand free and flattened her hand to his thigh. "The truth is," he said, "Andrea found Lucy and she's become CPD's number one suspect. I lied to my friend about Aaron. We were poking at the Conlons to see what might shake loose. We think that lighter could be an important clue to find her killer, but we can't exactly tell CPD that a ghost says there's a lighter somewhere in the alley."

Still sweating, Tripp burped and then swallowed. Nerves or nausea? "She says it's in the alley? It's not just, y'know, a symbol?"

Andrea chewed on her lip, pretending to think about what to say. She shook her head. "I'm not completely sure. The cops have been watching and I'm under suspicion, so we can't exactly go searching for it, but I'm trying to get Lucy to pinpoint its location."

"Candy could have any pick of lighters from the smoke shop," Glenn said. "He wouldn't much care or notice if he lost one."

"Candy's been cleared," Taka said. "He and Lucy were just two people who used to date."

"So, nothing y'all know about a silver lighter connected to Lucy?"

"Sorry, no," Glenn said.

"She, uh, liked bonfires," Tripp offered. "Maybe she's saying she wants to be cremated?"

A wild, inappropriate laugh flared to life in Andrea's chest. She forced herself to look Tripp in the eye. "That's a really good thought. She might be giving me her symbol, not mine. I'll ask her."

Tripp held up one finger, rolled out of his seat, and lurched away.

Glenn shook his head and sighed again. "Wait'll the wife hears all this. The commander's way overdone it being out most of the night, I don't know what's with Tripp, and now you turn out to be a psychic of all things. First you find Lucy, and now you've found that poor girl's bones? What will her parents think, her being right there on that property all these years they thought she was gone?"

Awful. That's how they'd feel. Just awful. Especially if her hunch was right. She leaned into Taka, chilled all over again with the car doors open. He put his arm around her and pulled her in close. She peered out of the open door at Tripp's hunched back. "Is he okay?"

"He's a good guy, always been a bit of a drama queen. I'll round them up."

"Wait," Taka said. "Can I borrow your phone?"

He handed it over and levered himself out of the car on stiff joints.

"I'm assuming you think one of them killed Lucy?" Taka hissed, watching Glenn pat Tripp's shoulder.

"I *know* one of them killed her."

"Fuck," Taka said. "I'm so fucking cold. Who do we call?"

"You said 'they,' is Jimmy with Scott?"

"And Karie. After the cruiser arrived, Scott picked the locks to get into the house. As far as patrol's concerned, you're home, with several visitors."

"He picked the deadbolt?"

"Not a skill I knew he had. Do you have a plan?"

"Get one of them to confess?"

"That's not a plan, that's an objective."

"Taka, my plan was to research my way into something to give Tamarin so he could catch the damn guy or at least shut Candy and the Conlons down. This..." She held her muddy hair out for him to see with one hand and swept the other out at Glenn and Tripp, walking further down the shoulder, having the same heads together, hand waving discussion as she and Taka. "...is your plan in action."

"I'll call Scott. Karie can talk to Louie. He can have someone keep an eye on the alley for anyone looking for something until we can, I don't know, set up a camera or something?"

Bowman stalked past the driver's side. He ripped the driver's door open and collapsed onto the seat. Leaning over, he reached into the passenger foot well and came up with another bottle of water.

"May I have another?" Taka said.

Without looking, Bowman chucked the one in his hand between the seats. Andrea caught it and handed it to Taka. He chucked a second one back and cracked the top on a third. He swished a big mouthful and spit it out before downing half the bottle in one go. With his back still to them, he said, "Who's Lucy?"

"Another woman the Conlons trafficked," Andrea said. "Only instead of OD'ing, she murdered her handler, and someone murdered her in turn."

Glenn slid into the passenger seat. "Feel good enough to drive?"

"Yes, sir," Bowman said and pulled his legs in and slammed the door shut.

Tripp had come around the back and with a nervous look at her, got in. Andrea slid as far as she could against Taka but couldn't avoid contact with Tripp. She didn't realize she was bracing for a memory until it hit. *Between Tripp and Candy, she's monkey in the middle of the pickup's front bench seat. The lap belt cuts into her waist as Tripp drives wildly over the ridge. She tilts her head back and laughs and laughs.*

Andrea knew it was Lucy's memory but didn't know what it meant. She focused on Taka's hands on Glenn's phone. The rapid movement of his thumbs over the tiny keyboard. And Lucy's laugh faded into the shush of the wet highway, the whir of the BMW's heater on high again, and the country song that Bowman turned up to stop them all from talking anymore.

37

"Hoyle," Pete Tamarin barked when Jimmy answered his phone. "You got eyes on Andrea Kelley?"

Jimmy's first instinct, he was stunned to discover, was to lie. But with a cruiser down the street, that'd be stupid. "No." He swallowed the "sir." Tamarin was at most his equal and he wouldn't be cowed.

"Your car's in her drive."

"Yes."

"How long have they been gone?"

"I was supposed to meet her here at seven a.m. When she wasn't here, I started calling around."

"We have cars rolling in Fayette and Clay Counties. Both sheriff departments are cooperating. Taka sent info to Fields yesterday evening that gives us new avenues of investigation. In addition, we've been monitoring Candy King's communications. This morning an analyst reported a forwarded link offering a man and woman in a flash sale. The photos appear to be authentic and appear to show Taka and Andrea Kelley in distress, timestamped last night. That link has led us to an encrypted human trafficking site. We have enough for warrants and we're hoping they haven't been moved before units are on scene."

"You know where they are?"

"No. We have two addresses for now. But no, we don't know for sure."

Karie came back into the kitchen from calling Louie.

Jimmy held his finger to his lips.

"Tamarin. I'm off duty. Give me something to do."

"I can't, Jimmy." For the first time in days, Tamarin sounded like himself. "This is a courtesy call. I know the last few days have made me look like an asshole, but I'm just doing my job. I shouldn't be calling you at all."

"Will you call me as soon as you have her?"

"Yeah. Look, keep that Wilson chick in check, too. And I'm not even going to say anything about one of Dewey's lackeys being there."

"Thanks, Tamarin."

Jimmy checked to make sure the call was ended before he spoke again. "Okay, that was weird." He relayed Tamarin's message.

"He lied to me," Scott said, a frown creasing his brow.

If Karie hadn't been there, Jimmy would've laughed at the absurdity of Scott being upset that he'd been lied to by Taka, the person he'd been lying to for months now.

"I'm sure he had a reason." Karie said. "Do we want patrol reporting they've shown up here before the raid happens?"

They looked at each other.

Jimmy clapped his hands. "We don't know, so let's go cautious. Try texting that last number, Scott. Tell them to either walk in or meet us somewhere else."

They waited in tense silence, Scott staring down at his phone for the reply.

He smiled. "Walking in."

WHEN THEY FINALLY DROVE DOWN the snow-covered, Christmas decorated cul-de-sac downhill from her own street, Andrea felt every hour of the last twenty-four hit her at once. The sky was a breathtaking jewel blue with no clouds, but the sun seemed very far away. A couple of kids played in the yards. She directed Bowman where to stop, near her downslope neighbor.

As Taka slid out, the icy air leapt in.

Andrea met Bowman's hard glare in the rearview mirror. *Her eyes were still black, and they were turning her on twenty-five-dollar tricks when Donny threw the paper on the dirty bed, a printed screenshot from Facebook.*

He turned his head to frown at her. "What."

"You come across a Donny associated with the Conlons?"

He gave her a tight nod.

"He called her Doll. And kept her in line."

He closed his eyes. "Her name was Becky."

"I'm sorry," she said.

Tripp was staring at her again, his mouth open.

"Call me if you need any more help with your Civil War research," Glenn said.

"Thanks, Glenn." She really hoped it wasn't Glenn.

Out in the bright cold, she stood still for a second, feeling all the open space around her and took a deep, clearing, cold-achy breath.

Taka shut the door.

The yard was unfenced and heavily wooded. They traipsed alongside the next-door neighbor's weathered privacy fence, threading between the dogwoods, rhododendrons, and maples to the large ditch that was her back property line. She stepped down sideways. Taka caught her arm and then they were both slipping down the steep slope on the fallen leaves and snow. They picked their way over the bottom and scrambled up the other side into the trees in her yard.

At the sight of Karie working on her laptop at the kitchen table, Scott sitting across from her, her legs went weak. She and Taka weaved like drunken sailors across the grass to her back stoop.

The kitchen door opened, and Jimmy took in their appearance. "Mud run?"

"Root cellar," Taka said.

Andrea shuddered.

The root cellar and thought of being sold against her will had been horrifying, but she'd known there was a way out. Being trapped in the car with a murderer had been terrifying. Now that she was home, she froze.

"Andrea?" Taka said.

Jimmy came out, scooped her up in one swift move, carried her through the kitchen, and deposited her at the base of the stairs. Vaguely, she heard Karie and Scott exclaiming over Taka. Jimmy herded her up the stairs to the bathroom and sat her on the closed toilet lid. "What happened?"

He turned the shower on and then knelt in front of her.

She opened her mouth, but her teeth chattered. "A woman Taka talked to. A f-f-ew days ago. At Xander Conlon's farm. Asked h-h-im to help her. It was a t-t-trap. They locked us. In a root ce-cell-ar."

"You need Karie in here?"

She shook her head, but then changed her mind, then changed it again. There was so much to do before tonight. She needed time to think. "I'm okay," she managed through the annoying chatter. "I'm cold. And . . . the shakes."

"The shakes will wear off. Don't turn the water up too hot. I'll make tea."

"Hooo . . . t . . . choc . . . late. Puuh . . . lease. My nu-nu-nipples are s-so cold they h-h-urt."

"I can't believe you just said that," he chortled.

"Mu-made you s-s-smile."

He cupped his hands on her muddy cheeks and kissed her hard.

DOWNSTAIRS, Taka was seated at the table with Karie, a blanket over his shoulders, tea in one hand, and a huge sandwich in the other. Scott stood at the stove, pouring soup from a can into a pot.

Jimmy lifted his chin towards Scott. "You tell him?"

"No."

"Tamarin called. They have a wiretap warrant on Candy and saw you'd been put up for auction. He's raiding the Conlons now."

Taka talked around his mouthful, "That why you told us to walk in?"

"We didn't know what was going on," Scott blurted. "You told us the Yukon broke down."

They'd been careful not to reveal their working relationship in front of Karie. But it'd be even harder now with Andrea and Taka in the mix. So far, Scotty had played Dewey's shill better than Jimmy ever imagined he could under the circumstances.

"Andrea said you'd understand."

Scott gave him a sheepish smile. "Karie said you'd have a reason."

"We didn't want the raid held up if you showed up before they execute," Jimmy said. "Should I call him now?"

Taka swallowed, finished off his mug of tea, contemplated the sandwich in his hand, and then took another giant bite. Scotty took the mug and refilled it with hot water and a fresh tea bag. Taka continued to think, so Jimmy pulled out a chair and sat down. Karie absently shoved his own half-drunk coffee in his direction.

He checked the time. Ten-thirty-five on a snowy Saturday morning full of anxious near-panic until this very moment. He was going to call that good. He got back up and pushed the liquor bottles around on Andrea's sideboard until he found the Jack Daniels. Unscrewing it on the way back to the table, he saw he had Taka's full attention.

He poured a shot in his coffee and when Scott set Taka's tea down, poured a shot into it without asking. Karie, who had been reviewing the recordings from Louie's after they'd exhausted their options for Andrea and Taka, tapped the rim of her mug. He shook the bottle at Scott, who picked up his empty water glass and held it while Jimmy poured. He set the bottle down, saluted them with his mug, and drank.

Taka finished his sandwich and then tucked into the loaded tea before he answered Jimmy's question. "I think we have to talk to Sweet Joe and Carson before we talk to Tamarin. Also..." He took another long swallow of tea. "There's a dead girl in the root cellar."

"Like, a fresh dead girl? Or a ghost dead girl?" Jimmy said.

Taka looked at Scott, who sipped his whiskey, while looking back.

"We told him," Karie said.

"Ghost dead girl and her bones. Lisa Elizabeth Townsend."

Before he finished talking, Karie was typing. "Oh. She's still listed as missing. Her poor parents."

Jimmy leaned forward, elbows planted on the table. "Can you run us through what happened from the top?"

A LOT warmer in dry jeans and her thickest sweater, Andrea met Scott properly. Taka handed him his coffee mug and went to shower. Scott rinsed the mug, pulled out a bowl like he'd been living with her forever, and poured her favorite soup into it from a pot on the stove. He popped a spoon in it and waved her to the table, where a steaming mug of hot chocolate sat waiting for her. She needed to tell Taka they were keeping him no matter what.

Jimmy held up the Jack. She nodded. The first gulp of hot chocolate and whiskey sent a path of warmth into her chest and then spread out. She was still cold. And tired. But wired, too.

"Wait," Karie said, staring at Andrea's hands. "Where's Louie's ring?"

"After jail and the hospital, I put it back on Louie's wall before we left yesterday."

"Thank God!"

"Right?"

Taka had given them the highlights.

"He said a ghost helped you," Karie said. Her notebook was in front of her, with another whole page of names and connections.

Andrea tilted her head slightly at Scott.

"We fucked that up," Jimmy announced. "And then filled him in."

"Okay, then," Andrea breathed. Was she just going to drag everybody in with her whether they wanted to know or not? "You're really okay with everything?"

Scott's mouth turned down at the corners. He waggled his head. "Yeah. I'm down with the supernatural. Your experience seems a little more intense than some flickering lights, but yeah. I'm good."

"Taka said he thought you had a plan," Jimmy said. "To trap Lucy's killer? But he didn't know where you were going with that."

"He told me my plan was an objective, not a plan." She eyed Scott. She shivered.

She couldn't tell them.

If she got Jimmy involved, he'd be interfering with CPD's case. But he was already involved as a witness and if they just happened to be at Louie's could he really get in trouble for that? How would Scott really take it if something happened with Aaron while they were there? Andrea shook her head. Karie would get it, but how could she help?

Jimmy started gathering the glasses, mugs, and plates off the table. "Eat. We can wait for Taka, so you don't have to explain it twice. I'm going to clean up. Scott's going to take in a little fresh air and check on the cruiser out front."

Scott stretched and got up, taking his time as he ambled out.

Karie smiled at her. "I'm so glad you're okay. I knew something had happened when you didn't call me about the reports Megan forwarded. Mrs. Dunbar's journals are only so long."

Taking the temporary time-out being offered, Andrea forced herself out of her head and dug into the soup. "The Ivystone burials?"

"She sent them to me and you and Talisha and Randy."

Although Scott didn't linger going through the front door, the cold drifted through the house and clung to her.

"Talisha and Randy and me, I get. How come she sent them to you?"

Karie grinned. "Because of the ghost story."

"Seriously?" Jimmy said and turned the sink faucet on.

Andrea relaxed into the comforting sound and Karie's excitement.

38

"First, the facts. All three graves were discovered along the southern exposure when Ivystone's sunporch was demolished and rebuilt. All of the corpses were partially mummified. Something about the soil and exposure. All the textiles were fragmented, but large parts were perfectly preserved, which is why your client was able to cut those drapery samples."

"I've been dying to know," Andrea said.

Jimmy snorted. Andrea blushed and flapped a hand at him.

Karie grinned and carried on. "One of the two older burials is a white man. A Confederate soldier, about forty years old. He was shot in the back with a shotgun. The other is a Black man around thirty. Now get this—they cleaned the Confederate soldier's handgun and proved the soldier executed the Black man. Shot him in the head. Their theory is the Black man was a Union spy who crossed the Potomac with Lee's Army during the retreat from Gettysburg." Karie's glee level jumped ten notches. "Guess what they found on him? You'll never guess!"

Andrea pointed her spoon at her. "A ring like Louie's."

Karie slapped Andrea's arm. "How'd you know?"

"I have a theory on this ghost thing. I'm calling it crossed circumstances. What about the third burial?"

Scott came back in. Instead of coming into the kitchen, he disappeared up the stairs. Taka's shower was still running.

"The burial shroud for that one is also drapery fabric, but it's a lighter type, popular from like 1870 to 1875. That body is also a Black man, also roughly thirty years old, but missing a leg. There was evidence he may have been ill before he died. The bone that formed his stump was eaten away by infection, so possibly septicemia or something similar. He had pneumonia when he died. No ring."

Although she'd bet dinner that Aaron was connected to Ivystone, none of it quite fit. Aaron appeared younger than thirty. Although he seemed to think of himself as a soldier, he'd never appeared to her in a Union uniform. Could he be the civilian? Although he'd used Louie's to get their attention, he had no ring. But he also appeared to have both legs. On the other hand, just thinking about it brought the burning pain of her leg in the vision back to her. "What about the ghost story?"

Karie turned her laptop so Andrea could see the photo she'd pulled up. Taken onsite at Ivystone Farm, two closed-face older men with shovels stood next to the bed of a pickup truck. It contained three long cardboard boxes, each filled with a rolled shroud. Numbered cardboard boxes stacked on the ground contained the grave dirt for filtering. A sheriff's car sat in the background.

"These guys," Karie said, "don't look like they scare easy. There were three of them altogether, plus a deputy. They claim they saw a young Black woman through the open kitchen window several times over the two days they were digging. Just glimpses through the open interior shutters. They could smell corn fritters and cooked apples with cinnamon. They'd met Mr. Pederson on the first morning, but then he left them to it. They just assumed she lived in the house. She never came out and they never needed anything from her.

"Right after this photo was taken, she came out and walked right up to the truck. One of the guys wrote down exactly what she said." Karie turned the laptop, clicked on something, and then read, "She said, 'I don't care much about that Reb, but you make sure those other boys get home to their family, wherever they may be now, you hear?'"

"They said they'd try their best and she turned around and marched right back into the house. They covered the boxes and stowed the shovels and considering her comment about 'the Reb,' one of the guys decided they should document any stories she might have heard before they left.

"He went to the kitchen door and knocked on it, but it swung open. The kitchen was in an abandoned state. Unused for decades at that point. The sixties-era stove was not only unusable, it was rusted out by an overhead leak at some point in the house's abandonment. They hightailed it out of there and called Pederson on the way, who confirmed no one was living in the house."

"Why do ghosts have to be so uninformative?" Jimmy complained. He'd finished and was leaning against the sink, arms folded.

Andrea rolled her eyes.

Karie laughed. "Right? I have no ghost stories in my files where the ghosts are straight up with their need and purpose."

"But the ring," Andrea said. "There's probably all sorts of variations on horseshoe nail rings. Can we ask them for detailed photos? Whay put a maker's mark on the one Louie has."

"Already requested."

"Taka'll be down in a minute," Scott said, coming into the kitchen and plopping down where he'd been.

Jimmy reclaimed his chair as well.

Andrea could already see how much harder she was making their lives. Although she hated that fact, she still needed them to help her. She set the dregs of her hot chocolate down. "Lucy Garcia recognized her killer's scent. It's distinctive. I recognized it, too, but she didn't think about him in a way that would tell me who he was. Then we got in the car today..." The scent filled her nose again like she was still trapped there with them.

"One of the VFW guys?" Jimmy said, his tone gentle.

"Not Bowman," she said. "Did Taka tell you about him?"

Nods all around.

"It's Glenn or Tripp."

Karie sat up straight. "Is one of them the Derek guy?"

"No, Taka would've recognized him."

Jimmy scruffed his head with both hands. "Tamarin's not looking for Lucy's killer anymore. He's sure she and Eddie killed each other.

There's no way to bring a scent to him without either further incriminating yourself or confessing you see ghosts."

"Which he'll just blow off," Taka said from the hallway. "What scent?"

Andrea sighed. "Either Glenn or Tripp killed Lucy."

"I got that much," Taka said.

"When are Sweet Joe and Carson coming?"

"Two hours," Taka said. "And they're arranging for Tamarin to come here later. We're not going to the station anymore unless one of us is being charged."

Someone knocked at the front door. They all fell silent. Another heavy knock.

Taka finally spun to answer it. He cracked the door open and then pulled it wider. "Dewey."

"Bought the Yukon, too."

"You didn't buy us. We were gone already."

"Au contraire," Dewey said and pushed forward. Taka stepped back. Andrea knew right then he always would. "Ah, you have company." He walked to the kitchen doorway, Taka following, and took a good look. He was, as always, his usual dashing self. "Now this is quite the crew."

"What do you mean," Taka said, arms crossed. "'Au contraire?'"

"I still bought you. You're mine now." He slid a sly smile Andrea's way. "Maybe not to play with, but you would have been hunted down unless I did. So you're mine now, it's recorded in a shared blockchain, and within days, anyone with a hand in the game will know you're both off-limits or they'll answer to me."

Andrea had no idea how to respond to that. None of them did.

"Unfortunately, the boys in blue acted on that link sent to Candy a lot faster than I thought they would, so I had to let them borrow the Yukon for a bit, rather than returning it to you in a grand gesture. I didn't want to be anywhere near the place when they arrived. It'll probably help the case against them anyway."

"You sent that link," Jimmy said.

"They haven't operated in Charleston this long without being smart about it," Dewey said, condescension dripping from his words.

"Bowman told you about the patrol car out front?" Taka said.

Self-satisfied, Dewey stuck his hands in his pockets. "Everyone knows you and I developed a friendship a couple of months ago. One literally forged in fire. Of course, I sent Scott around to find you when you didn't show up for our planned breakfast this morning. Of course, I've come myself, after learning Andrea is missing, too. Just checking in. Leaving Scott with Andrea's state policeman boyfriend and her new best friend so I'll be properly informed when CPD locates my good friend."

Again, Andrea could think of nothing to say.

"I can see I've interrupted whatever little plan you have to scare some poor fellow into a confession of wrongdoing. I've never seen Bowman on his heels before today."

Andrea covered her pang of guilt with the question that finally occurred to her. "Do you know the men with him today?"

"No. He's an independent contractor."

"They're veterans, they were with me at the smoke shop."

"Ah. I meet a lot of people. Can't remember them all. Now, I must be off. I hope you make your way safely back home soon. I spent a lot of Bitcoin on you." He gave one last considering look at Andrea. "Nice tits, by the way."

Jimmy stood halfway up, but Taka rolled his eyes and tipped his head back, sweeping his arm out towards the door. Dewey smirked at them and finally left.

"He's Machiavellian, isn't he?" Karie said after the door slammed shut.

"If that means a cunning asshole, then yes," Taka said.

"For God's sake," Jimmy said. "Before everyone knows except us, what's the plan?"

WHILE ANDREA and Taka huddled with Sweet Joe and Carson at the house, Jimmy and Jesus spent part of the early afternoon setting up three wireless security cameras while Scott and Karie kept an eye on either end of the alley to alert them if anyone decided to venture in from the street.

On Louie's office desktop, Jimmy watched Scott walk through the alley to make sure they had the angles right. "The van was here," he said, tapping the screen on camera one. "And her body was here, between these two bins."

"I looked at the lights in the alley," Karie said. "They're mostly just over the back doors, so if anyone comes looking, they'll be using a flashlight."

"Or night vision goggles, which, in this weather and at night—"

"In a mostly deserted location—"

"Would go unnoticed."

"Normally," Karie said. "Wait, do the cameras have night vision?"

Jimmy grinned. "They do."

His phone vibrated on the desk. Andy Detweiler. He debated with himself for a second and then picked it up. "Yeah?"

"My turn to bug you off-duty."

"And you see what I did?"

He could hear Andy rolling his eyes across the line. "You answered. But you're going to wish you hadn't."

"Let me guess. CPD is formally requesting assistance on a human trafficking case."

"Andrea already called you."

"We were supposed to have breakfast, but I was still in 'she'll show up' mode when she showed up."

"Well, CPD wants us, along with the feds. So we need you here. Nina's already helping with an encrypted auction site."

"Maddox doesn't want to put Mark or Oscar on it?"

"He says you and Nina are mostly up to speed and he's pretty sure you already know what went on last night." Andy's tone wasn't as sarcastic as it could've been regarding his relationship with Andrea, which was one reason Jimmy still liked him.

"But is Detective Tamarin okay with it?"

"Dude. Tamarin requested you. Says he needs someone with a handle on all the connections." Jimmy suspected Tamarin had a BCI birdie of his own and what he was after was whatever BCI had connecting Dewey to the Conlons.

Nina said something in the background and Bill replied. Andy kept talking. "CPD's got more than enough charges in mind for the Conlons without having to wait on the Lansing investigation, which you were clear of anyway, right? And the other one in the alley's wrapped up regarding the actual murders. The victims killed each other."

"CPD go public on that?"

"Read it in the paper this morning. They didn't mention the inconvenient ties to sex trafficking and the Conlons, so I guess we'll go after that separately."

Andy was obviously already on board for the multiagency task force.

Jimmy said, "Scott visually verified the house Dewey went to on Tuesday night as Anna Lansing's. Maddox agreed to withhold that visit from CPD. I'm good with sticking to that unless CPD starts squawking about Dewey while they're pinning Linda Conlon down at the Lansing scene."

"I fucked that up. I don't have a problem withholding it. I think we should decide together whether we share any Dewey info at all with other agencies. And I think we should collect and exploit any and all Dewey-related info or evidence in the various investigations that get launched under this task force."

Jimmy could get behind that. "When's the briefing?"

"You got out to talk to her?" Carson exclaimed during the first time they told their story.

Sweet Joe appeared sweet, in part, because he was less expressive than most people, and way less expressive than an agitated Carson. He kept his mild, perpetual smile in place as he shifted his laconic gaze from Carson to the recorder on the kitchen table to Taka and said, "Don't answer that. Keep going."

The recording was just for the lawyers to get an unpolished baseline and for later review.

They were entirely truthful except for how they located Lisa Townsend's useful bone in the dark. For everyone outside their small cadre, the bone was sticking up out of the dirt and once they had light, they'd realized what it was and replaced it with the rest of her, quickly restoring her resting place until police could recover her.

As Carson coordinated their approach to Tamarin and the announcement regarding their escape from forced captivity, Sweet Joe took Taka and Andrea into the living room to make a short recording that Tamarin could keep for the case or release to the media.

When they were finished, Joe took the footage into the kitchen to show to Carson.

Andrea checked the burner Jimmy had pulled from his car for them to share. "Jimmy's out. CPD asked for assistance from State and the Feds. His supervisor and Tamarin, of all people, want him as part of the task force."

"Tamarin's smart. That's the right move."

"I don't know how I feel about tonight," Andrea confessed. "I'm scared neither of them will show and I'm scared one of them will. I want justice for Lucy, but I don't want anyone to get hurt. I don't know if I want to carry. It didn't do me any good last night."

And still, the casual way the boy had held his gun made her belly churn all over again.

"I don't want you to carry. We're going into an unknown situation in the dark in a business district on a Saturday night. I'm going to steal your HK from your safe, though, because I don't think I can handle not being armed."

"I wish Jimmy was going to be there."

"We just need enough to give Tamarin another lead, just like with Anna last night."

39

E nsconced in Louie's office, Andrea watched all three camera feeds live on his computer and her and Karie's laptops. She was grateful to be warm, while feeling guilty about being safe inside. She could only see Karie, hidden in the shadow of the bakery's dumpster in a nest of worn blankets because she knew where she was sitting.

Wearing an orange beanie, a thrift-store jacket with a torn sleeve, and old jeans with leg warmers, and unknown to either Glenn or Tripp, Karie had volunteered to intercept anyone, including possible employees from the businesses lining the alley, who appeared to be searching for something.

Taka sat in the driver's seat of Scott's Firebird on Quarrier, watching feed two, aimed at the area where Lucy had crawled between two dumpsters and died, on a server's iPad. Scott was loitering in the small median park directly across Lee Street from the mouth of the alley.

Louie's dinner service was slammed.

The bars were slammed.

On one side of the alley, Capitol Street was packed with tourists and locals alike, enjoying the snow and cold and lights as a festive start to the holiday season. On the other side, Hale Street, always a little quieter, was booming in its own unique, off-the-beaten-path way.

Louie's contribution had made her day and revealed his secret. He'd pulled units from his staff and given each of them mini two-way radios they could pocket and earbuds with wireless around-the-neck microphones so they could talk to each other. No wonder he always knew each customer's name and service was seamless.

Hopefully she'd put enough pressure on Glenn and Tripp that one of them would show up tonight. Unless, of course, she was just completely crazy about the scent and on the wrong track.

As if she'd summoned it, she caught a faint trace in the air. The temperature in the office plummeted. Flushing, Andrea stood up. A wisp of white rose from under the office door and swirled into a cloud of white in the shape of a woman. Then the air warmed up as fast as it had cooled, and the mist dissipated, but Andrea could still sense Lucy Garcia's presence.

TAKA SAW the man's shadow in the door's rearview mirror just before he tapped on the passenger's side window. Prepared to ignore any distractions, it took him a hot second to recognize Commander Bowman.

He hit the door locks and then keyed the mic at his throat, hidden under the neck of his sweater.

"Commander," he said, after Bowman slipped in and shut the door.

Taka wasn't sure the draft of air was actually as cold as his body was insisting.

"Tripp doesn't work for the Conlons."

"The way you were watching him? How come I don't believe you?"

"I don't get him, but he doesn't work for the Conlons."

"Okay."

"Your girl used me."

"She's not my girl."

"*Your girl* really got to Tripp."

"Why are you here?"

"The reason Tripp was so nervous? He was worried she'd read his mind and out him. He's desperate that no one find out he panhandles for a living. He sleeps out on the street or in his truck most nights even though he owns a rundown shack west of here."

"The vagrant," Andrea said in his ear.

The guy who had covered Lucy with pallets. Was the lighter Andrea had seen and Tamarin never mentioned his? "It's a good cover," Taka said. "As a panhandler, he can both recruit and kidnap."

"He's not organized enough. He's unreliable. Almost everything he does is spontaneous."

"Why'd you bring him with you then?"

"He's very good at creating a distraction."

"So, we should be watching for Glenn," Scott said across the comms.

The commander himself was creating a good distraction.

Taka dropped his gaze back to the live feed. At the edge of the camera's range, someone was swinging a trash bag up and over into a bin. The screen was too small to see individual actions but within a few seconds, it was clear they were scrolling on their phone while smoking.

The commander continued to sit, watching the passing cars. Taka doubted Tripp's involvement, too, but only because his bet was still on Candy having called Derek to handle the situation. "Why are you here?"

"To see if he shows up."

"What does it matter to you?"

"That stupid move you made yesterday looks like it's going to topple the Conlons' little empire here in Charleston. Candy's skirting the edges. He stands a good chance of skating with just a couple of drug charges. Romeos are hard to prosecute.

"Bulldog's going to soak up Xander Conlon's local stable and keep getting them whatever they need to keep them working. But on the Conlons' party circuit? The handlers are scattering like roaches right now and taking all their victims with them. Someone will step up and code a new auction page or pimp exchange, and the show'll go on. So yeah, if Tripp shows tonight, maybe he saw something I want to know about."

Taka was used to small wins. Although he'd have preferred recovering trafficking victims with a more organized effort, the Conlons took themselves down by killing Anna Lansing so publicly just to prove their power. And they would have done it, proven that power, if they'd succeeded in disappearing Andrea and Taka. "You know who Derek is?"

"Derek's dead."

No one said anything.

A car beeped both in his ear and down the long block where Scott was lurking on Lee.

Taka decided he didn't really care about Derek, but... "What about the kids at Anna Lansing's?"

"I'd have asked if I had gotten to him first."

"Who was she to you? Elsa's mom?"

"My sister."

On the iPad, the smoker pulled the back door to Pies & Pints open and disappeared inside.

"INCOMING," Scott said. "Two men. White."

Once in the alley, they walked closer together, heads together. One of them laughed. Near the bakery, that one bumped the other against the brick near the door and they shared a long, leisurely kiss.

"Great," Karie said. "Flurries."

"I hope you mean flurries," Scott said. "Of snow."

"What do you think I said?"

"Furries?"

An employee threw the Adelphia Grill's door open and came out.

"Oh, Scott," Karie said with gleeful abandon. "We need to have a conversation."

Another employee in the doorway tossed four big bags of trash out. They must've been loud because the lovers broke apart.

"What are furries?" Taka asked.

The employees flipped the lid back on a dumpster and threw the bags in. They went back in, pushing and shoving at each other.

"Hush," Andrea said.

Holding hands, the lovers continued down the alley. One of them spotted Karie and took a startled step sideways into the other. "Hi," he said.

"Hi, cutie," she said.

"Hi, cutie?" Andrea said and Karie laughed.

The guys picked up their pace.

"Got 'em," Taka said. "They can't stop looking over their shoulders."

"You got ears on?" Bowman said. Like before, his voice was muted and faint, but clear.

"Yep."

Andrea thought he'd say something else, but he didn't. The bounce of a ball turned her head. The boy sat on the floor beside her chair, playing jacks. Nearly translucent, she could hardly make out his features. When she looked back at the computers, a jack sat between them. The boy blipped out.

She picked the toy up. It was solid. Metal. Small, and sharper than the modern-day plastic jacks. Then she noticed a pile of three on a stack of cookbooks on the corner of the desk.

Over the next two hours, people came and went in the alley. Karie scared a group of teenagers tagging dumpsters and doors before they could do much damage. Andrea was amazed at the three stumbling couples who could ignore the surroundings. One of them managed to get the deed done despite Karie's crazed rant for them to at least move to where she couldn't see them. She ended up covering her face and begging Andrea to tell her when they were done, with the guys laughing at her across the comms.

Jimmy texted on the burner: *Yukon and ALL guns recovered*, which she took to mean both their carry weapons and the rifle and guns Taka had reported as stowed in the rear safe. Thank God they hadn't ended up out in the world in the wrong hands.

Every little while, Andrea would hear the bounce of the ball and when she looked—at the shelves, the printer, the top of a picture frame —there was another jack. She collected them in a small pile in front of the computers.

Then Aaron showed up in his apron and boots. His long white sleeves billowed in a phantom wind stronger than the breeze blowing occasional bits of debris down the alley.

"Heads up. Aaron's in the alley across from Karie, looking towards Quarrier."

Several minutes of silence passed.

The burner vibrated.

Jimmy.

On my way.

Andrea quickly texted, *Aaron here.*

Taka said, "Incoming. Hooded jacket and gloves. Cart. Appears homeless."

Tripp? Or someone else seeking shelter from the cold in the form of a dumpster wind break?

"That's Tripp," Bowman said, from the well of Scott's car.

"Hold position," Taka said. "I've got him on camera two, now, Andrea."

The scent of Lucy's killer flooded the office.

Tripp paused thirty yards from Louie's back door, looking all around for anyone watching him.

Andrea stood, sending Louie's chair rolling away. She felt around behind her, grabbed her jacket, and yanked it on.

Pushing his cart onward, Tripp picked something from the top.

A powerful flashlight beam flared in the infrared camera before he swung it to the area where Lucy had been. Aaron disappeared as it crossed over him.

Staring at the video, Andrea scooped up the burner and the jacks, dropping them in her jacket pocket.

Tripp pushed his cart against one of the dumpsters after searching the ground around it. Leaving it there, he swept the light around the area between them. Since Lucy's death, a new collection of pallets filled the space where she had been. Getting down on his knees, Tripp searched beneath the dumpsters. When he found nothing, he tried to search the pallets, but couldn't hold the light and move the heavy wood.

"Go, Karie," Taka said.

Karie, already primed, left her nest. "Hi, whatcha looking for?"

Tripp leaped and turned, dropping his light, which tumbled halfway across the alley. Karie picked it up. "Need some help? I'd love company out here tonight," she said, pointing the flashlight back towards her nest.

Tripp didn't move.

Karie walked over to him and shined the light in his face. Although he wasn't close to the camera, he was unmistakably Tripp. "I don't bite," Karie said. "Are you going to set up or did you lose something?"

Like Bowman's, Tripp's voice came muted and faint through Karie's earpiece, but clear. "I lost a lighter. And, and, and a money clip?"

"Ouch," Karie said. "Any money in that clip?"

Tripp held up his hand to block the light and Karie pointed it away.

"Sorry about that," she said. "So, this money clip."

"I don't know if it's still here. The lighter is, though."

"How much money was in it?"

"Why? Did you find it?"

"Maybe?"

"I'll give you all the money if you give me the lighter and the clip. It's not mine. I don't know how—"

"You don't know how what?"

Tripp suddenly transformed, and Andrea could see it coming. He puffed himself up into Southern redneck aggression pose. It was way more terrifying in a dark alley than it had been when she and her friends laughed at the boys at school pulling it out whenever they felt threatened.

Andrea ripped the office door open.

"Give it to me," Tripp yelled in her ear, and it echoed off the brick walls and metal bins.

She ducked beneath a loaded tray of dirty dishes. The busboy yelped but stayed upright. The rest of the crew darted and moved out of her way, giving Andrea a path through the kitchen.

In her ear, rustling and clunks and a car horn and hard breaths and the pound of boots on pavement.

"Tell me why I should," Karie said with defiance.

"Get away from her," Scott roared.

In front of the door, the dishwasher looked up.

Never looking away from her, he reached out, snagged the handle, and wrenched the door open. Andrea leaped into the alley as Taka ran past and slammed into Tripp and Scott. Karie stepped backwards, in the clear, as they crashed to the pavement.

Coming up on top, Tripp saw Andrea.

The snarl on his face melted.

Scott rolled away and ninja'ed to his feet, ready to take Tripp back on. Legs trapped under Tripp, Taka shoved at the man, trying to kick free but stopped at Tripp's utter lack of response.

The flurries gusted sideways, cold and wet on Andrea's face, catching in her lashes.

"It's not mine," Tripp said to her. "It's not mine."

40

Lucy's killer's scent swirled in the space between them. Aaron coalesced beside Karie, from the inside out, from torn and bloody to whole.

"You smell that?" Andrea said.

"Smell what," Tripp wailed, tearing up.

Taka shook his head at her.

"I just smell the alley. And snow," Karie said, in both Andrea's ear and the alley.

Andrea fingered her mic off and saw Karie do the same.

Aaron lifted his head, looking again towards Quarrier Street.

Scott remained ready to defend, demanding of Tripp, "What does the lighter have to do with Lucy's death?"

Taka winced and pulled his earbud out.

"I didn't kill her," Tripp cried.

Taka grunted and jerked one leg free. He kicked Tripp off the other and scrambled up.

"I picked his pocket," Tripp said, still sitting on the ground. "I'm a pickpocket."

Aaron let himself fade, intent on Quarrier all the while. He twisted into a mist and drifted past Andrea. She lifted her finger. "Give me a second."

She turned and followed Aaron down the alley.

"I left them with her so they could find him. I don't know how they could miss them."

"They?" Taka said in her ear.

"The cops, the cops. I wore gloves, so they could get his fingerprints and they think she did it? How? How is that possible?"

If those were the same fuzzy winter gloves Tripp was wearing now, there'd be little hope of getting fingerprints off the lighter or the clip.

"And then Glenn, he had to open his big mouth and tell him about the lighter."

Aaron sped up and Andrea broke into a trot.

Scott's Firebird rolled across the mouth of the alley. In the streetlight, she could see the back of Bowman's head. Andrea opened up her stride. A tall, wide shadow broke away from the wall of the brick building across Quarrier and walked fast down the sidewalk. A man, in a long black wool coat and black beanie and beard.

The killer's scent enveloped her.

"Parker!" Tripp shouted. "He told Parker!"

Beard nearly ran into a woman and her kids leaving Super Weenie. She screamed as he grabbed her arms to keep them both upright. Her drink went flying. The kids ran into her legs. Beard pushed her back at the door to get around her and one of boys threw his hotdog at him, leaving a splash of mustard on the back of his coat.

"Who the fuck is Parker," Taka growled, from down in the well.

Beard took off running.

Karie's muted voice sounded far away. "Is Andrea running?"

A car stopped short in the middle of Quarrier to avoid hitting her. She slapped her hands on the hood and vaulted the front bumper. She ran up the street along the parked cars, her lungs already raw from the cold air. Beard slowed at the intersection of Capitol, looking left, but then pelted straight on.

Andrea didn't have the breath to yell.

Scott's voice crackled in over the distance. ". . . over. . . stay. . ."

"Andrea," Taka huffed into her ear. "Right behind you."

Andrea glanced over her shoulder, but he was too far back for her to see. A parked car door opened up ahead of her and she swerved between two cars and up onto the sidewalk. Beard opened a little more distance between them.

Warmed up, lungs over their initial burn, Andrea pushed harder. Except through the woods, she hadn't run in days. Muscles growing sorer every hour from the root cellar, she didn't know that this was what she needed. She stopped trying to see every obstacle and danger and centered her focus on the yellow splotch of mustard coming and going under the lights and reappearing between other people.

The crowd was thinning. Beard darted left onto Summers Street, nearly deserted at eleven on a Saturday night. Rounding the corner, Andrea pushed harder. She could hear Beard's whining breath as he struggled to keep up his pace. He looked back, losing more distance to her.

An SUV pulling out of the Summers Street parking garage forced him across the road, past the old Capital Center Theater. As the SUV accelerated away, Andrea pounded across the street. Beard flagged, again looking back at her.

"They're on Summers," Taka shouted from the corner. The slap of his boots stopped.

Andrea refused to look.

She ran.

She was close enough to see Beard's alarm and the snowflakes turning his beard white, the wet hair around his mouth as he gasped when he stumbled, glancing back yet again. The gauges in his ears.

The smoke shop.

The older guy. Tattoo guy.

The scarf he wore covered the crucifixion on his throat. Jesus hanging from his jaw, feet tucked in his collarbone.

This guy?

This guy beat Lucy Garcia and left her to die in an alley?

The snow fell harder.

Beard ran straight out into the traffic on Kanawha Boulevard.

A car slid sideways. The squeal of grabbing brakes hurt her ears. She didn't look. The crunch of tearing metal never came. Beard plunged down the steps between the entrance railing of the waterfront park. One stride carried her across the sidewalk, and another over the two low steps.

Beard zigged left on the path and then right onto the flight of stairs down to the wide riverwalk, slowing to a careful trot. Andrea tried to take two at a time, but the snow was already sticking, and the steps were slick. She crashed down onto her right hip, her breath exploding from her.

More brakes up on the boulevard. It occurred to her that she could hear Taka again in her ear. She rolled to keep Beard in her sights. The sharp jacks in her pocket stabbed her side. He was still making his way down. She planted her left foot on a patch of non-icy step below her and stood up. Pain shot down through her right hip all the way to her ankle.

She screamed out her anger, her hands fisting at her sides.

The jacks poked against her forearm.

She dug her hand into her pocket and yanked them out.

Swinging her arm down, she brought it up hard overhand, the hours of playing baseball with the neighborhood boys in Cross Lanes coming back to her. The jacks soared through the air over Beard's head, disappearing into the falling snow.

She swore she could hear every tinkle of the metal jacks hitting the concrete steps.

Beard went down hard and slid another fifteen feet, bumping and flailing, ending up face-down and sideways across the stairs.

Taka brushed by her in big cat mode, with his unreal balance, rapid sideways steps giving the wide balls of his boots the best traction downward. While still moving, he bent low and grabbed Beard's arm, tugging it up behind him, and then straddled him.

He drew his cuffs.

Andrea hit the mic at her throat. "Make them tight."

"Will do. You hurt?"

"I'll live, which is more than Lucy can say."

"Are you hurt, asshole?"

A muffled reply.

"Yep. I'd say that leg is broken."

"That guy hurt?" Bowman said from behind her.

She startled. Her heart thumped hard. Her hip throbbed. "Ow. You both need bells."

"Sorry," Bowman said, but he didn't look sorry. "CPD and a bus on the way."

"Bus?"

"Ambulance. That's Parker. When the Conlons bring their streetwalkers to town for a few weeks, he pimps for them."

A sound of protest in her ear. Taka didn't move. He crossed his arms. "I'm just gonna sit here, thanks. The view is nice."

The dark river eased by, under a bright sky, light glinting off the turn of the currents. Huge, slow snowflakes floated and eddied on the freezing air. They might take days to hit the ground. Her elbow itched and she wanted something she could almost taste and then she remembered Eddie. Eddie giving her, no, giving Lucy, a snort and an X-ie, after dropping off the other three girls to meet their lookout.

Parker.

Who came back to the van with the girls and found Eddie dead and blood on her hands.

Lucy's hands.

"Do you smell pine?" Christmas trees. Wreaths with red bows. Garland draped along the banister.

"No."

"And cinnamon."

Bowman's mouth turned down. "You having a stroke?"

"And vanilla."

"I smell pine," Taka said. "I need to call my mom about her tree."

And there she was, a gathering mist. "Lucy's standing next to Bowman."

Bowman tensed.

Taka turned his head, the light riding the angles of his face.

Under his focus, Andrea watched Lucy blossom into the woman she had been. She wore the short white-and-red dress and voluminous blue hoodie she had died in.

"Can you see her?"

"No," Taka said.

"She's magnificent." But then Lucy unzipped the hoodie, revealing her military uniform underneath. "She's in her dress whites."

"Once a Marine, always a Marine," Bowman said.

Lucy raised her closed fist. "Ooo-rah," she thundered.

"Taka, turn it down!"

Bowman leaned away from her.

Lucy gave her a smile, but her eyes were sad. "Good initiative, bad judgement. Semper Fi."

"Semper Fi," Andrea said.

Lucy looked up at the sky and the snow falling on her. She grinned, threw her arms out wide, and spun around once, letting go, and spread out into the night.

41

Taka considered the half-eaten bison slider in his hand. Apropos of nothing, he said, "Aren't crossover circumstances every circumstance? Every moment in time is dependent on all the moments before, right? So, all the intersections that happen to cross at one point of time—oh. They're all converging at that one time, making a unique circumstance that allows you guys to become aware of each other. Never mind."

"I think you need sleep," Scott said.

Jimmy stuffed another fry in his mouth. "I can't stop eating these."

"It's the truffle oil," Karie said. "How have you not had Louie's fries before?"

Bowman picked up the last slider on the platter. "Why'd I rent a place in Clay?"

"The bad guys live near there?" Andrea said.

Bowman dipped his head. "And I didn't know about Louie's."

It was three in the morning before both scenes were processed and statements given and Tamarin allowed Andrea, Taka, and Bowman to make their way back to Louie's, where they'd been greeted with hugs and food.

"You're welcome here anytime," Louie said. With a snifter of brandy in one hand and his long legs stretched out in front of him, he was the most relaxed Andrea had ever seen him. He noticed her watching him. "Aaron seemed to have his own crossover circumstances with Lucy Garcia, didn't he?"

"I think so," she said. There was something beyond both being soldiers and slaves, though. It was right there if she could just grasp it. Semper Fi. Always faithful. "I keep wondering what Lucy meant when she said, 'Good initiative, bad judgement.'"

With his mouth full, Bowman said, "Mistakes were made."

"What mistakes?" Jimmy said.

"No," Scott said. "That's what 'good initiative, bad judgement' means. It's military doublespeak for 'Mistakes were made.'"

"It's a good question, though. What mistakes were made?" She adjusted the ice pack on her hip.

Aaron, sitting in the chair at the end of the table, looked like just another one of them. "Mistakes were made," he said. He patted his leg and blipped away.

A completely new phrase with no prompting. That was interesting. Maybe communication took practice on both sides of the veil.

Karie stood up, picking up the platter and sticking the fingers of her other hand down in three beer mugs. "I'm getting Andrea more ice, and then we're all letting Louie lock up and going home."

Only they didn't.

They went home to Andrea's.

Even Bowman, deemed too tired and buzzed to drive, rode with Karie to the house.

Andrea gimped down to the kitchen at noon to find pancakes and bacon and grits and an overlap of voices in full swing. Jimmy pulled a chair out for her, and Scott tossed him an ice pack from the freezer. Taka set coffee down in front of her. Bowman and Karie were arguing over whether or not sea salt was superior to table salt when making chocolate chip cookies like they'd known each other all their lives.

By two, she was alone again.

She swallowed two Tylox left over from the time she broke her wrist and settled down to pull in her fishing lines on Candy King and the Conlons, cast more, and then read all the things Live Oak-and-Falling-Waters-and-Ivystone related.

JIMMY PLOPPED a bag down on her kitchen table Monday morning. "Gotcha a new phone. Hope you backed up the old one."

Andrea made gimme hands from where she sat with her leg propped up on a chair and Jimmy slid the bag to her. "I did. Thank you." ¹

"Your hip?"

"Hurts. Tell me something new," she said, dumping the phone box out of the bag.

"Harrison Conlon was not just paying homage to his brother by adopting Skinny as his nickname. He *is* his brother. And everyone knows it, including his wife who is not his wife."

"What happened to the actual Harrison?"

"Probably? He was the only one in Skinny's car when it went off that bridge. It's been so long, I don't know if we'll ever know for sure. He gave Skinny a way to claim the full family estate, disappear from law enforcement's radar, and fix his earlier mistakes in establishing his network."

"But he grew up here! Why didn't anyone recognize him?"

Jimmy shrugged. "He left here a young man and came back an older one. Most of his legitimate connections were made after he became Harrison. He was reclusive. Certainly, the senator knew he wasn't Harrison."

"Linda Conlon isn't his wife?"

A car pulled down the drive.

Jimmy's ears perked up.

"Karie. She's bringing me stuff from work."

Jimmy shook his head. "You're addicted to information, you know that, right?"

Andrea pointed at herself. "Archivist, remember? Linda Conlon?"

"They couldn't rock the boat on Skinny's identity. The first charges going through are false documents, but like the true criminal he is, his hands are clean. Linda's getting all of those."

"He faked his own death. He took over his brother's identity! Isn't that illegal?"

"It's not a crime to fake your death, and he didn't even do that. He just didn't stick his hand in the air when his car went off that bridge and it was assumed he died."

Karie kicked the mudroom door shut. "It's not a crime to fake your own death?"

Jumping up, Jimmy took a large cardboard file box out of her arms so she could take off her coat and shake off the cold. "No. Adults can choose to go missing if they want."

"When did Harrison go missing?" Andrea asked.

Jimmy slid the box onto the table. "Technically, he didn't?"

"Oh," Andrea said. "Because Skinny just carried on. But surely there's some sort of fraud involved in taking over another person's assets?"

Jimmy shrugged and put his hands in his pockets. "For the lawyers to argue, I guess. As Harrison, he didn't commit fraud by accepting any life insurance payout on his true identity. He didn't even make a claim on the wrecked car. He divorced Harrison's wife, gave her a handsome payoff, and took full custody of his nephew, who benefitted from Harrison's estate. As his real self, he and Harrison's son are the only heirs anyway and he claims he's acting on behalf of his brother who prefers to stay lost in the world. His lawyer brought the powers of attorney to prove it."

"Wow," Karie said, making a beeline for the coffee. "Those have got to be forged."

"That's what I was telling Andrea," Jimmy said, remembering where he was before Andrea stole his thought. "Linda Conlon is still Linda King. Skinny has no legal identity at all and Harrison legally owns nothing but the original bank account and its investments. The documents she used to buy the properties and cars in her 'married' name are all forged."

"Therefore, the first fraud charges are on her."

Karie brought her coffee to the table and took Jimmy's abandoned chair. "Was the commander right? Have any of their current victims been found?"

"Just the woman at Xander's house and the boy. She was recruited off the street by Linda. She seems to have no concept of how she's been used. She's mad at us for taking everything away from her. The boy's Xander's son. Mom unknown. He doesn't know anything besides the life, and he was just another commodity to Xander. He's going through drug withdrawal at the Children's Hospital right now."

Andrea heard the boy whooping in the snow again, his voice rising and falling over the hill above the root cellar. Every day he'd lived had been a lie. And to some extent, just like Tina, he'd been happy. How would he ever assimilate into a normal life?

"You heard from Taka yet?"

"No." He'd been called in by Ronnie Horton to meet with PSD's Greg Stack. Another Internal Affairs investigation so soon after the shooting didn't bode well. "He did text that they were taking him out to the farm. Want your burner back?"

"No. It's prepaid. Stick it somewhere you'll have it in reserve."

Her mind immediately went to the Charleston Gazette-Mail reporter who helped her leak ghost info as anonymous sources to the people who needed to know certain things in October. She'd caught plenty of info on her web hooks that could give a reporter plenty of fodder to help the new task force with the Conlons and their minions in exchange for quoted exclusives. The burner phone would come in handy for passing on everything she was dredging up.

"I know that look," Jimmy said. "I don't want to know what you're thinking."

He pulled his keys from his pocket, then circled his finger at the box. "Have fun."

When he was gone, Karie pulled out a folder from the top of the box. "These," she said, handing it over, "are Megan's notes on the contents of this box. And your work messages."

She made Andrea more tea while Andrea flipped through the concise, well-organized notes. A timeline of the house, all the owners of the house, plat maps, and a summary of General Lee's retreat through

Falling Waters from Gettysburg. It was a lot of good information that Mr. Pederson could exploit for marketing his bed and breakfast.

"Remind me to recommend Megan as a hire when she graduates."

"I'll second that," Karie said.

No Sally besides the neighbor. No Ned mentioned. No slave record, though Megan had noted possible slave labor, two cooks, three nannies, several field workers. None of them named Aaron. She pulled the sheet with her phone messages from the folder and shut it.

Karie grinned and leaned forward to snag another from the box. "And this is from Talisha."

It was thick.

The first three pages were meaningless to her. Photocopies of handwritten lists of names and locations she couldn't decipher. And then a multipage typed transcription from a Charleston, South Carolina harbor master's records. On the second page, a highlighted name, Aaron. Approximately fifteen years old. Leased from Sutter's Hill as a deck hand on Her Fair Mathilda for a period of no less than two years and no more than four, with the commensurate payment to be made in advance of any extension. Property to be insured and death benefit to be paid in full to Tarquin Miles of Sutter's Hill, Virginia. A report on Her Fair Mathilda followed. She was a coastal schooner making merchant runs, which included the transport of slaves, between St. Augustine and Boston.

"Oh my god," Andrea breathed. "She found him."

"She said to tell you not to get too excited. The rest of this box is all the useful paper there was from the house. It's both what Mr. Pederson pulled from his research and what was physically still in the house." She stood and started pulling the folders and setting them in stacks. They were all labeled by time period.

Andrea picked one up labeled 1890-1900 and riffled through it while Karie talked.

"There's virtually nothing from the mid-1850s to 1872, except tax records. Maybe because Miles was the only owner of Ivystone who didn't die there."

The folder held a decade's worth of official records, thirty or forty personal letters, two recipes, and photocopied ledger entries recording expenses and crop yields. It would take months to properly log, read, notate, and scan everything Mr. Pederson gave them, but Megan had done an amazingly fast job sorting and organizing. "This is amazing. Because I accidentally fell into the Antebellum field, the projects I get are usually completely abandoned or everything inside's been destroyed by weather and mice, or a previous restoration or owner tossed it all. I've never had a project site with this much personal history attached."

"Oh, I get it," Karie said. "A huge part of my investigations is digging through official records for former occupants, trying to locate them or their far-flung relations through whatever genealogy site is most current, and making a ton of cold calls to beg them for any family ghost stories or deaths related to the property or when that unpermitted addition was added to the house or their letters from grandma." She laughed. "In movies, no one's ever moved or thrown anything away, so there's all this stuff left over from previous owners just abandoned in the attic or basement. I wish!"

"I knew you collected stories, but I thought your projects were mostly physical debunking and ghost hunting with all the stuff you've brought to Louie's. I didn't realize you did all that, too."

"I'm trying to track down that shopkeeper you said you saw at Louie's. I'm hoping the boy with the jacks is related to her."

Andrea had only focused on any records related to Black men in connection to the building. "If CPD ever gives me my notes back, I can give you the history I found looking for Aaron." Thinking about the boy, she took the ice pack from under the top of her legging and tossed it on the table. "How can those jacks appear out of nowhere?"

"They aren't. Remember you told me about Billie Mae moving your earring? That's a really common type of ghost story. Those jacks are coming from somewhere."

"Like Louie's ring dropping onto the counter. I didn't think of that. I've been like, how did thin air become metal?"

"It's that Tylox you've been taking," Karie said with a laugh.

"It is!"

While Karie gathered her keys and coat, Andrea scanned her written messages from work. Glenn's wife had called three times and left the same message: *Please call me.*

TAKA STOOD outside the root cellar, cold to the bone in his CPD windbreaker.

Two techs were working elbow to elbow inside. They'd finish working the scene for the imprisonment and escape, trekking back and forth to the crime scene van with evidence. Now they were lifting Lisa Townsend's bones from the ground.

He hadn't expected a field trip from the meeting with Horton and PSD.

Without Sweet Joe present, he'd only read the statement they prepared together on Saturday and not answered any questions about his decision to stake out Skinny's house while on personal time, with a civilian, and then talk to Linda Conlon after representing himself as on official business.

Tripp's eyewitness account of Lucy's killing had justified his arrest of Parker.

The jacks that Andrea admitted throwing had gotten him off any police brutality for Parker's broken leg.

Tamarin had recognized the tread of Parker's boots from the bloody prints lifted from just outside the van and had the paramedics collect them from Parker's feet before they left Summers Street. That got him a search warrant for Parker's apartment, so at least he wasn't joining the dogpile.

But no one had told him yet if his job was safe or he had set it on fire.

They'd given Fields Lisa's case. Of course, Fields didn't know it was her yet. Once the ME gave him a description, Taka had no doubt he'd find her among the long missing and link her to her bones.

Fields stumped over from a huddle of techs still working the house, a CPD winter jacket in his hand. He shoved it at Taka. "Here. You're making me cold just looking at you."

Taka pulled it on right over the windbreaker, zipped it all the way up, and stuck his cold hands in the pockets. "Can I ask you a question?"

Fields glanced around. But no one else was nearby. "Yeah, man. Anything."

"Glenn Caulkey told Parker about Andrea and Lucy and the lighter. How'd Parker know Tripp would go looking for it?"

Fields rubbed his upper lip. "Okay. You didn't hear anything from me."

Taka nodded and looked at the frozen ground.

Just two guys waiting on the techs in the cellar.

"Tripp's an accessory," Fields said. "Parker saw him out on the street one night a few months ago. He was the only one to know Tripp was living a double life."

Him and the commander, but Taka kept his mouth shut.

"When Parker went to check on Eddie, Tripp happened to be on his route and joined him. After Glenn mentioned the lighter, Parker confronted Tripp. Tripp caved and said he'd try to go find it. Parker's lawyer is already saying Tripp beat Lucy and tried to frame his client by stealing and planting the lighter and money clip. Tripp had destroyed any prints on the lighter, but the lab lifted a match to Parker on the inside of the clip and off a fifty. And Eddie's blood is on his boots."

"What's Tripp saying? Why didn't he call nine-one-one if he was so worried about Parker getting caught?"

Fields snorted, which Taka had never thought him capable of doing. "Because he's got the emotional maturity of a second-grader, but the psychological manipulation of an Army-trained negotiator, which he is. Let me see if I can keep this straight. He loved Lucy, but Lucy never even looked his way. Which he got, because she was spying on Candy, so she needed to be close to him."

Taka frowned.

"Wait, it gets better. After Lucy went missing, Tripp figured she'd just been 'recalled.' That's how he said it. 'Recalled.' And Candy's his dealer and shares the women he meets with him."

"Grooming 101."

"Gross is what it is. Point is, he didn't want to give it up. But he liked Lucy. And, get this, she was just doing her job, he said. He wanted Parker caught, but he didn't want Parker, and, most importantly, Candy, knowing he ratted them out."

"Or no more drugs and sex."

"When Andrea came nosing around, Tripp attempted to stay on

Parker's good side so Parker wouldn't decide he was a liability by shifting focus to Candy, while also giving Candy a chance to deny his involvement. He also wanted to stay in good with Glenn, who he looks up to, by not admitting to knowing Lucy had a bigger addiction than pot. And he figured it wouldn't hurt to make sure Andrea only mentioned him as a good guy to us if she did actually call us about Lucy."

"You got a lot out of him."

"He's a thinker, but I'm not convinced he's completely sane. Runs hot and cold. One minute he's spelling things out point by point, the next he's out in left field."

"And he thought Lucy was a spy."

"Dead certain. And that Andrea's a psychic."

"That's fair. She did tell him that."

"He showed us the news reports of the girl missing from here. Maybe those bones really are her. Make my job easier."

The held-breath tension Taka had carried since Saturday night, waiting to see how his life was going to change, hoping it might not, eased a little. It looked like Lucy might get justice. Maybe Lisa's parents would finally learn what happened to their little girl.

42

"Are you sure your hip's not broken?" Taka asked on Wednesday morning as Andrea gimp-hopped from the curb on Hale to Louie's front door.

If the snow hadn't all melted, she'd be in big trouble.

Andrea stopped and held her foot off the ground for a second to let her hip uncramp. "Pretty sure. It only hurts when I'm moving." And sitting. And laying down. But she didn't need him any more stressed than he already was. "I have an appointment on Friday."

"Tell me you put off having it checked because you're arm-deep in Aaron research."

"You find out one thing. You ask about three more. You pull one document, it leads to four more. At some point, it goes from a slow accumulation to an avalanche. It's called research cascading. It's a thing. Look it up."

Jesus pulled the door open for them.

"Maybe you'd be less grumpy if you go now," Taka murmured.

"Maybe I'd be less grumpy if you stop bugging me about going."

"Maybe y'all would both be less grumpy if either of you got some sleep," Karie said from the dining room doorway as Andrea hopped in.

"I'm set up in here, so maybe we should meet Glenn's wife out there. What's her name?"

Andrea limped to the closest six-top and plopped down in the nearest chair. "I don't know. The messages just said Glenn's wife. And when I called her, she didn't pick up. She texted me about meeting."

Taka rolled his eyes.

Jesus closed the door. "I'm going to lock it, okay?"

"Thanks, Jesus," Taka said.

"Coffee?"

"We're coffeed out," Taka said, shooting a look at Andrea.

Andrea narrowed her eyes at him, but she really, really didn't want more coffee. "Thank you for offering, Jesus, we're all good."

"Yell if you change your mind," he said, already retreating.

Taka threw his jacket over the back of the chair next to Andrea and pulled it out at an angle so she could prop her leg up. Karie sat across from her. "Did Glenn's wife tell you what she wanted?"

"She didn't. She was just very insistent on meeting me."

"Maybe she needs a psychic," Taka said, standing near the door. "You didn't try very hard to get her to tell you what she wanted, did you?"

Andrea rubbed her fingers across a scar in the distressed wood tabletop. "If she's wanting a psychic reading, I'll connect her with Miss Ava."

The familiar swish of the kitchen doors announced Louie's arrival, a laden tray in his hands. "Good morning, how are you all today? Your leg, Miss Andrea?"

"It's better," she lied. "You shouldn't have, Louie."

"Least I can do." Instead of setting the tray down, he unloaded it onto the table, somehow placing everything in such a way that each of them could easily reach the croissants and sliced fruits and small samplers of various yogurts. "I'm thinking of doing a brunch service on the weekends. Let me know what you think."

Karie already had a yogurt and one of the tiny spoons Louie laid down in hand. "Did you make this yourself?"

Tucking the tray under his arm, Louie grinned. "It's the best recipe, I think, so far."

"Don't change a thing," Karie said, taking another dainty spoonful. "This is—I have no words."

Taka leaned in and stole a croissant. Half disappeared in one bite. He chewed twice. And stopped. Andrea wasn't sure she'd ever seen him so surprised over a mouthful of food. Then his eyes practically rolled back in his head as he savored the bite.

"Louie," Andrea said. "I think you found his Kryptonite."

Taka swallowed and lifted the other half. "You calling me Superman, Ands? This jam filling is brilliant, Louie. Thank you." Taka stuffed the rest of the pastry in his mouth.

"Fig," Louie said.

Jesus swept out with another tray, this one with pitchers of ice water and orange juice and nice, heavy bar glasses. As Louie helped him unload and arrange, Taka swung the door open. "Glenn's wife?"

She was white and somewhere in the vicinity of sixty, with dark hair streaked with grey, large dark eyes, and strong features. She wore jeans and a black turtleneck under a smart black peacoat and had a fat leather satchel hanging from her shoulder.

Andrea liked her on sight.

"That'd be me! Call me Sally," she said, bustling in.

Something fell smoking from the tin ceiling onto the center of the table. It bounced off the rim of the fruit plate and landed in a yogurt cup.

Déjà vu.

They all looked up.

Louie pinched the metal ring from the yogurt.

Jesus whipped the bar towel off his shoulder and handed it to him.

"Where'd that come from?" Sally said.

"Uh," Louie said.

"It must've been thrown," Andrea said. "Is there anyone else here?"

"It's Aaron, isn't it?" Sally said.

She couldn't help but look when a shimmer near the dining room became a translucent Aaron walking himself into existence. She ripped her gaze back to Sally.

Sally lifted her chin towards Louie. "Could I see that, please?" She held out her hand.

Standing now between Louie and Sally, Andrea wondered if Louie might not drop the ring into Aaron's hand for him to transfer it to Sally. She could see Aaron's long eyelashes. His five o'clock shadow, the slash of a small scar across the right side of his chin. The more prominent one bisecting the back of his left hand.

Louie held the ring out on his palm for her to see. Instead of taking it, Sally took a sharp breath and then let it out slow. She slid her hand into her jeans pocket and then opened it next to Louie's to reveal an identical ring.

Andrea's gaze flew to Aaron's. He said, "Sally."

"No shit," she said out loud, drawing everyone's attention. She clapped her hand to her mouth. "Excuse my French."

Taka said, "Here, let's sit."

He went wide around Sally, Aaron stepping aside as if Taka could actually run into him and pulled a chair out for her. Louie handed his tray off to Jesus, asking him to tell the sous chef to carry on, and sat down himself. Taka brushed a hand over Andrea's shoulder and sat down on her other side.

Louie weighed the ring in his hand and then slipped it on his right ring finger. "May I?"

Sally gave him her ring.

He pulled his reading glasses from the top of his head and examined the intricate crossing of the horseshoe nails before turning the ring to look at the band. He nodded. "It's Whay's mark."

"You know Whay?" Sally said.

"I do."

"How do you know about him?" Andrea asked. "How did you get that ring?"

"Several generations later, I'm white," Sally said. "No getting around that. But Aaron was my great-great-grandfather's cousin."

"How do you know that?" Andrea said.

She glanced up at the ceiling. "Before that ring fell, I was going to tell you how I couldn't believe it when Glenn came home talking about you. After Calvin Pederson bought Ivystone, I contacted him to tell him I might have information he'd be interested in. He called me just this week to give me your name and suggest I contact you. That you could decide if the info I have is relevant to his restoration of the house."

"Is Aaron related to Ivystone?"

"Aaron's buried at Ivystone. So is my great-great-grandfather. But I've been there and couldn't find the graves."

"Oh my God," Karie said, her voice tight with excitement.

Sally raised her brows in question, "What? Tell me."

Karie waited, giving Andrea the chance to think through her answer. "Mr. Pederson uncovered three graves when he demolished an old sunporch. A forensic anthropologist in Charlotte recovered the bodies."

"Three unmarked graves," Sally said.

"Yes," Andrea said.

"A white man and two Black men," Sally said.

Louie let a long breath escape him. "So one set of the remains really could be Aaron's."

"Bones," Aaron said.

Andrea tucked away the fact that he didn't need the spirit box to say it for him this time.

"Who's Ned?" Karie asked.

"My great-great-grandfather was named Edward."

"Edward, of course," Andrea said, in an aha tone.

"Ned's a nickname for Edward?" Taka grumbled. "Henry for Harrison, Ned for Edward, Jack for John. What's wrong with people?"

"My given name is Sarah," Sally said.

Taka's mouth opened, but Andrea shot him a glare and asked Sally again, "How do you know all this?"

"My great-great-grandmother was Delphia. She was owned by Tarquin Miles. After the war, she learned to read and write, and she wrote a memoir in the pages of her diaries. It's mostly about her life at Ivystone with Edward and Aaron. It was called Sutter's Hill back then."

"So you know what happened to them," Karie said. "The man who was shot-gunned, and Aaron and Edward."

"Ned," Aaron said.

"Wow," Sally said. "They could tell the Reb was killed by a shotgun?"

Karie met Andrea's darted glance at her. "The Reb."

"Delphia wanted to go home with us," Aaron said.

"I don't suppose you have any photos?" Andrea asked.

Sally yanked her satchel from the floor. "I do. And I have copies of everything for you."

"What happened to them, Aaron and Edward?" Louie said.

"I'm sorry, Louie," Andrea said. "We've not told you any of the details yet, have we? Please, go ahead, Sally."

She pulled two big envelopes out of the bag. While she talked, she took the packet of papers from one of them and slowly flipped through them. "Sutter's Hill wasn't big. Miles had four to six slaves at any one time. He brought Aaron there in 1856. He'd been a sailor for several years after leaving Live Oak.

"He worked in the fields and Miles leased him out as a breeder, what Delphia called a stockman. She had at least three babies with him. Two were sold at ages three and four. The other died. Then the war came."

Shhhh. This ain't forever. Andrea looked over at Aaron, but he was fixated on Sally.

"Miles left the farm in the charge of an elderly uncle and joined the Confederate Army, taking Aaron and another slave with him. He died close to home in July '61 at Hokes Run, so they carried him home. He's buried there at Ivystone. The uncle died shortly after.

"Since they had everything they needed to keep surviving there, the slaves just stayed on. Delphia had been the cook and she was a natural leader. Late that same year, Union troops came through and took most of their supplies. There were several runaway slaves with them, acting as spies. They'd cross the front lines, work in the Confederate camps for days or weeks, and then steal away to report back to their units, or leave their messages at safe houses, where they'd get passed on. Sometimes they took Union officers with them, helping them fit in, acting as their porters or valets.

"Aaron couldn't resist. Off he went to help the cause. In April '62, after helping defeat Stonewall Jackson's Confederate troops at Kernstown, Aaron came back to Sutter's Hill with his cousin, Edward, whom everyone called Ned. Delphia fell in love. Aaron and Ned continued to do what they could to help the Union, sticking to Northern Virginia and Maryland, so they could stop in frequently.

"Then came Gettysburg. General Lee's troops retreated through Falling Waters. After crossing the Potomac, a Confederate captain recognized Ned and shot at him, but Ned escaped. He took refuge at Sutter's Hill, happy to be home again. But the next day, the captain came knocking. He'd become lost in the dark during his pursuit of Ned. He wanted food and water and to get his bearings. Ned came in from the barn just as Delphia was giving the captain milk and cornbread. He executed Ned. Delphia, pregnant with Ned's baby, shot him in the back while he was trying to leave.

"With the help of a slave couple living there, Delphia buried them where they might not be discovered and then planted an herb garden over them. Aaron made his way home in '65 on one leg. He'd healed from injuries to his chest, but the scar tissue restricted his breathing. His stump never really healed.

"Because she'd buried Ned with his ring, Aaron gave her his before he died in '71 and she buried him near his cousin. She recorded a lot of his history as well, so that Ned's son would know who his family was as well as hers."

"Is that Aaron's ring you have, then?" Louie asked.

"Yes," Aaron answered at the same time as Sally.

"Did Delphia record which of Whay's sons Aaron and Ned descended from?"

"Ned from Tooar. Aaron from Tattio. Here," Sally said, passing Andrea a studio shot of a matronly Black woman and a man of around twenty. "This is Delphia and Ned's son. And here's Tarquin Miles in uniform with Aaron and Simon."

Andrea glanced from the second photo to Aaron, standing tall in his chambray and drabs. A little older, the angles of his face wider, lines of his skin deeper. He'd had the tall boots at the start of the war, looking well-worn already. Taka followed her line of sight and then the others did, too.

"Aaron's really here?" Sally said.

"A couple of feet behind you, between you and Louie." She thought about how to ask her questions.

Karie pushed her chair back, trotted into the dining room and came back with the spirit box, a digital recorder, and an EMF meter, which Aaron lit up all the way with a wavering squeal.

She set everything down and said, "Okay, Aaron," in a cut-it-out tone and the EMF went dark and silent.

She fiddled for a minute. "Okay, Andrea."

"Do you want your bones reburied?"

"Yes," Aaron said, too loud. "With Ned."

"Taka," she said, tilting her head at Aaron.

Taka crossed his arms over his chest and studied the fruit plate instead of trying to detect exactly where Aaron was located.

"At Live Oak?" Andrea asked.

"Wife." His voice echoed a little but didn't hurt her ears.

"Are you what," Karie asked Taka. "Shielding?"

"I don't know," Taka said, voice low. "I just try not to focus on anything in particular."

"Do you know where she's buried?" Andrea asked, still not quite sure he was referring to Delphia.

"No," Aaron said, his vibrant solidity fading. "She was in the wrong place, too."

"She was in the wrong place, too," Andrea repeated for the recorder. She wanted to remember her first impression later. "Do you mean the same place your bones are?"

He smiled at Louie. "Cleared a few things up."

"You did clear a few things up," Andrea said.

"Whay," Aaron said, lifting his chin at Louie. "He could track boar in the pouring rain without a single hound."

"Will you be moving on now?"

More transparent now, he looked right at her.

And laughed.

He was luminous.

The boy with the jacks peered over the bar at him.

"Waiting on Delphia. Wife."

"Okay," Andrea said. She'd do her best to find the woman. Talisha and Karie and, she suspected, Sally, would help her.

Watching him disappear a fraction at a time, Andrea blurted, "Was Lucy a spy?"

Almost nothing left of him. "Soldier." The word was a caress that wrapped itself around her. "Brother."

And he was gone.

For now.

"He passed over?" Taka asked.

The ghost boy ran down the bar, hooked a hand around the kitchen doorway, and flung himself through the closed swing doors. They quivered in his wake. A jack sat on the bar's countertop.

"Andrea?"

"He did not. He wants to be buried beside Ned and Delphia." She cast a wave at all the food. "Louie, he says you're very much like Whay, an expert in your field. I think he likes it here."

"So we have to find Delphia?" Karie said, scribbling in her notebook.

"Yes. Though I kind of expect Aaron may hang out until we find all seven rings."

"We know where four are now?" Louie said.

Andrea held up four fingers. "Yours is Boway's, right?"

At Louie's nod, she put one finger down. "Kitch's is buried with Stanley Orengo. Ned's is in Charlotte." Two more fingers down. "And now we have Tattio's through Aaron."

Karie flipped pages. "That leaves Jeer's, Tendy's, and Gowar's."

Louie shook his head. "He may be here forever if he waits on all of them."

"Why did you ask that," Sally said. "About Lucy. I assume you meant Lucy Garcia?"

"Crossed circumstances," Taka said, giving Andrea the same curious expression as Sally.

"And what would that mean?" Sally said.

Taka nabbed a pineapple slice and launched into a long-winded explanation of Andrea's theory and how Aaron showed up when Ivystone did.

"THIS IS IT. Close the door, please," Tamarin said as Jimmy and Andy Detweiler entered the conference room.

Jimmy nodded to the federal lead on the Conlon task force, Kate Bolling, a sharp, older woman with years of experience whom Jimmy admired. Looking around the small group, he wished he'd taken another antacid. This was just the core group. The four heads of the local, state, and federal investigation teams following up and coordinating other agencies in nine different locations on the Eastern Seaboard related to the Conlon investigation, plus two strangers.

Bolling said, "Several inquiries from a variety of sources and a Washington Post investigative journalist have been rather determinedly digging into Lucy Garcia's past. The task of these two Special Agents, whom I will not be introducing by name, and yourselves, from this point forward is to discourage and stonewall all further attempts to dismantle Lucy Garcia's cover identity at every level."

Son of a bitch.

Tripp wasn't crazy.

The female agent's voice was steady, but she didn't look anyone in the eye as she spoke. "Garcia was single, no family, a volunteer for the position. We became aware of Candy King as a Romeo through a missing person report filed by a congressional aide regarding a West Virginia legislative intern. It was a simple in and out, discover where the victims were being sold or pimped."

Jimmy unclenched his jaw. "So what happened?"

The male agent looked up for the first time. "We lost her."

Andy grunted and sat back in his chair.

"You lost her?" Tamarin said. "Like she failed to report? Or she chose to actively participate?"

"She managed several weeks of infiltration with the skills she'd been taught to avoid ingesting intoxicants. She did participate in protected sexual intercourse with two subjects just before she disappeared. She was making all her meets and drops. Because of the danger she might be made and trafficked, she was under close surveillance. She went missing during a botched shift change."

"Toxicology report was positive," Tamarin said. "The van driver's phone showed she called Candy King but made no attempt to contact her handler."

Bolling compressed her lips.

"She was gone ten months," the female agent said. "She'd been fully compromised."

"Mistakes were made," Bolling said. "This incident and her undercover identity will be denied at the federal level. We'd like your cooperation in quelling any rumors and keeping her real name clean. Within her department, she will be honored for her sacrifice internally."

Mistakes were made. Wasn't that what Andrea said after Lucy crossed over? "Why are you telling us this? Bringing more people into the loop risks discovery. We were blowing off the witness testimony."

The agents exchanged glances and punted to Bolling. "We need the full-court press called off."

Tamarin twigged before Jimmy. "You have got to be kidding me. How much damage can a librarian do?"

Before last week, Jimmy hadn't fully appreciated the depth of Andrea's commitment to the discovery process. She should be working for a law firm. And she was a fucking archivist, not a librarian.

"Knowledge is power," Bolling said. She aimed her next comment at Jimmy. "And connections network knowledge. It's fine if this lives online as a conspiracy theory, but we will not condone the smearing of a national hero's reputation."

"Or expose your own fuck-up," Jimmy said. "Message received."

"Do it without giving away the details," Bolling ordered.

Jimmy shoved his chair back and stood, Andy following suit. "Yes, ma'am."

He stalked through the maze of CPD's halls, unaware of anyone he passed, Andy on his heels. Out in the fresh cold breeze off the river, he stopped.

Andy dug in his pockets and came up with a pack of smokes. He lit up and took a long drag, letting the smoke slip into the wind. "What the fuck was that all about?"

"For you, Andy? A reminder not to lose your surveillance target."

"Fuck you, Jimmy."

Jimmy shot him the bird.

Maybe he didn't need to say anything to Andrea. Hounds got tired of the chase eventually, especially when denied the prize.

They walked through the flat light under the cloudy sky to Jimmy's Impala.

43

Working at the kitchen table was easier than at her desk, but two weeks at home was already two weeks too long away from Waltham-Young. Scanning her task list, Andrea decided to call Randy next, in answer to his email asking her to call with a hundred exclamation points.

He picked up on the first ring. "Tell me you're okay!"

"I'm okay. It's just a bone bruise." Though who knew bone bruises could hurt so much? "I'm on crutches and I won't be running again anytime soon, but I'm okay."

"My heart was in my throat when I heard! I'm glad you're tied down to a chair for a while. Now, guess what?"

Once again, flurries were falling, which had to be a record of some kind, twice before Christmas. She wished she could go running. With the proper shoes and her crampons for traction, it'd awesome to run in the lazy drift of the snowflakes. "It's snowing?"

"Is it snowing at your place? It hasn't started here, yet!"

"I give up, what's happening?"

"I asked that company funding the General Lee exhumation and DNA testing if they'd consider other testing and told them about the unmarked graves at Berrylane Plantation. They said absolutely!"

"What?" Andrea shouted into her cell.

"Really," Randy squealed like a teenage girl. "They said yes! They're super interested in posting DNA results online in hopes of tracking and interviewing descendants as a generational analysis of evolving culture. They're really just nosy about whether families stick to their behavioral and political patterns over multiple generations, but whatever, they'll definitely help you out on whatever you need."

"Randy. This is great news! Thank you so much."

"I'll send you contact info and the funding requests, okay?"

"Yes!"

"Come back soon, okay?"

"I will, Randy."

With both Berrylane and Ivystone in Falling Waters, she wondered if the Confederate captain who executed Ned would also be found guilty of the rumored executions at Berrylane. She owed the forensic anthropologist in Charlotte a call anyway to see if she had received the copies of Delphia's memoir.

A half-hour later, she had an agreement to test Great-Aunt Sally and Sally Caulkey for DNA related to Ned and Aaron's remains. Step one in moving Aaron from the wrong place, check. And she also had a partnership for exploration of the Berrylane burials if she landed the corporate funding.

Her thoughts were so loud, she missed Jimmy pulling in to have lunch with her.

The rattle of the mudroom doorknob got her attention.

But it was Taka who walked in.

"What are you doing here?"

"Can you break free? Take the afternoon?"

At eleven-thirty on a Wednesday, he was wearing his heavy leather coat rather than his black CPD jacket.

"What happened?"

"They let me resign in lieu of termination. I'm getting my mom her tree. You coming?"

"Yes."

JIMMY SAT in the courthouse parking lot to check his messages.

Raincheck? Andrea had texted. *They let Taka resign today. We're going to take a tree out to his mom.*

Resignation was better than termination, but Jimmy felt for him. Taka was a damn good cop. *Stuck in cort anyway. Gve T a hard manly pat on the shlder for me and then a big hug. CU at brkfst. I hve a Fruits of the Forest pie for U frm my mom.*

On the burner, two missed calls from Scotty, trying to return Jimmy's call from yesterday.

Dewey encouraging their friendship sparked a cool-headed debate between Maddox and the team as to the direction in which to carry the investigation. One, pull Scott out because Dewey would never make him privy to his inner sanctum with Jimmy around. Or two, reassign Jimmy to a state office out of town and let Detweiler move from co-investigatory lead to full lead. Or three, show Dewey a renewed friendship and possible path to the corruption of a state cop. Bribery was as good a charge as any to crowbar Dewey's other activities open for inspection.

Scott surprised him by answering right away. "I'm off. Just did a full search and sweep, but I'm at the mall anyway. Christmas shopping. We can talk."

"Good. I've got two things for you. We're going the friendship route. We'll let it build a few weeks, see each other more through Andrea and Taka."

Under the murmur of the mall crowd and a crying child, a Muzak version of Jingle Bell Rock seeped through the line.

"We need you deeper," Jimmy said firmly into Scott's continued silence. "However we can get you there. If this op fails, Dewey Sanderson gets free rein for who knows how long until he makes a big enough mistake to put him squarely back in our sights."

"Dewey's talking like Taka's coming to work for him."

"Taka's cop all the way through. It doesn't matter that he resigned. He's never going to work—"

"He resigned?"

Shit. "I thought you knew."

Scott cleared his throat. "I might have to come clean with him."

Jimmy rubbed his hand across his head. Scott didn't know Dewey and Taka had talked every day since the root cellar. Chances were Dewey already knew Taka had resigned. "Taka can't know, Scotty."

Kid still crying. Muzak still annoying.

"Tell me now," Jimmy said. "You want me to pull you?"

"No. What's the second thing?"

"The Beretta 92 wasn't a match to the senator's murder, but it was used to commit a murder in '81."

"Not by Dewey then."

"No," Jimmy laughed. "Not unless he came out of the womb shooting."

"You need me to find a way to permanently remove it?"

"From Dewey's personal collection? No. Stealing it once was risky enough. Just keep an eye out. See it stays there until we're done."

The tap on his window scared the bejesus out of Jimmy.

Nina.

"I gotta go," he said.

"See you tomorrow." Scott hung up.

Dinner at Andrea's. Jimmy hoped that meant Scott was all in.

He rolled down his window. "When did it start snowing?"

"Just now. Listen, I just heard from a tech at the state lab. They've been processing prints CPD pulled from Anna Lansing's house. She wanted to know if Andy Detweiler had been left off the list of law enforcement on scene for a reason or if she should add him."

Jimmy heard the words, but his brain wouldn't process them. "I don't understand."

"Andy's prints are at Anna Lansing's house. Should they be eliminated or not?"

Nina knew as well as he did that Andy hadn't been at the scene.

And he claimed he hadn't followed Dewey there.

"Can you find out where they were located?"

"A partial on one of the bed frames of the children's room and a full high on the interior of the back door."

"He was there that night," Jimmy said. "He's dating someone who was there, we don't want to say who, and went by. She can eliminate him."

"Yes, sir."

"No paper trail, Nina. No texts. No voicemail. If anyone discovers he was inadvertently eliminated later, it was a mistake. Got it? I'll get to the bottom of this."

"Yes, sir." She gave him a little salute, trying to look loose and failing, and walked away.

USING ONE CRUTCH TO BALANCE, Andrea stretched up to hang a bluebird ornament as high as she could in the tree. The bluebird ornament. It had been hers to hang for almost as many years as she'd known Taka, but it had been years since she had the pleasure.

"Ma'll love seeing that later," Taka said, coming back into the great room, one of the current Jack Russell crosses trotting after him. He stopped in front of the fire he'd built after cleaning out the old ashes, his broad back to her. The dog flopped down at his feet with its belly to the heat and sighed in unadulterated bliss.

Tucked up on a two-acre wooded lot above town, the house wasn't especially large, but with its sloped roofline and central living space, it was inviting. It used to be filled to bursting this time of year with music and running boys and screams of laughter and the wonderful smell of his mom's gingerbread cookies.

Now the crackle-pop of the fire was the loudest sound in the room.

She tipped over and lifted a red ball from the box at her feet. "I think she's better this year."

"Maybe," Taka allowed. "Y'all seemed to have a good conversation."

"We did. Were your ears burning?" She dipped back down for another ornament, came up with a plastic gold reindeer. There were at least six of them in there. "Sorry I wasn't any help this year."

"I got enough done."

She picked up a beaded Styrofoam ball, the ribbon glued around its middle coming undone. "This was Andrew's. You should hang it."

He looked over. For a long moment, Andrea thought he'd turn away again. But he came over and took the ornament from her. She dipped sideways and chose another deer while he considered the ball.

"I miss him," he said. "I miss my mom the way she used to be."

"So do I," she said.

He hung Andrew's ball at his mom's eye level. "Hey, you hung the bluebird."

"I did. Look, here's your favorite ornament," she said, holding up a Santa gnome wielding an AR-15 and a take-no-prisoners grin.

Taka rolled his eyes. "Good ol' Uncle James."

"Are you going to their Christmas bash this year?"

"I told Auntie I would. We should all go."

"All who?"

"You, me, Scott and Jimmy, Karie. Maybe the commander, since he doesn't seem to have anyone else?"

"I like him."

"Me, too."

They worked their way through the box, Andrea mostly handing the ornaments to Taka and pointing out decoration deserts on the tree. When they were done, Taka packed the various ball boxes and bubble-wrap scraps back into the storage box and took it back to the storage shed in the back yard.

He came back in with snow on his shoulders and hair, the angel for the top, and the tree skirt his mom had made years before by mailing out quilt panels and fabric markers to collect dozens of Taka's relatives' hand-written names and then sewing them together to form the skirt. Andrea loved his and Andrew's handprints and kid-name scrawls.

He handed her the angel and wrapped the skirt around the tree stand. "It took her most of a year for the family to get the panels back to her," he said. "She badgered them every chance she got."

Andrea supposed this was how the stories got passed down, the kids repeating what they heard each year. "It's priceless," she said.

Her own dysfunctional family's single holiday tradition was making Toll House cookies at midnight on Christmas Eve. Whether they had a tree or not, or all three of them were home on Christmas Day or not, or there was anything like a planned meal or not, or they were talking to each other or not, they were all in the kitchen at midnight for cookie making and baking and eating, whether there was milk or not. The irony of it was that it had been her father's family tradition and they carried it on even after he left.

Taka stood up and eyed the tree. "Okay," he said, turning around to face her. "Almost done. Give me that crutch."

"Oh, I don't think I can do that this year." When they were teenagers, she always stood on a chair to climb onto his shoulders and put the angel up.

He tossed the crutch over onto the worn leather couch.

"I won't hurt you," he said.

Not on purpose, she didn't say.

He pointed from the top of her hip to halfway down her thigh. "No touch, right?"

Don't tense up." He squatted and wrapped his arms around her legs just above the knee and hoisted her up, his head pressing against the outside of her good thigh and stepped back against the branches of the tree. "You good?"

"Yes." Bracing one hand on his shoulder, she trusted his strength and stretched hard to get the angel balanced just right. She pulled her fingers away. The angel settled, tilting to the right. She cocked her head. "Got it, it's good."

Taka took one step forward and slowly lowered her onto her good foot. He straightened up without letting go of her altogether. She held onto his waist. "I've missed what, the last twenty, twenty-one years?"

"Of what?"

"Cookies at midnight?" He'd always been with his own family, or overseas, or working. "You always give me cookies on Christmas. You think I didn't remember?"

She shook her head.

"I happen to know I'm off work this year."

She couldn't help but smile.

His eyes dropped to her lips. "I can't stop thinking about . . ."

She kissed him, just a brush of her lips and pulled back.

He studied her, gaze roaming her face. "It scares me. I don't want to lose you."

"Do you know you're the only person who's never left me?"

He frowned, looking away, and she watched him think through her closest relationships before he came back to her. Like he always did. "It's not you," he whispered.

"It's kind of hard to believe that from where I'm standing," she whispered back.

He let go of her to cup her face in both hands. "People don't leave because of you."

"I thought you were leaving me, too."

"I could never leave you," he said and lit that match that had always been between them.

She caught fire.

THANK YOU FOR READING
SPIRIT, THE ARCHIVIST BOOK 2

Andrea Kelley is back in WRAITH, The Archivist Book 3:
AVAILABLE NOW at your favorite bookstore.

READ ON FOR AN EXCERPT!

To sign up for notifications of new releases, giveaways, and free books: www.elleandrewspatt.com

Please consider telling a friend about Spirit
and maybe leaving a review or posting on social media. Both help other
readers find the book and that helps authors.

I truly appreciate you! ~ Elle

ELLE ANDREWS PATT

WRAITH

AN ANDREA KELLEY MYSTERY
-THE ARCHIVIST-
BOOK 3

CHAPTER I

WRAITH

The young woman perched in the backseat of Andrea Kelley's little Infinity FX seemed unaware of her surroundings. Although the windows were closed, her red hair blew around her face and licked her bare shoulders above her billowing white dress as her voice droned on. "Then Tucker says to me, them green beans need a'pickin' now. Go on up to Leah Beth's and fetch her girls down here'n. But when I get up in the holler, them girls ain't there."

Andrea glanced over at William Taka, her best friend, sitting bolt upright in the front passenger seat, his hair wet from a shower and jaw clenched, tee-shirt on inside out, jacket in his lap. Scott was working late so Taka had simply stayed after dinner, like so many times before. She reached over and grabbed his tight fist.

"They's gone a'sangin' down on Winslow crick. Ever-body knows that 'bandoned homestead's got haints that'll scare the skin right off-n yourn..."

In the rearview mirror, Andrea glimpsed the woman's thousand-yard stare again, before returning her attention to the road.

"Ever-body knows why them crossvines a'grow so thick down there at the homestead."

Taka took a deep breath, opened his hand, and threaded his fingers through Andrea's. "Was Jimmy okay?" he croaked through a tight throat.

"Yes, I think? He didn't say he wasn't." Andrea had dated Jimmy, a state cop, for a couple of months before they settled into a close, affectionate friendship. But Taka and Scott, who met at roughly the same time, had formed a tighter bond.

"There's love and then there's fate and then there's Robie Dawkins and that slip of a girl from Copper Ridge," the ghost said.

Taking her hand back, Andrea threaded the FX from Timber Way onto Greenbrier which ran south down through the hills where she lived and then straight across the flat valley of Charleston, West Virginia, all the way to the north bank of the Kanawha River.

"Take sixty-four, it's faster," Taka said.

She nodded. The hospital lay to the west, on Route 60, which Greenbrier intersected, but that way lay multiple stoplights and Friday night traffic through historic East End. I-64 would let the FX fly west with a short jog south to General, the Charleston area's only Level 1 trauma center.

"Dewey?"

Ignoring the ghost as she chattered on, Andrea illegally passed a green Ford Galaxy poking along at pot-head pace before she answered. "He's in surgery."

Scott worked for Dewey Sanderson, Charleston's own business magnate. Dewey and Taka had a complicated relationship that had once been intimate. They'd politely ignored each other for years until recently, when they'd both suffered at the hands of a man Andrea still didn't regret killing, though she did regret her inability to stop dreaming about it and, despite reassurance, her worry that he'd come back to haunt her. Literally.

As if answering that thought, the rambling ghost said, "... might could, missy, he might could. You'd be smart to be a'feared of that one. He slinks across the skin like cold water, liftin every hair. Leah Beth claims him breathe on her nape one—"

The ghost's hair whipped harder around her face and shoulders, like the FX were a convertible with the top down. Her full train dress streamed right through the backseat and trunk of the FX, catching Andrea's eye in the side mirror.

"What's her name?" Taka said.

"Whose name," Andrea said over the ghost, braking for a stoplight.

"The ghost in the kitchen. Before I went up to shower."

"She hasn't said," Andrea replied, her gaze drawn back to the rearview as that spectral wind calmed, but still tugged and pulled at the ghost.

"Do you know the damage bullets do internally?" Taka said, hands again fists on his thighs. "They cavitate. Do you know what that means?"

"Yes." She did. Bullets cause a shock wave that blows body tissue outward. The tunnel they create displaces everything around it, shifting tissues that should never be moved that far from where they attach to everything else. Massive trauma. "I do."

He shook his head. "I don't know how I feel about either one of them. But I can't lose them, Andrea." Looking over, she noted how tired he looked, the tight line of his mouth as he pressed his lips together. She hoped her busting in on his shower with news of the shooting wouldn't set him back in his therapy. She'd already caused him enough pain. "Wait. Is she here?"

"She is. She's talking and talking. I don't think she sees us."

He frowned at her. "How is that possible?" None of the ghosts Andrea had seen before communicated well verbally. Or traveled with them. The light turned green. Andrea pressed down on the accelerator and the FX shot forward into the intersection. Keeping her eyes on the ramp to westbound I-64, Andrea shrugged. How would she know? She just wanted her to stop talking.

"...cause that girl from Copper Ridge sees the future. Ever-body says so but I don't believe that. Now throwin' the bones, that there's different, but just a'closing your eyes and saying sumpthin' what rise up on your tongue..."

Taka asked for Scott at the emergency room reception desk and then they sat for ten long minutes. He leaned forward, elbows on his open knees, watching everyone who came and went, though he couldn't have described a single one even a minute later. A woman in a wheelchair was doubled over, arms wrapped around her middle and crying in quiet, hiccupping breaths. A small boy seated directly across from Taka caught his eye, but then his bright-eyed gaze slid past Taka and froze. He stopped swinging his feet, staring.

Taka's skin prickled, his heart giving an uncomfortable lurch. "Did she come in with us?"

"Yeah. She's sitting on the other side of you, still talking." Taka flushed cold but forced himself to remain still. Andrea leaned into his shoulder, her phone in her hand, the text screen open. "Jimmy's upstairs with his boss. They're waiting for word on Dewey. Chet's arm is broken."

Chet was Dewey's main bodyguard. They knew each other in passing, what with Chet lurking behind Dewey for at least the last three years. When Scott joined Dewey's security team, Taka had learned Chet was competent and street smart. That made the impossibility of an attack at the Coliseum, Dewey's club, even more incredible. Taka couldn't stop his mind leaping straight to a connection with the murder of Dewey's dad, Senator Dante Sanderson. Dewey had been there, too. Taka wondered now if his hunch that Dewey held the reins in that situation was wrong.

A man in blue scrubs stepped through a secure door next to the reception desk. "Detective William Taka?" They both jumped up, but once at the door, the man shook his head at Andrea. "He okayed Detective Taka. You're welcome to wait right here. It'll only be a few minutes, anyway."

Taka's stomach dropped. What did that mean?

"Is that good or bad?" Andrea asked for him.

The man gave them a thin-lipped smile and stepped back, giving Taka room to enter.

"Go check on Jimmy," he said, trying to ease the worry on her face. "I'll text you when I know." He hoped the ghost stayed with Andrea, even though he knew now that when it came to ghosts whatever he wanted didn't really matter.

Jimmy paced the second-floor hallway. His West Virginia State Police supervisor, Maddox, stood near the windows on one side of the large, open, surgical waiting area, barking as quietly into his phone as he was capable of. Uniforms, both state police and Charleston Police officers were posted where they were needed, including the trooper keeping an eye on Jimmy, and everyone else was still at the Coliseum processing the scene.

He shoved his hair off his forehead, smoothing it back with both hands. And then noticed the dried blood on his shirt. Scotty was his responsibility. His field agent. But Andrea and Taka were on their way and he needed to pull his shit together, so he didn't blurt that out. He and Maddox had agreed that Scott's true identity and his undercover status would remain in place unless Scott tapped out. Although he hadn't managed to collect any concrete evidence against their target, Dewey Sanderson, WVSP had made investigatory inroads into both arms and drug networks based on leads Scott furnished them through his proximity. Jimmy couldn't blow that for them no matter the circumstances.

"Jimmy," Andrea called out behind him as she entered the hall.

Jimmy spun on his heel, opening his arms as she rushed at him. Her warmth shocked him. He didn't realize how cold he was until she pressed against him and wrapped her arms around him.

"What happened?"

He wasn't supposed to tell her anything, but Scott would almost certainly tell Taka. They had hopelessly tangled their personal and work lives like damn rookies, both of them lying to Andrea and Taka. But Charleston was a small city in a state of small towns, and it was a rare cop that didn't have some sort of relationship with someone he shouldn't be talking to—a brother, a best friend, a sister-in-law.

They'd settled into a steady friendship that he still hoped might become more. But she wasn't the sort of woman to forgive a lie easily.

And he hated that disappointing her seemed inevitable in this rat's nest he and Scott had built without much thought towards the real-life consequences or the consequences of using Andrea and Taka as cover from Dewey.

Andrea pushed him away enough that she could see his face. "Jimmy?"

He glanced at Maddox, but he wasn't looking at them and the trooper shadowing him was too far away to hear. He wanted to reel her back in so he could hide from her, but he sucked it up instead, meeting her dark brown eyes as he said, "I shot him."

"Dewey?"

"Scott. I shot him."

"Why?"

Now was the time to come clean. That Scott was an undercover officer borrowed from North Carolina's State Bureau of Investigations. That he was Scott's handler. "It was an accident," he said instead, which was true. "There was an active shooter at the club. Not inside," he added when horror crossed her face. "Out back. Someone was trying to kill Dewey."

Andrea glanced down the hall at the scurry of nurses, a couple with their heads together down the way, but no one was paying them any attention. "Were you on surveillance?"

She knew his team was interested in Dewey's activity and a few months ago when Taka had been kidnapped, she'd seen them in action. "No, we've moved on," he lied. Because he really needed to lay any more thoughts she might have about that to rest. "I'd actually gone for a beer with Scotty and just left out the front when I heard the initial shot. Scott thought I was part of the attack and when I saw his gun pointed at me—I reacted."

"Is this related to Dewey's dad?"

Jimmy shook his head. "Too early to know. Dewey could have most anyone after him considering his activities." Suspected activities. Despite Scott being embedded for several months, despite the cover story of a long-term friendship between Jimmy and Scott as an unspoken invite for Dewey to try and corrupt Jimmy, they still had damn all hard evidence to prosecute Dewey for anything.

"The shooter?"

"Got away."

"...what's this? 'nother fair-haired boy. They's be a nickel to every dark-haired dime down's Jackson way. But he's not a'one. Not a'one them those bones be chatterin and clatterin on aboot."

Andrea's gaze shot to the ghost. Was she referring to Jimmy?

"I really fucked the pooch on this one," Jimmy said to the floor.

The ghost had her head lifted, as if scenting the air. "No one's so bright as them dark-headed lads what's been gone from Winslow's crick so long."

"You made a mistake," Andrea said, tone firm, still watching the ghost side-eye. They'd all just been through an officer-involved investigation with Taka. The suspect Taka shot had died. Please God, let Scott be okay.

"None's them touch don't feel it. Them bleeding-vines don't lie."

"What's wrong?"

Besides everything? Andrea tilted her head toward the ghost.

Jimmy raised his brows. "Visitor?"

"Chatty one."

"It's a hospital, I guess that's to be expected."

"Tucker sez they's just a'moved, gone away, but Leah Beth heard tell how's that one's a wraith and ain't it been seed a'sanging in the holler, diggin and pickin like it was still a'this world."

Andrea forced herself to ignore the ghost. Jimmy needed her. "She showed up at the house, a little while before you called."

"Nobody else?"

"A couple in the ER lobby."

"Where's Taka?"

The thing about Taka was, he acted as an amplifier. Whenever they were together, the ghosts she saw came through clearer, with more agency, and she saw more of them. They also saw more of her. Taka dialed up all the spirit room lights.

"They let him back, Scott gave them his name."

The red-haired ghost's reality and volume remained undimmed through the several feet of concrete between the ER and the second floor. Andrea's attention drifted back to her. She was wandering from wall to wall in the hallway as she talked on, turning circles when she strayed too far from Andrea. Two nurses and a worn, anxious woman walked right through her. And she kept walking through a state trooper standing further down the hall, pretending not to watch them.

Jimmy straightened up, looking past Andrea. "Doctor."

Andrea followed him closer to the waiting area. The doctor stepped onto the carpet and asked for Dewey's family.

An older man in a wrinkled suit and sporting a moderate beer gut drifted over from the windows, his cell phone still pressed to his ear. "I'm Major Maddox, State Police."

A subtle shift of focus rippled through the small groups huddled together in the area. Maddox dug in his suit jacket and brought out his badge to flash at the doctor. She stayed his hand and took a good look.

"Mr. Sanderson has no family present?"

"His mother lives in Florida, she's being contacted. I'm the lead state investigator on the shooting and we very much would like to speak with Mr. Sanderson."

"He's headed into surgery. There's a high probability he'll fully recover, but you won't be able to speak with him until late tomorrow at the earliest."

"Tomorrow is what Tucker always sez," the red-haired ghost piped up louder than before. "Tomorrow. Tomorrow. Tomorrow, Madeleine. I'll be a'taking yous home."

Was her name Madeleine?

"...trooper outside treatment," Maddox was saying. "We'll need him present at all times."

"He accompanied Mr. Sanderson to the OR and is standing in the hall to recovery."

"But he never done yet," the ghost wailed. "I wanta go home. A'want, a'want, a'want..."

"Can someone get him a chair?"

The doctor smiled for the first time. "Of course. I'll update you following surgery."

"Scott Fergusson?"

"I'll find out and send someone to let you know."

"Thank you." Maddox held out his hand like they were making a deal and the doctor shook it.

As she walked back past Andrea and Jimmy, glancing up in acknowledgement of their apparent unabashed eavesdropping, the ghost stopped talking. Stopped walking. Stopped fidgeting. Her gaze sharpened, following every bob and sway of the doctor's exit. Once again, she reminded Andrea of a hound scenting the air. And she was undoubtedly aware of the real world, if only for a moment.

Silent, alert, she darted after the doctor, leaning out around a cart in the hall as if hiding, her long hair swinging, as she peered after her. Then she followed, folding in on herself in a way that made the back of Andrea's neck crawl, until only a thin, unnatural shadow slid along in the doctor's wake, and right through the gap of the surgical doors as they swung shut.

WRAITH IS AVAILABLE NOW at your favorite bookstore.

ABOUT THE AUTHOR

Elle Andrews Patt writes speculative fiction and also works in telecommunications and data migration. In the past, she has made her living as a vet tech, pizza maker, and horse breeding farm manager among many other ventures.

Her published short fiction, novelettes, and novels have been recognized by The National Indie Excellence Awards, Killer Nashville's Silver Falchion Award, The Writers of the Future, and the Florida Writers Association.

Elle currently lives with her family in Tennessee.

Read a free story, sign up for her newsletter, connect with her on social media, and visit her website from one easy link:

https://linktr.ee/elleandrewspatt

Or visit www.elleandrewspatt.com

www.ingramcontent.com/pod-product-compliance
Lightning Source LLC
Chambersburg PA
CBHW021130260626
47169CB00005B/1534